James, Lorelei,
Kissin' tell /
[2013]
33305231043435
mh   12/05/14

T3-AOR-970

Kissin' Tell

Lorelei James

SAMHAIN
PUBLISHING

Samhain Publishing, Ltd.
11821 Mason Montgomery Road, 4B
Cincinnati, OH 45249
www.samhainpublishing.com

Kissin' Tell
Copyright © 2013 by LJLA, LLC
Print ISBN: 978-1-61921-133-9
Digital ISBN: 978-1-60928-848-8

Editing by Lindsey Faber
Cover by Scott Carpenter

This book is a work of fiction. The names, characters, places, and incidents are products of the writer's imagination or have been used fictitiously and are not to be construed as real. Any resemblance to persons, living or dead, actual events, locale or organizations is entirely coincidental.

All Rights Are Reserved. No part of this book may be used or reproduced in any manner whatsoever without written permission, except in the case of brief quotations embodied in critical articles and reviews.

First Samhain Publishing, Ltd. electronic publication: June 2012
First Samhain Publishing, Ltd. print publication: May 2013

Prologue

Tell McKay had a boner.

In history class.

At least it hadn't happened in math, where he'd have to stand at the board to solve a problem and then everyone could see...his problem.

His cheeks burned imagining how much that would suck.

He shifted in his seat and blamed his situation on the distraction seated in front of him.

The oh-so hot, oh-so-out-of-his-league, sweet, sexy and amazingly perfect class beauty, Georgia Hotchkiss.

Yeah, Georgia was always on his mind.

She was something else. A petite powerhouse. The ultimate diversion. Those damn short, damn tight cheerleading skirts that showcased her athletic body. If he angled his head to the side, he caught a glimpse of her muscular thigh instead of the back of her head. Not that the view was bad. Her hair was as black and shiny as a crow's wing in the sun. Add in her china-white skin, full ruby lips and Georgia could be a modern-day Snow White.

You're a real poet, McKay. More like a fuckin' pervert. Think about something else.

"Tell?"

Startled by the husky rasp of his name, he glanced up from his notebook, right into pale, icy-blue eyes that made him stammer like a fool. "W-what?"

"Did you do the homework assignment?"

Be cool. Do not imagine Hot Lips Hotchkiss whispering that in your ear. "Yep."

Her mouth curved into a smile. He wondered if the gloss glistening on her lips was flavored. Would it taste like bubble gum? Peaches? Ripe black cherries?

"Thank God. Can I copy it?"

Tell managed to rip his focus from her plump lips. Before he could speak, she cranked the charm on high.

"Please? You let me do it before. And I didn't have time because I was..."

Sucking face with your asshole boyfriend?

Not that he'd ever say that, but man, he hated Declan "Deck" Veldekamp; not just because the super jock—aka big man on campus—was dating the hottest girl in their class. The guy was a prick and a bully. And those were his best traits.

"You was what?" Tell whispered back.

"Bottle-feeding the replacement calves my dad got yesterday."

He snorted.

"You don't believe me? I'm serious. I had chores to finish last night."

"So did I. And I was up until three a.m. helping my brothers pull a couple of calves since my dad—" *was passed out in the barn,* "—needed some shut-eye and I still got *my* homework done."

Her tempting lips formed a pretty pout. "I don't see the big deal in you letting me copy it real quick."

You wouldn't.

Like you didn't see a problem asking me to help with prom decorations, and I ended up doing everything.

Like you didn't see a problem asking me to help with Fellowship of Christian Athletes concessions, and I ended up doing everything.

"Please, Tell? I'm desperate."

"Miss Hotchkiss," Mrs. Walls said sharply. "Stop flirting with Mr. McKay and get ready to turn in your assignment."

Swish. Her silky hair tickled Tell's knuckles as she whipped her head. The scent of cherries traveled from his nose straight to his crotch.

Fuckin' awesome.

"I'm afraid that's the problem, Mrs. Walls," Georgia intoned sweetly. "I seem to have...lost my assignment and I was just asking if he saw the paper fall out of my binder."

"Is that true, Tell?"

Now Miss Sweet and Sexy was asking him to lie for her? Bull crap.

"No, ma'am, that is not true."

"Well, then, what were you two whispering about that was so all-fired important that you disrupted my class?" Mrs. Walls demanded.

Tell knew the hard-nosed teacher wouldn't let it go. "Georgia and I were talkin' about the upcoming class project, bein's we're partners. She forgot the folder with our notes and discovered she'd slipped her assignment in it too."

When Georgia gaped at him, Tell allowed a smug grin, but stopped short of giving her a conspiratorial wink.

"I'll let it slide this time, only because I'm impressed you two have already started on the project," Mrs. Walls said.

Score! Now with Hot Lips as his partner for a major graded assignment, she couldn't back out. It finally gave him the chance to show her the real Tell McKay. Not the tongue-tied loser who sat behind her in history class and sniffed her hair.

"What's the subject matter?" Mrs. Walls asked him.

Crap. "Ah. Advances and setbacks in Wyoming livestock practices over the course of Wyoming statehood." Hey, that sounded pretty good, especially on the fly.

"Excellent. The rest of you might as well choose partners today— after you turn in your assignments. The bell rings in two minutes, so get cracking."

Tell's mind drifted into a soft-focus image of Georgia and him, alone, studying in the back of the library with their heads bent close. When they looked up simultaneously, Georgia would whisper his name and lick her lips, letting him know she wanted him. Then would he gently touch her face and slide his hand into that thick waterfall of shiny black hair? Or would he keep eye contact with her as he gradually moved in for a long, slow kiss?

No. He'd grab her, kiss her with all the bottled-up passion he hadn't had the chance to show any woman, let alone her. Passion that was just waiting to burst free. While they were kissing like crazy, her soft hands would be all over him.

No. His hands would be all over her. Slipping under her shirt to touch her boobs. Inching beneath the spandex panties she wore under her cheerleading skirt.

She'd be moaning, rubbing her hand against his fly. Then he'd pick her up—just like in the movies. He'd sweep all the books and papers off the desk—just like in the movies. Then he'd gently lay her across the surface, bringing his body on top of hers. For some of that sliding, pounding, pumping action—

"Tell?"

His guilty gaze winged to Georgia. "Ah, what?"

"Are you even listening to me?"

He stammered, "N-no. Why?"

"The bell rang."

Shit. "Oh."

"Why are you still sitting there?"

Because I have another freakin' boner. "Because I'm tired. I must've fallen asleep."

She blinked at him. "With your eyes open?"

Way to be an idiot. He shrugged and fought another lame blush. Please, don't let his face reveal that he'd been in a porn scene, dry-humping her to orgasm as she screamed his name. *Be cool.* "What's up?"

"I wanted to say thanks for covering for me, but I can't be your partner."

Every fantasy—and his dick—deflated. "Why not?"

Georgia gnawed on her lip. "Deck will get mad."

"So? It's for school. Say the teacher put us together."

"But Smitty was here. He'll tattle that we weren't assigned and us partnering up was your idea. Then Deck will want to, well...deck you."

"I'd like to see him try." *Ooh, such a tough guy, McKay. Deck would wipe the floor with your scrawny ass.*

"I can't do that to you, Tell."

Was her concern for him from fear? Or from something else? She *had* been talking to him a lot during class the last couple of months. Did she kind of...like him?

Wait. If he let Deck beat the ever-lovin' crap out of him, would Georgia feel so guilty she'd offer to kiss his injuries and make them better? For the first time ever, he really hoped a guy punched him in the crotch.

Nice fucking fantasy, perv, but it ain't ever gonna happen.

"You understand, don't you?"

His focus snapped back to her. "What's your grade in this class?"

She dropped her gaze. "I have a C. Minus."

"I have an A. This project could raise your grade to a B if you partner with me."

"Well, okay then. But we can't meet to work on the project during school hours where anyone could see us."

If he'd had an ego, it would've taken a massive hit. "Where we gonna work on it?"

"How about the public library? In, ah, Moorcroft." Her fingers nervously twisted the purity ring on a chain around her neck. "I'll meet you there tomorrow night."

That's when he knew he'd be doing the history project alone.

That's when he understood that *sucker* defined a guy like him, easily manipulated by a pretty girl.

That's when he swore it'd never happen again.

Chapter One

Ten years later...

"Tell McKay, you're a sight for sore eyes."

"BeeBee, darlin', I swear you get younger-lookin' every time I see you. Pretty soon I'm gonna be carding *you* to make sure you're old enough to be serving in a bar."

"Even an old broad like me ain't immune to that bullshit flattery." She opened the cooler. "You drinkin' Bud Light?"

"Yep." Tell caught the bottle when the bartender slid it across the bar top. "Thanks, Beebs."

"No problem. So where's the blonde from last week?"

He grinned. "It's a new week."

BeeBee flapped the bar towel at him. "You're such a McKay."

"I'll take the compliment. But you gotta admit I ain't as wild as some of my cousins in their heyday."

"I think you're worse, sugar, because you hide it better. Lord, them dimples of yours are deep enough to get lost in. And the ladies eat up that fun-lovin' gentleman cowboy bit you do so well." She shook her finger at him. "Don't deny it."

"I don't. But I'll point out I *am* a fun-lovin' gentleman cowboy, so it ain't like I'm pretending to be something that I'm not."

BeeBee's gaze flicked to whoever stood behind him.

Tell slowly turned around on his barstool to see a redhead glaring at him. Aw, hell. Not again. He remembered he'd done a little mattress dancing with this cutie last year, but he couldn't recall her name. "Hey, pretty lady."

She rolled her eyes. "Does that work for you? The 'hey, pretty lady' when you can't remember a woman's name after you slept with her?"

BeeBee snorted.

Tell grinned. "Yep."

The woman opened her mouth, no doubt about to read him the riot act, but he jumped in to head her off.

"Now, don't go getting all indignant, darlin'. We both had a great time—that part I do remember. I told you up front that's all it'd be."

She sidled up to the bar, telling BeeBee, "A honey Jack and seven with lemon, please." Then she cocked her head. "I'm Jamie."

"Well, pretty Jamie, I may've been fuzzy on your name, but I do recall one thing about you."

"What's that?"

Tell traced the line of her neck from beneath her jawbone to the hollow of her throat. "How much you liked havin' my mouth here."

Jamie's breath caught. "You are the devil. A handsome devil with dirty, sweet-talking ways and wicked, wicked hands."

"Mmm-hmm. But knowing that ahead of time still didn't keep you from sayin' yes to me, did it?"

"Because I didn't want to say no." Her gaze gravitated to his crotch and zoomed back to his eyes. "Then or now."

He raised a brow. "That right?"

She inserted her curvy body between his thighs and leaned into him. "Buy me a drink, cowboy, and we'll talk."

His night was looking up. "BeeBee doll, put Jamie's drink on my tab."

BeeBee snorted again.

"So, you here with anyone?" Tell asked.

Jamie took a healthy sip of her drink. "My friend Stephanie and some chick she knew in high school."

High school. A time in his life he'd rather forget.

He set down his bottle and said, "Dance with me."

There wasn't a band, just piped-in country music, but several couples were on the dance floor.

Three fast songs later, Tell led Jamie back to their seats at the bar. "I forgot that you're such a great dancer," she said breathlessly.

"Ain't a lot of other things to do around here on the weekends."

"But I haven't seen you in Ziggy's for a while."

He didn't mention he was in here every Tuesday night for dart league. "We just got done calving. Now I'm gearing up for rodeo season. Which means I'll be gone most Friday and Saturday nights."

She placed her hand on his chest. "Is that your way of warning me off?"

"Nope. Just stating the facts up front." He shifted against the bar and put his mouth on her ear. "So knowing that... What are the odds that you'll come home with me tonight?"

13

"It depends."

"On what?"

"On whether you still live with your brother."

His lips nibbled down her jawline to the column of her throat. "My brother was only staying with me temporarily. So it'd just be you and me. I'll be the only one to hear you moan when I do this." Tell parted his lips and sucked on the sweep of skin where her neck met her shoulder.

"God. You're good at that." She bared her entire throat.

"At what?"

"Seducing me with your mouth and the words flowing from it."

He chuckled against her neck. "So is that a yes, pretty—"

"Jamie?"

Tell froze. He recognized that smoky voice. Soft, sweet, unbelievably sexy. Been a while since he'd heard it. He lifted his head, but kept his face shadowed beneath the brim of his hat.

"Can't you see I'm a little busy?" Jamie said crossly.

"I wouldn't bother you, but Stephanie told me to tell you that your sister has called your cell about ten times. She thinks you oughta call her back in case it's an emergency."

Jamie stepped away from him, warning, "Don't go anywhere."

"I'll be right here, waitin' on you." As soon as Jamie flounced off, Tell raised his head, looking at the woman who'd starred in his teenage fantasies for three long years. "Hello, Georgia."

Surprise crossed her face. She stumbled backward and would've fallen on her ass if he hadn't lunged for her.

"Whoa, there."

"Tell? Tell McKay? *You're* the hot cowboy Jamie was talking about?"

Tell wasn't sure if he should scowl because of Georgia's shock or if he should grin because she'd called him hot. A smile won out. "Yep, that's me."

"Wow. You...look amazing." Georgia's gaze traveled over his shoulders, his arms, his chest and then landed back on his face. Her fingers tightened on his biceps as if she was testing the merchandise. "Like, really amazing."

He couldn't look away from her. Christ. Hot Lips Hotchkiss was still a knockout. Her ebony hair was shorter—shoulder length, rather than flowing halfway down her back in a tangle of black silk. Same lush mouth. Same startling blue eyes. She'd put on weight, which had softened the sharp angles of her face, and added some curves to her compact body.

"You're staring at me," she said in that low-pitched voice he'd dreamed about.

"You were staring at me first, darlin'. And I'm pretty sure you can let go of me now, unless you wanna challenge me to an arm-wrasslin' match?"

"Ah. No. Sorry." A hint of pink spread from her neck up to her cheekbones and she dropped her hands.

Interesting. Tell couldn't remember if he'd ever seen her blush in high school. "So what are you doin' here?"

"Having a drink with Stephanie. You remember her?"

Tell frowned. "Was she in our graduating class?"

"Yes. Stephanie Blackstone?"

"Ah. Now I remember. One of them smart girls. But I didn't know you two were friends."

Her eyes turned cool. "I couldn't be friends with a smart girl because I was a dumb cheerleader?"

Shit. He'd stepped in it with her first thing. He felt the knots tighten in his tongue as that stammering, apologizing, blushing boy from the past made a brief appearance.

No sirree. He was not going there. He hadn't been that kid for a long damn time. He reached for his beer and sipped. Then he granted her a slow grin. "Georgia girl, you were smart enough to get a boy like me to do your schoolwork, even when you were more than capable of doin' it yourself. So that snippy response don't hold true and you know it."

She laughed self-consciously. "I guess I deserved that."

At least she could laugh at herself. "I haven't seen Stephanie in years."

"Steph moved back to Moorcroft last year but she travels all over the state for her job."

"I haven't seen you in years either. What brings you back to Sundance?"

His cell buzzed before she could answer. Normally he would ignore it, but he'd been expecting—dreading—this call. He lifted a finger and said, "Hold on a sec. I gotta take this." He clicked Answer. "What's up?"

"Landon has been shrieking since you left him here. He don't wanna watch a movie. He ain't hungry. And the little sh— poop kicked

15

my dog. When I put him in time out, he smacked me in the face with his fire truck. Sorry, bro, but I can't do this alone."

Perfect fucking timing as usual. "Fine. I'll be there in fifteen." Tell finished his beer. He fished out a twenty and dropped it on the bar, signaling to BeeBee. "We square?"

"Sure enough. You're leaving so soon?"

"Gotta deal with a kid problem."

BeeBee frowned. "You've got Landon this weekend?"

"Yeah, and he's actin' up bad enough to warrant a call, so I gotta get. Thanks." Tell looked at Georgia with serious regret. "Sorry we didn't get a chance to catch up. Take care." He slipped on his PRCA jacket and hustled out the door.

Georgia watched the hot cowboy with the black hat disappear into the night. Tell McKay had been cute in high school in that sweet and dorky way. But now? The man was drop-dead gorgeous.

And built. Holy cow. She'd gotten a good grip on his muscled biceps when he'd kept her from making a complete fool of herself.

Now she felt totally perverted since she'd been sneaking peeks at Jamie and him on the dance floor, mesmerized by his fast, sexy, smooth moves. She'd kept watching them when they returned to the bar. Saw him draw Jamie in. He hadn't given a damn who knew he was seducing her. Jamie had been his only focus in a bar full of people.

Lucky, lucky Jamie.

What would it be like on the receiving end of such potent sexual attention? She'd know if she hadn't tuned Jamie out as the girl had regaled Stephanie with explicit details of her last hookup with the man she'd referred to as "cowboy hottie".

What an understatement.

She'd spiraled back ten years when Tell's eyes met hers. Even back then, she'd felt he saw so much more than other kids their age, which sent her into full retreat. Maybe she'd even acted a little cold to him sometimes because she hadn't wanted anyone—especially a sweet-talkin', sharp-eyed McKay—to see that deeply inside her, fearing he'd find her...shallow.

Georgia dodged dancers on her way back to the booth.

Stephanie stirred the ice cubes in her glass and watched her approach. "Jamie had to bail. Issues with her sister."

At least she wouldn't have to break the news to Jamie that Tell had left.

"I saw you talking to Jamie's mystery guy."

"So you didn't know the hot cowboy Jamie was going on about...was Tell McKay?"

Stephanie's eyes became enormous behind her purple glasses. "Seriously? Jamie never said his name." She groaned. "Then again, she did say she wasn't the type to kiss and tell."

Georgia choked on her vodka tonic.

"I shouldn't be surprised. That's how karma works."

"Karma? What are you talking about?"

"You. Running into Tell McKay. He always had a crush on you. But you were too busy being Deck's girlfriend to notice."

Wrong. She had noticed. But it wasn't like she could've acted on it. Deck had been insanely jealous, and enough bad blood had lingered between Deck and Tell in rodeo club that she hadn't wanted to add to it.

"Tell was surprised we were friends."

Stephanie shrugged. "Our friendship was off the radar. No biggie."

"Did that bother you?"

"Of course not. When we saw each other at school, you didn't pretend you didn't know me. I never understood what you did to earn such animosity from the girls in our class anyway, besides their bitchy attitudes being from stupid, petty jealousy because you were beautiful and dating the class stud. You weren't a mean girl, not like Sally Hermanson and her group. You just stuck with your own crowd—RJ, Deck and his groupies. Who can fault you for that? Besides, look at us now. We're still friends. Can either of us say that about anyone else in our graduating class?"

"No, but that's because you took pity on me after I divorced Deck and let me room with you in Laramie."

"It worked out for both of us. What else did Tell say?"

"Nothing." After the cocktail waitress took their order, Georgia steered the conversation away from her embarrassing run-in with Tell. "You know who else I ran into from our class? Maggie Malone. She looks exactly the same."

"That's it? You have been keeping a low profile since you moved back to Wyoming."

Moved back. Banished to purgatory was more like it.

"I've been busy the last week setting everything up to Barbara's specs."

Stephanie adjusted her glasses, which meant she was getting ready to grill Georgia. "I don't understand why your boss picked Sundance to open a branch office."

"It's not a branch office. Since she took over promotions for L bar K Rodeo, we have to maintain a physical presence throughout the summer rodeo season. Mostly to reassure the committees that hired L bar K that we plan on honoring those contracts. Plus, Barbara believed my former ties to this area would work in our favor now."

"So you won't be living here permanently?"

"No. But that tidbit has to stay strictly between us. You know how locals get about an out-of-state company relocating here temporarily for tax benefits and then pulling up stakes."

"But it still seems bizarre and...coincidental. How did a promotions and advertising firm in Dallas end up owning a small rodeo promotion company in Wyoming?"

That same question had crossed Georgia's mind, especially after Barbara's strange edict: take the job in Wyoming or lose her job in Dallas.

"L bar K has fallen on hard times and they approached Barbara about a buyout."

Both Stephanie's eyebrows rose. "Again with the coincidence."

"Barbara does this buyout thing all the time. And she's getting plenty out of this deal, trust me. Some of the rodeos around here are overlooked gems just needing the right PR company to put a shine on them."

"What are you getting out of it?"

"A promotion, if everything goes smoothly. In the meantime, I get to spend my summer at the rodeo grounds, instead of taking calls at my desk in Dallas."

"Does your dad know you're here?"

Georgia reached for her fresh drink. "He's probably heard rumors. Have I called him? No. Do I intend to? The jury's out on that one."

Stephanie sighed. "I don't blame you. But I feel the need to point out that people change. You have. Why couldn't you at least give your father the benefit of the doubt, just once?"

That comment made Georgia think of Tell. Not of how he'd changed, but what had remained the same.

His piercing blue eyes were the same.

That dimpled smile was the same.

His sweet, helpful disposition was the same.

"You've gotten better at evasion," Stephanie inserted. "You don't want to talk about your dad? Fine. We'll finish the conversation about Tell McKay. Did he recognize you?"

"He was too busy trying to get into Jamie's pants to pay attention to anything but her zipper."

"Not what I meant."

"Yes, he recognized me. Right away."

Stephanie said, "And?" with exasperation.

"And what? He was polite, even when I sort of freaked out on him." Georgia groaned and put her forehead on the table.

"That bad? Really?"

"Yes." Georgia raised her head and mimicked herself. "Wow, I can't believe you're Tell McKay! Wow, let me feel your big muscles! Wow, you look amazing! God, Stephanie. What was wrong with me?"

"You were sideswiped with lust?"

"Me and every other woman in the bar. But *they* didn't gasp and swoon. Can you believe I almost fell on my ass, so the poor man had to catch me?"

"He didn't *have* to catch you," Stephanie pointed out. "But the fact he did is great insight into his character."

Georgia wanted to roll her eyes, but her psychologist friend would read something into it. "I didn't talk to him long enough to find out anything about his character. Besides. What does it matter? He's with Jamie."

Stephanie shook her head. "Jamie's commitment issues preclude her from anything but casual relationships. After what she's told me, I'm assuming cowboy hottie, aka Tell McKay, is the same way."

Georgia wanted to point out she'd overheard Tell's phone conversation and he had a kid, but that didn't mean he had a wife or even a significant other. Just a baby mama, who was at home, dealing with his child while he caroused at the local bar.

Maybe Tell had turned into a player. Wouldn't be much of a stretch, given his good looks and the wild reputations the McKay men had built up over the years.

"You know, he could solve a major problem for you."

She glanced up. "What major problem? That I need to get laid?"

Stephanie laughed. "I don't know if I'll ever get used to hearing you talk like that, G. Anyway, maybe this will be a two-fer in the problem-solving department for you: you'll get laid and score a date to our ten-year class reunion."

"Uh. No. I'll take the sex but I'm not going to the reunion."

"Bullshit."

Georgia started to retort but Stephanie cut her off.

"You *are* going. You *cannot* not show up at our class reunion, Georgia. Especially when people find out you live here. Especially not after you and Deck were voted class couple *and* prom king and queen."

"Those titles worked out so well since we've been divorced for seven years," she retorted.

"Which is why you have to go. Don't let Deck have the upper hand. Plus, you know he'll be there with Tara-Lee."

She scowled. "All the more reason to skip the damn dog and pony show."

"You really don't care if Deck badmouths you?" Stephanie asked. "Because you know he will if you're not around to defend yourself."

"I dealt with the Deck drama a lifetime ago."

"That's why you have to show up at the reunion on the arm of a gorgeous cowboy. It'd give you cred. It'd give Tell cred because you're still the hottest woman from our class. Add in the fact Deck and Tell were rivals in rodeo club? Sweet, sweet revenge."

That would be a way to prove she'd moved on. That she no longer had that purity ring around her neck like a noose.

No. She could not possibly be considering the idea of attending that farce of a reunion. "Who are *you* taking to the reunion?" she asked Stephanie.

"No one. I'm going stag." Stephanie held her hand up again. "And before you blow a gasket, let me remind you that you were in the thick of things during high school. I was very happily in the background, observing."

"You're still observing."

"So make it interesting for me. Show up and show off. The introverted high school girl you were wouldn't dare ask Tell to go to the reunion with her. That's exactly why you *should* ask him."

"What if he says no?"

"I think you're more afraid that he'll say yes."

Chapter Two

Landon calmed down immediately when Tell walked through the door. The four-year-old crawled onto Tell's lap with his dinosaur blanket and promptly fell asleep.

"He prefers you, even to Brandt."

Tell glanced at his younger brother. "Only because Brandt hasn't spent much time with him, Jessie bein' pregnant and all."

Dalton shook his head. "It's more than that. I think Landon is drawn to you because you two look so much alike—like Luke."

Total bullshit, in Tell's opinion. His nephew had been born several months after their brother Luke's death. No one had known about the kid's existence until the boy was almost a year and a half old. Having a piece of Luke had been a catalyst for change in their family—some good, some bad. But it'd become important that Landon grow up around his family.

Tell was aware that he most closely resembled Luke—at least in physical appearance. In temperament he was light-years away from his hotheaded oldest brother. Every time he dealt with a frustrated Landon, Tell was reminded that he'd been the one to calm Luke down when his temper had gotten the best of him.

"I could use a beer, since my night of drinkin' was cut short."

Dalton brought back two bottles of Bud Light. He gulped down a mouthful before he said, "You're probably gonna need more than one when I tell you that Dad called."

"What'd he want?"

"To see Landon."

"Bullshit. He just wants to see if Mom's boyfriend will be along when she picks up Landon tomorrow."

"Probably."

"So what'd you tell him?"

"That you'd be at the park in Sundance tomorrow afternoon." Dalton shrugged and took another drink. "He probably won't show."

"I can hope." Tell let his head fall back on the couch cushion and closed his eyes. He did not want to think about the fucked-up family shit now when he'd have to deal with it again tomorrow.

"So who did I pull you away from at the bar that's put that crabby look on your face?" Dalton asked.

The thought of Georgia snapped him out of a potentially sour mood. He raised his head. "Georgia Hotchkiss. Remember her?"

Dalton whistled. "Of course I remember Hot Lips Hotchkiss. You had it bad for her."

He felt his cheeks heat. "I did not."

"No need to lie, bro. You let her run roughshod over you. But damn, I might've let her roll over me, too. She was all that and a bag of chips. A little stuck-up, though. She still that way?"

"No idea. You called right when I started talkin' to her. I haven't seen her since a week after graduation."

Dalton gave him a considering look. "Weren't you friends with her twin brother, RJ?"

"I knew him, pulled a couple pranks with him, but we weren't friends since he ran with Deck."

"You weren't around the summer he was killed. Sad deal."

Landon stirred.

Tell stood, carrying him to the spare bedroom and slipping the kid into bed. He pulled the blanket up and smoothed back the boy's hair. Then he returned to the living room, plopped back on the couch and stretched out with a sigh.

"I take it you're staying tonight?"

"Yep."

"What if I had plans?"

Tell quirked a brow. "At ten o'clock when we gotta be up at five?"

Dalton sighed. "I wish I had plans. Been awful damn hard getting back into the swing of havin' a social life after calving. Don't know if I'll ever catch up on sleep. Man. Was this year brutal or what?"

"We added an extra hundred head and Brandt is uptight and so, yeah, it was rough."

"Glad it's not just me bein' a whiny pussy."

"That'd make me one too."

"Now I feel better." Dalton drummed his fingers on the chair arm. "I heard something that might interest you."

"What's that?"

"It's all over for Jim and Charlene Fox—'cept for the fightin'."

Tell frowned. "Why would that interest me?"

"You dated Charlene, right?"

Dated. More like he banged her a couple times and then she married someone else. "Yeah. Like six years ago. Why?"

"She remembers your time together fondly. Hell, I think she remembers every man fondly, which is probably why her marriage is on the skids." Dalton smirked. "But she told me—in confidence—that when it gets down to the wire with Jim, she wants to sell off everything and move to Austin to live with her sister."

"When did Char spill her guts to you, D?"

"She stopped by here yesterday when me'n Landon were outside. Something about a cute kid makes a woman go all soft and talkative. Anyway, if we play our cards right, we could get first crack at it."

That caught his interest. "First crack at everything?"

"Yep." Dalton's face turned into pure business. "The land is already divided into two parcels. That larger section wouldn't be a bad investment. Especially if you were serious about starting a feedlot in a few years."

"I am serious. But given land prices, there's no way we can afford it. Even if she gives us a friends and former lovers discount, even with what we've got saved up."

"There's no way we can afford to *pass up* this opportunity, even if it takes us a few years to get the feedlot up and running. This time we wouldn't have to rely on someone else to run interference for us. We could handle the details ourselves and no one would know until after the fact."

They both had a bad taste after a land deal had fallen through a year and a half ago. "I don't know. I'd hate to get my hopes up again. We've been talkin' in abstracts. What if I'm wrong and a feedlot isn't viable?"

"You're not wrong. You're the smartest person I know, T, and if anyone can make it profitable, you can show us how. You've done more than talk in abstracts. You've already studied up on the regulations."

His brother's faith in him was humbling.

"And wouldn't it be sweet to stick it to Little Miss Know-It-All-Ecologically-Sustained-Agriculture after what she done to us?"

He spit out his beer at hearing Dalton refer to sweet Rory Wetzler in such a way. "Hey, you're the one who got drunk with Rory and spilled the beans about us wantin' to buy her mom's land so we could turn it into a gigantic feedlot."

Dalton sighed. "Yeah, that wasn't smart of me, especially since we managed to keep that part of our plan even from our cousin Ben."

"You should've expected Rory would blab to her mom right away, which is how Rielle ended up selling to Gavin so fast. Both Rielle and Rory have that hippie attitude and don't want any changes to the land."

"Well, they're getting their wish since Gavin hasn't done shit with it."

They chewed on that in silence.

"You be all right doin' chores Sunday morning alone?" Dalton asked. "There's a poker tournament in Deadwood. The pot is twenty grand."

"Go for it. Get drunk, get laid and win the pot. I'll need payback next weekend."

"Where's the rodeo?"

"Buffalo. Friday and Saturday night."

"Deal." Dalton stood. "Night, John-Boy."

"Night, Mary Ellen." Tell snagged the afghan off the back of the couch and let sleep overtake him.

The next afternoon after Tell got Landon cleaned up and fed, they headed to town. It was one of those perfect Wyoming days—the sun shining above an enormous, cloudless blue sky. Just enough bite of cold in the air to remind him winter had ended but summer wasn't here yet.

Landon exuded energy and ran from the swing set to the jungle gym to the sandpit and every place in between before he decided to shinny up the monkey bars.

Tell chased the boy, ran when Landon chased him, and let himself be caught and tickled. Finally Landon settled into the sandpit to dig— an activity that'd keep him occupied for more than five minutes.

Tell rested in the grass, letting the sun warm his face. It'd been a cold, snowy and gloomy winter. Seemed the sun hadn't shone at all, so he basked in the warm glow like a fat barn cat when he had a chance.

Not long after he hit that perfect relaxation point, a shadow fell across him. He inhaled a slow breath, expecting to open his eyes and see his father looming over him.

But Georgia Hotchkiss's beautiful face swam into view.

He grinned at her. "Well, it's my lucky week if I've seen you twice in as many days, sweetness."

"It is you. I wasn't sure."

"What threw you off?"

Her gaze moved along his body from his Merrell hiking boots up to his face. "Might've been that ball cap you're wearing instead of a cowboy hat."

Just then Landon skidded to a stop, spraying Tell's legs with sand. "Watch me!" The boy jumped over Tell and sped around the perimeter of the sandpit, making racecar noises.

"Pity the kid doesn't have any energy to burn off," Tell said dryly.

"How old is he?" Georgia asked.

"Four."

"What's his name?"

"Landon."

"Great name. Your son looks a lot like you."

Tell pushed to his feet. "Whoa. That's not my kid. That's my brother Luke's kid."

"Oh. Sorry. I just assumed..." She cleared her throat. "So are you babysitting for Luke or something?"

"Or something."

Georgia gave him a strange look. "Sounds cryptic."

"You probably haven't heard the story since you've been gone. Luke died a few years ago. Before he died, he'd stepped out on his wife and knocked up this chick he met in a bar. She didn't come forward until Landon was sixteen months old. So, as weird as it is, we've got an informal custody agreement with Landon's mom, Samantha."

Horror widened Georgia's eyes. "Oh my God, Tell. I had no idea that Luke had died... I'm so sorry."

"Thanks." He kicked a clump of sand. "I'm sorry about RJ. Losing a brother sucks ass."

"Yes, it does. I would've loved to have a surprise nephew or niece show up in my life." She scowled. "But that's an impossibility since my dead brother's girlfriend is now married to my ex-husband."

Tell laughed. "That situation is familiar. My brother Brandt married Luke's widow, Jessic."

Georgia smiled and Tell's heart skipped a beat. Goddamn. She still had that goofy smile. He was happy to see she hadn't perfected a fake, polite grin over the years. "What are you doin' at the park?"

"I'm out for a walk, enjoying this beautiful day." She tipped her head toward Landon. "Do you have him all weekend?"

"Me'n Dalton have had him the last two days. My mom lives in Casper now and helps Samantha with Landon's daycare and stuff."

"So your mom and dad...?"

"Got divorced." Tell tore his gaze away from her and looked for Landon. Sneaky kid was nowhere to be found. He said, "Gimme a sec," and jogged to the monkey bars.

Landon wasn't crawling around the jungle gym or sitting on the swings. Tell spun a slow circle and squinted at the flash of red by the picnic tables.

There the little bugger was. Tell froze when he saw his father sitting next to Landon on a picnic bench. He'd had to bribe Landon with ice cream to get the boy's attention.

Tell meandered over, feeling his skin tighten and toughen up. "Dad."

"You ain't keepin' a very good eye on my grandson, Tell. Anyone coulda snatched him up while you was yammering to that girl. You always did have the attention span of a dog with fleas. Praise the Lord I was here."

Landon jumped off the seat and wrapped his arm around Tell's leg. "Whoa there, buddy. Sit down. I'm right here. Didja tell Grandpa thanks for the ice cream?"

"Thanks." Landon ducked his dark-haired head.

"It's a shame the kid don't know who I am."

And whose fault is that?

"Your mother is probably poisoning him against me," Casper said with a sneer.

Tell wouldn't let that comment slide. "I reckon you're doin' that just fine yourself. If you want him to know you, you've gotta spend time with him. Which you haven't done, even when we've given you opportunities."

"Doin' the Lord's work keeps me busy."

And of course that was more important. Anything was more important than mending the rift with his family.

"I see your mother's got you jumping through hoops now too." He pointed at Landon. "How often does she ask you to watch the boy?"

Way too often, but Tell wasn't about to give his father that ammo. "Me'n Landon are pals, right, bud?"

Landon nodded.

"Where's my youngest son? Ain't you two joined at the hip?"

"Dalton helped with chores and then he took off."

"I ain't surprised Brandt didn't show up." Casper shook his finger. "Remind him he'd better call me when that baby arrives. I've already talked to my pastor about baptizing the child."

"You'll have to take that up with Brandt and Jessie, Dad. Leave me out of it."

"At least that's one thing your mother and I did right. Havin' all you boys baptized. Even if we didn't follow through and raise you up proper in the church."

Becoming a sober, born-again Christian hadn't made Casper McKay any nicer. It'd just given him faith that he'd be forgiven by God for whatever mean thing that spewed out of his mouth.

Tell studied his father, knowing he hated it. Casper had been sober for a year and a half. He'd lost all the puffy, pasty skin and bloated body shape that had been the result of years of alcohol abuse. He'd let his hair grow instead of keeping it short, strands of silver prevalent against the black. His eyes, identical to the ones staring back at Tell in the mirror every day, were clear, yet still filled with the disapproval Tell had felt his entire life.

Landon shouted, "Gram!" He raced across the park, throwing himself into Joan McKay's arms.

Tell couldn't help but smile. Landon loved his grandma, and his mother loved having a living reminder of the son she'd lost.

As she walked over, holding Landon's hand, Tell had to remind himself this relaxed, laughing woman was his mother. Not only did she look happier after leaving her husband, she owned an air of confidence—too much, maybe, to make up for the years she'd had none.

Tell whispered, "Lookin' good, Mama," and kissed her cheek. Then he offered his hand to her companion. "Bart. Nice to see you again."

"You too, Tell."

She looked at her ex-husband. "Casper."

"Joan." Casper gave Bart a full inspection, but didn't offer his hand.

"So everything went okay? No problems?" she asked.

"We had a great time like we always do, huh, Landon?" Tell said, ruffling the kid's hair.

"Yep. I got to ride on the four-wheeler three times! And Uncle Dalton buyed me a new toy, a backhoe, and we dug a big hole and he let me fill it with water!"

She laughed. "And I'll bet your uncle had to hose you down outside afterward."

"We had a water fight."

"Boys will be boys."

Casper snorted. "Dalton is long past bein' a boy. He needs to grow up and start actin' like a man."

Joan stiffened. "And just where was Dalton supposed to learn how to be a man? Because you're definitely not the example he oughta be following, Casper."

Shit. This was not good. He hated how they verbally assaulted one another and that his brothers were never around to witness it or help him break it up.

Bart said, "Tell, how about if you give me your keys and me'n Landon will get his stuff."

Tell tossed them over. Bart and Landon took off.

He didn't blame them. Maybe he should've gone along.

"You're getting mouthy in your old age, Joan," Casper said.

"And you're still an asshole in yours, Casper."

"Does that young fella sharin' your bed like your dirty mouth?" His eyes gleamed. "I remember when you used to—"

"Goddammit, Dad, that's enough."

Casper whirled on him. "Don't you be takin' the Lord's name in vain. God wouldn't smite me down for popping you one in the mouth for your blasphemy."

"Oh, give it a rest," Joan snapped. "We get that you've switched your allegiance from Jameson to Jesus. And don't forget—"

"That goes for you too, Mom. Stop it. Both of you."

"Fine. I need to get going anyway since we're meeting Brandt and Jessie for supper." Of course she had to get in another shot. She hugged him. "Thanks for everything, son. I'll call you."

She didn't even look his direction before she walked off.

"That woman needs—"

"I'm warning you to shut it," Tell said.

Casper muttered something about him still being a mama's boy.

"Look. I'll see you. I got things to do." That's when Tell realized his family drama caused him to forget about Georgia entirely. He looked over at the last place she'd been, but she was gone.

"Like what?" his father said to his retreating back.

Like walking into the closest bar.

He needed a goddamn drink.

Chapter Three

Tell ordered a beer and a burger. He'd finished half and most his fries when his buddy Thurman Watson showed up. Not only had he and Thurman been friends since fifth grade, these days they were the last bachelors in their group of friends.

"Since you called me... You buying my supper, McKay?"

"I guess."

The waitress brought Thurman a Coors and took his order to the kitchen. "Will you call me a pussy if I admit I ain't in the partyin' mood tonight?"

"Nope." Tell swirled a fry through a puddle of ranch dressing and popped it in his mouth. "How long you in town?" Thurman spent three weeks out of every month on the road as a long-haul trucker.

"Until tomorrow. I oughta have next week off, but I picked up an extra load going to Seattle. Then I hit Salt Lake and Denver before I get back."

For the next hour they bullshitted about family crap and work, drank and played pool. A few of their buddies showed up. They eyed the ladies trolling in the bar; most seemed barely legal. Tell was talking to Thurman's older brother, Warner, when Thurman stepped in front of him.

"You'll never guess who just walked in."

"You buyin' me a beer if I guess right?"

"Sure. 'Cause you ain't never gonna get this one."

Tell smirked. "Is it...Georgia Hotchkiss?"

Thurman's jaw dropped. "How the hell did you know that?"

"I've run into her twice, actually."

"And somehow you just forgot to mention that to me?"

"You said you weren't interested in partyin' or gossiping like an old woman tonight."

"Fuck off. This ain't gossip. This is news, my friend."

Tell rolled his eyes.

"I'm serious, McKay." Thurman looked around before he lowered his voice. "You had it bad for her."

"So did half the damn school. Which is why Deck gave her a purity ring until he could swap it out for a wedding band."

Before his friend could rib him any more, their buddy Ned showed up with his wife, Roxanne. Then Warner's wife, Leah, joined them. The group had grown to six, so they claimed a circular booth in the back corner.

After ordering a couple pitchers, talk turned to the weather, sports and kids. Warner still team roped on occasion and he and Tell talked about upcoming rodeos.

During a lull, Roxanne said to Tell, "I take it Jessie hasn't popped yet?"

"She's got three weeks left. If Brandt could hurry that baby up, he would."

"Then he'll wanna shove it right back in there after it's been cryin' for two days straight and it won't stop," Warner said.

Leah bumped him with her shoulder. "Says the big, tough daddy. Now all Desiree has to do is pout and Daddy gives her whatever she wants."

A skinny bleached blonde butted in and perched on the edge of the booth, right next to Tell. "If it isn't my favorite cowboy."

"Mira. How's it goin'?"

"Better now that you're here."

"And why's that?" God, he hoped she didn't ask him for money.

She leaned close enough to put her mouth on his ear. "Because I am so horny. Come outside and do me in your pickup. Do me anywhere." Then she blew her boozy breath in his ear and licked it. "Please."

The drunk woman used so much tongue Tell was surprised saliva wasn't dripping off his earlobe. Now he wished she had just hit him up for cash. He scooted closer to Thurman. "Sorry to disappoint you, darlin', but I'm just getting over a nasty bout of the flu."

"It don't bother me. Come on."

Tell had a hard time remembering why he'd ever found her attractive. He uncurled her fingers from his bicep. "I'm on heavy-duty meds and they have an...unfortunate side effect." He sipped his beer, waiting for the meaning to sink in.

31

Her painted lips formed an "O" of surprise. "You can't get it up." She popped to her feet. "Huh. Too bad. See you around." And she took off.

Ten seconds later the entire table burst into laughter.

"Man. Does that happen to you a lot?" Ned asked.

Tell nodded yes and said, "No."

More laughter.

"You ain't worried about her spreading rumors you can't get it up?" Thurman asked.

"Nope. There are plenty of women around who will dispute that statement."

"You're such a dog, McKay," Warner said. "How many chicks *do* you have on a string right now?"

"What day is it?"

Laughter ended abruptly and everyone looked at the end of the table.

"Hey, Tell. I just wanted to come over and say hello."

Tell felt that same *whomp* in the gut he had at age seventeen whenever their eyes met. "Georgia. Good to see you again." He stopped being mesmerized by her beauty long enough to say, "I'm sure you know most these folks we went to school with. Thurman. Ned. Roxanne—"

"I'm Ned's wife now," Roxanne said sharply. "And I doubt you would've remembered my name if Tell hadn't reminded you."

Wow. That was bitchy.

Leah folded her arms over her cleavage. "Yeah, I'll bet you don't know who I am either."

All eyes were on Georgia. But rather than lifting her chin and leveling them with a haughty stare, she took a step back. "Our class wasn't that big, Leah. Of course I remember you." She gave Tell a wan smile. "Sorry to interrupt. Have a good night." She walked off.

"Jesus, Roxanne, way to be a bitch to her," Ned said.

"Serves her right for all the times she was so stuck-up to me," Roxanne shot back. "Did she expect we'd give her a group hug?"

"She has put on a few pounds," Leah said with a cruel smile. "No way would she fit into that itty-bitty cheerleading skirt now."

Tell frowned. He'd never seen this side of his friends' wives and he really didn't like it.

"Sally Hermanson, who's running everything for the reunion? Said when she called Georgia last year to ask if she'd be interested in helping organize it? Georgia said no and she doubted she'd be attending the reunion anyway." Roxanne shrugged. "I sure as hell wouldn't show up if I was her."

"No kidding. Divorced from the guy you married right out of high school. I heard she lives with her mom in some hippie commune in Boulder."

"I've heard her dad doesn't have anything to do with her."

"Maybe that's why Deck kicked her out," Leah added.

"Or else she was too good to be married to a guy who became a pig farmer."

Both women snorted.

Tell slammed his beer glass on the table. "Jesus. Really? You guys haven't seen Georgia or talked to her in ten years and you automatically assume she's exactly the same person she was back then? Why? None of us are the same. Thank God we've changed, but you can be damn sure I ain't gonna stoop to your level and point them changes out, because they ain't all good." He stood, tossed a twenty on the table and went to find her.

Georgia had taken a booth in the center of the room. Some guy appeared to be harassing her. Tell tapped him on the shoulder and recognized him as Dalton's former classmate. "Monte. Been a long time. You waiting for the band to start?" He maneuvered him aside so he could slide into the booth opposite Georgia.

"Nah. I'm just looking for someone to take to my buddy Brad's party."

"Do you know Mira? Skinny blonde? She mentioned wanting to get wild tonight. Track her down. She'd be game."

Monte said, "Thanks for the tip, McKay," and loped off.

"I'm assuming you don't mind that I interrupted?" Tell asked, suppressing a grin. "Or were you interested in accompanying Monte to a kegger?"

She laughed. "No."

Her low-pitched, sexy laugh hadn't changed either. "So will you let me buy you a drink?"

Her face shuttered. "If it won't ruin your reputation being seen in public with me."

"I remember when you wouldn't be seen with me. So, it's a chance I'm willing to take."

A waitress took their drink order.

"So, I overheard part of the conversation with your friends."

"Which part?" Hopefully not Mira's last comment.

"The part about you having a bunch of women on the hook." Georgia cocked her head. "Embraced your McKay wild-man heritage after we graduated, did you?"

"With both hands. I had plenty of wild oats to sow and I've enjoyed the hell out of plowing up every single row." He adjusted his hat. "Sorry Leah and Roxanne went off on you."

Those pale-blue eyes searched his. "Not your fault. It's not the first time I've faced that kind of hostility since I returned to Sundance."

"Returned? You're not just visiting?"

She shook her head.

Well didn't that just present some interesting possibilities? "Fill me in on the last ten years in the life of Georgia Hotchkiss."

"If I bare all, McKay, you'd better be willing to do the same."

"Oh, I don't have a problem baring anything, sweetness."

She blushed.

Huh. How about that.

Once they'd been served their drinks, Georgia said, "When was the last time we saw each other?"

"After graduation. That night at the lake." She'd shown up in skintight Daisy Duke short-shorts and an icy-blue tank top that matched her eyes. He'd stood by the bonfire, mesmerized by the golden glow reflecting on her beautiful face, taking her from the realm of a pretty woman to that of a goddess. She'd only stayed long enough to forever burn that image of her in his mind.

"My life. Let's see... Deck and I got married the month after graduation. RJ died the next summer. Then my mom left my dad. I was divorced from Deck by my twenty-first birthday. I finished college in Laramie and got a job in Dallas. That's it."

Okay. Maybe he'd expected more. But...she had boiled it down to the basics.

She took a drink. "You know, I was so self-involved back then I have no idea if you went to college."

Tell shook his head.

"Why not? You were definitely smart enough. You graduated at the top of our class."

"There were only a hundred and thirty kids in our class," he said dryly.

"You never considered it?"

Even though ten years had passed, Tell couldn't confess there'd been no money for college. "I'm a generational Wyoming rancher. My life choices were decided for me when I was born." He sipped his beer. "But I did take off the summer I turned nineteen. Spent three months on the southwest rodeo circuit. Considered going pro." Part of him hadn't wanted to come back. But he'd felt guilty about leaving all the ranch work to his brothers, and he'd missed Wyoming more than he thought possible.

"That was the summer RJ died." She started picking at the cocktail napkin. An air of sadness softened her brusque demeanor.

It ripped at him, but Tell knew how that felt. Putting on a brave face or a funny face because that's what was expected. He covered her hand. "I'm so damn sorry."

Georgia didn't pull away from his touch. "Did you know my father went off the deep end two months after RJ's funeral?" Her gaze met his again. "Sorry. This is all old news to you. I'm sure the town gossips had a field day."

"I never heard anything about it," he lied.

"I don't know which is worse. Being the object of gossip. Or no one caring enough *to* gossip about you."

He had no idea what to say to that.

The band started tuning up.

Her melancholy mood disappeared and she offered him a dazzling smile that set off his warning bells. "Enough about me. So you're ranching?"

"Yep."

"You raising Black Angus? Or Herefords?"

Tell studied her. It'd been a while but he still recognized the switch—cranking the charm on high meant she wanted something from him. Time to let her know he wasn't the gullible teen boy he'd been. "Do you really care?"

That caught her by surprise. "Yes. Why would I ask if I didn't?"

"'Cause small talk ain't ever been your style."

She didn't deny it.

He took it a step further. "Besides, I get the feeling you came here tonight lookin' for me."

"Cocky much? I didn't ask you to join me, Tell. So feel free to leave."

And that retort was so old-school Georgia-like he had to grin. "There's the glare I remember. I prefer it to that fake flirting thing you do."

"Fake flirting? You don't think much of me, do you, McKay?"

"I haven't seen you in a decade and I ain't gonna pretend I know you. Likewise, you don't know me. So you oughta understand that I'm a straight-shooter. If you wanna continue this conversation, you'd best be up front about what you want from me, without dousing me with your feminine wiles."

Georgia laughed. "Now I remember why I always liked you."

"Because I was easily manipulated?"

"I see you're still tossing off those one-liners every chance you get in an attempt to charm and distract."

Ouch. He deserved that. It surprised him that she remembered that about him. He smiled. "Now we're getting someplace. So spill it, hot lips."

"You are right. I did come to the bar tonight looking for you to ask if you're going to the class reunion in two weeks."

"I'd planned on going to the Saturday night stuff, but not the Friday family picnic."

"Do you have a date?"

Why did his heart rate spike? "Not yet. Why?"

She blurted, "Will you be my date?"

After the shock wore off, Tell leaned forward. "For real, Georgia?"

"For real. I hadn't planned on going to the reunion. What a fun way to spend an evening, dealing with the stares, rude comments and whispers about why Deck and I are divorced. Or hearing about what a tragedy it was that RJ got killed driving drunk."

"So what changed your mind?"

Her pale-blue eyes remained on his. "Seeing you last night."

Don't fall for it. Demand a solid reason. "Because…?"

"Because you know how to have fun. And if I went with you, I might have a chance at having fun."

"Your change of heart about revisiting those glory days isn't because Deck hates my guts and it'd be a hard poke at him to show up with me on your arm?"

She allowed a tiny, embarrassed smile. "Okay. Maybe that's part of it. And you have to admit it'd be a great bit of drama if we showed up together."

He grinned. "That it might."

"And I can't go to the family picnic that Friday either. I'll be out of town for a job."

"I never asked what you're doin' for a living that allowed you to move back to Sundance."

"I work for an event management company out of Dallas. We have a PR arm and an advertising arm, and we mostly handle promotion for events like rodeos, concerts and benefits."

"What's the name of the company?"

"Barb Wyre PR. Ever heard of it?"

He had heard of it. Recently. "The committee that hired me as a judge for the rodeo in Buffalo next weekend mentioned L bar K had been bought out by another company."

Her eyes widened. "Wait a second. You're a PRCA judge?"

"For over two years."

"I'm not surprised. I figured you'd always have a foot in the rodeo world. Seems to be an addiction."

Tell knew that Deck was a judge too, but they'd never worked a rodeo together, and he'd always been thankful for that. "How many other rodeos is your company providing promotion for this summer?"

"Twenty, right now. We seem to add more every week. Why?"

Tell's mind was churning. This could be his chance not only to get more judging gigs, but to get Georgia Hotchkiss where he'd always wanted her: on his arm in public and in his bed. "Do you have judges scheduled for all those events?"

"I'd have to look, but I'm betting not. Not all rodeos are PRCA-sanctioned."

"I know. I've worked quite a few that aren't."

"How many PRCA events are you scheduled to judge this summer?"

"Only four. Which ain't bad, considering I haven't been doin' it that long and I've mostly been judging small rodeos in the area during the summer."

"Have you pissed off one of the higher-ups in the regional PRCA judge management?"

"Not so far as I know. The only thing I can think of is the committees that hire companies like yours are goin' with judges who have more years on the dirt. How am I supposed to get experience if I don't get the chance to judge?"

Georgia thoughtfully drummed her fingers on the table. "That is a catch-22, isn't it?"

"But you could help me change that. We could help each other out. If you like how I conduct myself, then you could drop my name to the committees that hire judges for non-PRCA rodeos. Extolling my...qualifications."

"And what would I get in return?"

Tell bestowed his most charming grin. "I'd be your date for the reunion. Might be fun, bein' the stick you use to poke Deck and anyone else who wants to take a whack at you."

A strange expression flitted across her face, but she hadn't automatically said no.

"What?"

"Won't our classmates think it's a setup? Or worse, that you're my date strictly out of pity? I don't want to be pitied, Tell."

That could be a problem for both of them. He snapped his fingers as a solution occurred to him. "Then we'll just have to convince everyone in town that we're crazy about each other in the next two weeks *before* the reunion."

"By pretending to be together?"

"Oh, sweetness, there wouldn't be no pretending. We'd be together for real."

"Define 'for real'."

His gaze encompassed her face, then dipped to her chest, and he didn't bother to bank his lust when their eyes met again. "You want me as your date for the reunion? I'll also be sharin' your bed."

Georgia's jaw dropped and she shrank back in the booth.

"Is that such a repulsive thought to you?" he asked sharply.

"God no. Not at all. You're just so—" Her mouth snapped shut on whatever she'd been about to say. "Who is gonna believe it?"

"Everyone, if we play this right." He leaned in, trying to hard-sell it. "See, we've already got the ball rolling. We were seen in the park together today. We're sitting in the Golden Boot right now. I told off my friends' wives for their bitchy behavior toward you, and Leah and Roxanne are two of the biggest gossips in town. It'll get around. Trust me."

"You defended me?"

"That mean-girl shit don't fly with me."

When Georgia continued to stare at him without speaking, he started to get annoyed. "Why're you so shocked?"

"Because I wasn't expecting it."

"You expected I'd be happy just holdin' your hand and smelling your hair?" Had he really said that? *Be a man. Be firm. You're no longer that eager-to-please pup.* "Wrong. Nothin' comes for free. We'll be lovers. Not friends. There's your deal. Take it or leave it."

"No room for negotiation?"

"Nope."

Georgia's chin came up and her eyes were pure skepticism. "Oh really? Not even when a no on my part could mean you don't get assigned to more rodeos?"

"Yep." He finished his beer and slid out of the booth. "Let me know what you decide, but I wouldn't take too long to make up my mind, sweetness, because you are not the only woman who's asked me to be her reunion date."

Damn hard to do, but Tell walked away.

When did you turn into a mouse, Georgia Hotchkiss?

She'd scurried out of the bar and was pacing in the parking lot, a little shocked by Tell's aggressive side. He'd always been so laid back. Then again... How well had she known him ten years ago?

Not well at all.

But she'd really like to get to know him now. On the most basic, carnal level.

What was the worst that could happen if she said yes to Tell's demands? Sex would be bad with him? Doubtful.

Still, Georgia couldn't shake the feeling this might be a game. He'd agree to attend the reunion with her, have sex with her beforehand, but back out at the last minute, just to get even with her.

She hated to think along those lines, but she had to put that possibility into the equation. Along with the fear that Tell was living out some high school fantasy. As soon as he bedded her, he'd revert to locker room behavior and brag that he'd nailed the homecoming queen.

Where did that leave her? Sorting fact from fear.

Fact 1: Tell McKay was undeniably hot.

Fact 2: He wanted her on his terms.

Fact 3: She could be the bold, sexually adventurous woman she'd always wanted to be.

Fact 4: She was leaving at summer's end.

So why was she debating the pros and cons in the dark parking lot of a honky-tonk? Because he'd unnerved her? Or because he'd made her panties wet with one simple demand?

She had nothing to lose...and everything to gain.

That cinched it. She'd become Tell McKay's lover for however long it lasted.

Mind made up, Georgia walked to the bar entrance. Who should wander out but Leah and Roxanne. They didn't act nearly so confident without a bar full of people bolstering their courage.

"You know the funny thing about returning here?" Georgia sauntered forward. "The length of time away is disproportionate to the level of animosity I faced when I lived in Sundance. I get that neither of you liked me during our years together in high school. But did either of you *really* know me?

"Granted, I didn't know you either, so I'll give you both a pass on that one. But what I *do* know? I didn't try and steal your boyfriends. I didn't snub you because you wore a purity ring. I didn't put gum in your hair. I didn't X out your face in every homecoming and prom picture. But you know what? Every one of those things was done...to me. So remember that when you embellish the past and paint me out to be some nasty bitch. I wasn't that way back then and I'm not that way now. It sucks if someone made your high school years hell, but that someone was *not* me. And my high school years weren't a bucket of fucking roses either. Think about that." She walked between them into the bar.

One monkey off my back.

The noise had increased exponentially. The lighting seemed dimmer. The air smokier. Technically smoking wasn't allowed in the bar, but folks in Wyoming didn't appreciate the government handing down decrees, so they ignored them.

Georgia scanned the line at the bar. The dance floor. The pool tables. Then she saw him. Her belly swooped. Her mouth dried. Her sex clenched.

Even in a room full of hat-and-jeans-wearing cowboys, Tell McKay stood out. A prize bull, a top stud, a virile male.

He studied her nonchalantly, as if trying to gauge her intent. Waiting for her to make the first move.

So she did.

Squaring her shoulders, she offered him a sexy smile and started toward him.

Chapter Four

The neon glow from the bar lights created a blue halo above her shiny black hair.

But she didn't look like an angel. She looked like a temptress.

Tell's eyes ate up every inch of Georgia's sexy body as she meandered toward him. He drained his beer and set the bottle aside, meeting her halfway. "You came back."

"Yes."

"Why?"

"There's something compelling about you, Tell. There always has been. I couldn't stay away."

He bit back a growl. "You know what that means."

"Yes, I do."

"Say it. Out loud."

"You'll be in my bed or I'll be in yours. Either way, we'll be lovers."

He ran his palm down her arm, from her shoulder to her fingertips. Her skin beaded and a tiny shiver rolled through her.

Now that's what I'm talkin' about.

Without asking, Tell clasped her hand and led her to the dance floor. Holding her felt as good as he'd imagined.

She was such a petite thing. The sky-high heels she wore put the top of her head level with his chin. She definitely had curves in the right places now, all luscious woman, not athletic girl.

"You haven't said much, Tell."

"Just thinkin'."

"About?"

"You. Bein' so short. Remembering when the cheerleaders threw you in the air at football games."

"They'd be hard-pressed to basket-toss me now."

Tell tipped up her chin. "You looked good then, but you look even better now."

She said, "Oh really?" as if she didn't believe him.

"Yep. Now I won't worry that I'll break you when I fuck you hard."

Those stunning eyes widened. With shock? Some. But mostly interest.

Tell just smiled and spun her around the dance floor.

They didn't speak through the next song; they held fast and learned the rhythm of their bodies until they were in perfect synch. Georgia followed his lead like she was born to it. Would she be that yielding in bed?

You don't want that. You want her all over you like a cat in heat. Hissing. Scratching. Rubbing. Purring.

"You okay?"

He refocused on her. "Yeah. Why?"

"You made a strange noise."

"Probably a growl." He bent his head closer to hers. "I suspect you'll bring out the beast in me."

"Are you trying to scare me off, cowboy?"

"Nope, but maybe this will." Tell twined a handful of her hair around his fingers, pulling those soft tresses to tilt her head back. He kept their gazes fastened as his mouth descended. Once their lips touched, he kissed her with the zeal of a seventeen-year-old boy, but with the finesse of a twenty-eight-year-old man.

She surrendered to him, kissing him with passion as alluring as the taste of her. The press of her lips, so pillowy soft, yet so firmly locked to his hungry mouth, sent a spike of desire straight to his dick.

Tell could've kissed her all damn night, but he'd taken things a step further than was smart. He released his possessive grip on her hair and broke the seal of their mouths, feeling her rapid exhalations on his kiss-swollen lips.

She opened her eyes. A mix of wonder and hunger flared in the icy-blue depths.

They began dancing again. "That oughta get some tongues a'waggin'."

Georgia didn't crack a smile.

"What?"

"Let's make their jaws drop. Come home with me tonight."

Immediately his dick was on board with her suggestion. But a quick fuck wasn't in the cards for them. He'd been waiting a long time for this, so she sure as hell wasn't getting instant gratification. A little sexual teasing would be good for her. For him too.

She brushed her mouth against the corner of his lips. "You know you want to."

"Like you wouldn't believe. But we're gonna do this the right way. We'll spend time together *before* we slip between the sheets."

Her eyebrows knitted. "I don't understand. Aren't we trying to convince them we're lovers?"

"If we want people to believe we're really a *couple*, then we need to be out and about doin' couple things, not just banging each other behind closed doors." Tell put his lips by her ear. "Once I get you nekkid—and trust me, sweetness, that will happen sooner rather than later—we'll be there for a while. A good long while."

Georgia shivered.

When the band switched to a fast tune, he led her off the dance floor and purposely sat across from her in the booth.

"What now?"

"You'll go home. I'll stick around here for another hour or so. Then we'll meet tomorrow."

Her eyes narrowed. "Let's get one thing straight. If we're a couple, then I expect you to only be with me."

He bristled. "You think the second you're out the door I'll take some other woman home with me? Wrong."

"You sure? Because you admitted earlier that you have a reputation as a player. I've seen the glances other women are throwing your way."

"I've got no control over who looks at me, Georgia. You either trust me or you don't."

She was clearly torn, wanting more assurances, but Tell offered her none. Finally a faint smile touched her lips. "Obviously I have some trust issues that aren't your concern. So what are we doing tomorrow?"

Tell brought her hand to his mouth and kissed her knuckles. "We're gonna have some fun. Because I get the feelin' you don't have near enough fun in your life, hot lips."

"Tell. You don't have to—"

"Get you to loosen up? Yes, I do. 'Cause that's one of the things I do best."

"What's the other thing?"

He raised a brow at her and smirked.

"You're such a guy."

"And proud of it. Mark my words, I'm gonna make you have fun tomorrow even if it pisses you off."

Georgia laughed. "What fun thing do you have in mind?"

"I'm takin' you out for ice cream. But first we'll meet in the park at the basketball court. Wear something casual and sporty, because sweetness, I'm gonna make you work for that very first lick."

Casual and sporty, he'd said.

Georgia checked her reflection in the bathroom mirror for the fourteenth time before she muttered, "Screw it," and sailed out the door. On the walk, she gave herself a pep talk.

Don't overanalyze everything. Have fun. Be sexy. Be flirty. In other words, act nothing like yourself.

No pressure.

By the time she reached the park, she'd calmed herself down.

Then she got a gander at Tell McKay and her heart rate zoomed into the danger zone again.

Uh, yeah. No mistaking him for a teenage boy now.

Tell wore black basketball shorts that hung above his knees and a sleeveless gray top that molded to his upper body. Over the years he'd bulked up, making his chest appear broader than she'd remembered. *And yeah, baby, check out those well-defined arms.* His skin was startlingly white from the ball of his shoulder to his muscled biceps, and from that point down, the length of his arm was a caramel brown. Even a farmer's tan looked good on him.

He noticed her and jogged over, holding a basketball. "I'm glad you came." His gaze moved over her body from her orange Lycra tank top to her gray cotton capris to her black athletic shoes. "You look great."

"You too." Without a cowboy hat covering his dark hair, she saw the ends held a slight curl. Such a tempting man, with his banging body, piercing blue eyes and those deep dimples. She wanted to lick him up one side and down the other. And that was a totally foreign feeling to her. She defined *reserved* in all matters of her life, especially in relationships with the opposite sex.

"You ready to play?"

"I thought we were going out for ice cream?"

"After." He dribbled the ball around her. Stopped and took a shot at the basket. Naturally, he sank it. He chased after the ball and bounced it as he returned.

"You're good. Why didn't you play in high school?"

"It conflicted with rodeo season. I like shooting hoops for fun. Not everything has to be about competition."

Her eyes met his in direct challenge. "So we're not havin' us a little contest?"

Tell laughed. "You mimic me pretty well, sweetness. Yes, we're havin' us a little contest."

"I can't go one-on-one with you, Tell. You're too big."

He eyes smoldered. "I've no doubt you could take me. Take all of me just fine."

Wasn't he just pouring on sexual innuendo today? And didn't she get a secret thrill out of it? When was the last time any man had cajoled her into having fun while making her think of hot skin, cool sheets, and a night without end? Never, probably.

"We're playing for ice cream?"

He shook his head slowly, gifting her with a sexy, sly grin. "If you win, *you* get to pick the place on your body I kiss. If I win, *I* get to pick the place on your body to kiss."

Her mind automatically compiled a list of spots, adding stars and hearts to her favorites.

"Earth to Georgia."

Her gaze zoomed back to him to see a sinful grin on his handsome face. "That sounds like a heckuva good deal for me. What do you get out of it?"

He loomed over, all hard-bodied man. "I finally get to put my mouth on you wherever I want."

"So confident you're gonna win?"

"I've already won." Tell pressed his lips to hers and let the kiss linger. No tongue, just the warm tease of his mouth. "I trust you know how to play horse?" he murmured between soft smooches.

"Yes. But I get to shoot first because you're going down."

"Or I'm goin' down on you." Grinning wickedly, he handed her the ball. "Show me whatcha got, hot lips."

Georgia had always hated that nickname, but coming from Tell in that husky male rasp...made it sound sexy. Standing on the right side of the basket, she shot and the ball bounced off the glass to the other side.

"Tough break. My turn." Tell performed some fancy dribbling maneuver around her. Stopping beneath the basket, he took the shot.

Nothing but net.

"And the crowd goes wild." Tell spun a circle, pumped his fist into the air, then passed her the ball.

Okay. She could do this. No sweat. She lobbed the ball at the basket and it dropped in. She must've had a surprised look because Tell laughed when he high-fived her.

He snatched the ball and lined up at the free throw mark. He bounced the ball four times and then let it fly.

Swish.

Dammit. She'd never make that shot. Georgia felt Tell move in behind her at the free throw line; his breath tickled her ear. "Don't forget. It was four bounces before the shot. If you don't do it exactly right, you'll earn a penalty."

She faced him. "That's not in the rules."

"There's one thing you oughta know about me, sweetness. I make up my own rules."

Tempting to break the rules just to see what he'd do. But Tell probably expected that. She dribbled four times and sent the ball into the air, only to watch it bounce off the rim.

"And she earns an 'H'. Better luck next time."

For the next two shots, Tell remained in the same place at the free throw line. He aced both baskets, which added an "O" and an "R" to her score when she missed both hers.

Tell slam-dunked the next one.

"Now that, Tell McKay, is just plain mean. I'm short. I need a ladder to make that shot."

"Or some help." He handed her the ball. "Hold on."

"What?" barely squeaked from her mouth before Tell wrapped his arms around her thighs and hoisted her up. "Omigod, I weigh too much for you to be lifting me."

"Bullshit. Now dunk that ball in the basket."

Using both hands, she slammed it in the hoop. She released a loud *whoop* and kept her eyes on Tell's as he allowed her to slide down his body slowly enough that every hard inch of his upper torso pressed into her thighs, belly and chest.

When they were eye to eye, Tell muttered, "You're just so goddamn tempting I can't help myself," and snared her mouth in a kiss.

Tell McKay kissed the daylights out of her. Even after he finally let her feet touch the ground, Georgia still had that floating sensation.

"I could get used to seein' that dazed look every time I kiss you."

"I could get used to you kissing me like that," she shot back. "But I know what you're doing."

"What?"

"Cheating. Trying to keep me off-balance."

"Yep." He flashed an unapologetic grin. "And I'm even gonna let you take the next shot."

"Only because you believe I won't make it."

He walked backward with his hands out. "So prove me wrong."

As Georgia scooped up the ball, she had a brilliant idea. She dribbled the ball until she reached the free throw line. Then she turned around.

"Georgia, what *are* you doin'? You're facing the wrong way."

"I know." With her back to the basket and her feet spread wide apart, she swung the ball between her knees and threw it over her head. She spun quickly, watching the ball hit the backboard, sloppily rimming the bucket before it dropped in. "Yes! Yes! Yes!" She skipped toward Tell, taunting, "In your face, McKay."

"You think I can't do it granny style, hot lips?"

"I'm sure you can. Just as I'm sure you'll make a crack about preferring to do it doggie style."

"Guess you'll find out, won't you?"

Georgia cooed, "I'm game for that right now."

Tell let the ball drop. He stalked her, but it wasn't like she tried to get away. He bent down and slapped his hands on her ass. "Jump up and wrap your legs around my waist."

"But—"

"Do. It. Now."

That bit of bossiness coming from him was hot. Soon as she moved, he lifted her, keeping a firm grip on her ass. Georgia emitted a little yelp, clutching his shoulders as he walked her backward until her upper body rested against the steel post.

His intense blue eyes were riveted on hers before he dipped his head. She expected fire the instant their lips touched, but Tell kissed her without hurry. Keeping the kiss soft, sweet and slow. As if he had all the time in the world to explore her mouth, to tease her tongue with little sucks and bites. To drive her to the edge of lust and hold her there for as long as he damn well pleased.

She tangled her fingers in his hair, drifting into a fuzzy state of pleasure. She couldn't blame the heat building between them on the sun. Just this man.

They only broke the kiss because someone whistled.

Tell's forehead met hers. "Damn."

"My thoughts exactly."

"What are we gonna do about this, sweetness?"

"I have a couple of ideas. Explicit ideas."

"So if I said, 'Georgia, let's hotfoot it to my place right now and get nekkid'...?"

"I'd race you to your truck. And I'd probably win."

He laughed. "Guess that settles my question."

"Which was?"

Tell studied her. "If you're shy when that bedroom door closes."

"No. But I'm not bossy, either."

"Good to know. Because I *am* bossy."

She expected him to laugh and say just kidding, but apparently he was serious. Very serious. She swallowed hard.

"Did you know I had a hard-on every damn day in history class?"

"Ah-hah!" Georgia poked him in the chest. "I *knew* studying the War Between the States got you all hot and bothered."

"Funny girl. *You* got me all hot and bothered. Every time your hair brushed across my knuckles, I imagined those soft strands teasing my dick. I'd stare at the back of your head and daydream."

"About my hair?"

He grinned. "No. Mostly about sex stuff that I had no experience with, but your cherry-scented hair played a big part in every one of those horny teen dreams. And I wasn't the only guy in our school who got hard just from lookin' at you. I hoped my boner would be gone by the time the bell rang. So you wouldn't notice."

A sudden feeling of guilt caused her to blurt, "What does that say about me, Tell? That I didn't notice?"

"It says you were a seventeen-year-old girl immersed in her own dramas. It also says for bein' the hottest girl in school, you were unaware of your appeal. I didn't bring it up to make you feel bad, Georgia. I only said it because I'm hard right now."

"I figured that out on my own."

He laughed. "See? You're much more observant now."

"So how long do you plan to keep me pressed up against this pole?"

"Until my flagpole impression goes away. Just give me a minute to...catch my bearings, because we still need to finish our game," Tell murmured in her ear.

"Huh-uh. I forfeit. You win. Now can we get ice cream?"

Tell kissed her and gently set her back on her feet. He picked up the basketball and held out his hand. "Where you thinking? Dairy Queen? Or the drive-in? Wherever we go, you cannot order a cone. No way can I hide an erection in these shorts if I watch that tongue of yours licking."

"Too bad. I'm definitely picking that." She yelped when he swatted her butt.

After piling in Tell's pickup, he patted the center of the bench seat and grinned at her.

Georgia rolled her eyes, but she scooted over.

The DQ parking lot was full on a Sunday afternoon.

Tell kept his hands on her shoulders and his body tucked in close behind hers as they waited in line. He read every item on the menu to her, and made every item sound dirty.

When she turned to warn him to knock it off or else she was ordering a chocolate-covered frozen banana, he kissed her. Not a quick peck either.

"Eww, Tell. I think I saw your tongue," a young male voice complained.

They broke the lip-lock and looked at the boy. Dark hair, blue eyes, wearing camo shorts and an orange Toby Keith T-shirt.

"Hey, Ky. Guess you haven't kissed a girl yet if you're still grossed out by it."

The kid blushed. "I coulda kissed a girl if I wanted to, but who'd want to?" Ky's gaze landed on Georgia. "Who're you?"

"Georgia Hotchkiss. Who are you?"

"Ky McKay. Tell is kinda my uncle." He threw back his thin shoulders, rising to his full height. "You're kinda short. I'm almost taller than you."

"And you're about to get extra chores for bein' rude, Kyler."

The man who'd spoken stood behind Ky with another dark-haired boy of about two resting on his hip. She'd never met him, and he was probably a dozen years older than Tell, but he was obviously a McKay.

"Aw, Dad, I was just kiddin'," Ky complained.

The man thrust out his hand and smiled. "I'm Cord McKay. Tell's cousin."

"Nice to meet you, Cord. Who's the little guy?"

Cord glanced down as the boy hid his face. "Beau. It's past his naptime and he's steppin' on his mama's last nerve today."

Another dark-haired boy, around age four, barreled up and head-butted Ky in the stomach. "You stole my toy!"

Ky looked innocent. "What? I don't know what you're talkin' about, Foster. You probably lost it."

"Give it back!"

"Don't be such a baby. It's just a stupid toy."

Foster growled and charged Ky again, but was handily stopped by his father. "Knock it off. Both of you."

A pregnant blonde stopped next to Cord, and Beau tried to jump out of his father's arms into hers. When Cord kept that from happening, Beau wailed.

Cord passed off the crying Beau to Ky and handed him a set of keys. "Take your brothers to the truck. But don't even think about starting it," he warned.

The boys raced out.

Cord put his hand on the woman's lower back and kissed her temple.

But the pretty blonde wasn't looking at her husband. She was looking at Georgia.

Tell said, "This is Cord's wife, AJ. AJ, this is Georgia—"

"I know who she is," AJ replied coolly. "We went to school together."

Georgia didn't remember this woman at all and she started to get that panicked feeling like she should know her.

"But she doesn't know me since I didn't have time to go to football games, dances and such. I was too busy working on the ranch."

"And that experience came in mighty handy when you married a rancher, didn't it?" Cord kissed her temple again. "Come on, baby doll, let's get you home."

Georgia said, "Nice to meet you." Cord nodded, but AJ didn't say anything.

Another snub.

"AJ's usually really sweet, but you wouldn't know it today. Sorry about that."

"Looks like she has her hands full." She smiled, trying to act like it didn't bother her. "I've decided on an Oreo Blizzard."

They finished their ice cream in Tell's pickup. Then Tell eased the seat back and patted his thighs. "You're lookin' a little cold. I'll warm you up."

She put her knees by his hips, facing him as she sat on his lap. "Checking out my nipples, were you?"

That bold observation seemed to shock him. "What? No. I saw you shiver."

"Uh-huh. Maybe I shivered because I saw you eyeballing my chest, Tell McKay."

He placed his cold lips on the hollow of her throat. "It's been distracting me all damn day because I know you ain't wearin' a bra."

Georgia rested her elbows on his shoulders. "Would I have had a chance at winning the basketball game today if you'd known I'm not wearing panties?"

"Nope. But the game would've been over before it began." Tell kissed her hotly, sliding his hands beneath her backside, urging her to her knees so he could run his hands from the curve of her hips, over her butt, down the backs of her thighs and back up.

Her fingers mapped the breadth of his shoulders and the cut muscles of his arms. Such defined biceps. Ripped triceps. Even his forearms were meaty. She let her fingers lightly trail back up to tangle in his hair.

The kiss turned playful. When his tongue tickled the roof of her mouth, she laughed and leaned back to look at him.

Tell had a slight smile on his face, but his eyes were dark with sexual heat.

So she took a chance that he'd act on it with a little encouragement. "Will you come inside when you take me home? Show me where you want to place the winning kiss?"

He traced her lips with his thumb. Then his finger drew a line down her throat to the middle of her chest. "You are so sexy, Georgia. I want you like crazy. But I've got things to finish before dark." He brushed his knuckles over the rise of her cleavage. "Once I get you in bed, we're gonna stay there awhile. That's not a possibility tonight."

Georgia spread his palms over her breasts. "I don't mind a quick tumble."

"I do." He moved his hands to her rib cage, his thumbs stroking her hardened nipples. "But that don't keep me from imaging how it's gonna be between us."

"So in your wildest imagination, what is the first thing you'd do to me?"

"Strip you to skin. Learn every inch of it with my mouth."

"Mmm. Would you get me off while you're touching me, or do you keep me hanging on the edge?"

"Definitely keep you hanging." His mouth skated across her collarbone. "Until you're begging."

"When you're tired of hearing me beg, do you use your fingers to make me come? Or do you use that wicked mouth between my thighs? Or maybe you'll go straight for ramming your cock into me." She'd started rocking her pelvis and she wondered if he realized he was pushing his hips up to match the motion.

"You like dirty talk?"

She sank her teeth into his bottom lip, tugging slightly before releasing it with a wet pop. The flame of want in his eyes burned hotter. "I love it. The dirtier the better."

"Prove it. Say something dirty.".

"Fuck me harder, Tell. Put your cock in my mouth, Tell. Bend me over the tailgate of your pickup, Tell."

His breaths were choppy. His jaw set. One hand squeezed her breast. The other hand gripped her hair. He rubbed his mouth over her ear, teasing her mercilessly until she was shuddering in his arms.

"Did that change your mind?" she whispered.

"No. It was freakin' hot. But here's a warning. You can say all the raunchy things you want. Get me so damn worked up I'm ready to shoot in my shorts. But guess what? The more you tease, the longer I'm gonna make us wait."

She couldn't help the bewildered, "Why?"

"Because, sweetness, I can." Then he kissed her. Not with the hunger, but with delicacy. Letting their harsh breaths mingle, thoroughly teasing her lips, making her want a firmer kiss. Making her want his unrestrained passion, not his caution.

Tell held her face in his hands and ended the kiss. "Let's get you home."

Dazed, and a little petulant, Georgia tried to return to the passenger's side, but he wouldn't allow her retreat. He pulled her back to the middle of the bench seat and rested his hand on the inside of her thigh.

He left his pickup idling by the curb as he walked her up the sidewalk. "Didja have fun today, Georgia?"

"Yes."

"Me too. Did you notice all the folks watchin' us? Ought to make for some interesting chatter around town tomorrow."

She'd had such a great time she'd forgotten that creating buzz about them being a couple was part of the deal.

He stopped in front of the door. "You busy tomorrow night?"

"More of this 'see and be seen as a couple' stuff?"

Bristling, he stepped back. "You can say no."

"I'm not saying no tonight, Tell." Maybe he wouldn't notice that came out kind of whiny.

"I know that too. What's with the snippy answers and the pouty face?"

"I'm not pouting."

"Yes you are." He pushed her against the door. "Gimme a smile, Georgia."

"No."

"You can give me a smile or I'll take it." He poked her ribs, trying to find her ticklish spots.

"No fair. Stop."

"I will. All's you gotta do is lemme see that pretty smile." More pokes.

She giggled. God. When was the last time that'd happened?

"A laugh will work too."

He kissed her cheek and tickled her until she shrieked, "Tell!"

He laughed. "Okay. I'm done." He stepped back. "See you tomorrow."

Chapter Five

The instant Tell popped out of bed he thought it'd be a damn fine day.

He couldn't wait to get outside and do chores. Or more to the point, finish chores so he could come home, get cleaned up for his date with Georgia tonight.

Hard to believe he had another date with Georgia Hotchkiss.

He'd wanted to hang out with her longer yesterday, but he knew they'd wind up in bed and he wanted to wait.

Why? Haven't ten years been long enough? Or are you stalling because you're afraid you'll disappoint her in the sack?

No. The younger version of himself might've been worried Georgia would find him lacking in bedroom skills. That definitely wasn't the case now. He wouldn't rush this; he had one chance to get it right.

Juggling his coffee, he drove to Dalton's place.

Dalton ambled out after Tell honked three times. His brother wore sunglasses—never a good sign. He was either hungover or he'd been fighting or both.

"Rough weekend, bro?"

"Might say that."

Tell pointed at his shades. "Take 'em off and lemme see how bad."

Dalton slid his sunglasses down his nose, revealing a blackened right eye. "Satisfied?"

"You wanna let me in on what happened?"

"Not really." He pushed the shades in place and adjusted his hat. "I'll just say the other guy looked worse than me."

"Where'd this happen?"

"What part of *I don't wanna talk about this* is confusing you?"

"Touchy much?"

"Yep, so maybe we oughta hurry this up today so you don't gotta be around my crabby ass."

"Nice try. We're fixin' fence when we meet up with Brandt."

Dalton groaned. "Fuck. Can't it wait another damn day? I'm whupped, T."

"Ain't my fault you played too hard. We gotta get that section fixed because Brandt wants to run the bulls in there after we're done turnin' them out with the cows."

"That's right around the time Jessie is set to calve."

Tell snickered. "I doubt she'd find the humor in comparing her to a heifer."

"No shit. She ain't finding humor in anything. Brandt told me she cried for an hour after she dropped a dish and she couldn't bend down to pick up the broken pieces."

"That don't sound like Jessie."

"That don't sound like Brandt, neither. He never tells me shit like that."

Tell downshifted as they crested a small rise. "He's just worried about this pregnancy. And who can blame him?" Shortly after their dad got out of rehab, Jessie had miscarried. In a moment of anger, Brandt blamed the loss on the stress their father caused. Being a total asshole, Dad said the baby dying was God's will.

Yeah, that'd been a fun day.

So Jess and Brandt hadn't announced her pregnancy until she'd reached the end of the fourth month. Everything was progressing normally. But the truth was, they were all a little anxious.

The pastures still had enough grass they hadn't needed to supplement feed. Funny how the only time cattle paid attention to them was when they were hungry.

While Dalton catnapped in the truck, Tell walked the fence line until he reached the first section they'd rip out and replace.

He and Dalton were unloading equipment when Brandt drove up. He was all business. "Mornin'. Let's only do the first half today. Jess has a doctor's appointment this afternoon, so she's home. And there's no cell service on this part of the ranch, so I—"

"Worry," Tell and Dalton finished simultaneously. Then they grinned at each other and high-fived. Eerie, how often they were on the same wavelength. Although he and Brandt were closer in age, Tell and Dalton had spent more time together as kids and as adults, because Luke and Brandt had been so tight.

"Looks like I'm workin' with Tweedledee and Tweedledum today."

Dalton poked at Brandt's belly. "Looks like we're workin' with the Pillsbury Doughboy today."

"Jesus, Dalton," Tell said with a groan.

The comment rolled right off Brandt. "Yeah, I know I've packed on an extra twenty pounds. But Jess is so damn self-conscious of how much she eats that if I'm not shoveling food in my mouth right along with her, she won't eat. That ain't good for her or the baby. So I'll deal with my flabby gut after that kid is out of my wife."

"If you need someone to be your fitness drill sergeant, I'm game," Dalton said.

"You just wanna stand over him and yell," Tell retorted.

"Yep. And ain't you jealous that you didn't think of it first?"

They dragged fence posts, a posthole digger, shovels, barbed wire and various hand tools to the first rotted post.

They'd done this enough times there wasn't need for discussion, which Tell knew would've bugged the crap out of most people. Silence ruled out on the western plains and between the McKays.

And if they'd had the radio blasting or been jawing about nothing, he probably wouldn't have heard the rattler.

He'd noticed a weird-shaped chunk of rock behind Dalton's boot. Then that rock rose up.

"Ah, Dalton. There's a rattler about a foot from your left boot," Tell said calmly. "It's ready to strike at something, so I suggest you don't move."

Dalton said, "Shit," but stayed put.

"Brandt, can you get on the back side of it?"

"What am I supposed to do? Poke it with a stick?"

"That's what Dad would tell you just to see if it'd strike you first. Hit it with a rock and see if it'll move away."

Brandt approached the snake with a spade and tossed a rock five feet behind it. But instead of it slithering the opposite direction, the snake moved forward, right between Dalton's feet.

Once the snake had slithered through, Brandt said, "Catch," and tossed Dalton the spade.

Dalton brought the shovel down hard, slicing the snake in two.

"Nice. You keeping the pieces to make yourself a snakeskin hat band?"

"Never. I don't even want the damn rattles." Dalton shivered from head to toe. "I hate them things."

"It's the season. Guess that's a sign to break out the tall boots from here on out," Brandt said.

Dalton and Tell groaned Most rattler bites happened below the knee, so thick leather boots that hit directly below the knee were necessary in the summer months. They all hated wearing them.

Even though it was just a little after one, they reloaded the equipment, deciding to call it a day.

Jessie's SUV bumped up the path to the fence.

Brandt was down the hill before Jessie opened her door.

Dalton and Tell weren't far behind.

The first thing Tell heard? Sweet Jessie snapping, "For Christsake, Brandt, will you move your ass and let me out of the damn car?"

Okay. Maybe she wasn't so sweet today.

"What's wrong?" Brandt demanded.

"Nothin' is wrong. I saw you forgot your water bottle and I knew it'd be hot out here, so I brought it to you." She hoofed it up the small incline and gestured to Tell and Dalton, panting, "Brought you guys some too."

Seemed Jess's belly had grown another six inches in the last week. She looked like she'd swallowed a beach ball.

Not that Tell would share that observation with her.

"Thanks, sweetheart," Brandt said. "That's mighty thoughtful, but aren't you supposed to be—"

"Locked in the damn house going out of my freakin' mind? I'm supposed to sit around with my feet up so I can watch my ankles swell up like toads?"

"Jess—"

"Don't you tell me to calm down or use that patronizing tone with me, mister. You'll be in the doghouse right along with Lexi. The little shit pissed me off today."

"Your dog pissed you off?"

Jessie's gaze pierced Dalton. "Yes. And if you spout off anything smart, Dalton McKay, you're liable to piss me off too."

Dalton's hands went up in the air. "Forget I said anything."

"Good idea." When she turned to her husband—too fast—and started to lose her balance, Brandt was right there, keeping her steady. He was smart enough not to warn her to be careful. Or to open his mouth at all.

"The other reason I came out here was because some guy called the house phone and needs to talk to you right away about irrigation sprinkler heads. Something about a back order? He's only going to be in the office another hour and then he goes on vacation for two weeks."

"Goddammit. Those have already been on back order for six weeks. I ain't waiting another month and a half for them. Let's go. I'll drive your car and Dalton can bring my truck to the house."

"You go on," Jessie said. "Now that I'm out of jail and see how nice it is, I'm taking a few minutes to breathe in some fresh air."

Brandt looked torn, wanting to command her to get in the car, but also wanting to keep his head attached to his body. "Fine. But don't wander off. Dalton just killed a rattler." He set his hands on her belly, kissed her—twice—and whispered something that made her smile. Then he whacked her butt before he jogged to his truck.

Once Brandt was gone, Jessie put her hands on her hips and squared off with both of them. "I lied about needing fresh air."

Awesome.

"I wanted to talk to you guys without your brother hovering."

Tell and Dalton exchanged a look. "What's up?"

"You tell me. Brandt is beyond tense. Like heart attack and stroke-level stressed out, and I'm scared. He won't talk to me. So I wondered if maybe something was going on with Casper or your mom or Landon or the ranch, or if you two boneheads are sneaking around, trying to buy some land again, and my husband is hiding all of this secret family shit from me so I don't get upset!"

Jessie's voice had become louder until she shouted the last part.

Dalton popped the tailgate on the pickup. "You can yell and scream at us all you want, Jess, but you're gonna do it while you're sittin' down. So park it."

Surprisingly, Jessie didn't quibble. "Sorry. It's just...you have no idea how on edge Brandt is."

"Yeah, we do. We were just talkin' about it."

"And did you come up with a solution to get him to calm the fuck down?"

Tell stepped in front of her, bracing himself for her wrath. "Know what I think? You need to calm the fuck down too."

Jessie's stubborn chin came up. "What the hell are you talking about? I *am* calm. I'm as calm as the fucking sea of tranquility! No one is more goddamn calm than me!"

A crow cawed in the silence.

Then Dalton started laughing. "Girl, that baby is gonna come out swearing a blue streak if you keep talkin' like that."

Tell started laughing too.

After a minute, she cracked a smile. "Pay no attention to the hormone-crazed pregnant lady cussing like a McKay."

"Look, Jess, you and Brandt are feeding off each other's anxiety. Brandt sees that you're uptight, then he gets uptight and paranoid that something is wrong with you or the baby, something that you're not telling him because you don't want him to worry. Which makes *you* even more uptight and you don't want to talk to him about it because you believe your worries will just add to his. See how this goes?"

She nodded and started to cry.

"Oh Jesus. Don't cry. Brandt will kill us both if he thinks we made you cry."

"These last two months I've cried enough that it doesn't even faze him anymore." She sniffed and set her hand on her belly. "Hey, little kicker, that was uncalled for."

"Can I feel it?" Tell asked.

Jessie placed his hand off to the left side. "He's too big to show off his soccer-player imitation, but he gives me plenty of knee and elbow action."

He couldn't believe how hard and tight the skin stretched over her belly was. Then he felt something move beneath his palm. "I know you're tired of bein' pregnant, but this is just so damn cool. Yours and Brandt's baby is in there."

She set her hand over the top of his. Tears filled her eyes. "Thank you. When I'm feeling bloated and I can't stretch my maternity shirts over this massive bump and I can't put on my boots and just want it to be over, I forget this is a miraculous thing. And I've wanted it for so long."

"I suspect things will settle down once the little bugger makes his appearance," Dalton said.

"I hope so. Thanks, guys. Now I know Brandt's tension wasn't just my pregnancy paranoia. I just wish there was something I could do for him short term that would relax him."

"I know *one* thing that will relax him completely. Guaranteed. A b—"

Tell shoved his younger brother. "Really, Dalton? That's how you help, by suggesting Jess gives him a blow job—"

"Whoa. No! I was gonna say a big tumbler of whiskey! Sheesh." Dalton shoved him back. "Perverted much, bro?"

Jessie giggled. "I have a hard enough time getting out of a chair, say nothin' of getting down on my knees."

"And with that...we're sending you home to your husband."

They followed her back to the house—still weird to think of it as Brandt and Jessie's place. After Casper sobered up, he'd announced he wasn't returning to live in Sundance and handed over his house to Brandt and Jessie. They'd hired Chet and Remy West for a complete remodel. Happy as he'd been for his brother and sister-in-law to have the family homestead, the place he'd grown up in wasn't his home any longer.

On the way to drop Dalton off, Tell asked, "Is it poker week?"

"Got postponed since everyone is scattered. Cam and Domini took their kids to Disney World. Colby is testing new stock at Cash Big Crow's, which means Cord and Colt are swamped. Kane and Kade are checking out a bull sale in Montana. Quinn and Libby and their kids are in Arizona at Gavin's, which means Ben's up to his ass. Keely and Jack are on some tropical vacation."

"Won't be long before the poker games end altogether."

"You're probably right." Dalton tipped his hat back. "You think Ben told anyone in the family about our card skills?"

"I doubt it. I will say that it does suck, pretending that we're lousy players."

"I remember someone talking about us havin' bad poker faces." Dalton laughed. "I wanted to prove them wrong, until I realized I *was* proving them wrong and they didn't have a clue."

"You never said if you won or lost in Deadwood."

Dalton cocked his head. "I didn't, did I?"

And he didn't intend to, either. "Asshole. Looks like you're gonna get that nap after all since we're done early."

"Thank God. What are you gonna do with yourself?"

"Make sure the baler is working. Ben said something last week about double-checking every piece of equipment before we get to haying. So I might swing by his place after lunch to see what he needs help with, since I doubt Brandt will remember to do it."

Dalton peered over the tops of his sunglasses. "Word of caution—never just drop by Ben and Ainsley's house."

Tell frowned. "Why? Because they're newlyweds?"

He emitted a strangled laugh. "Yeah, that's it."

Weird.

"Later."

Chapter Six

Georgia looked forward to her date with Tell, hoping that tonight he'd put his bold declaration that they'd be lovers into action.

She'd tried to work after he dropped her off yesterday, but her thoughts kept drifting to back to him. Starting with when she'd seen him in the park on Saturday. She'd watched him for a while before approaching, hesitant to interrupt the fun time he'd been having with Landon.

But Tell's happy demeanor changed when his father entered the picture. Tension rolled off him so thickly Georgia felt it on the other side of the park. She'd left soon after; she wouldn't want Tell to witness a dustup between her and her family.

As the afternoon had worn on and she hadn't accomplished a damn thing, she'd dug out her high school yearbooks.

Georgia had no interest in seeing pictures of her size-two self, not because of the twenty extra pounds she carried, but because when she saw at pictures of that young girl, her gut twisted thinking about all the losses facing her. The disappointments to come. Shaking off the morbid thoughts, she scanned the index for mentions of McKay.

There were tons of entries for Chase McKay and Keely McKay. A couple for his brother Brandt. Three listings for Tell. He'd kept a low profile their sophomore year. Then again, Georgia remembered both Chase and Keely had ruled the school that year—easy to be overlooked even if your last name was McKay.

She thumbed back through the pages. The first shot was of Tell in the lunchroom, mugging for the camera with his buddies Thurman and Ned—the trio called themselves TNT. The second pic was of rodeo club—not surprising he wasn't standing by Deck, but he wasn't next to his cousin Chase, either, who was front and center. The last entry was Tell's sophomore class picture. The kid in the pic was scrawny. His dark hair was brutally short and no hint of a smile lingered on his lips or brightened his eyes. She honestly didn't remember this somber version of Tell at all.

Georgia flipped open the next yearbook. Five mentions of Tell during their junior year. A picture of him at the first football game of the season. One of him in the buckin' chute as he got ready to ride. Another picture of him in rodeo club. A shot of him filling balloons for the junior/senior prom. And his junior class picture. At least he'd smiled in that one.

Guilt rolled over her, seeing the picture of Tell standing beside the helium tank. After being assigned the tedious task by Denille, the head cheerleader, she'd asked Tell to help. He'd made her laugh all the time in English class, so she figured he'd make even a crappy chore fun. But when Deck had found out who she'd asked to help her, he'd told her dad. And her father refused to let her spend time alone, unsupervised, with a godless, wild McKay boy. She'd been too mortified to explain why she had to back out, and poor Tell had gotten stuck doing all the work.

Come to think of it, that had happened more than once over their high school years.

If Tell was the vengeful type, agreeing to take her to the reunion and then standing her up would be a perfect way to get back at her.

The beautiful evening was impossible to resist, and Georgia sat on the front steps, basking in the sun's last rays as she waited for Tell to pick her up. She'd probably overdressed in capris, a sleeveless yellow shirt patterned with tiny daisies, and wedge sandals, given the fact they'd played basketball on their first date.

Her heart skipped a beat as she watched Tell saunter up the sidewalk. He wore that sexy grin and his usual cowboy finery that made him look smokin' hot, so she was glad she'd taken extra time with her appearance.

"You make such a damn pretty picture, sittin' out here with the sun shining on your hair, making it look like black gold."

"Listen to you, Tell McKay, talking so sweet."

As soon as she was upright, he tugged her into his arms. Then his mouth was on hers, reminding her that he knew how to kiss. Georgia's head was pleasantly muzzy by the time he pulled away.

"I like hearing that happy little hum when I kiss you. Gets me all kinds of curious about what other noises you make when you're turned on."

Georgia laughed softly. "Don't get my hopes up that you'll find out tonight."

Tell frowned. "What's that supposed to mean?"

"Nothing. Where we going?"

"To Bill's Burger Shack in Hulett. Best burgers around. Been there yet?"

"No. But first ice cream? And now burgers? You'd better have a plan to help me work off these extra calories, Tell McKay."

"I do."

"Which is...?" Should she mention sex burned a lot of calories?

"If I told you, it wouldn't be a surprise."

"I don't like surprises."

"So I gathered. Come on. Let's go."

The drive was beautiful. The years away from this area had allowed her to forget just how spectacular the scenery was. Had she ever really appreciated it?

They scored the last table in the burger joint. Between bites of an oversized burger, Tell asked about scheduling for upcoming rodeos. She responded as best as she could, but each event had different parameters and she hadn't memorized the details.

That didn't make him happy. She knew he was anxious to get scheduled to judge, but he'd brought it up on the drive back to her house after the trip to DQ too. Was that all he cared about?

Did he think she only cared about the reunion?

Maybe. To prove she had interest in his life, Georgia asked about his day. He mumbled about Dalton being hungover, his sister-in-law Jessie having a short fuse and broken fences that don't fix themselves.

Then he clammed up and this slid into awkward date territory.

Tell didn't talk to her but he sure didn't have a problem talking to anyone else—or everyone else that stopped by their table. When Tell introduced her, a few people remembered her; mostly they remembered her brother RJ.

While Tell chatted with yet another person she didn't know, she was reminded of her biggest mistake after moving to Sundance the beginning of her sophomore year: letting her high school boyfriend become her everything.

Deck's interests, activities and friends took priority over hers. Cheerleading was the one activity she could claim as her own. Being back here was a harsh reminder that she'd spent her high school years as arm candy. Virginal arm candy. Silent, virginal arm candy. A girl so sweet and demure sugar wouldn't melt in her mouth. A girl whose opinions were considered as fluffy as a bag of cotton candy. She snorted. There was a past persona to be proud of.

So as proud as she was that she'd grown a spine and left Deck, she knew few people would see the new and improved Georgia Hotchkiss—because no one had really known the old Georgia.

Tell leaned forward to capture her attention. "Sorry about that. Tim, from my dart team, tends to go on and on."

Georgia bit back her smart response, *I hadn't noticed.*

"He's one of those guys who believes we oughta have a strategy for winning the league. When most of us are just there to bullshit and drink beer."

"That'd be the only draw for me."

"Speaking of... Would you come to Ziggy's tomorrow night and watch the match?"

Nothing she disliked more than being a spectator at a guys' sporting event—she'd done that more times than she could count. But if she wanted to spend time with Tell, hopefully naked time, she'd have to take one for the team first. "What time?"

"League starts at seven. It's usually done by nine."

"I could show up for a little while."

He grinned. "Good. As far as tonight... Are you a fan of John Wayne movies?"

"I've only seen a couple, so I don't know if that qualifies me as a fan. Why?" *Please say we're going back to your place to watch movies. In your bed.*

"The Sundance Arts Council plays movies in the park every Monday night in the summer. They have a big projection screen by the band shell. You interested in checking it out?"

Tell wore such an earnest look she couldn't say no. "Sure, as long as it doesn't run past my bedtime."

"When's that?"

"Whenever you decide it's time to take me to bed," she purred. Then she stood, adding an extra wiggle as she dumped her empty cup in the trash.

Tell was a lot friendlier on the drive back to Sundance.

At the park, he spread out a blanket on the grass, away from the families with small children. She looked around, feeling so far out of her element she might as well be on Mars.

Then Tell's hand gently touched her face. "Georgia? Something wrong?"

I don't fit in here. I never have. "Just lethargic after eating."

He scooted back, stretching his legs into a V. "You can use me as a pillow."

Georgia crawled toward him. That bad-boy grin with smirking dimples was impossible to resist. She nestled her backside into his crotch, wiggling to get comfortable. Rolling her spine against his chest, she releasing a tiny sigh. Tell was so warm and firm. She turned her head to kiss the bottom of his jaw, getting a noseful of his pine-scented aftershave. "You are kinda hard for a pillow."

"And getting harder in some places." He set his chin on top of her head. "You feel good on me."

"You'd feel good *in* me."

He chuckled. "You never give up, do you?"

"Nope. So be prepared to be worn down by my feminine wiles, cowboy. Because not only do I talk dirty, I can act out all the dirty suggestions. Wanna see?"

"Maybe later."

The movie started and she blocked out all sounds, concentrating on the steady beat of Tell's heart and the rhythmic rise and fall of his chest. Onscreen, John Wayne was shooting at an outlaw. She tried to focus on the action, but her eyelids kept slipping shut. It wouldn't hurt to rest her eyes. Just for a couple of minutes.

A rough hand skated up her arm and she jumped.

"Relax. You conked out for the first half."

"It's not over?"

"Intermission gives the local kids' groups a chance to sell popcorn, candy, soda. The rodeo club is scheduled to work the concession next month."

"How do you know that?"

"I'm an advisor to the club. Some of these kids need direction. Plus, it's fun."

That surprised her. "What else do you do for fun in your free time?"

"I hang out at the trap club. My cousins Colt and Kane roped me into refereeing at Little Buddies/Big Buddies flag football and basketball games. I shoot pool with Thurman, Warner and Ned." He shrugged. "I'd rather do just about anything than stay home by myself. That ain't fun."

"That's completely the opposite of the way I am. I'd hole up in my condo in Dallas all the time, if I could."

"You love your place that much?"

No. I just don't have anywhere else to go.

Tell kissed her forehead. "Well, I aim to change your antisocial ways now that you're back here in the Wild West."

"And force me to have fun."

He grinned. "Yep. By any means necessary."

They wandered to the concession stand hand in hand. Tell struck up a conversation with the couple ahead of them in line.

The woman kept sneaking looks at her, until Georgia finally asked, "I'm sorry. Do we know each other?"

"I doubt you'd remember me. I graduated the year after you. We had gym together and Mr. Larkin partnered us for—"

"Tennis," Georgia finished. "We got second place. I remember that. You're Allison."

"Yes. And I was friends with RJ." She smiled sadly. "Then again, everyone was friends with RJ."

"My brother did have a knack for knowing everyone when he walked into a room." Kind of like Tell.

"RJ was a great guy."

That pang of sadness surfaced. "Yeah. He was."

Tell squeezed her hand.

But the encounter was a pointed and poignant reminder to her that this small-town stuff didn't appeal to her. Where everyone knew her sad family history. Where everyone paid attention to her purchases in the local grocery store, gossiping that she'd bought magnum condoms and a raunchy romance novel. She'd rather be anonymous in a big city than infamous in a small town.

She looked around the park. Everything seemed too perfect. Almost as if it'd been staged. Happy moms and dads resting on heirloom quilts while their kiddos ran wild. Friends laughing together. Reliving the types of memories she'd rather forget.

You don't belong here.

Georgia had such a sense of disquiet she abruptly let go of Tell's hand.

Tell frowned. "You okay?"

"Ah, yeah, I'm just going to use the facilities."

And she fled.

Maybe this hadn't been the best idea.

Georgia had been skittish all night. When she wasn't ignoring everything and everyone around her.

It bothered him that she hadn't joined in the conversations at the burger joint. Not that she'd been rude. She'd just seemed uninterested and entirely focused on her food.

Maybe she's shy.

That jarred him.

Georgia Hotchkiss...shy?

No way. She'd always spoken her mind.

Hadn't she?

No. If he remembered correctly, the only time she'd voiced her opinions was when Deck hadn't been around. Like in history class. The rest of the time she'd kept quiet. So she wasn't aloof or stuck-up, as most people—including him—had assumed.

As much time as Tell had spent watching her in high school, how had he not noticed that she was actually shy?

Because you were a teenage boy too busy imagining fucking her.

Seemed he, too, had seen only what he'd wanted to see.

When Georgia returned from the bathroom, her face was even more pale.

He was by her side in an instant. "What's wrong?"

"I'm ready to go. If you want to stay and watch the end of the movie, it's not that far to my place. I'll walk."

"Like hell you will." He loomed over her. "Stay here. I'll grab the blanket and be right back."

They didn't speak on the short ride to her house. After he'd parked in her driveway, he said, "You wanna tell me what's really wrong?"

She continued staring out the window for another minute before she faced him. "Now that I'm back in Sundance I see a lot of mistakes I made."

"Like what?"

"Like I didn't make much effort in high school to make new friends."

"Why's that? Because you're a little shy?"

Georgia looked at him sharply. "How'd you know?"

"Lucky guess." He kissed the back of her hand. "Go on."

"I'm not painfully shy or anything. I was just raised in a God-fearing home where men were masters of their domain. My mom was a foreigner and introverted, so I ended up like her, where RJ took after my dad and was outgoing. Took me a long time to figure out most people thought I was stuck-up because I wasn't like RJ."

"With the last name McKay, I've dealt with a lot of those preconceived ideas too. It sucks."

She nodded. "But mostly I didn't try to find a best friend because I already had one."

"Deck?"

She shook her head. "RJ. Whenever we moved to a new town, I didn't worry about fitting in because I had him. Then he took to Sundance like he was born here and he kind of left me in the dust, which is probably why I clung to Deck so much. Everybody knew RJ. Everybody liked him." She looked away. "I miss him. I know it's been almost nine years and it should be easier, but it still hurts. And being here makes me face it every day."

"Hey." Tell leaned across the seat, gently encouraging her to look at him. "I know how that feels. I still expect my brother Luke to barrel up when we're out fixin' fence. Course, he'd tell me I was doin' something wrong. That part I don't miss." He smiled. "But I miss him. Not the Luke who was a shitty husband to Jessie or the Luke who was Dad's favorite kid as well as his favorite whipping post. I miss Luke, my brother. The guy he was when it was just the four of us. Not trying to impress the ladies, or trying to piss Dad off, or trying to make Mom laugh when she was so damn miserable. But the guy who taught me stuff. The guy who listened when I talked. He's been gone almost five years and I still miss him every day. I know I'm lucky that I've got two other brothers. But neither of them replaces Luke."

Her eyes filled with tears. "Thank you."

"For what?"

"For understanding. For not thinking I'm some kind of freaky girl for crying over my dead brother."

Tell hauled her into his lap. "I'd never think that."

Georgia curled into him. "I'm sorry this has turned out to be a shitty date."

"Sweetness, it's always a good date when I've got you in my arms." He kissed her forehead.

"Sorry to rip you away from the end of the movie."

"I know how it ends. John Wayne wins."

"Wouldn't be much of a John Wayne movie if he didn't."

He stroked her hair. "Can I ask you something? I'm not clear on why you chose to return to Sundance. You had to know there'd be memories of RJ all over the place."

Georgia absentmindedly stroked the tops of his fingers. "Maybe I came back here to face my demons. Be warned: I've got quite a lot of them."

"Don't we all." Tell eased her back so he could take his time kissing her. Enjoying the feel of her soft body against his. Enjoying a lazy exploration of her mouth.

She slipped her lips down his chin, breaking the kiss. "We'd be more comfortable in my bed."

"Of that there's no doubt."

"Is that a no?"

"For now."

Georgia disentangled herself from his embrace and sat up. "Thanks for supper."

"My pleasure."

"I'll see you tomorrow night sometime."

Chapter Seven

Tell had sensed the change in the air when Georgia walked into the back room at Ziggy's. His eyeballs had popped out like a cartoon character's when he got a load of her outfit—a cleavage-baring black lace lingerie thingy topped with a sheer black blouse. Painted-on jeans that highlighted every juicy curve. Her inky-black hair was a hot mess, as if she'd just rolled out of bed. Her lips were glossy. And those eyes. God. Damn. Those eyes.

Georgia Hotchkiss was a fucking goddess.

Georgia Hotchkiss was here for him.

And Tell immediately staked his claim. Wrapping one arm around her lower back, curling his other hand on the side of her head, bringing her mouth to his for a possessive kiss. A public kiss that no one would mistake as friendly.

His dick performed a happy, hopeful salute whenever Georgia was around, so he hoped his friends wouldn't razz him about the tent in his jeans.

Throughout the game, his gaze kept zipping to her. She distracted him to the point he'd almost sent his last dart into the wall instead of the dartboard.

"Focus," Tim hissed.

Right. It was freakin' darts. But he also had the need to impress Georgia—and he hadn't done squat this round.

When his turn rolled around again, he threw perfectly and broke the tie to win the third game.

His buddies clapped him on the back and offered to buy him a couple of beers, but he only had eyes for her.

"Hey, hot lips," he said, pulling her to her feet.

"Hey yourself. Pretty impressive shooting at the end."

Tell put his mouth on her ear. "Between you and me? These guys take darts way too seriously."

"But you didn't want to let them down."

He inhaled and the scent of her hair filled his lungs. Lord, she smelled good. Like vanilla cupcakes. "No sense in doin' something half-assed."

Her sexy rasp of a laugh rolled over him.

"Come on. Hang out for a bit."

His friends had left one chair at the crowded table. Which meant Georgia had to sit on his lap.

Tell made introductions. During a lull in the conversation, to which she'd contributed little, she whispered, "Why am I the only woman here?"

He shrugged. "It happens sometimes. Most the wives and girlfriends work. Why?"

"Because I don't know anyone here and I shouldn't have—"

"Georgia? Is that you?"

Someone knew her.

They turned and saw Eugene "Smitty" Smith. A fellow classmate who'd hung out with Deck and RJ's crowd.

"It is you!" Smitty crowed.

"Hey, Smitty."

"What you waiting for, girl? Gimme a hug."

She hopped off Tell's lap and let Smitty scoop her up and spin her around.

Tell drained his beer.

"I haven't seen you in forever. You're still looking like a million bucks."

"Thanks, Smitty."

"What're you doin' here? Not in this bar," he clarified, "but in Wyoming?"

"I'm working in Sundance."

"No shit? Huh. Don't get over there much. Have you seen Deck?"

She dodged the question. "How's Janice?"

"Fat and mean-mouthed. In other words, the same."

"Didn't you always say it takes one to know one?"

Smitty's pseudo-friendly demeanor changed. "You seen Deck?" he repeated.

Georgia's fake smile faltered. "No. Why would I have?"

"So you don't know that him and Tara-Lee are havin' a kid? They've been tryin' for years."

"You'd think it would've happened sooner beings they'd been practicing since I was married to Deck."

Tell draped his arm over Georgia's shoulder. "Smitty."

Smitty's gaze winged back and forth between them. "You gotta be kidding me. You two are together?"

"Yep." He didn't elaborate. Neither did Georgia.

And Smitty fidgeted in the silence.

"I gotta get. See ya around." He scowled at Tell and lumbered off.

"Gee, if that's a preview of how the reunion is gonna go, I'm thinking I'll skip it."

Tell pressed his lips to her temple. "Now why would you wanna do that? This is just startin' to get interesting. You want another drink?"

"No. I should go."

He tipped her head back. "Why? You bored?"

"I feel like I'm intruding on guy time." Georgia gave him that sexy, crooked smile. "Besides, I want to spend time with you. Alone with you. Don't you want that?"

Well, hell, what was he supposed to say to that?

Say yes, you dumb fucker.

Georgia placed her hands on his chest. "Your lack of enthusiasm for that idea is giving me the impression this attraction is one-sided."

"Bull. You just wanna set the pace of how things are gonna go between us."

"That's because things aren't *going* anywhere."

"Where do you suggest we take things on our third date, Georgia? Skip the getting to know each other part and head straight for the nearest bed?"

She backed up. "You know what? You're right. I'm being pushy. I'll go. Thanks for the drink." She spun away from him.

Tell wouldn't have believed Georgia could run in such ankle-breaking heels, but she was hightailing it out the door.

Dammit.

Tim clapped him on the back. "So, McKay, when the fuck did you hit your head?"

Tell glared at him. "What the hell are you talking about?"

He pointed toward the exit. "Dude, you've got a screw loose if you'd rather be with us than her."

The guy had a point.

"Thanks for the kick in the ass, buddy, I owe you." Tell took off, catching her halfway across the gravel parking lot. He picked her up, covering her shriek of surprise with his mouth.

She fought him for about two seconds, then her arms wound around his neck and she kissed him back.

He didn't stop moving until he reached the back end of his pickup, setting her down long enough to drop the tailgate. He hoisted her onto his lap, facing him, crossing her ankles behind his butt.

The light in the parking lot allowed him to see her face, but the angle he'd parked his truck meant no one could see them.

"You flounced off in a snit before I got to say my piece."

"Because I've heard that particular piece before."

"Oh yeah?"

"Yeah. We're taking it slow. You're gonna spend two solid days in my bed once we finally get there...blah blah blah."

That seemed a little sarcastic. "But you don't believe it?"

"I'll believe it when I see it." Georgia let her fingers trace his jawline, the hollows of his cheeks, the corners of his eyes and the arch of his eyebrows. Then she murmured, "Look at you. So different now. You're all man. Hardly any trace remains of that cute high school boy I knew." Her mouth curled into a mysterious smile.

"That's an interesting smirk, hot lips."

"Just wondering if that high school boy still inside you is afraid I'll reject you if you try and touch me."

His jaw tightened beneath her stroking fingers. "Not true."

"So true." Georgia flicked her tongue across the seam of his lips. But rather than diving in for a kiss, she retreated. "Come on, McKay. Don't you want to get to second base with me tonight?"

Automatically his gaze dropped to her chest. Damn. She'd always had such a great rack. Now that he was inches away from those perfect breasts...the *go slow* portion of his adult brain was suddenly silenced by the *show me your boobies!* section of his teenage brain.

No surprise which side won.

"I'll admit that contraption you're wearing—while sexy as all get-out—is a little intimidating for a simple country boy like me."

"It's just a bustier."

"Mmm. The *boost-e-ay* needs gone." Tell's hot gaze hooked hers. "Untie the bow."

She curled the satin ribbon around her finger and gently tugged until the bow disappeared, leaving two short ribbons dangling along each side.

"Show me more."

The next two hooks didn't reveal much.

Georgia must've been impatient because she popped the last few hooks in rapid succession until the bustier hung open completely, and *goddamn* he could see smooth white flesh from her neck to her navel. And those pretty, perky nipples.

"Beautiful." He slid his hands up her back and around her rib cage to peel away the sides of the stiff material. His thumbs stroked the underswell of her breasts and the soft, plump sides. Each new stroke sent gooseflesh across her arms. Seeing her reaction caused his cock to jerk against his zipper.

"Tell. Please. Touch me."

Since she asked so nice... "Remind me again about second base. 'Cause I never got to it in high school."

"You're kidding me."

"Nope. I was a late bloomer, remember? So second base means I just get to touch? Or do I get to use my mouth?"

"Uh. It can be whatever you want."

"Oh. I want all right." Tell lowered his head and Georgia arched back slightly. He pursed his lips around the already hard nipple and sucked.

She groaned and bit her lower lip.

He delicately swirled his tongue around the crest of her nipple until she squirmed. Then he bit down with enough pressure to get her attention.

"What the..." She shuddered when he did it again.

Tell pulled her upright and pressed her against the hard planes of his chest. He brushed his lips over her ear, keeping his hand cupped around her breast trapped between them. "You like a little pain."

"I don't know what you're talking about."

"Liar." He pinched her nipple and she quivered.

"Tell—"

"Do you like that? Yes or no?"

"Yes, okay? Yes. Do it again."

Another pinch brought forth another moan from her.

"You will be honest with me, Georgia. Even if you haven't been honest with other men who've enjoyed your body. Maybe especially if

74

that's been the case." He blew gently in her ear. "Make no mistake. I will enjoy the hell out of this body, and I can give you everything you've been afraid to ask for."

"God, you're killing me. Please. More."

He growled and pushed her back. Squeezing her tits together so he could nip and suckle her nipples. Making her moan and thrash. The scent of her arousal teased his nose every time she rocked her hips forward. And damn if she wasn't riding the sweet spot on his cock. And double damn if he didn't just want to spin her around, yank her pants down and fuck her. Leaving suck marks over every inch of that beautiful skin. From beneath her strong, stubborn chin to the tips of these tasty nipples.

Georgia moaned louder; her fingernails dug into his biceps as she pushed her nipple against his teeth.

Fuck. She was hotter than fire. Tell sucked harder, switching between her left and right nipples. Licking. Biting. Devouring her until she released a long wail.

A pair of male voices echoed to them. "Did you hear that?"

"What? I don't hear nothin'."

"That's because you're drunk. Them grunting and moaning sounds mean someone is getting fucked good."

"Let's see if we can find 'em," the drunken guy slurred. "I wanna watch live porn. See some big bouncing titties."

They both froze. Tell's eyes met Georgia's. He mouthed, "Sorry."

She wasn't happy as she began to re-fasten the hooks with shaking hands. He didn't offer to help; he just kept his hands on her lower back, holding her steady. The only thing that'd stopped him from fucking her right there on the tailgate of his truck was...well, they were on the tailgate, in the parking lot of a damn bar. He wanted so much more than bouncing in the bed of his truck the first time he made her come undone.

Good timing, though, with the interruption from the peeping drunks. Tell had been seconds away from throwing common sense and caution into the wind, taking Georgia amidst the hay, dirt and tools in his truckbed. How fucking romantic would that have been?

She tapped his shoulder to get his attention. "You can let go of me now."

"Sure." Tell stood and set her back on her feet.

She made a big show of straightening her clothes and a big point of not looking at him.

"Georgia, I'm sorry—"

"Me too." Her gaze snapped to his. It wasn't embarrassment in her eyes, but anger. Or frustration?

He took a step forward only to have her take a step back.

"Stay where you are, Tell McKay. I seem to lose all rational thought when you put your hands on me."

Tell couldn't help but grin. "But, sweetness, that's the way it's supposed to be when I'm touchin' you."

"Not in public. Again. Not when you have no intention of following through after getting me so worked up. Again. I'm such an idiot. Again." Georgia took another step back. "Look, I have to go."

"But—"

"Do you want to come back to my place so we can finish what you started?"

When he didn't immediately answer, she released a harsh laugh. "I didn't think so." She whirled around and set off at a good clip across the parking lot.

He followed her.

She stopped beside a black Honda with Texas plates. "I'll see you."

"When?" he demanded.

"Not tomorrow. I can't...I have something else going on."

Why did he get the feeling she was lying? "Fine. Thursday night. I'll pick you up. We'll go out for a nice supper."

"Tell, I don't think—"

He closed the distance between them. "I will be at your place at seven on Thursday night."

"All right."

"And you are gonna give me a goodnight kiss."

"Why don't you just take one?" she taunted.

"Great idea." He clamped one hand on her ass and grabbed a fistful of her hair, angling her exactly where he wanted as he plundered her mouth.

They'd shared some hot kisses over the last three days, but nothing like this. This kiss was a primal preview of every raunchy, dirty, kinky thing he planned to do to her. At least three times.

Maybe he felt a little smug that Georgia whined a protest when he broke the kiss. Maybe he felt a little cocky, seeing the dazed look of need that had heated her pale irises to a deeper blue.

"Drive safe."

Chapter Eight

Trying to do twelve things at once, she let the phone ring six times before she brusquely answered, "This is Georgia Hotchkiss."

"Georgia. I had to hear from Smitty that you got a job in Wyoming?"

She'd wondered how long before the news reached her father. "It's been what? Four months since we've talked?"

"I'm calling you now. How long are you in Sundance?"

Why wouldn't he assume her job was permanent? "The event promotion company I work for has taken over the summer rodeo events for our latest acquisition. I'm here to ensure it all runs smoothly." She'd keep the conversation short. "Was there something you needed?"

"I can't even call my own daughter? You're too good to talk to your dad now?"

Georgia paced. "I'm not going to fight with you. I doubt you would've called me if Smitty hadn't mentioned he'd seen me at Ziggy's on Tuesday night, right?"

A pause. "Fine, I'll admit Smitty called me."

"I didn't realize you and Smitty were so close."

"We ain't. He's still good friends with Deck. He wondered if Deck would be upset when he heard you were back."

"Why would Deck be upset about anything that had to do with me? We've been divorced for seven years."

"You left him, Georgie. A man don't take that well, no matter how long it's been. No reason to rub it in."

She hated that he'd called her Georgie. Like a boy. Like the boy he wished she were. "The *reason* I left him was because I caught him in bed with Tara-Lee."

Her father harrumphed. "All men make mistakes."

"That was the proverbial straw for me, and his mistake cost him, didn't it?"

"Ain't nothin' as cut and dried as it looks. Anyway, I'm asking if you're going to your high school class reunion next weekend."

"Why didn't Deck call me himself and ask?"

"Because Tara-Lee would get upset. Not good for a woman in her condition."

"Terminally stupid is a condition now?" Wow. Had that bitchy comment just come out of her?

"Such a mean mouth. Just like your mama."

Georgia rolled her eyes. Her mom had a mouth so sweet honeybees swarmed around it. "Yes, I'm going to the reunion. With Tell McKay."

"Why him, Georgie? That's gonna cause a big ruckus."

"Deck and me being in the same room will cause a lot of speculation anyway. I don't owe my ex-husband anything, least of all any type of consideration for everything that man has..." *Taken from me.*

"You remember your actions reflect on you, not on him."

"I'm thrilled to hear that Deck is still golden in your eyes and he's become the son you lost."

"Now wait just a damn minute, Georgia Lou, that's not—"

"Sorry, Dad, you'll have to excuse me, I have a business call coming in on the other line." She hung up on him.

Beyond angry, she paced, hands clenched at her sides.

Even when her father finally deigned to call her, it hadn't been to see how things were going in her life. No, it was to poke at her.

Why are you surprised?

Needing to get out of her head, she cranked up her iPod and stormed outside.

She'd rented this small, two-story house because it had a great backyard. It wasn't until she'd signed the lease that the landlord informed her she'd have to keep up with all the yard work. It'd surprised her, how much she enjoyed mowing the lawn, especially on days like today, when exercise was the secondary goal. Something about the mundane physical task alleviated frustration.

Yard mowed and trimmed, Georgia weeded and fertilized her little garden. She watered the pots of flowers she'd planted and scattered about. She swept the patio and scrubbed down the porch swing. She eyed the scraggly lilac bushes. Best not to trim them in her present mood—she'd likely hack them to stubs.

In her frame of mind, she considered canceling her date.

But maybe being a little pissy with Tell would force him to see that she wasn't the purity-ring-wearing innocent he remembered.

Tell wanted her. He turned her inside out. She'd about come unglued—hell, she'd just about come period from those sexy love bites he'd given her in Ziggy's parking lot. Obviously the man had bedroom sexpertise if he could almost get her off with just his teeth on her skin.

So why was he so hesitant to take that next step with her?

A power thing?

A fear thing?

A little dick thing?

She'd find out tonight.

Tell held a bouquet of flowers behind his back as he knocked on Georgia's door. He heard the locks disengage and the door swung open.

"And of course you're right on time," she said.

He couldn't make his mouth work. She was breathtaking. Not because of her clothes, although her hippie-type blouse, flouncy miniskirt and high heels made her look even more like sex on legs, but because a kind of ethereal glow emanated from her.

You are a sucky poet, McKay. Do not share that lame-ass you glow, baby observation with her.

"Tell?"

His gaze met hers. "Damn, woman, you look fantastic." He remembered the flowers and handed them over. "For you."

"Thanks. Come in while I put these in water." She started down a hallway and disappeared around the corner.

Tell rested against the doorjamb into the living room and checked it out. Not at all what he'd imagined. The space was bland: white walls, beige-colored furniture. No pictures or books or personal items of any kind. Her couch wasn't overloaded with those annoying throw pillows most women were so crazy about. No newspapers, magazines or TV remote on the coffee table. The space looked as if it'd never been used. As if it was just for show.

Weird. True, she'd just moved in a few weeks ago, but he didn't see any boxes stacked around, waiting to be unpacked. After he'd moved in to Brandt and Jessie's old place, he'd made the place his own, right away.

His subconscious snickered. Putting in a seventy-two-inch TV didn't exactly make him Martha freakin' Stewart.

Georgia sashayed toward him, her heels clacking on the wooden floor. She set the flowers on the coffee table. Then she grabbed her purse and smiled. "Where are we going?"

"Up to you. If you want steak, the Twin Pines is the best option. If you want to get out of Sundance, there are a couple more casual places in Moorcroft."

"You choose. Just not Dewey's. I had lunch there today."

"Twin Pines it is."

He opened the passenger door, figuring she'd need a boost into his pickup. When he put his hands on her hips, she twined her arms around his neck and pressed her lips to his. Not in a chaste kiss, but a *let's strip and get wild* type of kiss. Her tongue was aggressive, her body so tight against his that he felt the rapid beat of her heart.

Tell's mind shut down to everything but the scent of her hair and the minty taste of her mouth as their tongues dueled. He slid his hands down to cup her ass, and he groaned as he squeezed those soft globes.

That's when Georgia broke the kiss and looked at him, her eyes shining with lust. "I'm an eat-dessert-first type of girl. Let's go back inside."

He grinned. "Nice try. We are eating *food* first. Then we'll see about dessert."

Georgia was quiet on the drive to the supper club.

She wasn't overly chatting during their salads either.

Maybe that's because your date has been interrupted half a dozen times by former female conquests.

Tell hadn't encouraged the interlopers, but he hadn't discouraged them either. He'd wondered if Georgia would mention it.

"So if the number of women who've dropped by to say hello are any indication, you've dated a lot of women."

Guess she wasn't the type to let it slide. Tell sipped his beer. "The word *dated* works better than some other words that come to mind."

"Meaning, you've slept with a lot of women."

"I guess."

His answer seemed to annoy her. But she didn't ask him to define *a lot.*

"Why? You worried I have herpes or VD or something?"

"No." She stabbed her lettuce, then shoved the fork in her mouth, chewing angrily.

"Georgia, you want to tell me what's goin' on?"

She wiped her mouth. "I needed fertilizer yesterday, so I went to the hardware store. It appears your plan of convincing everyone in town that we're a couple is working."

"And that's bad...how?"

"Evidently the store clerk has been on the receiving end of your sexpertise and she high-fived me."

When Tell shifted in his seat but didn't answer, Georgia added, "I didn't catch her name, but then again, maybe you don't remember it either? Rumor is that's a major problem with you."

That was a low blow. Or was it, since it was true?

Then she gestured to the space surrounding them. "Did you pick Twin Pines because you knew there'd be a bevy of women hovering around? So I could see how much sexy-man, town-stud Tell McKay is in demand these days?"

"Georgia. You've got it wrong."

"Do I? Want to know what else I heard today at Dewey's? From my waitress? Because evidently she's another one of your conquests. And I got an earful from her."

Oh fuck.

Georgia's fingers tightened around the stem of her wineglass. "Aren't you going to deny whatever she said and defend yourself?"

"Against what? I'm a guy. I like sex. What am I supposed to do when an attractive woman is throwing herself at me? Say no?"

Silence.

Jesus. He'd walked right the fuck into that trap.

And she didn't snap back a smartass comment. She didn't utter a sound. But the oddest, saddest expression crossed her beautiful face and he wanted to start this whole date over.

He reached for her hand, only to have her snatch it back. "It's different with you."

"Because I'm not an attractive woman?"

"No! Why would you even say that? You know I think you're gorgeous."

She shrugged and leaned back when the waitress brought their entrées.

As soon as they were alone again, Tell scooted forward. "I have an idea."

"So do I." She pointed to his plate with her steak knife. "Eat your steak before it gets cold."

He ate. And kept stealing glances at her.

But Georgia ignored him. She didn't shove the petit filet in her mouth in one bite, but damn close.

When she retreated to the ladies' room, he slumped in the booth. He had no idea what he was supposed to do to make this right.

If he took her straight to bed tonight, she'd never believe it wasn't a knee-jerk reaction.

If he didn't take her to bed, she'd assume he wasn't sexually attracted to her.

That brought up the question: why *had* he set these dating parameters? Because he wanted to show her that he was in control? Because he got off on making her wait? Or because he didn't want a fast and easy hookup with her? He wanted something more.

Yeah. Like she'd believe that.

Georgia returned and pointedly waited at the end of the table. Tell paid the check. He placed his hand in the small of her back as they crossed the parking lot to his truck. "About the ladies who kept coming by—"

Georgia held up her hand. "No need to explain further. In fact, I really rather you wouldn't even try."

This night had gone straight to hell.

Rather than take her home, Tell decided to follow through with his original plan.

If she recognized where he was taking her, she kept it to herself. He drove to one of his favorite spots with an amazing view of the valley.

Georgia didn't say a word until he shut off his pickup.

"Really, Tell? You brought me to Flat Top?"

"Yeah, why?"

"Because it's the local make-out spot!"

Again, not the reaction he'd hoped for.

"What is wrong with you?" she demanded.

"Excuse me?

"Are you living out some high school fantasy? Taking Hot Lips Hotchkiss to Flat Top?"

He bristled. "So what if I am?"

"Then you're an ass." Georgia opened the door and bailed out.

Dammit. That'd been the wrong thing to say. Tell followed her. With clouds covering the stars, it was darker than normal, and he was afraid she'd forgotten about the steep drop-off. "Georgia? Be careful. There's a—"

"Ledge. I know. It's not the first time I've been up here," she retorted.

"Then you'll recall this time of year, the ground is soft and it gives way easily."

"I'm not an idiot. But you're certainly treating me like one." She whirled around and crossed her arms over her chest. "Are you having a good laugh? Stringing me along these last few days? Did you even intend on taking me to the reunion? Or was that part of the joke?"

"What joke? I'm confused."

"That makes two of us. I have no idea what your game is, but I'm tired of it. Just take me home."

This woman ran hot and cold like no woman he'd ever met. "Huh-uh. You're gonna tell me where these accusations came from."

"Fine. This is our what? Fourth date? Let's recap our dates. For the first date, we played basketball and you took me out for ice cream. The next date, you fed me burgers and fries before dragging me to an outdoor movie in the park. The third date, I watched you throw darts at Ziggy's. Oh, we played a little grab-ass that night, but we had to stop, because we were in public. Now tonight it's flowers, dinner and a trip to lover's lane—where no doubt we'll hold hands and gaze adoringly into each other's eyes. What's next, Tell? Pizza and video games while we grope each other on the couch?"

"If you weren't havin' fun, you should've said something."

"I'm saying something now!"

More pissed off than hurt, he loomed over her. "So you're telling me that all the time we've spent together in the last couple of days...has sucked?"

She threw her hands up in the air. "I knew you'd take that the wrong way."

"How else am I supposed to take it?" he demanded.

"As constructive criticism! As a suggestion that this is not working. When you have dates with other women, what do you do?"

He tried to remember his last date. An actual date. Where he picked the woman up, took her to supper or to a movie. He couldn't remember.

It'd been a long time. A damn long time.

That's when Tell realized all his encounters with women in recent years had been hookups. Regardless if he met the chick in a bar, or at a rodeo, or at the poker table. He'd flirt. She'd flirt back. Then they'd be naked, fucking the night away. In the morning, they'd go their separate ways.

He didn't want that with Georgia. He wanted something...real. "Honestly, I don't even remember my last damn date, so maybe that's why I'm a little rusty. Why don't you tell me about your dates?"

That strong chin of hers came up. "Most guys at least *try* to get me in the sack on the first date."

Tell felt the strangest surge of jealousy. "And because I haven't tried to nail you the first week we've been together, there's something wrong with me?"

"Oh, there's nothing wrong with you. You're sexy, you've got an incredible body and I've no doubt you know exactly how to use it. You act like you want me. But there's no follow-through, just the constant tease. So can you understand why I'd be suspicious that this is a game? Since you couldn't have me ten years ago when you wanted me, but I want you now, you're going to lead me on and then change your mind?"

His mouth opened to deny it, but part of him feared she was right. If any other woman had been so hot to get naked and wild with him, he would've jumped her the first night. But he'd held back with her. Not just one night, but every time they'd been together.

Shit. Maybe he *was* turning this into a game. Despite his mortification, he looked at her. "What do you want from me?"

"I can tell you what I don't want from you. I don't want to neck with you in your pickup at the local make-out spot and get all hot and bothered. I don't want to watch you racing around half-naked on a basketball court and get all hot and bothered. I don't want to sit on your lap after your dart game and get all hot and bothered. I want more because we're not high school kids anymore, Tell. There's no reason for us to be worried we're taking it too far, too fast. My biggest worry is you see me as that purity-ring-wearing virgin and you won't take it far enough."

Silence.

Unable to come up with a clever response, he just said, "I think it's best if I take you home."

"That's it? We're not talking about this?"

"You've got my tongue so tied up in knots that I'll just say the wrong damn thing." He sighed. "Look, it's obvious I'm an idiot when it comes to this stuff, all right? Can we just go?"

After he helped her into his rig, she said, "Such a gentleman."

"That's who I am, Georgia. And for some reason, you bring out those gentlemanly qualities far more frequently than any woman I've met."

She touched his face and he felt as if he'd been zapped by a cattle prod. "Know what's funny?"

"What?"

"Your gentlemanly side brings out my inner whore."

Tell laughed softly, appreciating her attempt to lighten the mood. "That right?"

"Yes. So no wonder we're at cross-purposes."

The ride back to her place was mighty quiet, not that he'd expected Georgia to blather on. So her next question surprised him.

"Do you remember when you took me home that one time senior year?"

Like he could ever forget. Seeing her crying outside the gym, looking so lost and alone. He'd acted on instinct, trying to soothe her, trying to get her to talk to him. It'd shocked him that she had talked about bad choices and no choices. Then she'd asked him for a ride home and climbed in his dirty, piece-of-shit pickup. She'd left the window open and literally let her hair down, allowing all that black silk to flutter in the breeze. Georgia had been so preoccupied that she hadn't noticed him staring at her. She hadn't noticed that he'd almost wrecked his damn truck because he'd been staring at her.

"Do you know what I wanted more than anything that afternoon? To ask you to keep driving. To drive until we were a long way from Sundance."

"I would've said yes. I would've taken you anywhere you wanted to go." He'd ended up on the receiving end of Deck's fists for that anyway. Getting to spend more time with Georgia would've made those bruises a little less painful to bear.

Tell pulled up in front of her house. She hadn't left the light on, so he walked her to the front door.

She faced him. "Tell, I—"

"I don't expect you to lie and say you had a great time tonight."

"I didn't intend to. I want to know where we go from here."

"Are you asking me if I still plan on taking you to the reunion?"

"No. I'm asking you if you plan to take me to bed anytime soon."
"Define soon."
"Like right now."

Chapter Nine

Georgia watched the muscle in his jaw flex and his eyes darken.

His voice was dangerously low when he finally spoke. "Tell me what you want in that explicit detail you're so fond of."

Don't chicken out now.

She inhaled a deep, slow breath. "Don't get me wrong, Tell; I've liked spending time with you. But I'd really like to know what sound you make when my hand is on your cock. What sound you make when your cock is in my mouth. I want to feel your body on top of mine as you're fucking me. I want to feel your body behind mine when you're fucking me. I want to look down and see your face between my thighs. I want to see who Tell is when he stops showing me his fun, flirty, gentlemanly side and starts showing me the intensity I saw that first night you kissed me at the Golden Boot."

He stalked her until her back hit the door. "Think you can handle me when my fun, flirty, gentlemanly side is completely overtaken by a whole different side you haven't seen?"

She raised her chin a notch. "Why don't you try me?"

Then Tell's hand snaked out and curled around the back of her neck, pulling her so close their noses almost touched. "That's what you want, Georgia? Hard, fast, hot sex without the niceties?"

If his blazing eyes were any indication, she'd awakened the sexual beast inside him.

Finally.

Her gaze gravitated to his sculpted lips. She wasn't scared of his *no niceties* warning, and she said, "Yes."

He smashed his mouth to hers without warning, consuming her in a kiss so blistering hot it nearly melted her brain and started her hair on fire. His hands tightened in her hair, holding her head in place.

The kiss went on and on. A ravenous display of heat, raw power and sexual greed.

Georgia had never wanted like this. She'd never been wanted like this.

His mouth remained fused to hers as his fingers began to undo the buttons on her blouse. Once her shirt hung open, he stroked her damp flesh with rough-skinned fingertips, from the waistband of her skirt, up her belly, between her breasts.

He ripped his mouth free from hers. "No more public displays. Let's finish this inside."

Man. Tell had scrambled her brain so completely she'd forgotten they were in front of her house. She tried to pull her blouse closed, but his hands stayed the movement.

"Once the buttons are undone, they're undone. No goin' back. We do this my way."

Nodding, she fumbled with the keys to unlock the door.

Tell kissed her as he pushed her through the door and locked it. He kissed her as he pressed her back to the wall. He kissed her as he unhooked her bra and played with her nipples.

Her hands raced over him, eager to touch him everywhere at once. Bulging biceps, broad shoulders, thick column of his neck—God, too many delicious body parts to choose from. Her fingers tangled in his hair, pulling slightly when his teeth grazed her nipple.

He made a growling noise and said, "Don't. Move."

That terse command made her tremble with anticipation.

His mouth reconnected with hers as he slipped his hand beneath her skirt, stroking her over her panties.

She gasped when he pushed his finger inside her. He thrust in and out before adding another thick finger, which easily slid into her channel because she was so wet. When he rubbed his thumb back and forth across her clit, she whimpered.

His mouth was on her ear. "Come on my hand."

"Tell—"

"You want my cock in you? Fucking you like this?" He thrust his fingers in deep.

It felt so damn good she moaned, "Yes."

"Then come on my hand."

Georgia didn't have to tell him she needed him to stroke her clit faster. She didn't have to tell him to rub the tips of his fingers over the ridge of flesh on the inside wall of her pussy. Tell did that automatically. Perfectly.

"I wanna hear you the first time I get you off."

She was so close. And Tell's harsh panting in her ear really did it for her. Normally she had some warning before an orgasm unfurled, but not this time. This time everything happened in a rush. Her clit pulsed. Her pussy muscles spasmed around his fingers. She dug her nails into Tell's forearm, just in case he decided to pull away too soon.

He chuckled against her throat and the vibration traveled down her torso to where his magic fingers were still working her.

"Oh God."

After the last throb faded, his firm, warm lips ate at her mouth. He murmured, "I want you. Now."

"Yes. My room is upstairs—"

"That's too far. I want you now." He blew in her ear. "On the stairs."

On the stairs? Georgia shivered.

Tell eased his hand out from beneath her skirt. Watching her eyes, he yanked the blouse off her shoulders. Then her bra hit the floor. "Take off your panties, Georgia."

Dragging them down her legs, she kicked them away.

His eyes drank in her half-bared body as he unbuckled his belt and unzipped his jeans.

This intensity was intoxicating. No dimpled smile, just heat firing his eyes. The angles of his face seemed more pronounced. Edginess rolled off him as he pulled his T-shirt over his head.

He wrapped a hank of her hair around his fingers, using it to tug her closer until they were chest to chest.

She spread her palms on his pectorals, wanting so much to put her mouth and tongue where her fingers touched.

Then his mouth snared hers in a brutal kiss. Another hot, wet, deluge that left her teetering in her heels and on the edge of orgasm again.

During the all-consuming kiss, Tell maneuvered her to face the staircase.

He said, "On your knees on the second stair."

Her heart threatened to beat out of her chest as she did as he directed, resting her elbows on the fourth stair tread.

Hearing the crinkle of plastic, she looked over her shoulder at him as he rolled on a condom.

"Grab on to the spindles." His work-honed hands skimmed the outside of her legs and he pushed her skirt out of his way. "Spread your knees and flatten your back."

The carpet scraped her elbows and her knees as she widened her stance.

The tip of his cock circled her pussy. His strong fingers dug into her hips as he pushed inside her fully. Filling her so completely she felt the head of his cock bumping her cervix.

Yes. God. Yes, that was good.

He didn't say anything beyond a long groan.

Twice more, Tell eased in slowly and withdrew slowly.

Then no more niceties. He slammed into her and pulled out all the way, quickly slamming into her again. And again. And again. The sounds of bodies slapping and harsh grunts permeated the air.

Georgia arched harder. At this angle each stroke hit her G-spot with pinpoint accuracy. Each hard thrust nearly stole her breath. It certainly stole her wits; she couldn't think beyond *more*.

Tell fucked her without stopping. Without saying a word.

She'd never been…taken like this. Her body had never responded like this. Her skin tingled from her nape to her heels. Her blood burned hotter as it churned through her. She held on and held her breath as another orgasm rocked her.

His thrusts became frenzied and he released a long groan. His hips slowed from the relentless, pounding rhythm to small, rolling prods with his pelvis. His entire body shook as he fought for more breath.

Then she felt his hands moving up her back, releasing gooseflesh from every point of contact. Firm, warm lips kissed her shoulder. His hands swept aside her hair so he could string kisses up to her ear. "So beautiful." His palms followed her arms to her wrists. He curled his big hands around her fingers gripping the stair spindles. "Loosen up, sweetness, or you're gonna get a cramp."

Still such a concerned gentleman. She'd move. In a minute. When every part of her brain and body and soul wasn't so relaxed and floaty.

He chuckled. "You're a little out of it, huh?" He pulled out. She heard clothes rustling. His hand circled her ankle and he removed her shoes, sending them tumbling to the floor. Then he picked her up and carried her up the stairs.

Georgia let her head loll into his neck. He was so warm. So solid. And he smelled good. Like cologne, sweat, sex and man. She sucked in another lungful of him and let it out as a sigh.

"Which room is yours?" he said gruffly.

"The one with the big bed."

She thought she heard him growl again.

"You shoulda said the big pink bed."

"I'm a girl. I like pink."

He set her on the bed. Keeping her eyes closed, she stretched her arms above her head. "I'm so tired."

"Lemme help you get ready." Tell's hands roamed over her torso until his fingers reached the waistband of her skirt and he tugged it off. He settled her head on the pillow before tucking her beneath the sheets.

"Aren't you gonna stay with me?"

"Not tonight."

He stroked her cheek so sweetly, she angled into his touch. This floating feeling was marvelous.

"Thank you."

"For?"

"Turning my brain into mush. That was really fun. Can we do it again?"

"Anytime." He kissed her forehead. "Sweet dreams."

Classy, McKay. Fucking Georgia on the stairs. That was your big 'wait for it baby, it'll be phenomenal' sex play?

What the hell had he been thinking? Not even taking the time to get either of them completely naked? He'd just bent her over...

And found himself in heaven.

Georgia Hotchkiss was as hot-blooded and hot-bodied as he'd imagined. Those little moans she made. The way she'd given herself over to him without hesitation. If she hadn't forced him to look at why he'd been holding back with her, he wouldn't know the wet clasp of her pussy around his cock.

He'd come so hard he'd had to cage her body beneath his or he might've passed out.

Georgia had come twice. He'd made her come twice. And how fucking sexy had it been when she'd dug her nails into his forearm, not wanting that hand going anyplace? Or how about when she arched against him? Pushing herself deeper into his rapid thrusts. Wanting more, wanting everything he gave her.

These sex flashbacks aren't helping you get focused.

Right. He was supposed to be getting ready for the rodeo.

Tell slipped on his judge's vest and pass, heading to the livestock penning areas to inspect the rough stock. Rarely had he deemed an animal ineligible for competition, but the health and welfare of the animals were top priority for everyone involved. Tell had never run across a stock contractor who would put anything—money, or a shot at getting picked for NFR—ahead of the well-being of their livestock.

The outdoor arena in Buffalo was a mix of old and new. The stands were little more than wooden benches with a tin-roof covering. Spectator seats ringed the arena, reserved for sponsors and fans who were willing to pay a higher ticket price to get sprayed in the face with dirt.

At this particular rodeo, all the rough stock and timed events originated from the same end of the arena. At some venues, the rough stock chutes were on one end and the timed events were on the opposite end. Tell had worked the Buffalo Rodeo before, so he knew it ran very smoothly. At least it had under the other rodeo promotion company. It'd be interesting to see if anything changed under the company Georgia worked for.

After the fireworks and pageantry of the opening ceremony, including appearances by Miss Rodeo Wyoming, Miss Rodeo Montana, Miss Rodeo South Dakota, Miss Rodeo North Dakota, and Miss Rodeo Colorado, a salute to veterans, and the singing of the national anthem, the crowd was revved up and ready to rodeo.

Tell hit the dirt with his clipboard and took his place as the second judge.

The only time he paid attention to the crowd was if the judges were booed for what the audience believed was a bad score. It happened at least once during every event. He never took it personally.

The roster was pretty big for a small rodeo. Saddle bronc riders fared better than bareback riders, as far as making that eight-second mark. As the second judge, Tell wasn't required to be on horseback for the timed events.

Since it was a two-day event, purses and buckles weren't awarded, so the festivities wrapped up early. The other judge invited Tell to hang out at the local bar. He didn't jump at the chance like he usually did—because he was looking for a chance to jump Georgia.

He waited until the crowd thinned before he made his way to the business office. And he was still stopped half-a-dozen times by people he knew. He remembered how nervous he'd been the first time he'd judged an event. How he'd worried it would be like high school. Where the upper classman sneered at him as fresh meat or all questions would be about his bull-riding cousin Chase McKay, who'd seemed to get more famous every year. But now even that wild man had been tamed.

Speaking of wild...there she was. The hot little number he wanted to get wild with all freakin' night.

Her clothing was a mix of professional and accessible. No severe business suit; no-over-the top sequined rodeo-queen outfit either. Her denim dress was form-fitting enough to be sexy, but modestly cut. She looked good enough to eat.

After the group broke up, Georgia started gathering papers. She hadn't noticed him yet, or that they were the only ones in the room.

When she finally looked up, he hauled her against his chest and kissed her.

And kept kissing her, sinking into that sweet mouth. Sucking in her fevered response like oxygen. Aching to touch her, but keeping his hands spread across her lower back, knowing once he set his hands to roaming, he wouldn't be able to stop.

Georgia slipped her mouth free, leaning back to look at him. "Well. If it isn't Tell McKay. No *hi, how are ya?* No *sorry I didn't call?* You just waltz in here and kiss the crap outta me first thing?"

"Yeah. Is that a problem for you?"

She grinned. "Not. At. All."

"Good." Tell cradled her face in his hands. "I should mention that you are totally rockin' that dress. But I preferred what you were wearin' the last time I saw you."

"I was naked... Oh, ha ha. Real funny."

He feathered kisses across her lips. "As hot as it was between us last night, I intend to slow things down a bit tonight. So will you come to my motel room right now and let me show you?"

"Or we could go to my hotel. It's got a king-size bed."

"Better yet." Tell tucked a strand of hair behind her ear. "You have anything else to do around here?"

"I'm free to go. Someone else will lock up."

An odd expression crossed her face when he reached for her hand. "Is there a problem with your job if people see us together?"

"No. I'm just...surprised that you aren't keeping this under wraps. I mean, us being out together in Sundance is one thing. But here?"

"Why would here be any different?"

Her gaze dropped to his chest. "Because you have a reputation as a player, Tell. Rumor has it that as many buckle bunnies wait for you after an event as for the riders."

Tell grabbed her chin, looking into her eyes. "We are together, here, there and everywhere else. I won't deny my reputation, but I will point out that I don't fuck around. You are the only woman I'm with."

When Georgia still didn't look convinced, he picked her up and plopped her on the conference table. He made room for himself between her thighs and loomed over her, forcing her to rest her hands on the table behind her. "You want me to prove that right now?"

"That's not necessary—"

"Oh, darlin', I surely believe it is." He placed a soft kiss on the hollow of her throat. "Move your head to the side."

Georgia arched her neck.

He nuzzled that warm sweep of flesh, letting his breath tease before he used his mouth to kiss and suck. He dragged his lips over the smooth muscles of her throat. Inhaling her fragrance and absorbing the vibrations of her body reacting to his touch. When she began to squeeze her thighs together, he whispered, "Think I'd be embarrassed and back away from you if someone walked on us?"

"No."

"If I hadn't fucked you so fast and hard the first time, I'd fuck you hard and fast right now on this table."

Then her hands were on his chest, pushing him back. "Let's get out of here before the temptation is too much for me to resist."

Hot damn. "Can you leave your car here?"

"I guess. But I really hate being without a vehicle."

Tell brought Georgia to her feet. "I'll keep you too goddamn busy to even think about leavin'."

And didn't that put a hungry look in her eyes?

"I'll drive. You tell me where we're goin'."

As much as he wanted to run for his pickup, he didn't. As much as he wanted to swing Georgia into his arms and carry her, kissing that tempting mouth of hers the entire way, he didn't. He patted himself on the back for his control.

But as soon as they reached their destination? Tell knew his control would be nonexistent.

Georgia said, "I'm staying at the Holiday Inn."

Then he remembered he'd left his duffel bag in his motel room. "We have to stop by my motel first."

"Why?"

"That's where the condoms are."

"Oh." She smirked.

"What?"

"I'm pretty sure we won't be seeing that big bed at the Holiday Inn tonight." She picked up his hand and rubbed the back of his knuckles over her cleavage. "But at this point, any bed will do."

"Damn straight."

"Drive faster."

He hit the gas.

Chapter Ten

Probably it wasn't the first time pickup tires screeched to a stop at the Sage and Spurs Motel.

Tell had the old-fashioned key fob in his hand when he skirted the back end of his pickup.

When he went to help Georgia out, the woman launched herself at him and locked her arms around his neck. He clamped his hands on her ass and half-carried her to the door.

He released her long enough to get the key positioned. But with the way her hands were clawing at his chest, he fumbled the key twice before he fit it in the lock.

As soon as they were in the room, before he'd turned on a single light, Georgia was all over him. Her mouth attacking his throat as she started popping buttons on his shirt. Her pelvis rubbing against his. Making those sexy-ass moans.

He put his hands over hers, stopping her frantic motions. "Georgia. Hold that thought for a sec." He took off his hat, reached over and hit the light switch.

This was a pretty shitty room. Maybe keeping the lights off hadn't been such a bad idea. But then he looked at the beautiful woman standing in front of him. Her breathing uneven. Her lips so full and ripe. The blush of arousal on her cheeks, those magnetic eyes of hers so completely focused on him.

"Look at you. God. You are something else." He traced her prominent jawline with the backs of his fingers. "Take off your clothes."

That stubborn chin came up. "I'm not stripping solo again."

"Fair enough. Then I'll strip you." He yanked her denim dress over her head. He unsnapped her bra. He hooked his fingers into the sides of her bikini panties and tugged them down to her ankles.

Georgia tried to take a step back, but hobbled by her underwear, she fell ass-first on the bed.

Tell dropped to his knees in front of her. He kept his caresses easy, wanting to take hours to touch and taste every inch of her bared skin. The explosive passion wasn't going anywhere so he'd just put it on simmer while he savored her.

But Georgia seemed a little unsure about being naked.

He wouldn't allow it. He lightly pushed on the insides of her thighs and demanded, "Let me see you. All of you." He heard a swift intake of breath and then she scooted her bottom to the end of the bed.

"Watch my eyes. See how goddamned turned on I am by your body." He grinned. "And baby, if that doesn't convince you? Look at the crotch of my jeans."

That brought her sweet, lopsided smile.

He pressed a kiss below her belly button. Then lower. Then lower again. Leaving a longer kiss on the small strip of black curls pointing the way to his ultimate destination.

When his tongue followed that silken trail, she moaned.

He glanced up at her, his mouth hovering over her sex. Then he shoved his tongue deeply into her slick core.

So sweet. So wet. God, he wanted to suck and lick and make her come undone at least five times before he moved from this paradise. His intent to leisurely explore every delicate pink fold, to keep her hanging until she begged him to make her come...vanished.

Tell used his thumbs to pull her pussy lips apart, settled his mouth over the skin hiding her clit and began to suck.

Georgia's body quivered. A strangled moan escaped and she arched, shoving her pelvis forward.

He loved this part of sex. Losing himself in this first taste of her. Hearing her moan louder when he lightly flicked his tongue over that swollen little pearl.

Her fingers tangled in his hair as he kept up his relentless assault. She kept murmuring, "Yes, yes, yes..." Then her body went stiff and she cried out.

Georgia's sex pulsed beneath his lips and against his tongue. Tell stayed right there, his sucking mouth keeping rhythm until the spasms ended. He scattered kisses to the creases of her thighs, stopping to dip his tongue into that sweet, sweet honey again.

She rolled back onto the mattress, her body limp.

That was the only limp thing around here.

As he unbuckled his belt, she rallied and pushed upright. She didn't say anything, she just watched from beneath heavy-lidded eyes as he removed his boots, shucked his jeans, boxers and socks.

When his hand tugged on the remaining buttons on his shirt, Georgia shook her head. "I get to do that."

"That right?"

She still had her shoes on, so when she stepped off the bed, the top of her head brushed the underside of his jawline. "I've wanted to put my hands all over you since Sunday when we played basketball. Last night we were too..."

Tell touched her cheek. "Should I apologize?"

"God no. It was fantastic. One minute we're arguing and the next you're stripping me and fucking me." She popped the next button. "You had that look of animal lust and I..."

He stayed her hand. "What?"

"I liked that you didn't treat me like a fragile doll. You wanted me, you took me. That type of intensity is powerful, Tell. Especially when it's new to me." Her cheeks reddened. "I haven't been with a lot of guys. And it's been pretty basic sex." She met his gaze. "But from the first time you kissed me at the Golden Boot, I knew it'd be different with you."

Tell groaned. "And then what did I do? Became that same type of guy you didn't want. With the innocent dates and the waiting to get nekkid and wild."

"You don't need to read up on the *Kama Sutra* to impress me, but I don't want you to hold back." She focused on unsnapping his buttons and ridding him of his shirt.

Now that he wouldn't have to worry about holding back with her...didn't that just bust open the vault to all his kinkiest fantasies?

Georgia ran her hands over his chest. Tracing the ridges of his pectorals. Following the edge of his rib cage down to his lower abdomen. Then she locked her gaze to his as she wrapped her hand around his cock, delicately sweeping her thumb over the spot beneath the head.

As much as Tell wanted to see those hot lips circling his cock, it could wait. "We sorta slowed down. Maybe I shoulda gone with my first instinct and fucked you against the door as soon as we walked in." He bent to align his mouth with her right nipple. Licking the hardened point with the very tip of his tongue. "On the bed. Now."

Georgia placed a soft kiss on his sternum and scooted onto the bed.

Tell ripped open a condom, rolled it on and crawled across the mattress. She'd parted her thighs, keeping her arms above her head, making her body one long line of curves he couldn't wait to explore. Lowering himself over her, hips to hips, he fit his cock to her core, gliding into that tight heat. Then he ran his palms up her arms until he reached her wrists. Threading his fingers through hers, be began to move.

Her gaze never left his. For the several long, sensuous strokes, they stayed in that silent connection of bodies touching from feet to hands, being skin to skin.

"You're so beautiful, Georgia." He kissed her. Hungrily, frantically, even as he kept the same steady rhythm. His cock pausing outside her entrance on every fourth stroke before he snapped his hips, slamming into her to the root. Withdrawing slowly. Dragging out this pleasure as long as possible. Their mouths breaking only long enough to suck in more oxygen.

Georgia's fingers squeezed and released as her body strained to match the rhythm of his. He wanted to feel that same clenching and unclenching sensation of her pussy around his cock.

Tell kissed a path to the sweet spot below her neck. Then he rammed into her fast and hard on every stroke until she arched against him violently.

Her sexy wail burned his ear as her pussy clamped down on his cock. Her grip on his hands was almost painful as she rode out her orgasm.

The strong pulses and pounding rhythm were so perfect, his own release caught him unaware. He came hard and fast. A head rush. A brain freeze. Free-falling into the abyss. Then nothing but the decreasing *thud thud thud* of his heartbeat in his ears.

Georgia nibbling on his jaw brought him back to reality. He eased back and looked into the face of a satisfied woman.

Despite the cramp in his ass, and in his arms, he wanted to stay right here with her, just like this—sweat-soaked, sticky and sated. Possibly forever.

His cock was totally on board and his aches and pains disappeared.

He rolled his hips and she gasped. He whispered, "Again," and lost himself in her, half-afraid he'd never find his way back, half-grateful that he'd found her at all.

Wasn't Tell McKay just as cuddly as a kitten?

After he'd rocked her body—twice—she'd expected a sweet kiss and then he'd pull back.

But after he'd ditched the condom, he'd returned to bed, tucking her body against his, trailing his rough-tipped fingers up and down her spine as her head rested on his chest.

It'd be heavenly, if it weren't freaking her out.

Georgia couldn't remember the last time she'd been held so tenderly in the aftermath of spectacular sex.

Maybe never.

Wasn't that sad?

Deck had fucked her and reached for the remote.

Other lovers had fucked her and reached for their pants.

So she didn't have much experience with this...lying around in the afterglow type stuff.

Wouldn't that make an awesome confession?

Funny thing, Tell. I'm not used to the snuggly routine because previous lovers couldn't wait to get the hell away from me. Maybe they were disappointed in my bedroom skills, or maybe my O face is fugly, but sweetness after sex? Nope. Not familiar with that. So forgive me if I—

"What's wrong? You tensed up."

I'm a loser and a bad lover and too mortified to tell you, although you've probably already figured it out. "Nothing."

Tell put his fingers under her chin, lifting her face up. "Don't go silent on me now, hot lips. What's goin' on in that beautiful head of yours?"

"You were amazing."

He shook his head, placing a gentle kiss on her lips. "Huh-uh. *We* were amazing. Together. There are two people in this bed, Georgia."

"I know. Believe me, I know. I've never..." She rubbed her fingertips on the razor stubble that had sprouted on his jawline. "You're just overwhelming."

A tiny wrinkle appeared between his eyebrows. "You don't mean overbearing?"

"No. I... For supposedly being in charge of my own sexual needs and sexuality, I don't have much experience with men like you."

"Men like me," he repeated. "Meaning what?"

Georgia blinked at him, unsure the level of honesty she should strive for. Especially when he was naked and she was looking into a face that could make angels sing.

Yeah, saying girly stuff like that will make him take you seriously— not.

"Georgia?"

"Men like you who have the moves. The experience."

"You sound a little pissed off about that," he said tersely.

"Not at all. I'm not making any sense. Just forget it."

"Nope. Take a deep breath and time to gather your thoughts, because I ain't goin' anywhere."

She didn't want to screw this up. "I acted like a cat in heat around you last week because I thought it might get you to finally see that I'm not the goody-goody I used to be. Now I'm worried you're disappointed I wasn't a tiger in the sack. And I didn't live up to all the fantasies you've supposedly had about me."

"Jesus. Stop. You are sex on legs." Tell let the backs of his knuckles outline her face. "I want the you that you are now. Not the girl who sat in front of me in history class."

Relieved, she tossed off a flip, "Eh. She wasn't that cool anyway. A bit of a prude, I've heard."

He laughed.

She traced a scar on his rib cage. "This has been awesome."

"But?"

"I hate to bring this up now, but when do you plan to take me back to my car?"

"I thought you were stayin' here tonight?"

"When you were seducing me I would've said anything to get naked with you." Georgia kissed the frown lines bracketing his mouth. "I loved every second of it. But I do have to work in the morning."

"I can run you back to the rodeo grounds first thing."

"Tell. That's not the best option."

"Why not?" His lips flattened. "You sure you ain't embarrassed to be seen with me?"

"Can you hear me out without getting defensive and paranoid?"

"Fine."

Georgia smiled at his gruff tone. "I don't care who knows we're together. I do care about the walk of shame tomorrow morning in front of people on the rodeo committee if I show up in the same clothes and sporting sex hair."

Understanding flashed in his eyes. "Damn. I hadn't thought of that." Then his lips quirked. "Sex hair, huh?"

"With the way you always mess with my hair? I'm sure I look like I just rolled out of bed after a wild romp."

"It's a good look on you." He curled a hank of hair around his finger.

"So you're not mad?"

"Nope. But I expect you'll stay with me tomorrow night."

Of course he would. "Motel sex is pretty hot."

"You're pretty hot," he shot back with a sexy growl. "In fact, let's burn up the sheets once more before I haul your sexy ass back to your car." Tell flipped her on her back and rolled on top of her.

Her belly rumbled like an empty railcar.

He squinted at her. "Why didn't you tell me you were hungry?"

"The only hunger I cared about feeding was what I saw in your eyes."

"Now who's the sweet-talker? I'm still starved for you, sweetness." He kissed her three times, each kiss lingered a little longer than the last. "But you ain't gonna be able to keep up with my appetites if I don't feed you."

Georgia finished dressing and watched Tell tucking in his shirt and refastening his belt buckle. Something about getting dressed after experiencing such explosive heat together made her self-conscious of her rumpled state. She smoothed her hair and tugged her dress into place.

Then Tell was in her face, giving her the gentlest kiss while his fingers firmly held her chin. "Every time you get that embarrassed look, I'm gonna kiss it right off your pretty face. No matter where, no matter when, understand?"

He wasn't being his playful, fun self. She wondered how many women knew this side of him. Rather than speculate, she just asked. "Are you always this intense after sex?"

The heat in his eyes didn't dissipate. Tell slowly shook his head. "Apparently only with you."

Oh man.

They drove to a truck stop on the outskirts of town. Tell ordered the steak and egg platter while Georgia chose blueberry pancakes.

"We're lucky this place is open twenty-four hours."

He picked up her hand and rubbed his lips over her knuckles. "I'd like to keep you tied to my bed for twenty-four hours."

She blushed but held his molten gaze.

"That didn't send you running away screaming."

"Was it supposed to? Because the thought of you showing me all your sexual tricks and making me come so many times I lose track sounds like an awesome way to spend a day."

He laughed. "You constantly surprise me."

"That's me. Miss Unpredictable," she said with an edge of sarcasm.

"You don't feel that way?"

"Only with you."

Another kiss to her knuckles. "Then you should be around me all the time." He frowned and pulled his phone out of his pocket. "Hang on, I gotta take this. Dalton? Why're you callin' me this late? Uh-huh. No. That's fine, but it sucks. Yeah, yeah, yeah. I'll leave after the event tomorrow night. But just remember you can't do this next weekend. I'll be gone Saturday morning. Nah. I can do 'em Sunday but it'll be late. Fine. Drive safe." He laughed "Fuck if I'll tell you, perv." Tell hung up and looked at Georgia. "Sorry. Dalton is goin' to Colorado in the morning and won't be back until Monday. Which means I have to head back tomorrow night after the rodeo so I can do chores Sunday morning."

Georgia sighed. "I have to be here Sunday morning to wrap everything up. So much for us spending tomorrow night together."

"Come by my place on Sunday when you're done."

She paused a beat too long before saying, "Okay."

Tell's eyes were on her. "Something wrong?"

"Not wrong. I just wanna know that we're both okay with keeping this casual. Us hanging out until the reunion."

"Is that important to you, keeping things casual?"

She nodded.

"Sure." Tell fiddled with the straw in his water glass. "I just got to thinkin'. Aren't some of these rodeos small potatoes for a PR firm outta Dallas?"

"One of the stipulations when we absorbed the company was that we fulfilled the contracts of all the events, no matter the size."

"Did you have problems with other existing contracts?"

"A few. Mostly because the committee didn't want to work with an out-of-state firm. After the fifth cancelled contract, my boss decided to send someone to Wyoming as proof we were invested in the local community. Local meaning, within four hundred miles," she said dryly.

"Did you volunteer?"

"I was volunteered."

He glanced at her sharply. "You don't sound too happy about that."

Hedge. "No way do I want to think about work when I've got a gorgeous hunk of man sitting across from me," she cooed. "Can't we talk about something else?"

"Fine. Let's talk about you. What's the most exciting place you've been in the last ten years?"

"I went to Cozumel for a week."

A depraved look settled on his face. "Now I'm imaging you in a bikini, sipping fruity girl-drinks on the beach. I'd like to've been there to rub suntan oil all over your hot skin." Then suspicion entered his eyes. "Who'd you go with?"

"My mom. It was my college graduation present. I haven't been anywhere since." She took a sip of water. "How about you?"

"I spent the summer down south. A buddy I met on the circuit dragged me to a swamp in Louisiana and a beach in Pensacola. Went someplace in Mississippi where the drawls were thick as molasses and I couldn't understand nothin'. Guess that's how I ended up eating opossum and turtle."

Georgia laughed. "So were them tasty vittles?"

"I didn't know what it was at the time."

"Were you ever tempted to stay down there?"

Tell shook his head. "I'd got tired of the humidity, the bugs, the slower pace. I also figured out I didn't have what it takes to become a championship saddle bronc rider."

"What's that?"

"Money, mostly. It's expensive to keep competing if you ain't winning. Hell, it's expensive even if you are winning."

"I don't know how these rodeo cowboys do it. They're gone at least a couple times a week over the summer."

"It's no different than you flying off here and there to do your job."

"I'm the *remain in the office to put out fires* type of employee. No jet-setting for me."

Tell studied her. "When you're not working, what do you do for fun?"

"I'm happy to stay home on the weekends. I live forty-five minutes from where I work and the traffic is awful during the week. Sometimes in the summer I head to this small lake that has great walking paths. I pack a lunch and hang out all day."

"By yourself?"

"Yes. Why? Do I sound pathetic?"

He snatched her hand and kissed the inside of her wrist. "No. It does sound a little lonely, sweetness. So I'm glad you don't have to go back to that."

Georgia felt guilty for letting him believe she was sticking around. "Your off-the-ranch hours are packed with stuff. What else do you do besides play in a dart league, mentor the rodeo team, judge rodeo events and charm and bed all the women in the county?"

"Only one woman I'm interested in charming and bedding."

"Do I know her?" she asked innocently.

"Intimately. And if we weren't waitin' for some grub, I'd haul you out to my truck right now and we'd get reacquainted." He lifted a brow. "How come you're sittin' so far away from me?"

Georgia stood and scooted next to him in the booth, secretly thrilled he always wanted her physically close to him, not just in bed.

"Much better. So when you come over tomorrow, I've got a couple of fun things we can do. Since you don't like surprises, I'll give you a hint. It begins with Z."

"A visit to the zoo."

He rolled his eyes. "That would suck balls. Try again."

"You're taking me on a Zamboni ride."

"In Wyoming. In June. Nope."

"We're gonna catch some z's after you tie me to your bed for twenty-four hours," she purred.

"There's an idea, but nope. One last try."

She tapped her chin. "Does it have anything to do with a zipper?"

Tell grinned. "Partially. I'm takin' you for a ride on the zip line I built."

"Zip line. As in flying-through-the-air-with-no-safety-nets zip line?"

"One in the same."

"No way."

"It'll be fun. It's safe. I promise."

Her fingers pleated the paper placemat that boasted facts about Wyoming. "Sorry, but that's just not my thing."

Tell turned her face toward his. "It's not scary or steep. I built it for Landon. Try it one time. Please."

How could she resist those damn dimples? "Fine. But if I take an ass-buster—"

"Then I will kiss your ass until it feels better."

Chapter Eleven

Tell's phone rang at midnight Sunday night.

Never good.

Caller ID read: *Brandt*. "Brandt? What's wrong?"

"Jesus, Tell, Jessie is in labor."

"That's good, right?"

"No! She's two weeks early!"

"Is Jess all right? She's not havin' complications?"

"She's just...in so damn much pain she can't even talk."

Tell set his feet on the floor. "Where are you?"

"In my truck on the way to the hospital."

A loud female wail echoed through the phone. "Can't you make this fucking thing go any faster, Brandt? You're driving thirty miles under the speed limit."

"Just bein' safe, baby. Got precious cargo on board."

"Brandt?" Tell prompted.

"You're gonna hafta do chores by yourself, at least in the morning."

"I'm pretty sure I can handle it. You need to be focused on Jessie."

"Come on, Jessie, baby, breathe."

Another groan, followed by, "It fucking hurts to breathe!"

"Shit, bro, I gotta go."

He said, "Keep in touch," to the dial tone.

Georgia's warm, naked body pressed against his back and her chin rested on his shoulder. "I take it Jessie's in labor?"

"Yeah. And Brandt doesn't appear to be handling it any better than he did her pregnancy. They're on the way to the hospital."

"Wouldn't it be funny if they ended up sedating your brother instead of the pregnant woman?"

Tell laughed softly.

"Come back to bed. It's hours before we have to start chores."

He turned and looked at her. "We?"

"Yes, *we*. You said Dalton is gone this weekend and I know it's too much work for one cowboy—even a McKay cowboy—so I'll help you." She kissed the cup of his shoulder. "I'm not all city girl."

"I know that."

"Did you also know that I'm having a pain on my right butt cheek? From where I fell off the zip line."

He grinned. "You didn't fall off. Your arms gave out and you bailed off because you went on the damn thing like twenty times."

"But it was so fun!"

"See? I told ya."

"Don't be smug. Now get back under these covers and kiss my butt."

Tell kept checking his phone all morning, but he hadn't heard from Brandt and he was getting worried.

Georgia was a big help with chores. She'd brought all the paperwork for the upcoming rodeos and she started the ball rolling on getting him assigned as a judge. He was happy he'd be working fourteen more rodeos this summer, although none were PRCA-sanctioned, and not all of them were events she was working.

They'd finished a late lunch when his phone vibrated. He fished it out of his pocket. "Brandt. You have good news?"

"Yep. Jess had the baby about an hour ago. His name is Tucker. The boy weighed eight pounds."

"And Mama Jess? How's she doin'?"

"Weird to hear her called Mama Jess. But she's already taken to the little guy like he's been here forever..." Brandt cleared his throat. "She was in labor for five hours before she even told me, so it was eighteen hours in labor instead of just thirteen hours at the hospital. She's sleepin'. The nurses came in and took Tucker for some tests or something about five minutes ago."

"If Jess is sleepin', aren't you supposed to be with Tucker wherever he goes?"

Silence.

"Shit. You're probably right. I don't know how to do any of this stuff."

"It's no different than anything else. You'll learn as you go."

"Will you come to the hospital?"

"When?"

"Ah...now."

"You think that's a good idea, given Jess is sleeping? Who all have you called to spread the good news?"

"What do you mean?"

Jesus. Brandt was really a mess.

"You're the first person I called, bro. Jess called her mom." He exhaled a frustrated burst of air. "I better call Mom, huh?"

"And Dalton. And Skylar. If you call Keely, she'll make sure everyone in the McKay family knows."

"Good idea."

Was it funny or sad that neither mentioned calling their dad?

"Now go track down your kid, Brandt. That way when Mama Jess wakes up, you can fill her in on what happened to the little tyke. 'Cause she's gonna want to know."

"Thanks. I just... I need you here, okay?"

Had he ever heard such a note of panic in his older brother's voice? "I've got some things to finish up here first, so it'll be a couple, three hours before I'm there."

Georgia rubbed Tell's arm after he stood there for several long seconds without speaking. "Sounds like congratulations are in order."

"Yeah. I'm happy Jessie didn't have complications. But man. Brandt is still uptight as hell."

"Then it's a good thing you're going in. Maybe you'll calm him down."

Tell leaned down to kiss her. On impulse he asked, "Will you come with me?"

Regret flashed in her eyes. "No. The first time seeing your nephew will be special. Jessie will have a ton of visitors and I don't need to add to her stress, especially since she doesn't know me."

But I want her to know you.

Whoa. That'd come out of left field. Normally he kept the woman sharing his bed far away from the McKay family madness, so as not to give her ideas that he was serious about wanting her to become a part of his family.

"Besides, I have work to do today. Somebody—" she pecked his mouth, "—has distracted me. Not that I'm complaining."

"Good. 'Cause I don't plan to stop distracting you anytime soon."

She gave him that goofy smile. "Call me later?"

"Sure. I'll be in town. Wanna do something?"

"If that's your way of asking if I want you to fuck me senseless again? The answer is yes." One last kiss and she sailed out the door.

The odd thing was, Tell hadn't been talking about sex.

He killed an hour doing stuff around the house he'd been putting off. Stalling wasn't normally his style, but he suspected Jessie might be as overwhelmed as Brandt.

After he checked on Jessie and Brandt's dog, he stopped at the grocery store to grab some flowers. The selection was shitty, so he drove to Spearfish.

Somehow he managed to leave Walmart with flowers, a stuffed horse, a DVD of *Parenthood,* a box of chocolates and a bottle of booze.

He felt like a dork schlepping all the stuff into the hospital. When he asked at the visitor information center for Jessie's room number, the woman made him wait.

His heart sped up. "Is something wrong?"

The older gal shook her head. "Doc Monroe put a limit on visitors for the first twenty-four hours. The McKays could overtake the whole wing if y'all showed up at the same time."

He grinned. "That's true."

"You're cleared to go in, Tell. Room one nineteen."

He cut down the left hallway—due to various injuries over the years he'd been in this hospital several times—and stopped in front of the door. After shifting everything into one hand, he knocked.

Brandt opened the door a crack. Then he threw it open wide. "Tell. Man. I'm glad you're here. What took you so damn long?"

"Had to get a few things to mark the occasion."

Brandt's eyes were dark with guilt when he saw the bouquet. Dammit. His brother hadn't gone out and brought Jessie flowers yet? Dumb-ass.

Jess was sitting up, a blanket-wrapped bundle tucked against her body. She looked tired, but happy. She beamed at him. "Hey, Uncle Tell. Whatcha got there?"

"Flowers from your adoring husband. He asked me to pick them up for him because he couldn't bear to leave you guys." Tell passed her the bouquet of yellow, white and pink daisies.

Her lip trembled. She looked over at Brandt. "Thank you. Daisies are my favorite."

Brandt said, "I'll get 'em in some water."

Then Tell pulled out the tie-dyed plush pony. "Looks like a hippie horse, but I've heard babies like bright things. And so you didn't think I forgot you..." He waggled the two-pound box of chocolates and the DVD at her.

She laughed.

He took the bottle out of the paper bag. "My gift to the proud daddy. Koltiska liquor made right here in Wyoming. Figured my big brother and I needed to celebrate Wyoming's newest resident."

"Maybe you oughta give Brandt a shot now," she said dryly. "Anyway. Come see our son." Jessie peeled back the blanket covering the baby's face.

His eyes were squeezed shut. In fact, his whole face was squished and red—not that Tell would point that out. The baby had a full head of dark hair.

Jess murmured and stroked Tucker's cheek. His eyes opened.

"Whoa. He's lookin' at me."

"He's actually awake more than I thought he'd be."

"Heya, buddy. Welcome to the family." Tell kissed Jessie's forehead. "Ya done good, Mama. He's perfect. And so little."

She snorted. "He didn't feel little when I was tryin' to push him out."

Tell chuckled.

"Do you wanna hold him?"

"In a bit. He looks content. I ain't gonna mess with him."

Jessie frowned.

"Has Dalton been by yet?"

"He's on his way. Now that Tell's here to keep you company, I'm gonna fill out that paperwork." Brandt softly closed the door behind him.

Tell's gaze connected with Jessie's. "Is everything all right?"

"No. Brandt... He..." She shook her head. "This is gonna sound stupid, but I don't think he likes Tucker."

"Why would you say that?"

"Brandt was great during the delivery. He stayed right beside me and he didn't blink when I sort of...took a swing at him."

"Really?"

"Yeah. It didn't faze him. He just kept me focused on getting through the next contraction. After I delivered Tucker and it was just the three of us alone in the room, Brandt was so quiet. When I finally made him hold his son, he just looked at Tucker like I'd handed him a rabid raccoon." Jessie started to cry.

Tell was going to slap his stupid fucking brother right upside the head when he got him alone.

"What if he didn't really want this baby? What if Brandt just said he did to make me happy and now he regrets it—"

"Hey." Tell wrapped his hands around Jessie's face, wiping away her tears. "I promise you, I will find out what is wrong with him. But get it outta your head, right now, Jess, that he doesn't love this kid."

Silence.

Then Tucker squirmed and grunted and made the funniest face that both Tell and Jessie laughed.

Three knocks and the door swung open.

Keely McKay Donohue sauntered in, holding a shiny blue bag covered in rocking horses. "Thank God that baby is finally here." She hugged Tell and then hip-checked him, completely horning in on his spot.

He knew Keely would stick around awhile and he considered tracking down his shit-for-brains older brother. But he opted to stay in case Keely needed encouragement to leave because Jess was too nice to point her toward the door.

"Do you wanna hold him?" Jessie asked Keely.

"Yep. Lemme pull a chair over first." She scooped Tucker up like a pro. "He's hefty. Colt and India's McKenna weighed in at seven pounds. That one pound makes a big difference."

"Tell me about it."

Keely kissed Tucker's forehead. "God. I love the way babies smell. And they're so warm and cuddly."

"After that remark, you know I'm gonna ask when you and Jack are going to start a family," Jessie said.

"I know." Keely fussed with the blanket. "Can I ask you something? On a scale of one to ten, how bad did it hurt to have these eight pounds squeezed out of your va-jay-jay?"

Jessie paused. "A nine."

Tell did not want to hear this conversation but now he was trapped.

"Crap. That's what I thought. See, AJ spews this 'it's a beautiful thing' when she talks about giving birth, even when I saw her screaming at Cord when she was in labor with Beau."

"Yikes."

"And that was her *second* baby."

"Well, it hurts like nothing I've ever felt. I mean, I wanted to punch and scratch and scream at Brandt because I had to go through all of this and he didn't. Yet the baby would still be half his. How is that fair? At the very least he should have to suffer somehow, right? I mean, months of being sick, being hormonal, being fat, being so desperately horny and then wanting to chop off Brandt's hand or his dick if either so much as touched me again."

Tell's legs automatically snapped together.

"And now after the blessed event, not only is there no sex for six weeks, I've been warned that my nipples might crack and bleed while I'm breastfeeding. Not to mention milk leaks everywhere. And I have this extra pooch of skin on my gut that I'll probably never get rid of. I'm pretty sure my hips or my ass won't ever be the same pre-baby size."

Maybe they wouldn't notice if he dropped to the floor and crawled out. Knowing women talked about shit like this and hearing it? Two. Different. Things.

"See?" Keely pointed out. "Pregnancy sounds like a raw deal for women, doesn't it?"

Jessie's face softened. "But look at him, Keely. He's so perfect. He's part me and part Brandt. I just stare at his sweet little face and wonder if he'll have my personality or his father's, or maybe his own. I wonder who he will look like."

"Hate to break it to you, but this boy already looks like a McKay. He's beautiful." Keely sniffled.

Holy fuck. His cowgirl-tough cousin was...crying?

Jessie's voice dropped to a soothing timbre Tell hadn't heard from her. "What's this really about, Keels? Being scared of labor isn't really what's holding you back from having a baby. Is Jack pressuring you?"

Keely wiped beneath her eyes. "A little. I love Jack like crazy. I love our life together. I never thought I'd be this happy. What if having a baby screws that up? What if everything in our life becomes about being parents? What if I lose myself in motherhood? We both know we won't stop at one kid. Plus, I don't think I'm cut out to be a full-time, stay-at-home mom. And I'm afraid that's what Jack wants, because that's what we both had growing up."

"Have you talked to Jack about any of this?"

"No. He's my best friend—hell, he's my everything—but I don't think he'll understand. I can't talk to AJ because she's glowing with pregnancy. My mom had five kids by the time she was my age. My single friends remind me I'm only thirty and there's no rush to motherhood. My sisters-in-law and my cousins' wives nag me to get on the ball so mine and Jack's kids will be raised around cousins like I was. I just feel that no one understands my fears, even when they sound stupid when I say them out loud."

Tell sat up a little straighter. Could that be the issue with Brandt? Some unnamed fear and he felt he had no one to talk to about it?

"It'll cause problems if you don't talk to Jack about what's holding you back as far as planning a nursery and picking baby names. Trust me on this. Brandt is holding something back from me and it's frustrating. So I imagine Jack might feel the same way."

Keely snickered. "GQ practically shoved me out the door to meet the newest McKay. I think he's hoping new-baby pheromones give my biological clock a good swift kick." She glanced down at the bundle in her arms and her nose wrinkled. "He just filled his diaper."

"Hand him over. Will you get the diapers and stuff over by the window?"

Brandt walked in, his gaze firmly on Jessie's face. "What's goin' on?"

"Diaper change."

"Oh."

Tell watched his brother standing there, just watching Keely help out, not offering to do anything.

Enough.

He grabbed the bottle and clapped Brandt on the back. "Come on. I could use some fresh air."

"Keely's gonna stick around for a bit, so I'll be fine," Jessie said.

Tell sent Jessie a reassuring glance before following Brandt out the door. He headed to his pickup and dropped the tailgate. He took a seat and watched Brandt pace. "Let's make a toast to your son."

"I don't think that's a good idea."

"Why? You figure we're gonna get arrested? If Cam's on duty, we won't even get a warning for open container."

"Fine. Gimme the damn thing."

"Huh-uh. I get the honors." Tell twisted the cap off. "Welcome to the world, Tucker McKay." Then he handed Brandt the bottle.

Brandt took a long swallow and passed it back to Tell.

After Tell drank, he said, "Your turn to make a toast."

"To Jessie. The best woman in the whole damn world."

By about the fifth toast, they'd knocked back a third of the bottle. Finally, Brandt stopped pacing and hopped up on the tailgate.

"Sharing a bottle takes me back. Remember that time Luke dragged all of us to the lake to go fishin'?"

Tell nodded. "We never even dropped a line on the water, bein's he stole a bottle of Dad's cheap whiskey."

"First time Dalton ever got drunk."

"First time *I* ever got drunk," Tell reminded him.

"Man. Dad whupped Luke but good. Gave him the punishment for all of us because as the oldest, Luke shoulda known better."

The liquid in the bottle sloshed as Tell helped himself to another swig.

"I miss him."

"I do too."

"I still expect him to show up where we're workin'. Skidding to a stop in his truck, the tires spraying us with dust, and then him saying, 'If ya ain't dirty, you ain't workin' hard enough'."

Tell chuckled.

"I can't really talk to Jess about it," Brandt said softly. "Not like I used to."

"I don't imagine you can. But you can talk to me, Brandt. Both me and Dalton. Neither of us wants to forget Luke like he never was."

Brandt didn't respond.

"Are you talkin' to Jess about anything? And before you deny it, it's obvious something ain't right. You wanna tell me what's goin' on?"

He sighed. "It's been goin' on a while. Since Jess miscarried. She just fell apart, convinced she'd never take a baby to term. We were shocked to find out she was pregnant so soon after. When she got past the six-month mark, that's when she began to breathe a little easier. But me? I couldn't breathe at all."

Tell tipped the bottle and drank.

"I worried about every damn thing. Her health. Money. The baby's health. Each month her belly got bigger, so did my fears."

"Is there one fear that's bigger than all the rest?"

Brandt looked away.

"Come on. It's me. This is eatin' you alive, bro. And that ain't good."

He scrubbed his hands over his face. "What if I turn out to be the same kind of father as Dad?"

Tell's stomach dropped.

"Don't tell me that it won't happen. To hear Dad's brothers talk, he wasn't always a total dick either."

"Did the uncles say when Dad changed?"

"Yep. After he and mom started havin' kids."

Jesus. No wonder Brandt was freaked out. Especially when their dad had always claimed Brandt was more like him than any of his sons.

But his brother wasn't an idiot. Couldn't he see that by closing himself off from his wife and his brothers that he was falling prey to that mindset and becoming like their father? That maybe he'd already slipped into that cycle?

This was totally fucked up. Tell mentally flipped his dad the bird. But he wouldn't stand by and watch that bullshit destroy any more lives, especially not the great life Brandt finally had with the woman he loved more than anything.

Brandt closed his eyes. "So now that I have a kid of my own, I need you to do something for me."

"Anything."

"Keep me from turning into Dad. I understand it ain't your responsibility, but you know the signs, Tell. I can't rely on Jessie in this. You will see when I've stepped too far over that line and you will need to jerk me back to the right place."

"Since you brought it up, you *have* stepped over the line in the last few months."

"Shit."

Tell waggled the bottle at Brandt but he shook his head. "You need to talk to Jessie. Yeah, some stuff can be between us. But the big stuff? She needs to know. She ain't gonna judge you. And without stepping in it too deep, Jess is afraid you regret havin' Tucker."

Brandt's mouth fell open in shock. "Why would she think that?"

"No idea. But you'd better figure it out fast. Tonight, before you're overwhelmed with visitors tomorrow."

"Jesus. Fine." Brandt sighed. "Uh, thanks for saving my ass with the flowers."

"No problem."

"I've gotta stop walking around in a fog, so damn...scared I'm gonna break Tucker if I hold him. He's so freakin' little." He scrubbed his hands over his face. "God. How can Jess think I don't want him?"

"No clue, but I expect you'll fix that issue right away or I will kick your ass until you're a broken heap on the floor. Then I'll turn Dalton loose on you. You ain't Dad. None of us are. None of us ever hafta be."

"What if I don't know how to do this?"

"Cut yourself some slack. The kid is a few hours old! And you know more than you think you do. You've watched our cousins become fathers. They all seem to be doin' pretty well. I'm bettin' every single one of them felt the way you do at first."

"Even Cord?"

"Nah. He's perfect. He's never fucked up anything in his life."

Brandt laughed. "Asshole."

Dalton's pickup zipped into the parking lot, music blaring. He trotted over like an eager pup and jerked Brandt into a big hug. "Congrats, bro! How's it feel to be a daddy?"

"Scary as shit."

"No doubt. Luckily you've got me and Tell to keep you on the straight and narrow in not turning into Dad. 'Cause I gotta be honest, B. The way you've acted a couple times in the last few months really reminded me of him."

Leave it to Dalton to cut to the chase.

Dalton spied the bottle. "Really? You guys started celebrating Tucker's arrival before I got here? For shame. I'm just gonna hafta catch up." He raised the bottle and drank.

"I'm done," Brandt said. "I wonder if Jess will let me hold our son with booze on my breath."

"You ain't had nearly as much as me." The shots seemed to hit Tell all at once.

"I'll hold off on any more then," Dalton said to Tell. "So I can get you home."

"Thanks. But I probably won't be goin' straight home. I'll probably just walk over there."

"Over where?" Brandt asked.

"To Hot Lips' place." Dalton took another drink.

Brandt looked confused. "Who's Hot Lips?"

"Jesus, Brandt. Get with the program. Georgia Hotchkiss. The chick Tell has been hangin' out with all week. Everyone in the whole damn McKay family knows about her."

Great. But it bothered Tell that his older brother hadn't been paying attention to things going on in his life. Then again, Brandt hadn't been paying attention to anything.

You cut him too much slack.

Dalton smirked at him. "Didja finally get into her pants?"

After several belts, Tell didn't have the tact to deal with his younger brother, so he ignored him and slid off the tailgate. He looked at Brandt. "I know you'll get a handle on this. Call me if you need anything."

Chapter Twelve

Georgia was mighty shocked to see Tell on her doorstep.

"Tell? What are you doing here?"

"I was at the hospital to meet my nephew. Brandt and I knocked back a few celebratory shots, and I realized I oughten be drivin', so I walked over to see if you'd be interested in goin' out for supper with me."

"That's thoughtful, but I just finished cooking."

He took a step back. "I probably shoulda called first. No big deal. I'll go."

She grabbed a fistful of his T-shirt, holding him in place. "Not so fast. I have plenty of food if you'd like stay and eat with me."

Tell curled his hand around her cheek. "You're so damn sweet. Thank you. I'd like that. A lot."

Just the simple stroke of his thumb made her belly flip. "I hope you like curry."

"Don't know that I've ever had it."

Georgia stood on tiptoe to press her mouth to his. "So come in and try it."

He let her lead him into the kitchen after protesting that he needed to remove his boots. She gently shoved him into a chair and grabbed another plate from the cupboard. "Tea would be better for you than beer."

"Yeah. I ain't drunk, but I'm definitely feeling the shots."

"How is the newest McKay?"

"Perfect, strapping, eight-pound baby boy."

"And your sister-in-law?"

"She's doin' great." He frowned and traced the edges of the place mat.

Between Tell showing up unannounced and the uncertainty surrounding him, Georgia knew something was up. If he wanted to talk about it, he would, but she wouldn't pry. She dished up two plates of basmati rice and poured coconut chicken curry over the top.

"Georgia, darlin', this smells awesome."

"It's a little spicy." She filled two glasses of iced tea and sat across from him. "Dig in. Don't be shy."

Tell stirred his food before taking a bite.

Georgia waited to see if he made a face. She remembered from living with her dad and Deck that cowboys weren't adventurous eaters.

He swallowed and immediately scooped up another forkful. "Hey. This is tasty." After a few more bites, he reached for his tea and sputtered. "Is there sugar in here?"

"Yes."

Tell shook his head. "Iced tea ain't supposed to be sweet."

"Sweet tea is the norm where I'm from in Texas."

"So you ain't claiming Wyoming as your home at all?"

She shrugged. "We moved a lot before we ended up in Sundance. I might've considered it home if I'd stayed married to Deck."

He dumped his tea in the sink and refilled the glass with water. "You've never talked about your life before you moved here."

"It's not that exciting. Me and RJ were born at Fort Bragg. My dad was stationed at two different army bases before he got out of the service. After that we moved to Nebraska. When Granddad died, my dad and his brother sold the farm, split the money and went their separate ways. My dad had always wanted to live in Wyoming, so he bought a small ranch and cattle operation."

"Your mom didn't mind movin'?"

"If she did, she didn't say anything." Georgia swirled her fork through the mixture, thinking back on those years. When everything thing had been somewhat normal in their family.

Startled by the rough fingertips caressing her hand, she looked up into Tell's beautiful blue eyes. "I didn't mean to upset you."

His concern touched her, because she hadn't expected it. "You didn't. It was just a reminder that Sundance will never be my home." She managed a smile. "So what do you think of the curry?"

"I really like it."

"You want the recipe?"

"I'm not really much of a cook."

It amazed her how many bachelors were clueless in the kitchen. "So what do you eat?"

"I stick to the basics. Meat. Potatoes. Chili. Eggs. Sandwiches. Frozen dinners. Or I eat out."

"I'll bet lots of ladies offer to fix you a home-cooked meal."

"I usually take them up on it too." He gave her a sly smile. "But none of those vittles have ever been as good as this."

Georgia rolled her eyes.

"I'd offer to whip something up for you, but now that I've admitted I'm a lousy cook..."

"I'll take you up on the offer, McKay, if for no other reason than to watch you squirm."

His gaze settled on her chest. "I know a thing or two about making *you* squirm, don't I?"

He laughed when she blushed.

After they finished eating, Tell insisted on doing the dishes. She wandered out the back door onto the patio.

The backyard was enclosed on three sides by a six-foot wooden fence with no trees obstructing the view of the sky. She'd even planted a vegetable garden, something she hadn't done since living at the ranch. The lush green grass was soft beneath her bare feet. She spent most nights out here. Gazing at the stars. Listening to the night noises that were absent in a big city.

The screen door banged. Then Tell's arms were around her. "I wondered where you'd gone off to." He kissed the top of her head. "I checked your bedroom first."

"Were you disappointed not to find me there?"

"Nope."

Georgia spun around and faced him. "It's peaceful out here."

His eyes were so serious. "Is that what you're lookin' for? Peace?"

"I don't know," she answered honestly.

"That makes two of us." Tell spread out the blanket from the porch swing on the grass. He'd taken off his boots and his socks. And did he ever look sexy: dark stubble on his lean cheeks, wearing a tight T-shirt and low-slung jeans, his feet bare. He dropped onto the blanket with a deep sigh.

And Georgia continued staring at him.

"Something wrong?"

"No. You're just so easy on the eyes, Tell McKay."

"You're just sweet-talkin' me, hoping it'll get you laid."

"Is it working?"

Smirking, Tell crooked his finger at her. "Gotta come closer, my sweet, to find out."

She straddled his groin, pinning his arms above his head. "Whatcha gonna do now, cowboy?"

121

"Remind you that what goes around comes around."

Angling across his body, she smashed her breasts into his chest, taking one teeny nibble of his bottom lip. "That sounds intriguing. What does that mean?"

"That means...restraining me now gives me the right to do the same to you in the future."

"Just like this? Just my hands?"

He shook his head.

Wow. Tell's dark look of challenge unfurled a long lick of want inside her. Imagining her arms tied behind her back. Or in front of her. Or above her head. Or tied to a four-poster bed.

"Sweetness, gazing at me all wide-eyed like that is bound to get you...bound in all sorts of interesting ways."

"Promise?" she whispered against his lips.

Tell made a low growling sound and took her mouth in a savage kiss. Swamping her body with a wave of heat. His tongue swirled around hers aggressively as he cranked her lust higher.

Georgia returned his passion, rolling her hips against his pelvis and across the hard ridge in his jeans.

He dragged an openmouthed kiss down the center of her throat, commanding, "Shirt off. I want your nipples in my mouth."

She released his hands long enough to yank off her shirt and pop the clasp on her bra. She expected him to gather her breasts in his hands, feeling that delicious shock of wet heat as his mouth enclosed the tip.

But Tell's arms remained above his head. His gaze hooked hers. "Bring them to me."

She scooted up, bracing one hand on the ground as she leaned closer to his open mouth, intending to tease his lips with the hardened tip, then pulling away when his wicked tongue popped out to lick.

He had other ideas. He arched his neck and sucked the tight point, closing his eyes as he attempted to work more of her into his mouth.

Gooseflesh broke out, starting at her nape, inching down her spine a vertebra at a time with every rhythmic pull.

He bit down harder than she was expecting and she jerked back, which allowed him to shift oral focus to her other breast. "Stay. Still."

She tried, but her body was twitchy.

He'd latch his suctioning mouth to the hard point and then back off, teasing with little whips of his tongue. Blowing a stream of air on the wetness. Rubbing his face over the center of her breasts, scraping the bristly five o'clock shadow across the puckered tips until they ached. She ached. Everywhere. She wanted more.

She shifted, putting both hands on the ground, and began to grind on him.

Tell released her nipple. "You can grind on me all you want, but you don't get to come."

"Why not?"

"'Cause I said so."

Georgia glanced at him. The ferocity in his eyes was a little scary, until she remembered this was Tell. Laid-back Tell. Tell with the sexy, dimpled grin. Tell with the dancing eyes. Tell with the silver-tongued sweetness. Fun-loving Tell who teased her.

But there was not a hint of that man staring back at her right now.

"Why do you have that deer in the headlights look?"

"Because I remember you looked at me like this the first night you kissed me when we were dancing."

"And how did I look at you?"

"Like you owned me."

"Does that scare you?"

"A little. But it mostly...excites me."

Then he was upright, his hand gripping her hair with enough force her scalp stung. "You like that take-charge side of me?"

She whispered, "Yes."

"Get undressed."

His command sent a shiver through her. She rolled off his lap and rested on her knees on the blanket.

He tugged his T-shirt over his head. Withdrew a condom from his front pocket and shucked his jeans and boxers.

Georgia was so busy watching Tell reveal his magnificent body that she'd forgotten what she was supposed to be doing.

All he had to do was lift a brow at her and she started stripping.

Then she was unsure what to do next.

"You're kinda far away. C'mere." Tell rolled down onto his back. Grabbing her hand, he murmured, "I liked how you were on me before."

"On top?" she asked, wondering if he could see her blushing.

"Yep. And hurry up, 'cause I'm dying to see how beautiful you are when you're ridin' me."

She straddled him, pressing her palms against his pectorals, squeezing that warm, hard flesh.

Tell reached up and traced the inner rim of her lip with his thumb. "Put me inside you."

Circling her hand around his shaft, she adjusted her hips. The instant the tip connected with her opening, Tell's hands landed on her hips.

"Slowly," he murmured.

Georgia lowered herself a little at a time, aware of how wet she was. Aware of Tell's hungry gaze on her. She looked up when his cock was inside her to the root.

"Put your hands on my thighs."

Arching back gave him full access to her clit.

"Ride me like this. Bring me all the way out of that tight pussy and then take me deep again."

Every time she lifted her hips, letting his shaft slide out, he'd swirl his thumb over her clit. Her body quivered from the effort as she kept the maddeningly slow pace. Her thighs were sweating. Aching.

When he pumped his up to meet her downstroke, she switched gears. She fell forward, dropping her hands above his shoulders. Sliding so they were skin on skin, which felt amazing. God. He was so pretty to look at as she was on top of him, fucking him.

His hands cupped her ass. "Impatient?" he murmured.

"Yes. This is so good." She rolled her torso, her breasts rubbing against his chest hair as she increased the tempo.

Two sharp smacks on her bare ass surprised her.

She froze. "What was that for?"

"For takin' over." He smacked her butt cheeks again. "Some other time when you get it in your mind to be in charge, I'm gonna put you over my knee."

Her pussy clenched at the image of lying across his lap as his big, rough hands connecting with her butt.

He chuckled. "Oh, sweetness, you'd like that, wouldn't you?"

"Maybe," she said, gliding back down his body like a cat, pushing him in deep. Then almost kissing him as she pushed herself forward. "But I'd really like to see that *holy shit* look in your eyes when I make you come."

He pressed a kiss to her lips. "Take us there."

Her instincts took over. She picked up the pace, sliding skin on skin until their torsos were damp and sticking together. Mouth dry, head roaring, every inch of her skin prickled with awareness as she pushed toward that point of no return.

Tell whispered, "Breathe, baby. Lemme help you." His grip on her ass tightened as he helped her move to shorter, faster strokes.

That little changeup flipped a switch, sending her straight over the edge. "Yes. Oh God." She threw her head back in sweet anticipation of that first hard pulse.

The automatic sprinklers went off as she started to come. She gasped from the shock of the cold water spraying on her hot skin. The *tick tick tick* of the sprinklers was synchronized to the contractions in her pussy, to the throbbing in her clit, and to Tell's sucking kisses on the pulse point in her throat.

By the time the climax slowed, she was soaked.

Then Tell flipped her on her back, trying to protect her from the sprinkler stream. Resting on his forearms above her head, fucking her with power, but tenderness dominated his eyes. "Watch what you do to me." He groaned and his back bowed as he peered at her from beneath lowered lashes. His mouth tight with tension, then slack with pleasure as he emptied himself into her.

There wasn't time to cling to each other, whispering sweet words as bodies and breathing returned to normal.

Tell twitched. "Goddammit. That sprinkler head is spraying me right in the ass."

Georgia snickered. "You won't need an enema."

"I can't believe you said that. Just for that..." He withdrew from her body and rolled to his feet, ducking out of the way so the sprinklers hit her from every direction.

She shrieked and scrambled upright, grabbing the corners of the blanket before she ran to the patio, where Tell was shaking with laughter.

"I shoulda left your clothes out there," she grumbled, dropping the wet bundle on the cement.

"Probably." He pulled her wet, naked body against his. "But won't you feel a little bad for me, drivin' home in wet clothes? While you're all nice and warm, wrapped in a fluffy robe?"

"Nope. Not a bit."

He whacked her ass and covered her mouth, stopping her squeak of protest.

The kiss was pure seduction. So hot her lips seemed to burn. So sweet her teeth ached. So thorough she felt as if he'd taken her body again.

"I just can't get enough of you, Georgia." He gifted her forehead, temples, cheekbones, jaw, the corners of her mouth with soft kisses. He murmured, "Being with you... There's never been anything like it for me."

For her either. And he seemed to be as perplexed by it as she was.

"I hate that I hafta go."

"Do you want to wait until your clothes are dry?"

"Nah. I've worn worse than this."

Her fingers traced the cut muscles in his chest. "At least let me give you a ride to your truck."

"The walk will do me good. But I appreciate the offer." He snatched his wet clothes and only grimaced a little when he slid them on.

When she returned from donning a robe, Tell lounged by the front door. "Thanks for supper tonight. And for—" his hungry gaze swept her from head to toe, "—dessert."

"Anytime."

"Will I see you tomorrow?"

"If you want."

His knuckles followed the curve of her jaw. "Oh, I want." Then he slipped out into the night.

Chapter Thirteen

Georgia spent way more time on her hair and makeup for the reunion than she'd planned. Pointless fussing as she was torn on which image she wanted to project to her classmates. That Georgia Hotchkiss hadn't changed in appearance at all? Or that Georgia Hotchkiss had changed completely?

She scrutinized her reflection. Her hair, a solid foot shorter than in her teenage years, was sleek and professional.

Wait. Why did she want to look like she'd just stepped out of a board meeting? Why wouldn't she prefer to look sexy?

Dammit. None of this shit mattered.

Georgia fluffed up her sleek style into a tousled look. As if she'd just rolled out of bed after a bout of hot, hair-pulling sex. Tell would appreciate it.

She was wearing a sleeveless, form-fitting dress in a pale blue. With a modest bodice, the fabric was shirred from the empire waist to the froth of tulle at the hemline, two inches above her knees. With her funky platform heels in a blue cheetah print and a rhinestone clutch, she'd probably added fashion violation to her list of worries, which was already too long.

Seeing Deck for the first time since the dissolution of their marriage.

Seeing Tara-Lee, pregnant.

Seeing the girls in her class who hated her.

Seeing RJ's friends.

The doorbell rang.

Georgia gave herself one last look and headed downstairs.

Tell hadn't waited for her to open the door; he'd just waltzed right in.

And wasn't it ironic he was standing at the bottom of the stairs waiting for her, just like she'd seen in all those teen movies where the guy showed up to take the girl to the prom? To top it off, Tell had a look on his face she'd never seen on any man.

"My God, Georgia. You are a fucking goddess."

"Thank you."

He stopped her before she reached the bottom stair, setting his hands on her hips. He still topped her by a couple inches.

"What?"

"You look so damn perfect I'm afraid to touch you. Afraid I'll muss you up."

Her shoes dangled from her right index finger. She propped her forearms on his broad shoulders and let them hang between his shoulder blades as she rubbed her nose to his. "I love it when you muss me up. In fact, if you wanna ditch this whole reunion idea right now, I'll take you upstairs and let you muss me up however you want. All night."

Tell laughed. "Mighty tempting offer, hot lips. Now you gonna let me give you a proper kiss?"

"Please."

His mouth came down on hers with more force than she'd expected. He dove in for a tongue-teasing, openmouthed kiss that utterly overwhelmed her. His fingers tightened on her hips. And he blew every one of her circuits.

Then he eased back and made her weak-kneed with his dimpled grin. "See? I didn't muss you up at all."

Not on the outside. But on the inside? Different story.

"You ready?"

"Just have to put my shoes on." She used the newel post for support as she shoved her feet in the heels and checked out Tell's attire.

A black western-cut sport coat worn over a pristine white shirt, a bolo tie at his neck. Jeans, boots and his black hat. Yummy. "You are quite the head-turner, Mr. McKay."

"Thanks." He seemed embarrassed by the compliment.

Georgia grabbed her clutch. As soon as they stepped outside and approached his truck, Tell apologized.

"I'm afraid we ain't showing up to the school tonight in a fancy sports car. The only person I know who has one is Keely's husband, Jack, and it seemed a little forward to ask to borrow it."

She waited while he opened the door. Then he helped her into the cab. She wrapped her fingers around the braided leather strings of his bolo tie and pulled him closer. "I'm very fond of this truck. Especially after last night. Now I know it *is* possible to steam up the windows in July."

Tell held her hand on the short drive to the school. She checked her reflection again, adding a coat of lip gloss.

The parking lot was nearly full, and her stomach tightened.

This was it.

As they walked up to the gymnasium doors, Tell casually asked, "You nervous?"

"A little. How about you?"

"Nope." He tucked her hand around his bicep. "I'm with the hottest girl in our graduating class, who also happens to be the sexiest woman I know. I remember promising myself ten years ago that I'd show up at this reunion bein' the envy of all the other guys."

"Did that fantasy include making all the girls in our class take notice of what a gorgeous hunk of man you turned out to be?"

Tell grinned. "Busted."

"Then it appears both wishes will come true, since I will be the envy of all the women."

"And that would be different from high school for you...how? Didn't everyone want to be you?"

She didn't crack a smile.

"What?"

"That's an ironic statement because *I* didn't want to be me in high school." She withheld a frustrated sigh. "Do you think that's what tonight will be about? Just an exercise in our classmates going out of their way to prove how much they've changed?"

"Possibly." He smoothed a piece of her flyaway hair back in place. "Isn't that why we're here?"

"Now that I am here, I'm wondering why I came. Can we just go? Out for dinner or something? I'll buy."

"No. But I promise we'll leave if it sucks, okay?" He kissed her. "I like the coconut-flavored lip gloss."

The registration table was directly in front of one set of doors. And who was manning the table? Denille Swedlund. A fellow cheerleader. An easy piece for any of the jocks, anytime they wanted—a fact Denille used to brag about to Georgia, staring with disdain at her purity ring. Denille had offered Deck a hand job—a fact Georgia had found out from Denille herself after Deck had taken Denille up on the skanky proposition.

Denille looked good—but Denille wasn't scoping her out at all. Her gaze stayed glued on Georgia's date. "My God. Tell McKay, is that really you?"

"Yes indeed. Nice to see you, Denille, you haven't changed a bit."

Denille preened and handed over his badge. "The number on the bottom is the table you've been assigned."

Tell raised his eyebrows. "You're kiddin', right? About the assigned seating?"

"No. The committee thought it would be fun."

The other woman at the table, Nicki DeSoto, was also ogling Tell. "Hey, Tell, remember me?"

"Of course I do, Nicki. We had geometry together. So I'm guessing, since you were good at math, you're an engineer or something?"

Nicki laughed. "No. I'm married. Living in Lander." She scooted her chair out and patted her rounded belly. "Our first baby is due in October."

"Congratulations."

Denille finally deigned to look at Georgia. She handed over the button and said coolly, "Georgia. You're looking...well."

Georgia smiled. "You too. Do you still live in Sundance?"

"No. I live in Longmont, Colorado. I teach high school biology and I'm the head cheerleading coach."

No surprise Denille taught biology since she'd had so much previous experience with male anatomy. Ooh. Snap. And as long as she was being bitchy, the phrase *you can always tell the head cheerleader by her dirty knees* popped into her head, which allowed her to give her former nemesis a genuine smile. "That's great, Denille."

"We weren't sure whether you were even gonna show up," Denille said.

"Someone convinced me it was a good idea," Georgia said, slightly nudging Tell.

Tell plucked the button out of Georgia's hand and murmured, "Hold still, sweetness," pinning it above her left breast. Then he straightened it, letting his fingers brush over the swell of her cleavage with obvious familiarity. "There. Perfect."

And perfectly sweet, his *I'm with her* display. "Thanks."

He draped his arm over her shoulder, said, "See you lovelies inside," to Nicki and Denille, and led her into the mouth of the beast—aka the gymnasium.

Georgia hadn't realized she was holding her breath until Tell leaned over and whispered, "Come on, baby, breathe."

A bar had been set up in the far back corner. He ordered a vodka tonic for her and a Bud Light for himself. Tell tapped his bottle to her plastic glass. "To makin' our own rules tonight."

"Good plan."

Popular music from their senior year flowed from the speakers. They drank in silence, watching the action up by the makeshift stage— not that they could see much through the crowd. Georgia's spine stiffened when she realized the crowd was gathered around Deck.

"You'll spill all over your pretty dress if you keep crushing the glass."

She glanced down. The sides of the cup were dented in. God. Why was she hiding in the corner? It wasn't fair to make Tell her babysitter because she didn't want to see her ex-husband and his groupies.

Like it or not, she had to deal with Deck, and it might as well be on her terms, not his. She drained her drink and set the empty on the closest table. "Let's get the bullshit out of the way."

"Now?"

"Right now."

Tell grinned. "There's my girl. Not a wallflower, just balls to the wall." He drained his beer. Then he put his lips on hers. "Let's go stir things up."

Once they reached the group, people began to recognize her and hugs were exchanged. She was on the receiving end of some dirty looks too. Tell laughed and joked with several guys, but he was never more than an arm's length away from her.

No one came right out and asked them about their relationship. Because it was obvious they were a romantic couple? Or because it was old news? She estimated more than a third of their graduating class still lived in the Sundance area and gossip was a way of life around here. And she and Tell had been all over the place in the last two weeks.

Deck was at the center of it all. Smitty said something in his ear, and Deck turned and looked at her.

Georgia could admit Deck looked good. He hadn't packed on a beer belly or spare tire like many of their male classmates. He hadn't gone bald; he still had a head of wavy blond hair. His face showed more creases than the last time she'd seen him seven years ago. But he was still a handsome man.

He seemed to be sizing her up. He kept his arms crossed over his chest and a scowl on his lips. She was grateful when Tell placed his hand on the small of her back, possessively sliding his fingers around the curve of her hip.

"Hello, Deck." Thankfully her voice stayed friendly and not cold.

"Georgia. It's been a while."

"Yes, it has."

"I was surprised to hear you're living in Sundance now."

"For about the last month."

"Funny. You couldn't wait to get the hell out of Wyoming and yet...here you are. Back again."

She shrugged.

"Robert said he talked to you last week."

"It'd been a while since we'd spoken."

"I know." Deck rolled his shoulders back. "He said you ain't gonna come see him."

"I never said that."

"That's not what he said."

"Well, I'm pretty sure he knows the road runs both ways."

All the talking around them had stopped as everyone listened in to their conversation.

Deck's eyes scanned Tell head to toe. He didn't offer his hand. "McKay."

"Veldekamp."

Deck pointed with his head to the woman next to him. "This is my wife Tara-Lee."

Tell said, "I remember Tara-Lee. You graduated a year behind us."

"I didn't look like this the last time you saw me." She laughed and lovingly rubbed her hand over her contoured belly.

Georgia didn't acknowledge the woman at all. Too much risk of saying *the last time I saw you, you were bouncing on my husband's dick.*

Sam, one of Deck's longtime buddies, started talking about some of the crazy stuff they'd gotten away with senior year. Georgia listened politely, not remembering those memories with such fondness.

When Deck's friends started chiming in, talking about RJ, Tell discreetly pushed her to the edge of the group to make their escape. And he didn't stop moving until they were hidden by the bleachers.

He framed her face in his hands. "You all right?"

"Yes. I really am."

"Good. Let's fuck up Sally's seating chart. I see my buddies are here. Or is there a group you'd rather sit with?"

"Just you. But we need to save a seat for Stephanie."

They shared a table with Thurman, Leah and Warner, Roxanne and Ned, and Stephanie, who'd brought Len Allen, the president of the chess club. Now the guy looked like he could be president of the steroid club.

Leah and Roxanne were surprisingly friendly, and had both her and Stephanie laughing at the stories about the hair and nail salon they co-owned.

When she turned to say thanks to Tell for bringing her another drink, he was a kiss away.

The kiss, while short, was shockingly possessive. As was the hand sliding up her thigh. The man just smirked at her, silently daring her to move his hand, because guaranteed, he'd slide it up higher.

Every time Tell looked at her with heat in his eyes, she felt the answering fire ignite her blood. And Tell didn't care if everyone else noticed. The connection between them was getting stronger, despite Georgia reminding herself it was just sex.

"They're setting up the buffet," Tell said.

"Think it's better than cafeteria food?"

"Probably not. Think Sally will act like the grumpy old lunch lady, Miz Farnsworth, and dismiss us table by table to get in the chow line?"

"Probably. She was a control freak."

"So let's freak her out and cut to the front of the line."

"You're such a bad influence on me, McKay."

He whispered, "Admit the good girl in you always wanted a bad boy."

"And lucky me, now I've got one."

"At least for the rest of tonight, right?"

That off-the-cuff comment left her a little unsettled. Like this was the last night they'd be together.

Isn't that what you wanted? A date to the reunion and hot sex?

Maybe at first. But everything had changed in the last week. Or at least since the night Tell had shown up on her doorstep after his nephew's birth, so sweet and vulnerable. Then so unbelievably hot and forceful during their sexy romp in the backyard. Although she'd known

Tell was okay to drive home, she still called him to make sure he'd arrived safely, and they'd ended up talking for another hour.

Then they'd yakked on the phone for several hours the following night, during Tell's last-minute trek to Casper to stay with Landon overnight. As much as she admired his dedication to his family, she couldn't help but suspect his family took advantage of his good nature and willingness to always lend a hand.

Wednesday night they'd met at the Golden Boot for a night of dancing and managed to stay through the band's first set. But they were so desperate for a physical connection, they hadn't even made it onto the bed in her room; Tell had taken her on the floor. Dragging out the passionate encounter until they were both soaked in sweat, shaking and sated.

She would've been happy curled up on the couch with Tell watching a movie Thursday night, but he had other *see and be seen* plans. Fun plans. A scavenger hunt picnic, where they picked up a food item from each restaurant in town and ate it at the park. Followed by an obstacle course race on the playground—which he'd won. Then dropping by the bingo hall for a game of bingo—which she'd won. And ending the evening with them jockeying for position for who got to be on top in her bed. They'd both won that one.

Georgia found him incredibly easy to be with. The thought of this ending, just as it'd gotten started, gave her a tiny feeling of loss. But she wouldn't push him for more, especially since he hadn't brought up extending their agreement.

She'd enjoy it—and him—while she could.

After a bit she excused herself and headed to the restroom. Unlike high school, there wasn't a line of girls gossiping at the mirror. She checked her makeup, smoothed her dress and walked down the hallway.

Straight into Deck.

She attempted to sidestep him, but he blocked her. As she looked up at him, she experienced a punch of bitterness that she'd wasted part of her life on this man. Being this close to him again, Georgia was hard-pressed to remember any happy memories. "What do you want?"

Deck loomed over her. "Bet you think you're clever, showing up here in front of the whole class, like you've got a real thing going on with McKay. But I know better. It's all bullshit."

"I stopped giving a shit a long time ago about what you think, Deck, not to mention not caring what anyone else thinks. I *am* with Tell."

"He's a fuckin' loser. Always has been, always will be."

"That's what sticks in your craw, isn't it? Were you afraid I might act on that attraction to him back in high school and I'd figure out you weren't half the man you pretended to be?"

A mean smile distorted his mouth. "You were only trying to make me jealous back then and you remember exactly how I handled shit like that."

With his fists.

"You're still trying to make me jealous. Guess what, Georgie? It ain't workin'. Tara-Lee is my life now. You're nothin' but a memory."

"So why did you follow me out here?" she demanded. "What does it matter that I know how much you adore your wife? I'm nothing to you."

"I know you're jealous that life could've been yours."

"Would've been a little crowded, with Tara-Lee in our bed and all."

"Your daddy would be so ashamed of your crude mouth, Georgia."

"He stopped being my daddy when he became yours," Why had she blurted that out?

Deck gave her that mean smile again. "See? You are jealous."

"No, I'm heartsick that my father accepted you as a substitute for RJ."

He stepped back as if she'd slapped him.

Good.

"Georgia, darlin'? Is everything okay?"

Deck looked over her shoulder at Tell approaching her from behind. "Don't get your jock in a twist, McKay. She's fine."

"I'll make that determination since she ain't your concern anymore," Tell said evenly. "You probably better get back inside anyway, bein's your baby mama is lookin' for you."

Giving them both another scowl, Deck retreated.

Georgia didn't have time to say anything before Tell took her hand, leading her deeper into the bowels of the school. "The reunion is the other direction."

"I know. Which is why we're goin' this way." They cut through the hallway to the main floor. As soon as they reached the locker bay, he crowded her against the cool metal, bracing his hands by her head. "I imagined doin' something like this every damn day for almost three years. Since the very first time I saw you."

"Imagined what?"

"Pressing you up against the locker and kissing the livin' hell out of you." Then Tell lowered his mouth and did just that. Turning her anger into passion. Passion he could coax forth with just the touch of his lips to hers.

The potent kiss hit her like a fifth of Scotch.

He broke the kiss and buried his face in her neck. His hot breath teased the damp skin and she shivered.

"Did reality live up to the teen hype?"

"Way better." A grinning Tell stepped back and grabbed her hand. "Come on. I have another fun idea." He towed her behind him through the hallway, stopping in front of room 226.

"Mrs. Wall's classroom."

"Yep."

Butterflies took wing in her belly when Tell asked, "How adventurous are you feelin', Miss Hotchkiss?"

"Very."

"Remember you said that."

Chapter Fourteen

He propelled Georgia into the room and shut and locked the door.

"I had at least one class with you every year, throughout high school. And every one of those years I had a fantasy of some sort about you and me."

"What did these fantasies of yours include, Mr. McKay?"

He ran the backs of his knuckles over her jawline, tempted as always by her soft skin. "Typical teenage guy stuff. Groping. Kissing. More groping. You whispering in my ear what a stud I was, because I didn't have a freakin' clue about sex."

"You're telling me that your fantasies about me were innocent?"

"Back then? Yep. But now that I've got the experience... Well, I'll remind you that I ain't exactly tame these days."

"Thank God for that."

"You willing to do a little play actin' with me? Takin' a trip back in time?"

"What do you have in mind?"

"Revisiting history class. Senior year."

"Sure." Georgia smiled and fingered the ends of his bolo tie. "Lose the sport coat and the hat. The you from ten years ago wouldn't have worn those to class."

Hot damn.

Tell took his seat, his heart pounding ridiculously hard. "Start at the front of the classroom and walk to your desk like you always did."

Georgia wandered up to the front of the classroom. She took her time reading a laminated sign. Then she walked to the other side of the chalkboard and studied the fire escape route and building layout placards.

Tell was getting antsy. He almost called out to hurry up, but he realized this was part of the game. Every day he'd been in his seat early, waiting for that first glimpse of her as she sashayed into the room. On game days, she'd worn the super short, super tight cheerleading uniform. He'd always loved game day.

Georgia took her seat, not looking at him at all. No different than when they'd been in class together. She tossed her head and the aroma of her hair wafted back to him.

That sweet blast from the past hit his lungs and traveled straight to his groin.

Then Georgia stretched her arms above her head and released a soft groan. Twisting her upper body sent her hair flowing back and forth, as mesmerizing as a pendulum.

Years before, he'd been too afraid to touch her. But he wasn't now. Keeping his hand as light as a helium balloon, he stroked that black silk. So tempting to twine his fingers through it and tug to get her attention. But he reminded himself that Hot Lips never paid him any mind unless she wanted something from him.

She turned in her chair to face him, gifting him with her megawatt grin. "Tell McKay. Just the man I needed. I'm hoping you can help me out."

"With what?"

"The assignment. I didn't get my homework done because I was up late cleaning stalls, since we've got four horses set to foal at any time."

"And?"

"And I need to copy yours."

"Georgia—"

"Please? Just this once. I promise I won't ask again."

Dammit. Tell remembered how easily she charmed, tempted and cajoled him into doing whatever she wanted.

But he wasn't going to make this easy on her. He leaned forward and murmured, "*Just this once* has been ten times over the course of the year."

Her haughty look was hot as hell. "I didn't realize you were keeping track."

Tell shrugged. "I just think it's time *I* got something in return for helpin' *you* out."

"What do you want?"

"What do you think I want?" he countered.

Georgia trailed her fingertips across his rough knuckles. "I never noticed how large your hands are. I think you want to put these hands all over me."

He quickly wrapped his fingers around her wrist. "Wrong. I want a kiss. Not a peck on the mouth. A real kiss. With tongue and everything."

"Okay." She bit her lip. "I can meet you after school."

Tell shook his head. "Right here, right now."

"Why can't it wait?"

"Because I know you. You'll have second thoughts just like you did with the project. So if you want to copy my homework, you'll let me taste my fill of them hot lips. Right now."

Desire flashed in her eyes. But she still played the game. "I don't want to get busted for a PDA."

"The teacher ain't here." Tell brought her palm to his mouth and placed a kiss in the center. "And I don't give a shit what anyone else says or thinks."

She finally sighed. "Fine. Pucker up. The bell is about to ring."

He laughed softly. "Not so fast."

"But—"

"Come closer."

Georgia complied with just enough trepidation to make it believable.

They met in the middle of his desk. The angle was a bit awkward, but this was how he'd imagined it.

Her lips were so full and ripe he ached to take a bite. He skimmed his mouth over hers, catching the edges of her upper and lower lips with the soft, smooth inside of his. Letting the moist undersides cling together before following the contour with a painstakingly slow glide.

Her breath came in short bursts, mingling with his measured exhalations. When he swept the tip of his tongue across the seam of her lips, she moaned, opening for him fully.

Tell curled his hand around her neck, taking possession of her mouth. His tongue warred with hers; every swirling stroke kicked his need higher. Each suck, each lick, each slide of wet lips urged him to drag her out of the seat. Urged him to press and grind their bodies together.

When she eased back, he focused his attention on the section of her throat where her pulse jumped. He could feel her body vibrating, and he realized the kiss had shaken her as much as it had him.

"Georgia." His teeth scraped her throat. "I want you."

"God. Yes. Don't stop doing that."

As many times as he had imagined this scenario as a seventeen-year-old boy, he hadn't choreographed the logistics. He didn't want to bend her over. He wanted to look in her eyes as he slid home. The student desks were too small and unstable for what he had in mind.

But the teacher's desk was perfect.

"Baby, we gotta move."

She attempted to smooth her hair back into place as she slid out from the desk.

He laughed and hauled her close. "Your hair is gonna look a whole lot messier by the time I get done with you."

"Tell. I don't know about this." She squirmed out of his hold and started backing away from him.

He stalked her. "You drive me outta my fuckin' mind, Georgia Hotchkiss."

"Maybe we should sneak out and do it in your truck."

"Maybe you oughta get it through that pretty head of yours that I'm gonna have you. My way. Now." Tell had let her retreat until she'd literally backed herself into a corner. He slapped his hands on the chalkboard beside her head.

Just as he leaned closer, she snaked her arms around his neck, and stole the kiss from him. Her body movements were porn-star-worthy as she made those fucking needy little moans.

He had years' worth of fantasies revolving around him and Georgia alone in a classroom, but dragging this out wasn't an option.

"Are you wet for me?" he whispered.

"Sopping wet," she whispered back.

"Who'da thought such a pretty mouth could be so dirty?"

"Show me dirty." She nuzzled his neck. "I've wanted you for so long. So, so long." Her tongue zigzagged back up to his ear. "Fuck me, Tell McKay. Fuck me now. No one ever has to know."

A primitive growl was the only sound he could manage. He held on to her biceps as he pulled her away from the chalkboard and spun her toward the desk. He kicked the chair aside, releasing her only long enough to sweep all the papers off the surface, just like in that teenage fantasy.

She emitted an *eep* of surprise as he picked her up and set her on the surface. Her heated gaze met his when he unbuckled his belt.

"Pull that dress out of my way."

The fabric clung to her thighs as she inched the dress up to her hips. She twisted a finger in the elastic band of her silver thong. "You want me to take these off?"

"Yes."

He watched with his damn tongue hanging out as she whisked that scrap of satin down her trembling legs, then fingered herself with a soft moan of delight.

Then he was wedged between her thighs. Condom on, he lightly pushed her shoulders with a murmured, "Lie back." Soon as she was, he slid into her. Easily. Fully. He slanted over her, taking her mouth the same way he took her body. With unrestrained passion.

Georgia arched; her tits bounced into his chest with his every aggressive thrust.

Everything spun into a vortex of pleasure: the tight clasp of her pussy, the sound of his flesh slapping hers, the taste of her mouth and the need building between them with every stroke.

She broke the kiss first. "I need...more."

Curling his hands around the steep angle of her high heels, he brought her knees above her hips and spread her wider. Fucking her harder, deeper. "Like that?"

"Yes. But I'm sliding around too much."

"Hold on to me."

She reached up, grabbing his biceps.

"God, I fuckin' love it when you dig your nails into me," he panted.

Gasping, she rocked her hips into his every thrust.

"Look at you. So damn hot. So much better than any fantasy."

"Tell. Please. Make me come."

He repositioned his pelvis so he connected with her clit every time he plunged to the root.

"So close. So..." A long moan flowed from her mouth as she unraveled. Completely. Her body arched and her face became lost in pleasure. He couldn't tear his eyes away from Georgia, beautiful in abandoning herself to passion, to the moment, to him.

Tell wasn't far behind. He pumped into her three more times and he was done. His eyes rolled into the back of his head as her cunt clamped down and milked him dry.

Holy fuck. He opened his eyes and saw Georgia was still as out of it as he was. He ditched the condom and had his pants buckled before she stirred. When he ran his hand up the inside of her thigh, she flinched. "You okay?"

141

Georgia wore a dreamy smile as she stretched her arms above her head. "I feel like an ungrounded wire. In a good way."

"So I gathered." Tell snuck another kiss. This one sweet and lazy. He rested his forehead on hers. "Thank you. That was amazing."

"Mmm-hmm. I'm still feeling a little dizzy. A shot of you is so heady." Her fingertips outlined his face from his temples to his jawline. "I don't want to go back in there."

"Just for a little while."

"I must look well fucked. You think anyone will suspect what we've been up to?"

I hope so.

She laughed. "You are so transparent, McKay. You want me waltzing into the gym with my hair a mess, my dress wrinkled, my grin ten miles wide."

"Busted." He slipped on his sport coat and watched as she fussed with her dress and her hair. "Ready?"

"I guess." Georgia started toward the door.

Staring at her backside, he muttered, "Shit. Wait a second."

"What?"

"Ah. You have chalk marks on your ass."

"Seriously?" She tried to look over her shoulder at her butt.

"Hang on. I'll brush them off." As he swatted, he noticed the perfect bounce in those round cheeks.

He had a flash of spanking her ass until those cheeks were pink and hot. Usually he kept his fun-loving persona at the forefront when he took a woman to bed. But sometimes he'd wanted more. Not a longer connection but a more intimate one. He'd finally had the guts to show his intense side to Georgia and she liked his sexual demands. He wondered how far she'd let him take it.

"So, are you about done smacking my ass, cowboy?"

Tell pinned her back to his chest. "And if I say no?" He nuzzled her ear. "If I admitted my other fantasy was tyin' you up and spanking your butt until you came, would you be willing to give it a go?"

Her breath hitched. It took a few long seconds before she answered. "If I didn't have to obsess about it beforehand. If we're in a moment..."

"And if I decided that's what I wanted from you in that moment? You'd be okay with that?"

"Yes."

He growled, "You've been a naughty girl, Miz Hotchkiss, getting fucked in the classroom. That behavior is against school policy and will result in a trip to the principal's office for proper punishment."

She peered over her shoulder. "Principal McMasters kept a paddle in his office."

"A bare hand is a much better instrument than a paddle for spankings anyway."

"An instrument of what? Pleasure? Or pain?"

Tell smirked at her. "You'll just have to wait and see which one you like better, won't you?"

The dancing was in full swing when they returned to the gym.

"What's shaking, kids? Where you been?" Stephanie asked.

"We toured the school. You know, reliving old memories." He grinned when Georgia smacked his knee under the table. "Why? What'd we miss?"

"A fucking limbo contest, if you can believe it," Roxanne grumbled. "Who did the planning for this event? Chuck E. Cheese?"

Georgia choked on her drink.

"No wonder no one wanted to help Sally. And can you believe she tried to assign us seats?"

Stephanie leaned across the table. "I had a run-in with Sally. I told her if she pulled a bitch move and tried to get you and Deck to dance together as the class couple, I would make myself projectile barf all over her."

"Thanks for having my back, Stephanie."

"Always."

The dancing ended and Sally took the stage to hand out the decade awards.

And just like high school, the awards were stupid, dragged on way too long and were handed to the popular crowd. With the exception of Georgia. Her face was a blank mask so Tell had no idea what she was thinking.

"The award for most changed goes to...Tell McKay."

"Christ. Really?" he muttered.

"Tell, you have to go up there," Georgia said.

He drained his beer before heading to the podium.

Sally gave him a hug and the small trophy. He started toward the stairs, but someone yelled, "Speech!"

Fuck. He hated talking in front of people. "I, ah, think everyone in this room deserves a trophy, because it'd be a sad freakin' thing if we

143

all stayed the same people we were in high school." He walked off to meager applause.

"Now we look back on the classmates we lost." The first picture on the screen behind the stage was of Matt Wilson, who'd died in combat in Iraq.

Sally went on about all that Matt had accomplished before his death. She called Matt's widow to the stage for a memorial plaque from the class.

The second picture on the screen was of RJ Hotchkiss.

Georgia tensed, but there wasn't a perceptible change in her expression. When Tell noticed everyone in the room looked for her, he reached under the table and set his hand on her knee.

Sally talked briefly about RJ, mostly about his life because his death wasn't noble. Then she called Georgia to accept the memorial plaque.

She didn't budge.

Tell squeezed her leg. "Georgia. You have to go up there."

"I can't."

"Yes, you can. Go on now. I'll be right here when you're done."

Georgia walked toward the stage like she was facing an executioner. She let Sally give her a stiff hug and she read the plaque before she glanced up at the crowd.

"It'll be nine years on August third since I lost my twin brother, my best friend, the person who meant the most to me in the world. I know you all remember RJ as the guy with the perpetual smile. The guy who lived for a dare. The guy with a larger-than-life personality. I remember him as all those things too. But he was so much more. I miss him every day and I wish..." Georgia looked at the plaque, her hair falling forward to obscure her face.

When her shoulders started to shake and Sally made no move to comfort her like she had Matt Wilson's widow, Tell was on his feet, his heart in his throat. He couldn't stomach seeing her standing up there alone, forced into public grief.

He scaled the steps, sidestepped Sally and stood in front of Georgia, blocking her from the room. "Georgia. Come on, sweetness, I gotcha."

Georgia peered up at him. "Please get me out of here."

He tucked her into the side of his body as they left the stage. Stephanie intercepted them with Georgia's purse and they made their way out the door.

Tell didn't stop until he reached his pickup. He dropped the tailgate and lifted her into his arms. Then he sat, holding her tightly as her body shook.

Her voice was whisper-thin when she finally spoke. "I'm sorry."

"Don't be." He kissed the top of her head. "Let's go."

Chapter Fifteen

She'd cried. In front of a room full of people.

Most of them had probably been happy to see her break down. They probably thought she deserved misery in her life after leading such a supposedly charmed existence.

The memory of RJ complaining he never won anything had hit her as she'd accepted the award. There was no irony in that, only sadness.

And then Tell had been there. Rescuing her. Going above and beyond. Showing her yet another facet of his personality—a protective side. She'd only scratched the surface in getting to know the man he'd become and she wanted so much more than the small glimpse she'd had the past two weeks.

Before he started the truck, he said, "You okay?" and brought her hand to his mouth for a gentle kiss.

"Yes. Thank you for..." She cleared her throat. "It's weird to think back on the awards they gave out senior year right before graduation. RJ was so bummed he hadn't won class troublemaker."

"It wasn't for lack of tryin'," Tell muttered.

The hair on the back of her neck prickled. "What is that supposed to mean?"

Tell shifted in his seat.

What was up with his guilty look? "Something you wanna share with the class, Mr. McKay?"

"Not really, but I'm sure you won't let it go now."

"You'd be right about that, especially if it has something to do with my brother."

"It does." He ran his hand through his hair. "You know me'n RJ had shop together senior year? We were partnered during the sheet metal unit. RJ came up with the idea to make an animal trap. We worked on that sucker for a week and grumpy Mr. Krystanski gave us a D on it, citing a design flaw. So RJ decided we should prove Mr. K wrong by trapping an animal in our new, improved cage and showing him that it *did* work."

Georgia stared at him. "You and my brother were responsible for letting the skunks loose in the school?"

"That's the thing. The mama skunk and her four babies were in the cage the night we snuck it into the classroom. So when we saw the cage was empty the next morning...we had no idea what'd happened. Mr. K never said a word and me'n RJ chalked it up to a failed prank...until a few days later—"

"When the entire school reeked like skunk."

"Hey, we had no way of knowin' the mama skunk had escaped and took her litter into the ductwork. By then, no way could we come clean, since they had to rip out the ceiling to free the skunk family and neither of us wanted to pay for the damage."

She smirked. "So Mr. K was right? Your trap had a design flaw since the skunks escaped?"

He shrugged. "Or someone let them loose. "

"And which one of you initially rounded up the skunks?"

"It was a joint effort after I told RJ I'd stumbled across a nest. The buggers are cute when they're little. But the mama was pissed we were touchin' them."

"Did she spray you?"

"Both of us."

Georgia wrinkled her nose. "I don't remember RJ coming home smelling like skunk."

"That's because we snuck into the showers at the truck stop and cleaned ourselves up. Hell, I think we even tossed our clothes."

"No one ever knew?"

"Nope. Me'n RJ swore we'd take the secret to our graves." Tell went motionless after he said that. "Shit. I'm sorry. I wasn't thinkin'."

She leaned across the seat, bussing his cheek, feeling an odd kinship with him for the secret he'd shared with her brother. "It's okay. I'm pretty sure RJ won't mind that you told me."

He rested his forehead against hers. "You ready to go to my place?"

"As long as you have ice cream. Because I'm in the mood to eat ice cream and wallow in front of the TV."

Tell grinned. "I have such a bad sweet tooth that I have four different kinds of ice cream."

They didn't speak on the drive to Tell's trailer. When they started down the long driveway, Georgia realized she hadn't brought other clothes. "You've got an extra T-shirt I can borrow?"

"Sure. But it's gonna cost you."

"Cost me what?"

He didn't respond until he'd parked. He faced her with a lascivious grin. "Two things are gonna happen if you borrow one of my shirts. One, you don't get to wear a bra. Two, I can ask for my shirt back at any time."

"Which means I'll be naked."

"I'll let you leave them sexy panties on." He smirked. "Unless they're in my way and then they're gone too."

"Is this your way of distracting me?" she asked softly.

He touched her face. "One of the ways I've got planned for tonight."

She bit back a girly sigh.

It was stuffy inside. As Tell started opening windows, Georgia looked around. The space was as tidy as the last time she'd been here.

"It'll cool down fast, but we might wanna sit outside until it does."

"Do you want me to dish up the ice cream?"

"You'd better ditch that sexy dress first so you don't spill on it. Hang tight. I'll be back with something for you to wear."

She wandered to the kitchen and opened the cupboards, looking for bowls. Why did she have a pang of sadness at seeing his meager selection of dishware? He had five mismatched dinner plates, four mismatched salad plates and three mismatched bowls. The plastic bowls were adorned with characters from animated movies: *Cars*, *Finding Nemo* and *Toy Story*. The selection of glassware followed those same lines: four Tupperware plastic glasses from the 1980s, a few small, plastic Happy Meal cups, three beer mugs, two wineglasses and four coffee cups.

What did it say about her that her cupboards looked like his? She'd left everything behind when she left Deck, except for one suitcase full of clothes and one box of personal items. When she got her own place, purchasing matching dishes and household items hadn't mattered. Sort of pathetic that she'd never cooked for anyone in her condo in Dallas besides her mother.

As busy as Tell's social life was, it didn't appear that extended to his home.

Strong arms hauled her back against a broad, hard chest. "Didja find anything interesting while you were snooping in my cupboards?"

"No. But I am wondering if I'll have to fight you for the *Toy Story* bowl. Woody is my favorite."

"I have a woody for you," he breathed in her ear.

Georgia faced him, noticing he'd changed into a tight black tank top and athletic shorts. "Your woody will have to wait. I'm fixated on ice cream right now."

"Then I'd better get you outta this dress. Does it come off over your head? Or drop to the floor?"

"To the floor."

Tell slipped his fingers beneath the fabric above her cleavage and followed the neckline to her shoulders. He peeled it down her arms and tugged the dress over her breasts and hips until it pooled at her feet.

Then he unhooked her bra. But this time the tease wasn't in how slowly he removed it, but what those clever fingers were doing to her nipples after her bra was gone.

She stayed still, although the way he was touching her made it damn difficult.

He murmured, "Hands up."

A super soft, super large T-shirt dropped over her head. The hem grazed her knee. "I could wear this as a dress. Except for this part." The deep V-cut of the neckline would reveal both her breasts if she bent over.

"I happen to like that aspect of the design." Tell pulled the fabric to the left, exposing the hardened nipple. He bent his head, pressing a soft kiss on the tip, before he straightened the shirt. "You're distracting me, woman. I'm supposed to be givin' you ice cream choices." He retreated to the freezer. "Looks like...rocky road, butterscotch ripple, cookie dough or chocolate and caramel swirl."

"A scoop of chocolate and caramel swirl and a scoop of rocky road, please."

Tell dished up two identical bowls and handed her one with a spoon. "You wanna sit outside on the back deck? It's a beautiful night."

"I'd love to."

They sat at a small wooden picnic table. It was too dark to see the view beyond the fence line, but she remembered the McKay Ranch had diverse vistas. "How long have you lived here?"

"A little over a year. This used to be Brandt and Jessie's place. Before that I lived in Luke's old place. Before that Dalton and I shared a crappy trailer. Now he's livin' in Luke's trailer."

"Sounds like your family plays musical houses?"

"Death, divorce and discontent sorta forces it. I think we're all kinda lazy because we like where the houses are located. Close, but not too close."

Georgia let the last bite of chocolate and caramel swirl melt on her tongue. "Do any of you get along with your dad?"

"Some days we all do. But they're few and far between. I never expected his sobriety would stick. I'm glad it has, because he was killin' himself. But the really sobering part for all of us? It wasn't the alcohol that made him a mean, grumpy jackass. Take away the booze? He's still a mean, grumpy jackass."

She threaded her fingers through his.

Surprisingly, Tell kept talking. "There are times when I wish he'd just go on a mission trip indefinitely. When he's not around, I feel guilty as hell for thinkin' that, then he shows up, still actin' like the same SOB he always was, minus the blackout-drunk moments. Ever since I was a little kid, the man terrified me. He did all of us. We were all afraid of doin' something wrong to earn one of them ass-chewings that strip you down to nothin'. Might sound stupid, but after he got done rippin' into me, I wished he'd taken after me with a switch. At least them marks would heal. The lash of his tongue always hurt far more than a belt."

This was the most he'd ever spoken to her of the issues he had with his father. And her heart hurt for him. It got her to thinking... Was a mean father worse than one who preferred a stranger to his own child?

Tell shoved his bowl aside. "Do Deck and Tara-Lee live with your dad?"

"I don't know. Deck and I lived with my parents until RJ died. When Dad bought the hog farm, we had a small cabin to ourselves on the property. Deck didn't like it because it was pretty basic, so he stayed in the house. And I didn't like being in the house with my parents because they fought all the time, so I slept at the cabin. Because Tara-Lee and RJ were supposed to get married that fall, Tara-Lee had already moved in with my folks, so they let her come with us to the new place. I was still in grief, still trying to take college classes. I'll admit I wasn't the most attentive wife."

"That didn't give Deck the right to cheat on you," Tell said hotly. "For Christsake, you'd lost your brother, you were forced to move, your parents split up. He shoulda been takin' care of you."

"Thanks. Evidently my dad didn't see it that way since he took Deck's side. When I talked to him last week, he basically defended his actions and Deck's by telling me nothing is as cut and dried as it looks. He doesn't understand why I don't just drive over to his place and we can hug it out."

Neither said anything for a few minutes.

Then Tell stood and held out his hand. "I wanna show you something."

"Is this more of your forced fun?"

"Yep and there's gonna come a day when you don't dread that word, sweetness."

Georgia allowed him to lead her down the steps and around the corner of the trailer. A two-person hammock was set up on the rise of a small hill. The ground was rocky and rough—no soft, pampered grass here—and she sucked in a breath when something jabbed the bottom of her foot.

Tell lifted her into his arms, carrying her the rest of the way.

As much as she liked being held against his warm, hard chest, she couldn't help but snicker. "Is this where you call me a tenderfoot?"

He grunted with exaggeration. "I'm stoically bearing the pain for you, little lady, 'cause that's what us cowboy types do." He set her down and stretched on the hammock before extending a hand to her.

It wobbled, but she found a balance point, which placed her right on top of Tell, luckily for her.

She sighed. "It's the perfect temperature."

"I crash out here in the summer when it's too hot to sleep inside."

"Don't you get eaten alive by bugs?"

"Nah. I must not be sweet enough."

"I think you're plenty sweet." She kissed his pectoral and snuggled into his side.

Tell shifted to tangle their legs together.

All the turmoil from the last few hours faded, and a feeling of contentment filled her as he trailed his rough fingertips over her skin.

After a bit, Tell said, "So what's the craziest, riskiest thing you've ever done?"

"Nothing."

"Come on, there's gotta be something."

"I've always done what was expected of me. Either by my parents or by my boss." Rather than dissect her boring choices, she posed the same question to him. "What's the craziest, riskiest thing you've ever done, wild man McKay?"

He continued stroking the underside of her arm from her wrist to her armpit. "I was tired of bein' the poor McKay relation. So I took all my money, except for fifty bucks, and entered a poker tournament. I was either gonna go big or go home broke."

"So what happened?"

"It paid off. I won first place. So I banked half of what I'd won, and used the other half to enter another tournament the next weekend."

"And?"

Tell chuckled. "I had a winning streak that lasted an entire year. Made a really good chunk of change. Dalton was my partner in crime, so to speak, so we won enough to buy more land to add to our part of the McKay ranch."

Georgia raised her head from his chest and looked at him. "Good for you. But now that you've told me, a game of strip poker ain't in the cards for us."

"You'd win. I'd get you half-nekkid and I'd start thinkin' raunchy thoughts..."

She smiled. "I like your raunchy mind."

"And sweetness, you ain't seen the raunchiest parts." He nipped the top of her ear. "Yet."

"Are you still sandbagging tournaments?"

"Once in a while. Dalton is still goin' strong. That runner's high after winnin' big is dangerous stuff. But it ain't like he's blowing money left and right. We are each other's checks and balances system, so it didn't happen to either of us, because we saw so many guys who fell prey to that mindset. Always wanting that next big win. Quarter of a million dollars one week; then they'd lose it all the following week. We treated gambling like a business. Only playing one type of game. Only entering events where the buy-in was high because the payout was high."

She stared at him, fascinated again by another facet of this man. "I've never heard you talk about this."

"That's because me'n Dalton keep it to ourselves. Brandt knows we won some money because he's on the land deed. Our cousin Ben knows because we tried to do a business deal with him a year and a half ago, but it fell through. But no one in my family knows and that's the way we wanna keep it."

"I won't breathe a word, I promise." She sighed. "I'm boring compared to you. You have this secret life and—"

Tell stopped her protest with a kiss.

After he released her mouth, she rested the side of her face on his chest. He nuzzled the top of her head and continued his caresses on her arm.

A soft breeze blew. Between the sway of the hammock, the comforting beat of Tell's heart beneath her ear, and the chirping crickets, Georgia could've easily fallen asleep. Being with him like this settled every ragged nerve inside her.

"You up for more ice cream?" he murmured a little while later. "Because one bowl doesn't count as wallowing."

"Sure. But I am pretty comfy right now."

"I could tell, bein's you were snoring."

"Maybe I did doze off. But I'm blaming you. You're so easy to be with."

"I don't know whether I oughta take that as a compliment or not," he grumbled.

Georgia pecked his pouting lips. "Fine. I'll eat another bowl of ice cream if it'll make you happy. How do we get out of this contraption?"

"Straddle me."

She sighed. "Nice try, Mr. Insatiable."

He grinned and lightly tapped her ass. "I'm serious. You bein' on my center of gravity will stabilize us."

"Okay. But if I feel your dick get hard, I can't be held accountable for attacking you." She balanced one hand on his shoulder and threw her other leg over his pelvis.

"Too late. I'm always hard around you. Hang on." Gripping her hips, Tell twisted and the hammock swung upward as he dropped both feet to the ground. Then he stood, sliding his hands down to cup her ass as he carried her into the house.

"You don't have to carry me everywhere," she said halfheartedly.

"I like it. You're pocket-size." He laughed when she drummed her heels into his butt. "Besides, you ain't wearin' pants. It's the least I could do."

Tell set her on a kitchen chair. Looking at him now, she understood Mr. Sweet and Funny had taken a powder, leaving Mr. Intense in charge.

"I'm gonna want that shirt back now."

Her heart rate sped up and a tingle of anticipation rolled through her.

"Also, I don't want you dripping ice cream on your panties, so you'd better take them off too."

Once she stood naked before him, he offered a wolfish grin. "I'll be feeding you. My way. If you don't stay still, well, darlin', I'm gonna be forced to tie you up."

Her midsection went hot and tight. And wet, a little further south.

"Understood?"

She nodded.

"Good. Now sit in the chair so I can reach all parts of you while I dish up."

What the heck did he mean *so I can reach all parts of you?* Georgia slid her naked, flabby ass to the edge of the seat. But being short, it put her head and her neck at a weird angle. She'd been so busy trying to get herself situated that she hadn't noticed Tell stood not two feet away, holding a bowl.

He frowned. "That ain't gonna work. Hop up on the table."

Although it was still warm in the house, the table surface was cool on her butt. Her legs dangled over the edge and she braced her hands behind her.

When she saw the flour sack dishtowel in Tell's hand, she said, "What's that for?" with just a little trepidation.

"To keep your arms outta my way. 'Cause I have the feeling this is gonna make you a little jumpy."

Georgia didn't fidget as he bound her, but her body was hyperaware of his. Then he ran his fingertips up the outside of her arms, over her shoulders, stopping to cup her face in his hands.

"Ready for your ice cream?"

"Umm. Yeah."

"Open up."

She closed her eyes after he spooned in the first bite of butterscotch ripple. The creamy goodness slid down her throat.

"Huh-uh. Eyes on me."

She gazed at him as he slipped the spoon into her mouth. As soon as she swallowed, Tell's lips were on hers; his tongue was diving into her mouth. The shock of his warm tongue against her cold one, the sweet taste of the ice cream and the familiar taste of Tell had her moaning. She wanted to curl her hand around the back of his neck, holding him in place as she lapped up every bit of this new taste combo, but her hands were out of commission. So when Tell broke the kiss, she whimpered.

"Take another bite before it melts." He fed her three bites, hungrily watching her mouth as she licked her lips. After the next spoonful, he kissed her again. Talk about melting. Hot and cold. Sweet and intense.

Keeping his lust-filled blue eyes on hers, he held the spoon at chin level. He tipped the spoon to the side and ice cream dribbled on her breast, sliding down the center of her chest.

She gasped.

"Oops. Looks like I'll be havin' a taste too." His tongue started at the bottom of the drip and he slowly licked up, savoring her ice-cream-flavored skin.

With the way Tell stood between her thighs, he had to know how wet this was making her.

The next pass, he used the end of the spoon to paint her lips with ice cream. Then he licked and nibbled, teasing her endlessly with mouth-on-mouth action, but denying her a full-blown kiss.

Talk about erotic. He'd feed her a bite. Then he'd hold the spoon just out of her reach and angle it, so the thick droplets never landed in the same place on her body twice. And only once on her nipple.

But he cleaned off every last speck of melted ice cream. Suckling to the point that she started to shake. Inside. Outside.

Georgia was damn close to begging.

And he knew it.

Then he hooked his foot around the chair, bringing it to the table, sitting so close her crotch was right in his face.

Her entire body flushed at the intense way he stared at the most intimate part of her.

"Goddamn, you look so pretty like this." He traced her slit from the top of her pubic bone down to her entrance. "Judging by how wet you are, you must really like ice cream."

"Tell. Please."

He looked up at her, desire burning in his eyes. "Oh. Sorry. I'm bein' selfish. Did you want another bite?"

She shook her head.

"Then you don't mind if I finish it off?"

Dear God. She would not survive this. Would. Not. Survive.

Georgia was helpless to do anything but watch as Tell used one hand to pull back the skin surrounding her clit. Then he took the spoon out of the ice cream dish and placed the cold metal directly on that swollen flesh.

Her body jerked and she yelled, "Sweet Jesus, that's cold!"

"Really? Huh. Imagine that. Lemme warm it up for you." He removed the spoon and placed his mouth over the spot.

His hot, wet, sucking mouth.

But he only sucked briefly. He switched it up and licked her pussy as if he were eating an ice cream cone. One long lap after another. Then he nuzzled the inside of her thigh...and again reached for the spoon.

"Oh. No."

"Oh. *Yes*. 'Cause you don't know how much I love me some sweet, sticky cream." Tell coated the back of the spoon with more melted butterscotch swirl. Except this time, he squeezed her nipple as he placed the spoon on her clit.

Georgia bowed back as if he'd attached jumper cables to her body. Every pulse point screamed for release. Even her toes were twitchy. Her mind was focused on one thing: *must come.*

Tell left the spoon in place, rubbing the curve over the sensitive nub until the metal warmed from her body heat.

This was torture.

"Georgia. Look at me."

Her gaze winged to his. He exposed her swollen clitoris. He lowered the spoon, tilting it so the drop of ice cream landed right on her clit.

This time, she screamed. One more drop and she'd explode.

And like he'd read her mind, he poised the spoon higher above her sex. When he tipped it, the droplet hung in the air, falling in slow motion. When that icy drop connected with her hot button, she started to come.

Then Tell's hot mouth was there, sucking on her ice-cream-cooled clit. Tonguing her through an orgasm of epic proportions. When the powerful climax ended, she floated down to the table like a butterfly.

Her butterfly haze didn't last long.

Tell pulled her up by her shoulders and put his mouth on her ear. "I need to fuck you, Georgia. Given how hard I am, it's gonna be short."

But not sweet.

He flipped her over on her belly. Something soft and nubby kept her hips from digging into the edge of the table. With her hands bound and her feet unable to touch the floor, Georgia was completely at Tell's mercy.

Callused hands lifted her butt higher. Then the head of his cock nudged her wet center and he snapped his hips, driving into her at full throttle. "Come for me again."

"I can't. The last one—"

"I can feel it, baby, it's right there."

He bottomed out on his next thrust and she almost lost her mind. He fucked her so hard the table moved. He fucked her so hard each fast stroke was like a mini-orgasm—the head of his cock scraped her G-spot and then immediately connected with her cervix, making her pussy muscles repeatedly spasm around his thick shaft.

On the next plunge, Tell roared his release. The frantic pumping of his hips slowed and stopped, although he maintained a firm grip on the outside of her thighs, as if he needed something solid to hold him up.

Georgia felt the hard wall of his chest and stomach when he layered his body over hers.

His breathing was ragged. His body shook. Heady stuff that she affected this man this way.

"Baby. You... Wow. That..." He laughed softly. "There are no words for what that was."

Such a sweet, hot man. She turned her head and kissed the corner of his mouth. "For me too. But cowboy, I think my arms are numb."

"Shit. Sorry." He stood and pulled out slowly. When he tried to set her on her feet, her knees buckled.

"Whoa, darlin'. Hang on. I gotcha." Tell swept her into his arms and headed to his bedroom.

She rested her face against his neck, still happily muddled from the hour-long—or so it seemed—orgasm. He held her closely against his strong body. She felt his erratic pulse beneath her lips and tasted the salt on his skin. Everything about him was so devastatingly masculine.

He gently set her on the edge of his bed and reached around to undo the towel. As soon as he freed her, he massaged her wrists, forearms and biceps. "You okay?"

"Mmm. Tired." She rubbed her mouth on the dark hair bisecting his torso from his chest hair to his groin. He smelled so good right there. All warm, musky male.

"Stop tempting me to go another round with you tonight, woman."

"But you could, couldn't you? Go another round."

Tell tipped her chin up to peer into her face. "That's the sex-drunk part of you talking." He brushed his thumb over her lower lip. "But yeah. All I have to do is look at you and I want you."

This man could undo her on more levels than she had brain power to contemplate.

"Good to know. But you wore me out."

"So crash. It's been a long night. I'm draggin' ass myself." He pulled the sheets back for her and she crawled in.

As she nestled her head into the pillow and drifted off, she wondered if she should ask him what happened next, not only tomorrow, but next week and in the next month, now that the reunion was over.

Chapter Sixteen

Georgia woke up alone. Not the first time that'd happened when she spent the night at Tell's place. The man had to get up at the crack of dawn every morning—didn't matter if it was the weekend.

A soft breeze wafted through the bedroom window. She rolled onto her stomach, stretching out on the cool sheets that smelled like Tell. She'd never paid much attention to a man's scent before, but his was so distinctive—sunshine, salty musk, the subtle aroma of laundry soap and a hint of lime shaving cream.

Mmm. She wondered if his scent would linger on her skin all day. There was incentive not to jump in the shower. Maybe if she remained naked, when Tell returned, he could rub that scent all over her body again.

She was imagining Tell's very inventive ways of waking her up, when voices drifted down the hallway. She rolled and jackknifed, clutching the sheet to her bare chest. Who was here at—she squinted at the alarm clock—nine thirty on a Sunday morning? She listened. She couldn't discern the words, but she made out two distinct male voices.

Relax. Probably just one of his brothers.

Wasn't like she could go out and meet the fam. She'd have to stay put because her only clothing was the fancy dress she'd worn last night. A dress that Tell had thoughtfully draped over the chair. When had he done that?

Was it a prompt for her to get dressed? Since he'd also set her underwear, bra, shoes and purse on the dresser—directly in her line of sight.

Her doubts from last night pushed front and center.

What happened now? He'd taken her to the reunion; she'd lined up judging gigs for him. Technically they'd each gotten what they wanted. Tell hadn't mentioned wanting more.

Neither have you.

So what were her options?

Crawl back in bed and yank the covers over her head?

Get dressed and face the day—and Tell?

Option two won out.

When she entered the kitchen, Tell didn't hug her or kiss her. In fact, he didn't even get up from his seat at the table. He just gave her a once-over and a small smile. "Morning."

"Morning."

"This is my brother Dalton."

Her gaze winged between the two men. Same dark hair, same blue eyes. Dalton had rugged features where Tell's were sharply defined. Dalton was a big guy—he had a couple inches on Tell and thirty pounds—all muscle, from the looks of it. Most likely Dalton had the same shit-eating grin as his older brother. But there was no sign of it as his gaze moved over Georgia. She fought the urge to fuss with her disheveled appearance, choosing instead to raise her chin a notch and give him an equally cool stare. "Hey, Dalton. I remember you."

"Georgia. You're lookin'—"

Tell smacked him in the back of the head. "Shut it, asshole. Why are you even here? Don't you have something to do today?"

Dalton scowled. "Not me, *we*. I'm waitin' on you, because we both have to deal with that one thing, remember?"

"What one thing?" Tell asked with confusion.

"You know. That one thing."

"Oh. Oh! *That* one thing. Gotcha."

Talk about vague. Was "that one thing" some secret man code for *lemme help you get rid of your pesky overnight female guest?*

Yes, if the looks exchanged between the McKay boys were any indication.

Georgia's cheeks burned. Yeah, she was some class act the morning after her high school reunion—wearing last night's wrinkled clothes, smelling of sex, sporting bed head and dragon breath. No wonder Tell had the look of a trapped animal. Was he worried she'd somehow embarrass him in front of his studly younger brother? By acting clingy? Or worse...by making herself at home?

Screw that. She'd hold her head up high. She could act casually slutty, as if rolling out of a man's bed after a night of hair-pulling, toe-curling sex was a regular occurrence for a tigress like her.

Big talk, Hot Lips. You'd run out the door if you could.

Her fingers tightened on her purse. "I know you're a busy man, Tell. But I'm afraid I'll need a ride home."

"No problem. I'll take you now."

"Want me to ride along?" Dalton asked.

Both she and Tell froze, but they didn't look at each other.

"Nah. I'll be back in thirty and we can go do that one thing."

So Tell wasn't planning to hang out at her place.

Georgia could feel Tell's gaze on her as he held open the front door. She never pulled the I'm-so-busy-I'm-constantly-needed-on-my-cell-phone type of avoidance—but she was doing it now.

She was so engrossed in the info on her phone she didn't even glance at Tell after he helped her into his pickup. She was so immersed in the text scrolling across the screen she paid no attention to Tell McKay at all. Muttering to herself as she pretended to ignore the Wyoming countryside rolling by out passenger side window.

"Something wrong?" Tell finally asked.

"No." She paused, wondering if she should take the chance and ask if she'd see him this week.

"I'm sorry Dalton showed up this morning. I completely forgot I told him I would—"

She held up the hand that wasn't poking keys on her phone's keypad, but she didn't deign to look away from the screen. "No need to explain. I had to hit the road anyway, I'm just sorry I had to tear you away from your plans and you have to give me a ride. This is why I insist on driving. I hate being stuck somewhere without my car."

"Takin' you home ain't a problem, Georgia."

The hard set to his jaw and the clipped tone belied that statement. "I see my boss left me several e-mails about expecting updated status reports on three projects I was supposed to have finished last week. Now I know what I'll be doing this week."

"What?"

Georgia heaved a heavy sigh. "Burning the midnight oil. I won't have time to breathe, let alone do anything else." There was Tell's opening, if he wanted it.

But he didn't take it. He didn't counter with a list of things he needed to accomplish this week and then ask if they could carve out time for each other at some point.

Tell left the engine idling when he pulled into her driveway. He didn't offer to help her out of his truck like he always did. But he did reach for her hand.

Georgia looked at him. Damn man was so freakin' gorgeous it was unreal. And it smacked her pride that he was done with her. Fine. She'd be done with him too.

Better to end it now rather than dragging it out until the end of summer. Didn't last night with all the people in this town who are happy to see you miserable just prove that nothing, not even a smokin' hot, super sweet cowboy who rocks your world in bed and comforts you when you cry, will convince you to stay in Sundance, Wyoming, anyway?

That snarky little conscience of hers had taken on a southern drawl and prompted her back to the cold reality of this situation.

Sweet Tell brought her knuckles to his mouth for a soft kiss. "I had a great time with you last night."

"Same here."

They stared at one another.

He said, "Georgia. I—" at the same time her cell phone rang in her hand.

Dammit. And it was her boss too. Calling her on a Sunday. She hadn't been lying entirely; she had a shit ton to do this week.

Tell retreated. "You'd better get that, bein' you're so *busy* and all."

Georgia snatched her purse and bailed out without looking back.

Late Monday morning, Tell drove to Ben's place to work on the baler.

They'd been wrenching on the machine for over an hour when Ben said, "I'm takin' a break before I haul out the sledgehammer and use it to try and fix this piece of shit."

"Good idea." Tell threw his tools onto the canvas cloth.

"So how was your reunion?"

He wiped the sweat from his brow. "All right, I suppose. Didn't seem a whole lot different from high school, except for the bar in the gym." And for the fact he fucked Georgia in the history classroom.

Ben chuckled. "Booze was the only thing that made mine bearable."

"It helps if you've got a hot woman hanging on your arm."

"I wouldn't know. I went to my reunion solo."

That surprised Tell. "Really?"

"Yep. I wouldn't have gone at all except I found out the girl I'd been crushing on for years was coming. Naturally I wanted to show her how much she'd missed out on by not getting with me back then, and by giving her the chance to rectify that."

"And did it work?"

He grinned. "Oh yeah. We drank. We danced. We ignored everyone. We ended up doin' it in the boys' locker room and missed the awards ceremony. Then we went back to her hotel room and fucked all night. Her plane left early the next morning.

"We went our separate ways. We both got what we wanted. No regrets, no promises, no invites to become Facebook friends. Just one night of turnin' those teenage fantasies a reality." Ben popped the cap on a bottle of water and drank. "Did it play out that way for you too?"

Tell leaned against the side of the barn, dreading that scenario. "It's different for me because Georgia is back in town for good."

"So what's the problem?"

"Along the lines of what you said. Wondering if we just scratched an itch."

"You thinkin' that's all there is?"

"No. I know there's more than that since we've been hangin' out the last two weeks. But that don't change the fact the only reason we started spending time together was because she needed a date for the reunion. Now that it's over... I don't know where we go from here."

Ben frowned. "You haven't discussed it with her?"

Tell shook his head. "I'm the fun hookup guy, remember? My morning after conversations are more along the lines of, *Hey, darlin', have you seen my pants?*"

His cousin laughed.

"Then Dalton showed up Sunday morning two hours early. We'd promised Brandt and Jessie we'd be at their place when Dad came over to see Tucker. But my dumb-ass little brother made it sound like some big, stupid secret, callin' it *that one thing* because neither of us wants to talk about our fucked-up family in front of someone that ain't family."

"So Georgia thought you were what? Tryin' to get rid of her?"

Tell groaned. "Yep. Then she was dismissive. Like she couldn't wait to get the hell away from me. And she was goddamn vague about her plans for this week. Complaining about bein' so swamped she'd barely have time to breathe. Basically, she said don't call me; I'll call you. So see why I'm stuck on what to do?"

"Yeah. I guess if she ain't goin' anywhere, I don't see the harm in letting it ride. Give yourself a couple of days away from her to figure out if you wanna continue what you started and let her do the same."

Sound advice. Not what he wanted to hear though. "Thanks, man. I appreciate it."

"No problem. You gonna be crushed and moping around like a kicked dog if she's done with you?"

Probably. "Fuck you."

He grinned. "Couldn't resist. But seriously, why aren't you talkin' to your brothers about this?"

"I would if I could catch Brandt between diaper changes and Dalton between poker games."

Ben's eyes narrowed. "Left you holding the bag again, did they?"

"Like that's a surprise. You know how it goes, Ben. Seems us middle kids—you, Colt and me—always get stuck with a shit ton more chores than the oldest or the youngest."

"No sir. It doesn't have to be that way. Just because Brandt has added on the responsibility of parenting a kid doesn't give him the right to blow off his ranch responsibilities. I know you and Dalton shouldered way more of the work in the last six months. I've been there, cuz, and it sucks ass."

"You had that issue with Quinn?"

"Yep. Prince Adam arrived and Quinn's priorities shifted, which meant the day-to-day ranch stuff shifted squarely onto *my* shoulders. Chase wasn't around. My dad tried to pick up the slack, but shit wasn't getting done. Pissed me off. I let my brother know it. Was ugly for a couple weeks, because Quinn is one stubborn cuss, but he got back on track. It would've gone on for as long as I let it go on. Confront your brother, Tell, or nothin' will ever change."

"I hear ya. I guess if it was just ranch issues with my brothers, I'd be okay, but family stuff can eat away at me until I've been chewed up and spit out."

"Something going on with Uncle Casper?"

"No, Dad ain't the problem, if you can believe it. My mom... Jesus. She's so involved in her own life she can't see that other folks have lives too."

"Meaning what?"

"Meaning, she expects me to..." Tell shook his head. "Never mind. I feel like a fuckin' whiner. No one can take advantage of me without my permission, right? So I just gotta buck up and remember to say no."

"Good plan. As far as Dalton not pulling his weight?"

Tell shrugged. "He ain't bad. He covers for me about as much as I cover for him. It's just Brandt who's the deadweight."

Ben shot the baler a disgusted look. "Speaking of deadweight... I'm sick of fucking with this thing. It's plain wore out. Time to put in a request for a new one."

"After all the times it jammed last summer, I'll back you on that request."

"This ain't the only piece of equipment that's seen better days. Seems everything breaks at the same damn time."

Ainsley's car pulled up and Ben's entire demeanor changed. "Looks like my lunch is here."

Didn't sound like Ben was talking about food.

Tell took that as his cue to leave.

On Monday, Georgia loaded her briefcase, trying not to dread the process of cold-call sales pitches. It'd be easier to drive the ten blocks to Sundance's main drag rather than hoof it in four-inch wedge sandals. The day was much warmer than forecast, and she'd be sweating like a whore in church by the time she reached her destination.

She waited in her car for a moment as she scanned the list of possible advertising sponsors for the Devil's Tower Rodeo program guide. Barbara's suggestion of hard-selling the locals—especially after the previous rodeo promotion company's lack of communication—scared Georgia a little. They'd both agreed playing catch-up at this late date might mean no business owners would be interested. No sales would reflect badly on her, so she had no other option but to channel her inner saleswoman and sell, sell, sell.

Luckily the committee that handled hiring the stock contractor, the entertainment, the rodeo announcers, the special guests and the individual chute sponsors also had commitments from the banks in Sundance for major sponsorships of the rodeo itself.

Her idea—albeit not an original one—was to get the businesses in Sundance, Moorcroft and Hulett to sponsor a grand prize called the cash cow, where the winner could choose between a fully processed and packaged whole cow or the cash equivalent. Their company had

165

seen success with this type of promotion for a small rodeo in Oklahoma, and the participating businesses had a big uptick in the amount of walk-in traffic to their stores.

Georgia inhaled a couple of breaths to calm herself and smoothed the wrinkles from her khaki linen skirt. New businesses had popped up in the years she'd been away, so she'd start there.

Fields, an upscale restaurant that featured locally grown ingredients from vegetables and grains to beef, pork and chicken, took out a big ad.

The hardware store bought a full-page ad. As did Lettie from the Golden Boot. Then Georgia had to wonder if some of the businesses were doing it out of pity because she was a poor pitchwoman.

So? Her inner demon argued. A sale was a sale. And if she had to answer gossipy questions to make that sale, so be it.

She'd convinced the dentist's office to advertise. As well as the feed store. The local implement dealership was providing ball caps, T-shirts and Frisbees for the breaks between events, and they placed a quarter-page ad anyway.

All the places agreed to allow promotional signage and flyers in their establishments, in addition to the entry boxes for the grand prize.

When her stomach growled, she realized she'd missed lunch. She ducked into Dewey's for a quick bite.

The restaurant was nearly empty. Thankfully the waitress who'd filled her ear with nastiness about Tell wasn't serving. She ordered the soup and salad special, shuffling through her notes while she waited. She had quite a few businesses left to approach in Sundance and she hadn't even started in Moorcroft or Hulett.

The server set the salad down first and spilled the soup. When she swore in Russian, Georgia's gaze snapped to the willowy blonde. Then she apologized in English. "Sorry. It's pretty obvious I haven't filled in as a waitress recently."

Georgia said, "No worries,"—in Russian.

That startled the woman. "It's not often I run across someone in Sundance who speaks Russian."

"My mother is from Russia."

"Ah. I was born in the Ukraine. I knew many women who found husbands here. Do you speak Russian fluently?"

"Just passably." Georgia slid her paperwork aside and pulled the salad and soup closer. "You're welcome to join me if you're not busy."

The woman smiled. "Really? That would be great. Let me grab the iced tea." She returned and refilled Georgia's glass. "Busy lunch. Feels good to be off my feet." She took a long drink of tea. "I'm Domini."

"Georgia."

"Named after Soviet Georgia?"

"Yes, few people catch that. I haven't seen you in here before."

"I'm usually in the back, making schedules and placing orders. I used to cook, hostess and serve, but I'm part time now." Domini shrugged. "Most people think I'm crazy for working at all when I have six children at home."

Georgia nearly choked on her soup. "You have six kids?"

"Yes. All of our sweet darlings came to us through adoption. While I love being a wife and mother, I need something for me too."

"My mother didn't understand that until she divorced my father." Georgia stabbed a few pieces of lettuce onto her fork.

"So your mother...?"

"Was basically a Russian mail-order bride? Yes. It's strange to say, even now. How about you?"

Domini shook her head. "I came to the US with a church group. Became a citizen and met my husband here a few years later. I spent most my life in an orphanage, so I am grateful that Cam has a large family in the area and they're willing to help out with our kids. Are you from around here?"

Georgia shared the edited version of her life, finishing with, "It's strange to be back. We had our ten-year high school reunion Saturday night."

"My husband is a deputy. He was disappointed the police didn't get called to the gym to break up any fights."

"Who is your husband?"

"Cam McKay."

Didn't it just figure? Another McKay. "Tell was my date to the reunion."

Domini pointed at her. "Aha! You're the one they were talking about. The beautiful woman from Tell's past."

She muttered, "We didn't have a past."

"Maybe that's the problem? Tell's definitely got a past now, with his love 'em and leave 'em reputation. So watch your step with him. Now that I've done my duty in warning you—" Domini gestured to the pile of papers, "—what are you selling?"

"Ads for the Devil's Tower Rodeo program guide." Georgia grinned. "Wanna buy one or ten? All the other restaurants in town have bought space."

Domini rubbed her hands together. "Absolutely. Can't let our competition get the jump on us. What are the options?"

When Georgia hesitated, Domini said, "My sister-in-law Macie McKay owns this restaurant, so I do have the authority to make these decisions. But you can call her directly if you prefer."

"No. That's okay. It's just... I thought the McKays were ranchers."

"Most are. But one McKay spouse or another owns each of the businesses on this side of the block. And Keely's husband Jack owns the whole building. But that is a good thing because you're involved with Tell. They should all be easy sales for you."

Before Georgia could assure her she'd never use Tell that way, Domini gave her a shrewd look. "I'll make you a deal. If I buy ad space, will you help me out? The community center is hosting a heritage festival Thursday night. In addition to the ethnic food, I planned on teaching the kids how to count to ten in Ukrainian. If you came, you could teach them to count in Russian. It'd only be for two hours."

Her knee-jerk reaction was to say no. But it'd be good for business if she showed a presence at and an interest in community events. "I don't have to wear a costume or anything?"

Domini laughed. "No *kokoshnik.* I promise."

"Well, since you're not insisting I wear one of those weird Russian headdresses my mother tried to foist on me... I'll do it."

By the time seven o'clock rolled around, Georgia had taken a break from the task lists Barbara had e-mailed and had poured herself a glass of white wine. She curled up on the porch swing, soaking in the last golden rays of sunlight. When her phone rang, she had the tiny hope it was Tell. But it was her mother. "Hey, Mom."

"*Moyah krasivaya doch.*"

Her mother always called her *my beautiful daughter.*

"I haven't heard from you. How was the reunion?"

"Meh. It was sort of fun to see everyone, with the exception of Deck and Tara-Lee." She pushed off the railing, setting the swing in motion.

"No issues with Deck?"

"He cornered me. But it got handled." Georgia sipped her wine. "The worst part of the night was when they did the memorial tribute to RJ."

Her mother was very quiet. "Have you been...?"

"No. Not yet. I'll go. I promise."

"I know you will. You're a good daughter and a good sister." She laughed softly. "I had a weird flashback the other day. A coworker's daughter is getting her tonsils taken out, and I remembered when you had your tonsillectomy. When they finally brought you back to your room, RJ wouldn't leave your side. He just crawled right into your bed with you and announced he was staying there all night because he didn't want you to be scared." She sniffled. "The little sneak had packed his backpack with a flashlight, your favorite stuffed animals and a bag of marshmallows because they'd be soft enough for you to eat."

Georgia closed her eyes against the grief that could still slice her to the bone. For all his wild ways, RJ had always been so sweet and protective of her. He'd brought the flashlight so they could cuddle up under the covers and read his comic book stash, trying to convince her that being in the hospital was just like camping out, so she wouldn't be afraid. "I'd forgotten about that. I do remember that RJ convinced the nurses we had to have ice cream every hour. "

"My boy did inherit his father's knack for using charm to get what he wanted." She cleared her throat. "Speaking of... What did your father have to say when he called you?"

Georgia frowned. "He called you after he talked to me, didn't he?"

"Yes."

"How often does he call you?"

"Every couple of months. Usually after he's been drinking. That's the only time he can open up."

"Mom. You don't have to—"

"It's fine. I can handle Robert. So anyway... How is work?"

"All right. You know how much I dislike cold-call ad selling, which is probably why Barbara is making me do it. So far I haven't run into any businesses that were screwed by the promotion company we took over."

"And it's okay? Being back in Wyoming?"

"I guess. I just keep telling myself it's temporary."

"I might drive up to see you."

She closed her eyes. "I'd like that."

They talked for ten more minutes, firming up the date for her mother's visit. After she hung up, Georgia had a melancholy feeling she couldn't shake. After spending the last two weeks with Tell, it'd hit her tonight, how alone she was in her life. Physically distant from her mother. Estranged from her father. If she was honest, her friends in Dallas were her coworkers and she wasn't close to any of them. She didn't know her neighbors in the gated community where she rented her condo. She went to the movies alone. She ate dinner by herself in front of the TV most evenings. She occasionally went out on a date. Most men weren't what she expected and certainly not what she wanted.

Definitely none were as fun, funny, insightful and sexy as Tell McKay.

It'd been one day and she missed him.

Looked to be a long week.

Chapter Seventeen

Georgia hadn't called him Monday. Not that he'd expected it. He'd spent way too much time thinking about her, weighing Ben's advice against his gut instinct of driving to her house and kissing her stupid as a conversation starter. But he held off. Going a couple days without contact wouldn't hurt either of them. He told himself that, yet he couldn't figure out why he was on edge with an odd feeling of gloom until he realized it was because he missed her.

So when Tell's phone rang on Tuesday afternoon, he was disappointed it wasn't Georgia's number on the caller ID.

"Hey, Mom, what's up?"

"Samantha has a last-minute overnight seminar in Riverton. I already promised Bart I'd go to the VA in Cheyenne with him for his outpatient surgery, and I can't bring Landon along."

No *Hi, son, how are you?* No *What's new in your world?* She cut straight to the chase; no pleasantries. Just like his father did. "So you're callin' because you need me to baby-sit Landon again."

"Yes. I know it's last minute, but I have no choice."

But I do. "I'm guessing you expect me to drop everything right now and drive to Casper? I'm sorry. I can't."

Her silence felt accusatory and Tell almost caved in.

"What's going on with you?" she demanded. "You never—"

"Say no?" Tell paced to the window. "I have plans tonight." No point in wishing he'd told his mother no last week when he'd cancelled a date with Georgia, but he could change the parameters from here on out. "Did you ask Dalton or Brandt if they could help?"

"Brandt and Jessie have their hands full right now, doncha think?"

"Yep. But I'm plenty busy myself picking up the slack around the ranch since Brandt is embracing fatherhood."

"What's going on at the ranch isn't my concern," she said with a sniff.

"That's because Landon had been your only concern the past few years." *Just like Luke was always your number one priority.*

Childish, probably, but accurate, and not the first time he'd had that thought. But it was the first time he'd voiced it to her.

"Tell McKay. That's not true. I thought you liked taking care of Landon."

"I do. I love the kid. But I hate that the only time I see him is when I'm the last resort for childcare. How long before Landon will resent getting shuttled off to his bachelor uncle's at the last minute?"

"Now you're just being ridiculous."

"That's me. Silly Tell, flitting around like a damn butterfly without a care in the world."

A long pause. "Son. Have you been drinking?"

He forced a laugh. "Look, Mom, I gotta go. I'll talk to you soon, okay?"

"You're really saying no?"

"Yep, I really am. Bye." He hung up. And it felt good.

An hour later Tell was thinking about a prime rib sandwich as he got ready for dart league, when he heard someone at his door. Doubtful it was his sweet woman, but he kept a goofy smile in place just in case as he snapped the last pearl button on his short-sleeved shirt and answered the door.

But his brother Brandt stood on the front porch.

"Hey, bro. Is everything all right?"

"Not according to Mom." Brandt bulled his way inside.

"Mom called you?"

"Yep. She thought you were drunk or high or some damn thing, so she sent me to check on you." Brandt squinted at him. "Are you?"

"Drunk? No. High? No."

"Pissed?"

Tell shrugged. "Getting there, since my mommy called my big brother to make sure I wasn't being naughty or pouting. So maybe it'd be best if you skedaddled on home to the wife and kiddie."

Brandt didn't budge. "What's goin' on? You never have words with Mom."

"Wasn't really an exchange of words—except for the one word she didn't wanna hear when I said no to drivin' to Casper to take care of Landon tonight."

"She mentioned it, and I don't see what the big deal is."

That got Tell's back up big-time. "Yeah? Then why don't you hop in your truck and do it?"

"Because I have a wife and a kid to take care of."

"And because no one believes I have a life outside of ranch work, my free time is up for grabs? Ask Tell to make a three-hour trip, he won't mind. Guess what? I *do* fucking mind."

Brandt's mouth dropped open.

"What? You were expecting I'd be cracking jokes?"

"I guess I was."

"Too bad I'm fresh out of funny."

They stared at one another. "How many times has Mom asked you to watch Landon in the last year?"

"At least twice a month. Except it's gotten more frequent since calving ended."

"And you say yes every time she asks." A statement.

Tell nodded. "Except for today. That don't mean I'm gonna stop helping out entirely; I'm just not doin' it today."

"Now that I've heard your side, I'm glad you stood up to her, because Mom has gotten...pushy lately." Brandt sighed. "Some days, she reminds me of Dad."

"Glad I'm not the only one who's seen it."

"I've noticed it and so has Jess. But I know you, Tell. That alone ain't enough to set you off."

Set him off? He'd been downright pleasant to his mother. How would people react if he really went off?

"You poke at me until I start talkin', so I'm gonna do the same to you, bro. What else is on your mind?" Brandt asked. "'Cause you've been actin' pissy. I suspect it's got something to do with me."

Tell counted to twenty in an attempt to temper his response, but maybe it was better to let fly. "Fine, Brandt, here it is. You've been a shitty ranching partner the last six months. I understood your distraction when Jessie was pregnant. But now that Tucker is here, I've waited for you to step up and do your part and it hasn't happened yet. I'm frustrated and tired of cuttin' you slack. I'm forced to make decisions because you won't, and then you question me on every damn thing I decide. Me'n Dalton are tired of it."

Brandt's face turned a mottled red.

A few excruciatingly tense moments passed and Tell wondered if Ben had given him bad advice all around: about confronting the family problem head-on with his mom and Brandt, as well as staying away from Georgia.

Then Brandt dropped onto the couch. "Fuck. When did I become that guy? The guy who does the minimum amount of work, who comes in late, leaves early and puts his life ahead of everything else?" Brandt chewed that over for a bit. "Christ. I'm actin' just like Luke did."

"I wouldn't have said that, but since you did... Yeah. Maybe a little."

"I'm sorry, Tell. There ain't no excuse."

"Nope."

"Won't happen anymore. I promise."

"Good to know."

Brandt pushed to his feet. "So, you tired of riding herd on me yet?"

Just like that, Tell knew Brandt's slacker days were behind them. Neither needed to beat this issue to death; it was over and done with and they'd move on. Now he wished he would've said something sooner. "Maybe a little." He grinned and lightly punched Brandt in the arm. "Hey. Maybe Dalton will fuck up and you'll be off the hook."

"Wouldn't put it past that kid. He's always got some damn secret." He snorted. "Kid. Now I really sound like Luke. Anyway, thanks for the kick in the ass before you had to kick my ass." Brandt cuffed Tell on the arm. "So as long as we're bein' all touchy-feely and shit... Jess wants you to come over for supper tomorrow night."

"Thanks, but I can't. I'm working a rodeo in Belle Fourche all day tomorrow that lasts into the evening."

"Guess I deserve to do chores by my lonesome for a change, huh?" He smiled and punched Tell in the arm just a little harder than the first time, which was a sign things were getting back to normal. "Come by anyway if it ain't too late, because we're usually up." Brandt smirked. "I promise we won't ask you to baby-sit."

"Not that it ain't great to see you, Thurman," Tell said, sliding into the booth at Ziggy's, "but you don't normally call on league night lookin' for a drinking buddy. What's up?"

Thurman swigged his beer. "I'm not lookin' to get drunk. I'm headed outta town tomorrow and I wanted the lowdown on you and Hot Lips, since you guys took off so fast Saturday night. How're things goin?" He waggled his eyebrows. "Planning that trip down the altar yet?"

"Fuck off. She's busy this week so I haven't seen her." That sounded plausible. Casual. Not like she'd dumped his ass. "I've been dealin' with ranch stuff and the always fun family shit anyway."

"Does the fun family shit have anything to do with Dalton?"

"No. Why?"

"I've heard a couple of things. Normally I don't put much stock in rumors...but this one about Dalton caught my interest."

Thurman wasn't the type to gossip, so Tell immediately went on alert. "Don't keep me in suspense."

"Evidently he rented a motel room in Hulett sometime in the last month. Claimed he was trying to set a new McKay record for the most women fucked in a single night."

"Jesus. There's a life goal. And he's makin' it sound like all the single McKays ever did was sit around bragging about female conquests."

"Your family has a reputation, Tell. Whether it's bullshit or deserved, ain't my concern." Thurman shrugged. "I just wanna make sure somebody knows what Dalton is up to and that he ain't knocking up half the young ladies in the damn county."

Their food arrived, which gave Tell time to consider this news regarding his brother.

Something had changed with Dalton right around the time their father had checked into rehab. With so many other things on his mind, maybe he hadn't paid as much attention to his little brother's escapades. But Dalton was a twenty-five-year-old man, not a child. He didn't need a baby-sitter.

"You're awful quiet, Tell."

He looked at Thurman. "Just debating on whether it's my responsibility to check up on him."

"No, it ain't. I didn't tell you this because I expect you'll stake out the Shady R Motel in Moorcroft to see if Dalton's truck is in the lot."

"I appreciate it, even though it don't make me happy." Tell signaled for another beer. "Curious, though. Did your source say how many women Dalton...serviced that night?"

"Why? You think your record might have his beat?" Thurman teased.

Tell flipped him off.

"I heard Dalton was with thirteen different chicks."

"Thirteen? Holy shit."

Thurman shoved his plate aside and leaned closer. "But that's not the kicker. My understanding is he did it with all thirteen women in the room with him. And these ladies were giving him pointers and feedback."

"Like a sex focus group?"

"Or a sex seminar."

Tell shook his head. "Damn. I don't even wanna think about twelve women standin' around, watchin' me have sex with another woman and critiquing my performance."

"You and me both."

"Even when I was a teen and my dick was hard all the freakin' time, I don't think I jacked off thirteen times in one day, say nothin' of getting it up and getting off that many times in a few hours."

"Boggles the mind, don't it? I'd guess he's beat Chase and Colt, who I'd lay odds were previous McKay record holders."

"It's not like I'm gonna ask them."

"Dalton might. Just for bragging rights." Thurman drained his beer. "Come on. Forget about it. I'll let you lose a game of pool to me before you lose at darts."

On the drive home, Tell realized he hadn't managed to put Georgia out of his mind, even for three hours. He'd found himself looking around the bar, hoping she'd show up.

He missed her. Given his schedule, tomorrow was a wash as far as reconnecting, but if he hadn't heard from her by Thursday night, he was showing up on her doorstep.

Wednesday morning, Georgia tackled the businesses on the other end of the Sandstone Building. First stop: Healing Touch Massage.

A soft chime sounded as she walked through the door. The space had been decorated with western touches—fake cowhide print chairs in the reception area, a coffee table crafted from logs. With mocha-colored walls and plush carpeting, the area embodied a sense of calm.

From the back, a voice trilled, "I'll be out in a sec." Then a drawer slammed and the pregnant blonde Georgia had met at Dairy Queen ambled around the corner.

Oh hello, hostility. This was going to be a fun sale.

Georgia smiled brightly, hoping it didn't look cheesy. "Great place you have, AJ."

"Thank you. Are you here for a massage?"

"No. I'm selling advertising space for the Devil's Tower Rodeo program guide."

AJ rested her folded arm on her belly. "I bought an ad last year and I didn't see the benefits."

"That's why the committee hired a new PR company. We're expanding the guide this year."

"I never asked where the ad money actually goes."

"A portion goes to printing the brochures. A portion goes to the local committee. They use it to try and bring in bigger sponsors."

"So local sponsorship by local businesses isn't enough? If you've got bigger fish to fry, why should I fork out my money?"

Talk about prickly. "Let me explain. Bigger sponsors will provide bigger payouts for the event purse, which will attract better competitors, which will bring more people into the area and into the area businesses. We aren't looking to replace the business ad you'd place with one for a bigger sponsor."

"Uh. Well, that makes sense."

"Would you like to see examples of ads we're doing for other businesses? And hear the promotion I've sketched out, which requires little to no effort on the part of the advertisers?"

"I guess."

When Georgia had shown AJ all the options and the pregnant woman's only responses were a sniff, a grunt or a shrug, Georgia lost all confidence in herself and any hope of a sale. She tidied up her papers. "Thanks for listening."

"That's it?" AJ's eyes narrowed. "If you're done, why do you still look so tense?"

"Because you make me nervous."

AJ blinked with total distrust. "Because you want me to buy an ad that badly?"

"That's not it." She blew out a slow breath. "Between us? Cold-call selling is not my strong suit. Add in trying to convince people that I'm not the aloof cheerleader they remember, but a professional woman...isn't exactly a cakewalk." *Why don't you just blurt out all your insecurities in front of a potential client, Georgia?*

"I understand where you're coming from because I'm definitely not the mousy girl I was in high school. And thank God for that." AJ stepped out from behind the counter. "Come on. I'm gonna give you a little shoulder massage. On the house."

Georgia blurted out, "Why?"

"Because I can feel the tension rolling off you. I have a Swedish in thirty minutes and it'll be good to limber up my hands." AJ led her to what looked like a beauty chair, but in reverse form, with an open oval to place her face in and padded arms beneath it. The footrest was adjustable, she could put her feet in front, or behind like she was riding a motorcycle.

"You'll need to take off your jacket. The blouse can stay on." AJ leaned closer and tugged on the material. "It doesn't look like it'll rip."

Rip? Like AJ planned to massage her violently enough to tear clothing? "Ah. I don't know—"

"Relax." AJ stood beside the chair, tapping her foot almost in challenge, waiting as Georgia climbed into the contraption.

Deep breath.

"There. Now just pretend we're two friends chatting at the beauty shop."

Friends? Right. AJ could teach torture tactics. Georgia gasped when two fingers sank into the skin beside her shoulder blades, almost to the bone.

"You have had a massage before, right?"

"Uh, yeah." Just not like this. Then she felt several hard pinches up the back of her neck.

"So as to not keep you in suspense, I'll buy an ad," AJ said.

"Good," she choked out.

"Has your business been doin' well?"

More pressure as AJ ground her thumbs across Georgia's shoulder. "It's not my business." Georgia explained, glad AJ couldn't see her face when she grimaced in pain.

"When I graduated from trade school and set up shop in Sundance, I wasn't sure I could make a go of it. Now I've got a steady enough clientele that I could be open eight hours a day, six days a week if I chose, but I keep it part time." She grunted. "So you've hooked up with Tell."

Didn't take her long to bring that up. "We've been hanging out."

"I heard you two were a couple."

Georgia purposely ignored the past tense form *were*. "We went to our class reunion together."

"I skipped my reunion. Keely and Chase were stars of our class anyway." AJ pulled on a section of skin. "Kind of like you were the star of your class."

"Not something I wanted, believe me. And I never felt that way."

"Really?"

"Deck was the star. I was the girlfriend in the background with the cool, fun brother everyone loved."

AJ's hands stopped moving so vigorously. "Aw, shoot, Georgia, I forgot that your brother died. I'm so sorry."

"Thanks. In some ways Tell reminds me of RJ. He's outgoing."

"Which means Tell goes out all the damn time. He's had a lot of girlfriends, I mean *a lot*, but he's never had a serious girlfriend."

Rather than gasp and say *I had no idea he was such a stud*, she casually remarked, "Yes, that has come up in conversation."

"Good. We're all a little protective of him."

Oh for Godsake, really? Like Tell McKay needed protection from her? She couldn't let that comment slide. "Because innocent Tell has absolutely no experience with women like me, right?" Georgia said with an edge. "I'm the ball-busting bitch from his past who's set her sights on breaking his poor little heart?"

"Ooh, snap," AJ said.

"You're not the first one to warn me off sweet, funny, perfect Tell McKay, AJ."

"I never said he was perfect, but I'll agree he's sweet and funny. And I wasn't warning you off him as much as I was just warning you. Tell isn't ready to settle down. So don't get your hopes up."

Then it felt as if AJ were slicing along both sides of her spinal cord to make it easier to rip the bones clean out. With her bare hands. Or perhaps her teeth.

Finally AJ said, "Done."

Georgia pushed herself up. "Thanks for the massage. Once I have a better handle on my schedule, I'll book a full appointment." She slipped on her jacket. "Let's get the ad set up before your next victim arrives."

She smiled cheekily at AJ and was totally shocked when the cranky pregnant woman laughed and said, "You know, cheerleader, I kinda like you."

Despite the sale, Georgia was feeling less than confident at the next stop: India's Ink and Sky Blue.

A woman and two small boys sat at a child-size plastic table by the front counter. A dark-haired baby bounced on the woman's knee.

The woman wore a flowery sundress and a whole lot of tattoos. Her short, dark hair had randomly scattered streaks of electric blue. "Hi. If you're here for a tat, it'll have to wait until my husband returns for my little helpers."

"I'm not here for that."

Suspicious eyes zeroed in on Georgia's briefcase. "Who are you and what are you selling?"

How many freakin' times would she have to go through this spiel?

As many as it took to fill up the damn program guide.

Before she could regurgitate the pitch she'd committed to memory, the oldest boy said, "Mama, look! I drawed a fish!"

"That's real good, Hudson baby, see if you can draw another one."

He scowled at his mother. "I'm not a baby."

"Sorry. I forget you're a big boy now."

These kids were the most beautiful children Georgia had ever seen. Had to be McKay kids with that black hair and those vivid blue eyes.

"You were saying?" the woman prompted.

"Sorry for staring, but your children are gorgeous."

She smiled. "Thank you. They get those genes from their daddy." She held out her hand. "India McKay."

Georgia shook it. "Nice to meet you, India. It seems you're busy, so I can come back later."

"No. Stick around. I don't usually bring the kids to work with me, but every once in a while I don't have a choice." She kissed the top of the baby girl's head. "Show me what you've got. Spread out on the counter, away from madly coloring little boys."

"Good plan." After Georgia lined up the pieces and made her sales pitch, she felt India staring at her.

"Now I know why your name is familiar. You're dating Tell."

That connection took all of thirty seconds. "I guess."

India's blue gaze sharpened. "What do you mean *you guess*?"

How could she admit that the R word had never come up between them during the two weeks they were boinking like bunnies? "Umm... It's complicated."

"Not when it comes to a McKay male. They are highly territorial."

Georgia wondered if the guys in the McKay family would take that as an insult or a compliment.

"So? What's the deal with you two?"

This woman just expected her to blurt it out?

India laughed. "Oh, I get why you're hedging about your relationship status and using the word *complicated*. Because Tell is in the d-bag stage right now." She patted Georgia's forearm. "Don't sweat it. We've all been there."

After the contracts were signed, a loud crash sounded behind them. The youngest boy had kicked over the table and was smacking it with a fat table leg.

"Ellison McKay! Drop that and park your butt on that chair right now, mister."

"No!"

"Don't make me start counting."

"No!"

"Okay. One."

Ellison threw himself on the floor and started crying. His brother seized the opportunity to jump on him. Which only made the boy shriek louder.

"Hudson! What on earth is wrong with you? Get off your brother."

The boys paid no attention. They rolled around on the floor. Dodging punches and punching back. Yelling. Crying.

The baby girl suddenly let loose a loud wail.

"Come on, McKenna baby, not you too."

Georgia gathered her stuff, thankful they'd concluded business before the tantrums started.

The door chime jangled, but that didn't end the chaos.

A wolf whistle pierced the air. Then a man separated the boys. "Hey, hey, you two. No hitting."

"Just in time, Colt," India said.

The younger boy clung to the man's neck when he stood. Colt settled the kid on his hip and smoothed the older boy's hair. "You wanna tell me what's goin' on?"

Hudson shook his head.

Then the man briefly looked at Georgia. And she just about choked on the puddle of drool forming on her tongue. This guy... Wow. Yeah, the kids had definitely inherited his amazing looks.

But he only had eyes for his wife. "Sorry to interrupt, Indy. I'll get the boys outta your hair."

"That'll work. But you should meet Georgia Hotchkiss. Georgia, this is my husband, Colt McKay."

"Georgia. As in Tell's Georgia?"

And she thought the people in Sundance were gossipy? They had nothing on the McKay family.

India elbowed him. "Sometimes there's a disconnect between your mouth and your brain. Yes, this is the Georgia who knows Tell. No, she doesn't belong to him, caveman McKay."

Colt grinned. "Nice to meetcha, Georgia. I'm gonna hafta rib my cousin, because he's dating way out of his league."

Georgia blushed.

India bent down to hug Hudson. Then she stood and kissed Ellison's cheek. "Be good for Daddy today, boys." She turned away.

"Hey, Mama. Where's my kiss?"

She sighed and stood on tiptoe to reach his lips for a quick peck. But Colt wrapped his hand around the back of her neck and held his wife in place as he gave her a very thorough kiss.

Georgia felt like a voyeur, seeing the intimate connection between these two, surrounded by their rambunctious kids, but existing only in the moment with each other.

Would she ever allow herself to have that kind of deep connection with a man? Or would she always pull back?

Like you're pulling back with Tell? Like you've pulled back with everyone since RJ died?

She shoved everything into her briefcase. The tattoo art on the inside of the glass case caught her eye. Some designs were really cool, especially the memorial tattoos. Some were portraits, some were just dates, some were crosses, or some were a combination of all three.

"See anything you like?" India asked.

"Are all these your designs?"

"Most of them."

"They are amazing."

"Thank you. Were you considering a memorial tattoo?"

Georgia looked up. "I never have before now. But it seems..."

India patted her hand. "It's hard to mark a sad event. But if you decide to do it, I can design anything from gaudy to discreet."

"I'll definitely be back."

That night as Georgia wrote her sales report for her boss and mapped out her plan for the businesses in Moorcroft the following day, she kept sneaking glances at her cell phone. Checking it like some smitten teenage girl, wondering if her phone was somehow...broken because another day had gone by and she hadn't heard from Tell.

So call him.

Right. After hearing his family's concerns that she was some sort of femme fatale heartbreaker? Now she was uneasy enough about the situation that she wouldn't call him first. Not out of pettiness; out of self-preservation.

Chapter Eighteen

Early Thursday morning, Tell glanced at Dalton, standing on his left. Man. His baby brother looked like roadkill. Then he noticed Brandt yawning. They were a lively bunch.

Cord had called a meeting at the sorting pens, which was neutral ground and the center of the ranch.

Pickups were parked in a lopsided circle. His cousins were spread out in groups of brothers. Kane and Kade were in a deep discussion. Colby, Cord and Colt were laughing about something. Quinn and Ben were standing together, not talking at all.

He spoke to Brandt. "You have any idea what this meeting is about?"

"Nope. Wish I'd brought more coffee. I am draggin' ass today." He yawned again. "Tucker cried all night. Woke us up every hour."

"That sucks."

Brandt offered a small smile. "Oh, it ain't so bad. It's just frustrating when we can't figure out why he's cryin'. The only thing that calms him down is bein' held, so me'n Jess take turns."

Dalton leaned closer. "Either of you got any Tums? I'm about to blow chunks after way too much drinkin' last night."

"There's some in the glove box," Brandt said. When Tell gaped at him, he said, "What? Jess ate Tums by the handful when she was pregnant. I kept 'em in my truck since I was her chauffeur."

"That ain't what surprised me. It was the fact you didn't go all 'you're a dumb-ass' on our little brother."

"I'm too fuckin' tired to care." Brandt shot him a smirk. "And I'm practicing not bein' a dick."

Tell snorted.

Cord stepped forward and all conversation ended. "We haven't had a formal shareholders meeting since around this time last year, so I figured we'd get it out of the way."

"So we're doin' this without the previous McKay generation in attendance?" Quinn asked.

"Technically, they're shareholders, but they gave up voting rights when they passed us the reins."

It went unsaid that none of them wanted to deal with Casper after what'd happened last year. An endless prayer followed by an endless litany of criticism and complaints.

"I don't gotta go over the financials because you all got copies relating to your shares. We all had a record year last year and so far it's lookin' like this one might be even better."

Heads nodded.

"That said, we've gotta replace a lot of equipment, and that's expensive, but since it's equipment we all use, the purchase will come out of the main ranch account."

"We're payin' cash?" Ben asked.

"That's what we need to vote on," Cord said. "Whether we wanna take out a loan or use the cash reserves."

Colt spoke up. "I'd rather we used some of the cash, say thirty or forty percent, and finance the rest. If we've still got a solid amount of cash this time next year, then we can look at payin' off the remaining amount. Or extending the loan another year."

"I agree," Kade said. "Who knows what the economy, the price of feed and the livestock market will do in the next twelve months? Better to play it safe."

"Any other comments or suggestions?" Cord asked.

Ben raised his hand. "At the risk of ruffling some feathers, I suggest we make sure we're getting the lowest rate from Settler's First Bank before we commit to borrowing money from them."

"Sez the competing bank president's husband," Tell said dryly.

Everyone laughed.

"I agree with Ben," Brandt said. "It wouldn't hurt to talk to American West Bank to see what they'll offer to get some of our business."

"And just to be clear, I won't be involved one way or the other. I just wanted to mention it," Ben added.

"So, show of hands on usin' a partial down payment?"

All hands went up.

"Good. Show of hands on me, Kade, Brandt and Quinn finding the lowest loan rate?"

All hands went up.

Cord stroked his goatee. "Motion passes and all that shit. What's next?"

Kade said, "As long as we're talkin' about joint expenses, something's gotta be done with that bunkhouse. Over the last few months, me'n Colby found a ton of beer cans inside and outside. All the wood we had stockpiled has been burned, so someone has been livin' there. Or more likely, kids have been usin' it as a party house."

"Once it becomes party central, it's gonna be hell to get them kids to stop goin' there," Colby added.

"And Cam can't patrol that area all the time because it's abusing his position," Colt pointed out. "Any ideas on how we oughta handle it?"

"I say all ten of us sit inside. When the little shits show up, we reinforce with ten loaded shotguns that they're trespassing on private property," Dalton suggested.

Chuckles.

"I vote for burning it down," Tell said. "Ain't like we use it all that much anymore anyway. Not during calving season, and we haven't played poker there in well over a year."

Everyone looked at Tell like he was holding a can of gasoline and a blowtorch.

"Jesus, Tell, can't you be serious for one fuckin' second?" Kane demanded.

Tell hated how his face heated. "I *am* serious. It ain't like we can move it, since we poured concrete footings. We used cheap materials to build it and we haven't been takin' care of it, so it is gonna fall into ruin. Better we torch it ourselves than to wait for some dumb fucking teenagers to accidentally light it on fire, as well as the damn grass surrounding it."

"Just torch it?" Kade said. "Seems wasteful."

Discussion broke out. Tell knew nothing would be decided today. He whistled and everyone stopped talking. "I believe there are two options on the table. Cord? Let's vote."

Cord cocked his head. "You're pushy today, Tell. What's up? Got someplace to be?"

"Maybe he's volunteered to walk a group of senior citizens across the street," Colt said.

"Or maybe he's gotta polish up his comedy routine for Wyoming's Funniest Person contest at Cheyenne Frontier Days," Colby quipped.

"Or maybe he's judgin' a swimsuit contest in his bedroom," Kane said.

"I'll bet he wants to get out of here because he's got a hot date with Hot Lips," Dalton said slyly.

Tell pushed him. "Fuck off." He looked at his cousins. "All of you can just fuck the fuck off."

"Speaking of... I met your woman at India's shop. She is a knockout. Indy says she's sharp." Colt paused and smirked. "So what in the hell is she doin' with you?"

Laughter.

"Really funny, cuz."

"You know, AJ mentioned that your latest squeeze had shown up at Healing Touch. Evidently you were a main topic of conversation," Cord said.

Tell muttered, "Fuckin' awesome. Now I have to wonder if India tattooed Georgia before or *after* her massage with AJ."

Colt shook his head. "She wasn't getting a tat. She was selling advertising."

"Come to think of it, Skylar told me about this charming little bombshell from Sundance who stopped in to the Sky Blue manufacturing plant and dropped your name."

Tell's gaze zoomed to Kade. "When was this?"

"Wednesday."

"Sounds like your lady was makin' the rounds," Kane drawled. "She showed up at Ginger's office too."

"Wanna take bets on whether she approached Domini at Dewey's? I'm guessing she hit Keely up for ad sponsorship too." Dalton looked at Ben. "How about Ainsley?"

"Ainsley approved an ad for American West yesterday. And she took out a personal ad for my furniture business after Georgia mentioned she loved the coffee table I'd made that she'd seen at Tell's place."

Tell could just see Georgia sauntering into his cousins' wives' businesses and cranking the charisma on high. His gut seized and his heart stopped. Jesus. Georgia hadn't shared any private stuff about them, hoping it would spur a sale?

"Sounds like this juicy Georgia peach you're banging is beautiful, smart and on her game. How long you think you'll last with her?" Colby asked with a grin.

More chuckling.

"At least until she's sold ad space to all of Tell's relatives for the rodeo program guide," Dalton said. "Then she'll probably dump his ass."

"Ha. Fuckin'. Ha." The teasing pissed him off. It shouldn't be a surprise his cousins were still doing what they had always done; making him feel like he wasn't up to McKay standards. Like it was a miracle a sexy, smart, savvy woman like Georgia would be interested in him.

But maybe...there was a grain of truth to that. Georgia had made it plain on Sunday she'd be busy working this week.

Evidently she'd been busy all right... Busy hitting up all his goddamn relatives for money.

"Back to the business at hand, let's vote on the bunkhouse," Cord said. "Who wants to torch it?"

Tell raised his hand and looked around. Not even his brothers backed him on the idea? That sucked.

"Who wants to discuss this at a later date?"

The majority of hands went up.

Kade shook his head. "Fine, we can table it for now, but we need to do a daily check until we make a final decision, since we're headed into fire season. And that means everyone will do his part. I'll write up a schedule and give everyone a copy. In the interest of fairness, we'll take one-week shifts and go from oldest to youngest."

Colby playfully punched Cord in the arm. "That means you're up first, old man."

The meeting broke up. Brandt, Tell and Dalton were the last to leave. And because Dalton had opened his big mouth, he was about to get an earful.

"Thanks for bein' a dick in front of everyone."

Dalton frowned at him. "What was I a dick about?"

"Bringing up Georgia."

"Come on, Tell, don't be such a fuckin' girl. We give each other shit like this all the time. And if it'd been somebody else, you'da jumped in too."

Tell knew his brother was right, but it still stung to be on the receiving end.

"You oughta be glad I did, 'cause it sounds like you didn't have a clue about what she's been doin'." Dalton gave him a curious look. "You haven't heard from her at all since we saw her on Sunday?"

Damn annoying to admit, "No."

"I'm not surprised. She was awful damn detached that morning. Like adios sucker, I got what I wanted from you—a date to the reunion—and now I'm gone."

"And she couldn't possibly want more from me than that?" Tell demanded.

Dalton rubbed a spot between his eyebrows. "Look. I don't know why you're shocked that she's takin' advantage of her connection to you to sell advertising to our family members. Georgia Hotchkiss is a user. She always has been. She always will be. Them type of people don't change, Tell."

"Bullshit."

"You've always jumped through hoops for her. No matter what she's asked you. You didn't moon over her like a lovesick fool, but you were a damn sight giddy whenever she asked for your help with some stupid school project."

Tell fumed, but he didn't lash out, which Dalton took as a sign to keep talking.

"Who ended up filling a thousand helium balloons for junior/senior prom? You. Was Georgia there after she begged you to help her? Nope. Who had to work the concession stand at the Fellowship of Christian Athletes events? You. And you never was the churchy type like her. Was Georgia there? Nope. Who ended up doin' all the research and work for the history project senior year? You. Did your partner Georgia help at all? Nope."

"None of that shit from the past matters. She has changed. And none of us can be held accountable for who we were in high school." Jesus. He was beginning to sound like a broken record.

Dalton started to open his mouth, but Brandt elbowed him, warning, "Leave it be."

"No. If Dalton's got something else to say, let him, because God knows he ain't held back so far."

"Come on, Tell, you'd see it if you weren't lookin' at her with stars in your eyes. Georgia is back in town to show the people that she ain't the goody-goody she used to be. Who better to have in her bed for a few weeks before the reunion than a wild McKay? The same McKay her ex hated. The same McKay she's always easily manipulated. The same McKay who's been crushing on her for thirteen years."

"That's enough," Brandt snapped. "Tell's a big boy. I have a hard time believing he wouldn't see through that bullshit."

While Tell appreciated Brandt sticking up for him, he knew that Dalton's speculations weren't that far off base.

But he had no fucking idea what to do about it.

One thing was for damn sure; he wasn't gonna let it ride.

Chapter Nineteen

Georgia never imagined that community events were this much fun.

The years she'd lived in Sundance, she'd only participated minimally in club, school and community events because her parents preferred she devote her free time to church activities.

Her nervousness about helping out at the heritage day event quickly disappeared when tons of kids showed up at the booth, eager to learn. They'd begged her to recite the alphabet after hearing her count to ten in Russian, telling her how cool it was she knew another language. Which was ironic, because she'd been embarrassed by her mother's ethnicity as a kid and had hated it when her mother spoke to her in Russian.

Because this was Sundance, she recognized a lot of people. Not only schoolmates, but teachers and ranchers and people she'd known from church and those who knew her father and mother.

During a lull, a young blond boy raced up to the booth and bragged he spoke Portuguese. He rattled off numbers and phrases, only to be contradicted in Portuguese by a dark-haired girl who appeared to be his little sister.

"You don't know everything, Sophia," he scoffed.

"Yes I do," she retorted.

A devious smile settled on his lip and he asked Georgia, "How do you say *big mouth* in Russian?"

The girl growled and pushed him, sounding like she was cursing at him in Portuguese.

A shrill whistle had them breaking apart.

Georgia looked at the trio moving toward the kids. Two good-looking men—one fair and blond, the other man dark-haired with golden skin—and a petite woman. With a hint of Native American heritage and the gait that said real cowgirl, Georgia recognized her immediately. "Chassie West?"

The woman stopped and handed the dark-haired toddler sleeping on her shoulder to the blond man. She cocked her head. "As I live and breathe, Georgia Hotchkiss, what the devil are you doin' back in town?"

Georgia headed straight for Chassie and gave her a big hug. "You look great! I wondered if you were still around here."

"We took over my dad's ranch a few years back." She patted her kids on their heads. "I see you've met our oldest kids, Westin and Sophia."

"They were explaining they speak Portuguese."

"That's because he's from Brazil." Chassie gestured to the stunning dark-haired man. "That's Edgard." Then she pointed to the blond guy grinning at the little girl skipping around them. "This is Trevor. They are the kids' fathers."

Edgard offered his hand. "Always enchanted to meet a beautiful friend of our Chassie."

Trevor rolled his eyes. "Brazil nut there always has to be the charming one. Nice to meet you, Georgia. You must've gone to school with our Chass?"

"No, we went to the same church. But I'll admit the last time I set foot in it was at RJ's funeral."

"Same thing happened with me after Dag and my dad died."

Georgia and Chassie exchanged a long look. Some people mired in grief turned toward the church for solace. It was rare to find another person who'd purposely turned away from the church, when those familiar rituals and tenets seemed like meaningless platitudes. Understanding passed between them as they recognized they'd both lost more than just family members by making that choice.

Chassie reached out and squeezed her hands. "So what are you doin' back in Wyoming?"

Georgia gave her the condensed version.

"I'd love to get together sometime," Chassie said.

"Me too. What's your number?"

"I know it!" Sophia said and rattled it off in English. Which prompted Westin to repeat it in Portuguese. Which prompted another argument that Edgard and Trevor immediately nipped in the bud.

Chassie jotted down her number. "Give me a call."

"Yes, please call her," Trevor said, kissing Chassie's cheek. "She don't get out as much as she should."

"Because I'm happy at home with you guys," Chassie protested.

"And we with you, *querida*, but sometimes it's good to mix it up, no?"

Chassie snorted. "You're both just hopin' Georgia takes me out drinkin' so I come home and get wild."

"We love it when you're wild, darlin'," Trevor said. "You turn into something extra special."

Edgard and Trevor looked at each other and laughed when Chassie hip-checked them both.

"Now that my men have thoroughly embarrassed me, I say we go get a drink right now."

"But Mama, you promised we'd make cookies tonight," Sophia complained.

"No worries, Chassie. I'll take a rain check. And I will call you, I promise." The family walked away, and Georgia grinned at Westin shouting goodbye to her in multiple languages.

As the two-hour event wound down, she glanced across the aisle to India, who was applying a fake tattoo to a pigtailed blonde girl. The women she'd met who'd married into the McKay family were all so different. Not at all like the traditional ranch wives she'd known growing up. Georgia remembered that Chassie West was related to some of the McKays, and it appeared she wasn't living the traditional lifestyle either.

Georgia had thirty minutes to wander through the exhibits before the event ended. Most the booths were dedicated to agriculture. A few civic organizations, the western preservationist society, the banks, restaurants, and even a couple of local bands had set up displays. For some reason she wasn't nervous at all about approaching these people and striking up a conversation. Probably because she wasn't selling anything.

As she turned the corner, she saw the Sundance High School Rodeo booth. And sitting at the table was Tell McKay.

Her heart stumbled a little. The man was something. Even wearing a scowl as she approached him.

"Hey, Tell. I'm surprised to see you here."

Tell seemed equally shocked to see her. Not in a good way. "Georgia. Didn't think community things were your style."

That was kind of snarky.

"You here beating the bushes for business?"

"No. I was just—"

"Oh right, that's because you've already tackled that problem this week, haven't you?"

"What are you talking about?"

He pushed to his feet and leaned so close, with such hostility, she was tempted to take a step back. "You know exactly what I'm talkin' about. Don't play innocent, Georgia, it'll just piss me off."

"Are you complaining because I've been so busy this week that I haven't had time to call you?"

"No. The fact I haven't heard from you ain't really a surprise because you got what you wanted from me. I thought it'd be different with you this time. But it sure as fuck smacks my pride when your user tactics are pointed out to me by members of my own goddamn family."

She gritted her teeth and waited for him to get to the point, since it was obvious he'd just gotten started.

"I don't know how in the hell I didn't see past the way you've showed up in Sundance actin' like you own the place, leading me around by my nose."

"No one has a leash around your neck or your balls, least of all me. So quit giving me the wounded man routine and get to the real issue."

"The real issue is you approached all my cousins' wives about buying sponsorships for the rodeo program. Actin' like we're a couple to guarantee a sale."

"That's crap, Tell."

"Is it? So you haven't been asking members of my family for money?"

"I have, but it's—"

"It's complete and total bullshit that you used me to get to them. I'm beyond pissed off about this, Georgia."

So am I. She stared at him, biting her tongue, attempting to remain civilized.

"Don't got anything to say?"

"Yes, I have something to say. I don't know if you've noticed a quirky little thing about the greater Sundance, Moorcroft and Hulett metro area, but quite a few of the businesses are owned by someone in the McKay family. So yes, I approached AJ, India, Skylar, Domini, Ginger, Keely and Ainsley.

"I also approached the owners of all the bars, restaurants, retail stores, the dentist, the doctor and the sheriff's department. So I didn't single out the McKay family for my nefarious plan of promoting a rodeo that will benefit all the business owners in the area. FYI: I didn't drop your name. *Your* family members brought up our intimate involvement, not me. And I'll remind you the *see and be seen* strategy of convincing everyone in town of our couplehood before the reunion was *your* idea. Now you're pissed off it worked? Or were you just hoping people would believe it long enough so you could brag to your McKay cousins that you finally nailed the prom queen?"

That retort caused the vein in his temple to pulse. "Don't you twist this—"

"Don't you act like this is a personal assault on you. It had nothing to do with you until you made it about you. I sure as hell don't need your permission to do my job. Get your facts straight before you start tossing out accusations."

Her heart raced. Her body vibrated with anger and outrage. And hurt. God, it hurt that Tell thought so lowly of her. The man who'd talked so boldly about people changing...believed she hadn't.

His eyes flashed a warning, but no guilt. "This is not the time nor the place to have this discussion."

"You started it!" *Take it down a notch. Act cool.* "Besides." She flipped her hair over her shoulder in complete dismissal. "There's nothing to discuss."

"Bullshit. I will be at your house as soon as this thing is over, so you'd better be ready."

"This thing is already over." Georgia turned and walked away, ignoring his attempts to get her attention, fighting her impulse to flip him off.

Call her contrary, but she didn't trot home to wait for Mr. Accusatory. She headed straight for the Golden Boot.

She slipped into a booth and ordered a vodka tonic and a grilled ham and cheese sandwich.

Tell's anger surprised her because she hadn't seen him angry. He was so easygoing at times she wondered if anything made him mad. She'd seen his intense side. His bossy side. But neither of those could be mistaken for anger.

He had no right to be angry. And she was so fucking pathetic for wondering what angry sex would be like with him that she didn't notice she'd drained her entire drink in about one minute.

"Georgia?"

Startled out of her glum mood, she glanced up to see Leah and Roxanne standing at the table edge. "Hey ladies, what's up?"

"Are you waiting for Tell or something?"

"No. I helped out at the community center and stopped in—" *to avoid Tell, actually,* "—for a bite to eat."

"Mind if we join you?"

She managed to hide her surprise. "That would be great."

Roxanne and Leah already had drinks. Pink ones. "What are you drinking?"

"Cosmos. Ned teases me endlessly about my love of girly drinks. But if I drink beer, I feel like shit the next day."

"Bull, Rox. You feel like shit because you're usually doing tequila shooters *and* drinking beer."

"True. So let's order a cosmo for Georgia so we don't look like lushes."

After they toasted, Leah blurted, "You are so different from what I remember."

"Is that why you've had the big change of heart? Did I pass some secret test?"

Leah looked thoughtful. "Well, we did take a hard look at our small-town, bitchy selves after what you said in the parking lot that night."

"And we've gotta respect you called us out on it. Plus, it took a lot of balls to show up at the reunion. Not only because Deck is now your ex, but also because you lost RJ." Roxanne patted her arm. "I can't imagine losing my sister. Sometimes she annoys the piss outta me, but she's my best friend."

"That's probably why I didn't have many close girlfriends in high school—because I had RJ."

"Well, you've got us now, and we're making up for lost time." Roxanne smiled. "Now that we're pals and all, I gotta ask you something. And be warned, it's personal."

"Geez, Rox, way to put her on the spot," Leah grumbled.

"You can ask, but that doesn't mean I have to answer," Georgia said coyly.

"Were you really a virgin throughout high school?" Roxanne leaned forward. "I mean, you proudly wore a purity ring. And Ned said Deck got pissed whenever someone asked him if you two were doin' it. But I'll bet you were doin' the nasty and lying about it."

"Technically, yes, I was virgin."

"Technically?" Rox repeated.

"Deck and I didn't have intercourse until we were married."

"So in other words, you messed around."

"A lot. I had broad knowledge of certain non-penetration acts involving my hands and mouth." She smirked and pinned Leah with a look. "How about you and Warner?"

Leah laughed. "We didn't save it for marriage. But you probably got the better end of the deal by holding Deck off for a few years."

"How so?"

"The benefit of lots of foreplay because that's all you could do. Once you start screwing...that groping, grinding and crazy-kissing part of sex becomes less important."

"I never thought about it that way."

"What the hell does any guy know about sex at age sixteen anyway?" Rox sighed. "Maybe that's why I was bitter about you wearing that purity ring. I shoulda waited."

"I know part of the reason Deck and I were at the altar a month after graduation was so he could finally fuck me."

Roxanne choked on her drink. "No shit?"

"Not a good way to start a marriage," Georgia said dryly. "Because the deed lasted less than a minute."

"What was the other reason Deck married you?" Leah asked.

"To go into the family cattle business with my father and RJ."

"My parents weren't happy about me'n Warner tying the knot when I turned nineteen. They wanted us to wait. We didn't."

The sandwich arrived and the conversation lagged while she ate.

As soon as Georgia finished eating, Leah whistled for the waitress. "A round of shooters."

Those shooters went down the hatch pretty damn easily. Especially when the toasts were directed to *our new fun friend, Georgia.*

I do too know how to have fun, Tell.

And Georgia was having a great time. Amidst Leah and Roxanne's heated discussion about the TV show *Tabatha's Salon Takeover*, a couple of young, good-looking guys came by the table and hit on them. Georgia might've felt self-conscious that two married women were more accomplished flirts, but these ladies were just too damn entertaining. Somehow the duo convinced the guys to buy them another round of shots and then charmed them into leaving.

Leah and Roxanne called their technique for procuring free drinks the power of the cleavage.

A power Georgia breezily admitted she'd been born without. Which sent her new pals into hiccupping laughter.

Roxanne got that look in her eye again and Georgia braced herself. "Okay, Miss G-Thang. Next snoopy question. Can you still do a herkie?"

Georgia rolled her eyes at Roxanne. Miss G-Thang was her new nickname? "Those are easy."

"Prove it."

"What? Now?"

"Yep. You're the one who said it's easy," Leah said with sweet belligerence. "So do one."

She could stall. The chatty pair would probably forget about it and move onto another topic. "I'll need another shot."

Leah motioned to the cocktail waitress and she dropped off three tequila shooters.

Roxanne smirked. "Are you gonna do the shot before you jump? Or after?"

Now she was stuck. "After."

The women clapped and whistled like her private cheering section.

Georgia scooted out of the booth. She'd done this many times, piece of cake. She briefly closed her eyes—whoa, not good for her balance after a few drinks—and reopened them, smiling, bouncy, peppy, in total cheerleader mode. She clapped her hands twice and followed it with a double fist pump.

"You're on a roll, sista. Do it!" They chanted *Georgia, Georgia, Georgia.*

She brought her body into alignment. She threw her arms in the air, performing back-to-back herkies. And she added in a pike, just to mix it up.

Applause broke out. Even some catcalls.

Breathing a little hard and thankful she practiced Pilates to stay limber, Georgia knocked back the shot and exchanged high fives with Roxanne and Leah.

"Now one of you has to do something since I totally humiliated myself."

"I know!" Leah said, sliding out of the booth. "Ever seen the movie *Coyote Ugly*? That's me'n Rox's favorite. And sometimes, if it's kinda slow in here, Lettie lets us do that boot-scootin' dance on the bar. Let's ask her."

"But only if you'll do it with us, Georgia." Roxanne cocked her head, sizing Georgia up as she scooted from the booth to stand beside her. "Men love to watch chicks' body parts bouncing. If you did a couple cheerleading jumps off the end of the bar? All sexy-like? Dude. We'd be drinkin' free all night long."

"Hells yeah, that's what I'm talkin' about," Leah said, giving them each a fist bump.

"Sorry, ladies, but that ain't happening."

Georgia's heart jumped into her throat when she heard Tell's voice behind her. She turned around and looked into his furious face.

"Hi, Tell," Roxanne said brightly. "What are you doing here?"

"Trying to spoil our fun, sounds like," Leah said suspiciously, "which is ironic since Tell McKay is the self-proclaimed king of fun, right?"

Tell's eyes never left Georgia's. "I'm lookin' for her."

"Why? Didja have a date?"

"No," Georgia said to him. "But if you wanna hang around, after I'm done dancing on the bar I'll sell you some ad space for the Devil's Tower Rodeo program guide."

"Not. Fucking. Funny. Say your goodbyes, Georgia. We're leavin'."

Then Roxanne and Leah were flanking her. "Not so fast. You're looking a little pissed off, McKay."

"I am pissed off and this doesn't concern you, Roxanne. So butt out," Tell said in a measured tone.

Leah wagged her finger in his face. "According to the girlfriend code—"

Tell put his mouth on Georgia's ear. "You can walk out. Or I carry you out. Your choice."

His he-man tactics ticked her off, making her bolder than usual. Or maybe that was the booze. Putting her hand on his chest, she pushed him back. "*You* butt out, McKay."

Roxanne and Leah released a chorus of *oohs*.

Georgia turned her back on him and continued the conversation, although Tell's angry gaze was hot enough to burn holes in her clothes. "Do we choose our own music for the table dance? Because 'Girls Just Wanna Have Fun' would be—"

Her sentence ended in a shriek as Tell picked her up and tossed her over his shoulder.

"What are you doing?"

"Makin' good on my warning."

She kicked and thrashed until he clamped his arms more tightly around her legs. She beat on his butt with her fists. "Let me go, you jackass."

Tell strode away. Jeers, whistles and more catcalls followed them outside.

So did Roxanne and Leah. They were trying to free her from Tell's fireman's hold until he yelled, "Enough! This is between me and Georgia. Now go on home to your husbands before I call them myself and tell them what you've been up to tonight."

"How do you know what we've been doing?" Roxanne demanded.

"Because I've been watchin' you for the last two hours."

Silence.

"Uh. Georgia, we had a great time tonight, but we'll see you later." Leah made the universal hand signal for *call me* and their boots were smoking, they took off so fast.

Traitors. Leaving her with a pissed-off Tell.

"Put me down."

"If I put you down, I'm putting you over my knee."

"Try it and I'll rack you," she snarled.

"Tough girl, are you now?"

"Caveman, are you now?" she mimicked.

His response was a low-pitched warning growl.

She thrashed, smacking her hands into his butt as he carried her to God knew where.

"That's it!" Tell flipped her around and set her on her feet. Then he pulled her blouse over her head and down to her wrists, tying some cowboy knot that immobilized her arms from hands to elbows.

"Are you fucking serious? You tied me up with my own goddamn shirt?"

"Yep. And if you keep bitching at me, I'm gonna gag you with your bra too."

She gasped. "You wouldn't dare."

Tell was right in her face. "Try me."

Shit. His *don't fuck with me* male thing was a total panty-dampening turn-on.

What the hell is wrong with you?

That made her rally. "If you think for a second I'll let you—"

200

"Hush." He rested his hands on her shoulders and placed his thumbs over the pulse points in her neck. "Two things. First: do you really think I'd hurt you, Georgia? Out of anger? Because if your answer is yes, well, then the second thing don't matter."

Her eyes searched his. Tell might push her boundaries, but he wouldn't do anything she didn't want him to. "No, I don't think you'll hurt me."

"Good. Second thing: we're gonna air out our differences."

"Will I be tied up during this discussion?"

"Do you wanna be?"

She opened her mouth to deny it, only to have Tell's mouth on hers. Kissing her with such potency she felt her resistance melting into a warm puddle alongside her sanity.

The longer he kissed her, the more she understood the different ways he could communicate everything about the way he felt, just with his wicked mouth.

He released her mouth in tiny increments, smooching, nibbling, nuzzling, leaving tiny love bites until they were both breathing normally again. "Now, see? Ain't it better that I didn't gag you?"

She sighed.

"But I am gonna keep you trussed up for a little while yet. Gives me all sorts of interesting ideas. Hang on." He swept her into his arms, carrying her to the passenger side of his truck. "And you might as well relax, 'cause it's gonna be a long night."

Chapter Twenty

Once they were in Georgia's house, Tell made his move. Before she turned the lights on.

Not that she could with her hands tied.

Good thing she couldn't see his smug smile about that fact.

They probably oughta talk, because unresolved issues hung between them, but talking wasn't his strong suit. He always said the wrong thing, which made the situation worse. Or he cracked the wrong joke at the wrong time. When he tried to be serious, no one took him seriously—another drawback from being known as the fun-lovin' jokester. Everyone expected him to be that way all the time.

He crowded her against the wall, bracing his hands by her head. Then he began the seduction, whispering, "Close your eyes," into her ear.

"Umm. What happened to us talking?"

"I said we were gonna air out our grievances." He nibbled on her lobe.

"Without words?"

Tell pressed an openmouthed kiss behind her ear. "Actions speak louder than words, don't they?"

She shivered.

"The words will come after."

"After what?"

"After I touch you." He rubbed his mouth over her skin. "After I taste you. I'm dyin' for you, Georgia."

Another shiver, followed by a moan.

"Arch your neck." He trailed sucking kisses down the cord straining in her neck. Stopping to sweep his lips across her collarbone. "Be honest. Me goin' caveman on you turns you on."

No response.

He bit down on the skin between her neck and shoulder.

Georgia's entire body vibrated.

"Answer me."

"Yes, you jerk. You know it does."

"How does knowin' what you like make me a jerk?"

"Because whenever you use that bossy tone and then put your mouth on me, I lose any rational train of thought. And I'm mad at you."

"I'm mad at you too. So maybe it's not my mouth you oughta be worrying about, sweetness, but my hand."

"What?"

"Remember when I warned you that anything you did to me, I'd do to you? Do you have any idea how many times your hand connected with my ass tonight?"

She immediately stiffened. "No! And even if I did, they shouldn't count because I was under duress!"

"Duress?" he growled. "Hot lips, *I* was under duress seein' you drinkin' with them wild women, wondering what all you were tellin' them about us."

Her eyes locked defiantly to his. "I had four drinks over two hours. And I didn't tell them anything. What goes on between you and me stays between you and me. I don't kiss and tell, Tell." She snickered, but her humor faded when he didn't laugh. "You still look surprised that I'm not blabbing far and wide, so you really must think the worst of me."

"Georgia—"

"Why are you here if I'm such an untrustworthy blabbermouth?"

He rubbed his jaw along hers. "You know why."

"No, I don't. Especially not after you accused me of taking advantage of your family because we are...whatever this is."

Looked like it was up to him to define it. "*Whatever this is...*is a relationship. Although neither of us wanted to name it, that's what it's been since day one." He eased back and peered into her eyes, half-afraid she'd deny it.

"You're good with that?" she asked carefully.

"Yep. Are you? If we continue to keep it casual?"

Georgia lifted her chin. "Just sex?"

He shook his head. "It's been about more than just sex for us since day one too. I can admit that now. Can you?"

"Yes." She briefly closed her eyes and pressed her mouth to his. "I missed you this week. I thought about you a lot. And I'm sorry that I was too unsure about us and this...relationship just to pick up the damn phone and call you."

This sweetness was one of his favorite things about her. "Same here. For us supposedly bein' ten years older and wiser, we sure acted like teens a snit, didn't we?"

She laughed softly. "Let's not do that anymore. We'll act like adults. So should we spit on our hands and shake on it? Or will a pinkie promise work better?"

Damn woman made him laugh. "How about if we just seal the deal with a kiss?"

"Deal." She took his mouth like she owned it. And damn if that didn't make him hard as a fucking fence post.

Once he caught his breath, he said, "As long as we're clearing the air, I'm sorry I listened to bullshit speculation from my family before I talked to you. You deserve better from me. I was a dick. It won't happen again. I promise."

Georgia seemed taken aback by the apology. She was even more surprised when he murmured, "That said, darlin', you're still getting a spanking." Then he fused his mouth to hers. Kissing her until his cock was hard as concrete and her lithe body bowed into his.

When they came up for air, Tell loved the bee-stung look of her lips after his harsh kisses.

After untying her shirt and freeing her arms, he said, "Turn around." As soon as she was in position, he nuzzled the back of her head, breathing in her scent. "Since I'm feelin'...generous, I'm gonna let you keep your pants on."

"So it won't be your bare hand on my bare ass?"

"You sound disappointed."

"I'm not."

"Good thing. Because you earned fourteen pops on this perfect butt of yours." He kept his mouth by her ear, teasing with his hot breath and hotter words. "How pink you think your ass will be when I get done?"

She squirmed.

"I guarantee we'll both feel the burn, even through the denim." He traced the curve at the top of her ear with a fleeting lick of his tongue. "But if you were bare-assed, I'd use my tongue to cool down those flaming cheeks when I finished." His nose slipped behind her ear, following that section of skin to the hollow below the lobe. "Can't you just feel my mouth all over your sweet ass?"

He felt her swallow hard.

"Bend over and brace yourself."

Georgia flattened her palms on the wall, making her body into a ninety-degree angle.

Goddamn she looked beautiful. He ran his hands up her spine and across the compact line of her shoulders. There was just one problem. He slid his hands into her hair and tugged her head up. "Better. Stay like that."

She glanced over her shoulder at him, not defiantly, but warily. "Why?"

"I'm gonna need to see your face, sweetness. See if you like what I'm doin' to you."

"And if I don't?" she asked softly.

"Then tell me to stop and I will."

Georgia broke eye contact first.

Tell let his hands roam over her. Never staying too long in one place. Rubbing. Stroking. Petting. Building the tension. He finally gave in and smacked her left butt cheek.

"Oh." She dropped her chin to her chest and seemed to gather herself. Then she raised her head, ready for the next one.

But Tell had no intention of dragging this out or making her count the strokes. He swatted her ass with hard, fast strokes. By the time he finished, Georgia had been pushing back into him for each spank. Her breathing came in short pants and she whimpered softly. Sexily.

Slapping his hands on the wall above hers, Tell caged her body beneath his.

Georgia cranked her head around to get at his mouth. Kissing him crazily. Hot flashing tongue, lips shifting on his as she tried to swallow him whole.

That buzz of need became louder and louder until Tell had to force himself to stop kissing her. "I gotta know... Are you wet?"

"Yes," she practically sobbed. "I never knew it could be like that... God. That was nothing like the spankings I got as a kid."

He released a strangled laugh.

She rolled her spine against his chest, pressing her ass into his groin. "Please. I feel like I'm about to burst."

After one last nip to her nape, Tell pushed upright. Then he tugged on her shoulders and spun her back into the wall, again trapping her body beneath his. "I want you in my mouth."

"Yes."

Another soft pass of his lips over hers. "And I want your mouth on me."

205

"Oh." A pause as his intent became clear, then, "Oh!"

"Lift your arms." As soon as she did, Tell whisked off the lacy camisole and filled his hands with her breasts. He pressed kisses from her mouth, down her throat, between her cleavage, lowering himself to his knees, continuing his southerly progression, only stopping when he reached the waistband of her jeans. Stopping to marvel that this beautiful woman was sharing so much with him besides her body.

"Tell?"

"Mmm. Sorry. Just takin' a minute to admire the view."

"Ah. Could you admire and take my jeans off faster? Because you've got me all kinds of worked up."

Smirking at her, he fingered the button before his thumb flicked it open. Then he worked her zipper down slowly. Such a fucking rush, watching the heated impatience warming those icy-blue eyes.

Georgia lifted a brow. "Remember that whatever you do to me, I do to you—the exact same way."

He laughed and yanked her pants to her ankles. "Step outta them shoes." After she kicked them and her jeans aside, he placed his mouth over her mound. Tonguing her clit through the silky fabric. Breathing in the scent of her arousal. Snaking his tongue beneath the elastic to taste her.

"God. Do that about a hundred more times, won't you?"

"In a minute." She really got squirmy when her panties were gone and no barriers remained between them. He slid his hands up the inside of the thighs, intending to spread her open for a little kiss, when Georgia clamped her hands around his face and her legs shut.

"Huh-uh. My turn. Stand up so I can strip you." She smirked. "And play with you a little." When he was on his feet, she pushed him against the wall.

Jesus.

Georgia attacked the buttons on his shirt. Once it hung open, her hands were everywhere on his chest. The way her nails scraped down his pectorals hardened his nipples and his cock, making it damn hard to swallow. She swirled her finger inside his belly button. She traced each rib. She outlined every cut muscle. With her tongue. Oblivious to the way his body shook, she played with his nipples. Sucking, biting. Twisting with just the tips of her fingers.

Generally driving him out of his fucking mind, which he probably deserved.

She knelt at his feet and said, "Gimme your heel so I can take off your boot."

"That's okay, I can do it."

"You'll either let me do it, or that big cock of yours isn't going in my mouth."

A little shocked by her vehemence, Tell lifted his foot. "Who made you boss?"

"You just did." She cupped her hand around the bootheel and pulled up. "Next."

This was weird. And thank God he'd put on clean sweat socks today. Ever since he was a kid, he'd been self-conscious about his smelly feet. He reached down to pull her up before she could get a whiff, but she slithered out of his grasp.

"I mean it, Tell, knock it off. You keep your hands on the wall and let me do this."

"Why?"

"Because I want to."

"What if I can't?"

"What's the problem?"

Be honest. "Because...fuck. My feet smell like something goddamn died in my boots, okay? I don't want you..."

Georgia merely blinked at him as she tugged off his sock. Then she bent down and...

No. Holy mother of God, no...

She licked his foot, straight across the knuckles of his toes. Twice. Then she slipped her tongue between the webbing of each toe. Twice.

Fuck. His knees damn near buckled. He just about shot in his jeans. Who knew that was so erotic? And goddamn she turned an embarrassing moment into something so sweet and hot.

Tell didn't protest when she removed his other sock. But he was in no way prepared for when Georgia licked and sucked on his toes. Who knew an invisible line ran from his feet to his balls? Every lick felt like she had her tongue on his sac.

Enough.

When she rose to her knees, he grabbed her biceps and hauled her up so they were nose to nose. "Your pussy in my face. Now."

"Uh. Okay."

He picked her up and carried her into the living room, setting her on the reclining chair.

Georgia's eyes were enormous and brimming with heat. He stripped off his jeans and boxers. His gaze encompassed the reclining chair as he walked toward her.

"Should that wild look in your eyes scare me, cowboy?"

"Only if you're not flexible enough for the way I wanna try this. But I saw you doin' them cheerleading jumps, so I don't think it's gonna be an issue, bendy girl."

"Now you've got my attention." Her eyes ran the length of his body and zeroed in on his cock. "But then, you've had it since the instant I saw you tonight."

"That right?" Tell set his palms on the cushiony armrest and kissed her. "Remember when you said you'd take me any way you could get me? Inside, outside, upside down? Well, sweetness, we're about to test that last one." He patted her thigh. "Spin around so your head is in the seat and your legs are on the backrest.

She shot him a crooked grin and flipped around.

And motherfuck if it didn't make his mouth water, seeing her legs splitting into a V, showing that juicy pussy. He grabbed a pillow off the couch and nestled it behind her butt.

With the recliner back a click, her head hung off the edge of the seat and her legs were splayed around the sides of the chair.

Georgia's breath caught when Tell widened his stance and rested on his forearms on the arm rests. Then he put his mouth on her wet sex.

She moaned.

He could feel her ragged breath on his shaft. The first tentative lick. The wet heat of her mouth enclosing the tip. Then her fingernails raking up the insides of his thighs to reach his balls.

Christ. He was not gonna last.

Without the use of his hands, he had to get creative with his tongue and lips and teeth on her pussy. When he pulled back from jamming his tongue in that creamy channel, he let his five o'clock shadow lightly graze her clit.

That caused her to arch, which sent his cock all the way into her throat.

Don't come.

Georgia clutched the outside of his thighs, setting the pace of how deep and how fast she'd take him. And holy crap could she take him deep in this position.

He lapped at her clit. Swirled his tongue around it. Flicked it, teased it until her legs shook and her belly muscles tightened. She was close.

And thank you, Jesus, because he didn't know how much longer he could hold off. With her jacking motions and the saliva from her wet mouth making his cock so slippery and ready to blow.

Tell zeroed in on that swollen pearl. His face was coated with her juices, and as he licked that swollen nub, his tongue still sought out more of her creamy taste.

Never enough. He'd never get enough of this woman.

She nearly arched off the chair when she hit her peak.

His cock had slipped out of her mouth as she wailed a long stream; the only discernible word was his name. Her pussy spasmed against his mouth with such strong pulses he wanted to roar with pride that he'd brought her to this point.

With just his mouth. Heh heh.

Tell nuzzled the inside of her thigh and the top of her mound as the orgasm wound down. Wishing he could use his hands to stroke and soothe her as well.

Then that wonderful, wet, sucking mouth was on his cock again. Focused on the head while her fingers stroked his balls and shaft. When he pumped his hips, she moved her hand faster.

That spark of release began in the base of his spine and traveled up, slowly, like a roller coaster climbing that first hill. His stomach was tight; his ass was clenched waiting for that first drop...and then *bam*. Plummeting into a chasm of dark pleasure. Come shooting out the end of his dick in hot bursts, and a thick tongue swallowing and a soft muscle milking the head until he had nothing left. Not seed. Not breath. Not sanity.

Whoo-ee.

After he'd realized his arms were quaking, he stood.

His head was still spinning, his heart still thumping, and he glanced down at Georgia to see the same dazed look on her face. Her upside-down face.

Then she grinned at him and waggled her eyebrows.

In that moment he knew this woman was everything he'd ever wanted.

When she spun around, he hauled her into his arms, giving her flirty kisses and a slap on the ass. "You." Kiss. "Knocked." Kiss. "My." Kiss. "Socks." Kiss. "Off."

"Actually, I pulled them off, but I'll take the compliment, sexy beast that you are." She smoothed her hands over his chest. "So are we okay? Is there anything else that happened this week that I need to explain?"

"No. I meant what I said, Georgia. I should've come to you first, instead of showin' up all pissed off after the fact."

"Is that an apology for throwing me over your shoulder and hauling me out of the Golden Boot?"

He flashed his teeth in a predatory smile. "Nope. I'm not sorry about that at all. I shouldn't have been so pigheaded about callin' you either." He brushed her wild strands of hair back in place. "I'm not good at this datin' stuff. I've always claimed I don't like playing games, but it appears that's what I was doin' with you. Testing you to see if you really wanted to see me after the reunion. Waitin' to see if you called me first." His cheeks burned. "I know. What am I? Fourteen? That was just fuckin' stupid."

"It's sort of unsettling that we both keep reverting to adolescent behavior."

Somehow Tell kept himself from making farting noises. Although Georgia probably would've laughed. "I'll try harder."

"Me too."

"Now how about if we get cleaned up, pop some popcorn and make out on the couch for a little while before I have to go home?" He saw disappointment in her eyes. "I'm sorry. I can't stay tonight. Can you come to my place?"

"No. I have to leave early for the two-day rodeo in Evanston."

"I wish I could go with you." Sometimes being a rancher sucked ass. "But I promise I'll have a fun surprise planned for when you get back."

"Fun," she repeated. "Should I be scared?"

"Probably."

Chapter Twenty-One

"Miniature golf," Georgia repeated.

"Yep."

"You want me to play mini golf with you?"

"Yep."

"That's your big, fun surprise?"

He grinned. "Come on. Admit you weren't expecting that."

"Uh, no. And I'll admit I don't know why you picked it."

"Because you need fun in your life. And as the McKay who's been called the ambassador of fun, aka the boy who won't grow up, I have much better ideas on how to have fun—with our clothes on—than you do."

As flip as his answer sounded, Georgia read between the quips. "Do your cousins call you that because they believe you're out having fun all the time, while they're tied down with wives and kids? Do any of them know how hard you work on the ranch? Or how much time you volunteer to the community? Or how much time you spend helping out your immediate family? If anyone deserves to cut loose, it's you."

His beautiful smile faded and she wanted to kick her own butt for causing it.

"Tell. I'm sorry. It's none of my business."

He curled his hand around the side of her face. "I'm surprised by what you pick up on that most people, even my own family, don't. The truth is, there wasn't a lot of fun in my house growing up, so I learned to make my own. That way when I was away from home, I couldn't blame anyone but myself for how things played out. Havin' fun didn't come natural, as my brothers can attest. Dalton is better at cutting loose than Brandt is, just because he's younger and I could beat it into him."

She laughed softly, even when a little pain had lodged below her heart.

"So what do ya say? A trip to Spearfish for putt-putt golf and a steak dinner?"

"How could I resist?"

After the ninth hole out of eighteen, Georgia realized why she never played mini golf: because she sucked at it.

She sighed and smacked the crap out of her stupid pink ball, and it bounced out of the stupid maze into the stupid grass.

"Ah, sweetness? That was your eleventh stroke. Why did you hit it so hard?"

"Because I was hoping the ball would blow up so I didn't have to finish this dumb game."

He grinned and his damn dimples winked at her.

Argh. She wanted to whack the golf club against the wooden bridge out of pure frustration. How could Mr. Mini Golf Pro Tell have such a great disposition when she was having a lousy time?

Then those devilish dimples were right in her face. "Such a sexy pout."

"I'm not pouting."

"Yes, you are. Want me to tickle a smile out of you again?"

Georgia swung the golf club like a baseball bat and snarled.

Tell held up his hands in surrender and backed off. "Okay, I'd rather see you pout than let you brain me with a putter because I'm winning." His lips twitched. "So let's see if we can't make the game more interesting."

"How? Are you gonna let me turn that replica gold-miner's shack into a real fire trap when I throw a match on the roof?"

He sighed. "Ever notice you have violent tendencies when you're not winning?"

"Who likes losing?"

"It's a game. It's supposed to be fun. F-u-n, Georgia. Spell it with me."

"F-u-c-k your f-u-n, McKay."

The man busted a gut, which made it impossible to stay mad at him. She smiled. "Fine. What's your suggestion for f-u-n?"

"Since you went thirty-seven strokes over in the first round, let's make the extra strokes...count in the second game."

This could be entertaining. "I'm listening."

"Every penalty stroke—meaning anything over six shots per hole—will earn you a penalty when we get home."

"What kind of penalty?"

"A hard smack on your butt. You across my knee. Bare-assed." He shrugged and tossed the neon-green golf ball in the air and caught it. "I'd probably tie your hands. Maybe even gag you."

Gulp. "And what about you?"

A smirk. "Same deal."

"But that's not fair! You haven't had a single hole over three strokes this entire game!"

"Then you'd better concentrate, hadn't you? If you don't want your ass smarting come morning." He plundered her mouth with a toe-curling kiss. "You can ask for my assistance at any time. Because, hot lips, you're gonna need all the help you can get. I am so lookin' forward to meting out your penalties."

Hah! She'd show him. She'd win this damn game. Or at least keep herself from getting a minimum of nine butt slaps.

That's when Georgia started to have fun. Tell teased her endlessly. Trash-talked her at every hole. Copped a feel whenever possible. Snuck kisses. Touched her just because he always had to be touching her. Which was really hot. He touched her in a way that was sweet to her, but held the *back the fuck off she's mine* vibe to any guy giving her a once-over.

By the time they reached the last hole, she'd had a miraculous improvement in her golf game. Only three penalty strokes, which Tell offered to waive if she gave his cock three long, thorough strokes. With her mouth.

Heckuva deal, in her opinion.

At Applebee's, Tell insisted on sitting on the same side of the booth as her. She ordered a dirty-girl lemonade and he opted for Crown and water.

They talked while waiting for their food. Easy conversation about their work plans for the upcoming week. She told him about the rodeo, but decided not to mention the committee had hired Deck as a judge.

She felt like a complete idiot that she'd missed Deck's name on both the PRCA and non-PRCA judges' list. Granted, his name was at the bottom, since he didn't judge much, but after their run-in, she'd flipped through her paperwork and discovered they were working at another event this summer. All three of them—Deck, Tell and her. Together. That oughta be a laugh riot—*not*.

She decided to avoid mentioning it until right before the actual event. It wasn't worth getting Tell's back up or setting them both on edge. And who knew what would happen between her and Tell between now and then? Maybe they'd break up.

The thought of that caused her stomach to somersault. Letting him know she was leaving at summer's end would be the responsible thing to do, but the more time she spent with Tell, the more time she wanted to spend with him. And she knew if she told him, he'd end it now. She wasn't ready for that.

Georgia sighed softly and laid her head on his shoulder—just because she could.

"Be honest. Did you have fun today?" Tell had one arm around her and gently trailed his fingertips across her bicep.

"Yes. I always have a great time with you. No matter if we're having a popcorn fight, or if we're out at a bar, or if we're in bed. I like being with you, Tell."

He cupped his hand around her jaw, turning her face toward his. Georgia expected a gentle peck, but he flipped all her switches to overload with a hungry kiss.

The insistent mating of mouths was a little much for a public restaurant. But again, Tell lived in the moment. He'd just told her he felt the same way, without saying anything at all.

"For pity's sake, Tell McKay, what is wrong with you?"

Tell didn't rip his mouth from hers as he ended the kiss, but every muscle in his body seized up. He glanced at the man standing at the end of the table.

The resemblance was obvious.

"Dad. What are you doin' here?"

"Didja forget I spend Sundays in Spearfish goin' to church? Not that you've ever bothered to visit my house or the Lord's house."

The man's mean blue-eyed gaze landed on Georgia. "Who're you?"

"Georgia Hotchkiss. Who are you?"

"Tell's father. Not that I wanna claim him some days when he does stupid stuff like this."

Before she responded, Casper McKay slid into the opposite bench seat. He scrutinized Tell. "So I hadta hear from my brothers the annual meeting was held last week. Why didn't one of you boys tell me?"

"Because you can't vote, and after what happened last time, you can't honestly be surprised."

"Sure, they can talk about drinkin' and whorin' all day long, but when I asked to say a prayer before the meeting started, you'da thought I'd asked to rape a goat."

Tell's cheeks turned bright red. "Jesus, Dad. Do you have to do this now?"

"Watch your language," Casper snapped. "I can't imagine this lady wants to hear your filthy mouth."

Oh, I wanna hear his dirty talk more than you can fathom, you clueless SOB.

Tell said nothing. Just sipped his drink.

"I haven't heard from Brandt since I saw my new grandson last Sunday. You were there when he promised to call me."

Georgia realized *that one thing* Dalton and Tell had referred to was code for a family situation involving the prickly Casper. What a relief.

"I imagine he didn't call because he's tired of hearin' you just rag on them to get the baby baptized according to your time frame."

Casper's nostrils flared. "Always gotta place the blame on me, doncha?"

"That's because it usually falls on you."

What was taking their food so long?

Georgia looked up to see Casper staring at her. "Hotchkiss, huh? You Robert's kid?"

"Yes."

"Huh. What church do you go to?"

"Dad, that's not—"

"It's okay, Tell." She smiled at Casper. "When I lived here before, we were Evangelical Free."

"Georgia recently moved back to Sundance from Dallas," Tell offered.

"The girl can speak for herself, can't she?" Casper retorted. "It's so like you, boy, always trying to smooth things over. We're just talkin'. Ain't like I'm gonna tell her embarrassing secrets about you."

"Dad. Stop."

Casper stretched his arm across the back of the booth. "Didja talk to your mother about her?"

"Her name is Georgia. And I don't see how it's any of your business what Mom and I talk about."

Casper grinned meanly at Tell and addressed Georgia. "Better watch this one. He ain't interested in settling down. Especially if he ain't mentioned you to his mama yet."

Tell drained his drink.

Georgia hadn't been raised to backtalk her elders. So as much as she wanted to brag that the kinky, anything-goes sex was keeping her interest, not the chance to snag a McKay, she wouldn't dare. But it broke her heart to watch Tell being miserable.

"His mother and I got divorced," Casper said out of the blue.

"My folks got divorced too, after my brother, RJ, died in a car accident."

"I remember that. But it wasn't no accident. He was drivin' drunk, wasn't he?"

"Yes." *And thank you for pointing that out.*

"I done my share of that. Ain't proud to say it even when I know now I had angels watching over me. Praise the Lord he's on my side, helpin' me stay outta the bottle. You're lucky he didn't take no one else with him. Not like what happened with my oldest son, Luke. Some jackass didn't know how to drive in the fog and my boy paid the price."

Finally their food arrived and Georgia hoped Casper would take a hike. But she feared he might be inclined to stay and say grace.

Tell started shoveling in the side of mixed veggies.

Casper said, "You know it wouldn't kill ya to say thanks to the Lord for all you've got before you eat like you've never seen food."

And Tell kept chewing.

"You are stubborn." Then Casper addressed her. "You wanna hear stubborn? When Tell was about fourteen, we had this old, worthless fishing boat. He thought he could get it runnin', despite the fact he's hopeless when it comes to mechanical stuff. I told him he was wastin' his time. He spent every wakin' hour workin' on it when he wasn't doin' stuff around the ranch. Somehow he convinced Luke to help him haul it to the lake." Casper grunted. "That sucker sank like a rock, with the bow sticking straight up. So when we're in the midst of a drought, that end sticks out 'cause the water table is so low. Since Tell fastened some kind of ridiculous pirate flag on it, everyone knows it's his. Everyone sees his mistake. Stubborn kid shoulda listened to me."

Tell looked up, his eyes dark with anger. "I'd appreciate you leavin' now, Dad. I am on a date. You're the third wheel that nobody wants."

Georgia's face warmed from Tell's harsh words.

But it didn't faze Casper. He slid out of the booth. "Fine, I can take a hint. Be seein' you." And he was gone.

She focused on her pasta. When she glanced over at Tell, he'd stirred his food but hadn't eaten much. Poor baby. She wanted to wrap her arms around him, but he'd see it as pity, not comfort.

He must've sensed her staring. But he didn't lift his head. "Sorry about that."

"Like you had any control over where he showed up for supper."

"Yeah. Well. Can we just forget it?"

Tell only ate half his steak and the waitress boxed up the remainder. Georgia sensed his impatience for her to finish so they could get out of the restaurant.

In the truck, he didn't pat the seat for her to scoot over. He didn't snatch her hand. Tell just hunched over the steering wheel and drove in silence.

Halfway home, she peered around the invisible elephant in the truck cab. "Is it always like that with your father?"

"No. Sometimes it's worse."

"I just want to say—"

"Don't say anything. Can't we just drop it?"

"No. You're upset and hurting and I want to help you." Georgia picked up his hand and kissed his palm. "Please. You've been there for me and you have no idea how much I appreciated that. You need to talk about this, Tell. And I'm right here. Ready to listen. Without judgment."

A few long miles passed. Then he said, "He got worse after Luke died, but that nasty attitude is just who he is, whether he's drinking or sober with the light of God shining down on him. No one in our family can stand to be around him. You can see why.

"I don't know how my mother put up with it for as long as she did. She finally chose a different life and I'm happy for her. Yet that leaves me'n my brothers dealing with Dad without her as a buffer."

Georgia knew exactly how that felt, but this was about Tell. Not her.

"It never changes. God, he's been embarrassing me my whole life. I wish I could say it wasn't as bad because at least he wasn't drunk. But I still hold my goddamn breath anytime he opens his mouth in public. And usually with good reason."

She waited for him to continue.

He sighed. "Look. I appreciate what you're wantin' to do, but nothin' is gonna get rid of this lousy mood anytime soon, so it'd be best if I took you home."

"Not happening. We can chill out at your place, but I'm not leaving you alone to wallow. We wallowed pretty good together last time, if I recall."

217

Tell shot her a look. "You expecting ice cream will help?"

She leaned over to smooch his strong jaw. "Ice cream always helps. But this time I get to dish it up."

Tell needed to clear his mind after the run-in with his father. He'd cracked open a couple of beers, but they were basically untouched on the coffee table, and he and Georgia were entwined on his couch, attempting to watch TV.

"You still seem tense."

Lie. Make light of it. Crack a joke. But he couldn't. "I am."

"I can help with that."

He raised an eyebrow. "Yeah? And how's that?"

"Take off your clothes and I'll show you."

Didn't have to tell him twice. He got naked, whipping his shirt and his camo shorts on the floor.

She watched as his sleeping dick stirred. "Lie back."

Tell stretched out with his arms folded behind his head, letting her look her fill.

Georgia scooted between his legs. Running her palms over his thighs, she stopped to trace the muscles in his quads with her fingertips. Using such tender caresses it seemed every hair on his thighs stood straight up, vying for her attention.

"Is this your way of distracting me?" he asked.

She touched his knee. "One of the ways I've got planned for tonight."

He remembered he'd said that to her the night of the reunion. But the look in her eyes wasn't soft or sweet. Just determined. "Are you gonna torture me?"

"Maybe. I like touching you. Don't you like it?" Her fingers fluttered around his groin, but she didn't touch his dick.

At all.

"I'd like it better if you were touchin' me in one spot in particular."

"I will." She spread her hands over his pecs and kissed his sternum, keeping her eyes on his. "Maybe I wanna drive you a little crazy. Like you do to me."

"I drive you crazy?"

A dangerous smile curled her lips and Tell wondered if he should be worried. "You know you do."

Her soft, warm lips followed the slope of his shoulder.

First thing she did was kiss him. Taking over his mouth completely. Sliding her tongue deep. Sucking and swirling and licking until his body was racked with need.

From just a kiss.

He went to move his arms, to try and regain some control, but her fingernails dug into his biceps. She lifted her lips briefly to warn, "Leave 'em there. And drop your head back. This stubborn chin of yours is in my way." She placed kisses in a straight line from his chin to his collarbone. The wet glide of her mouth over that section of skin caused gooseflesh to erupt from the back of his neck to his knees. He must've made a noise because Georgia just kept right on doing it.

As her hands traveled all over his lower belly, he found himself clenching his fists. His jaw. His butt cheeks.

"This is supposed to be relaxing you," she murmured, kissing his lower ribs.

"The last thing I wanna do with your hands on me is zone out."

"Then this oughta keep you awake." She licked his shaft from his balls to the tip like his cock was a meat Popsicle.

Goddamn that felt good. He about choked on his tongue when she stuffed his entire shaft into her mouth. Sucking so hard her cheeks hollowed. Taking him so deep the head of his cock bumped her soft palate before slipping into her throat. Making a little hum of happiness that vibrated from his balls to the back of his neck.

Then she released his cock gradually, stopping to let the lower rim of his cockhead catch on her bottom teeth. She tongued the underside with hot, wet lashes. Once he got used to the ticklish sensation and anticipated another sweeping lick, Georgia backed off.

His thighs shook. He gritted his teeth against bumping his pelvis up as her lips firmly enclosed the crown. She suckled gently, when he ached for that fast, wet push and pull of his dick plunging in and out of her mouth.

Georgia teased. Rolling his sac with a tender touch. Sucking on his balls as her hand jacked him slowly. Then she'd switch it up, squeezing, licking, lapping with abandon, and she jerked his shaft hard and fast.

Pure. Fucking. Torture.

Soft hands. Warm mouth. Heated breath. Wicked tongue. Tell's body vibrated. He squeezed his ass, his abs, his calves, attempting to hold off and prove...what? That he had stamina?

Fuck stamina. He needed to come now. "Enough. Finish me."

She released his cock, angling her head to nuzzle the inside of his thigh, keeping those sexy eyes on his. "How do you want me to finish you?"

"Hands on my thighs. Lean in, but arch back. That's it." He fisted his shaft, still slippery from her saliva. "Open your mouth."

Tell beat off, each stroke faster. That tingle in his tailbone was a brief warning and a drop of come landed on her chin before he shoved his cock between her lips and groaned, "Suck me down. All of it," as he shot his load.

Georgia's cheeks indented and her throat muscles kissed his cockhead with each swallow.

Hot. Wet. Tight. It felt so goddamn good. Keeping his grip on her head, he closed his eyes, bumping his hips into her face with each pulse, letting himself drift into the peaceful place she'd brought him to.

Teeth sinking into his cock stirred him from his orgasmic stupor.

He swept his thumbs across her cheekbones as he withdrew from the haven of her mouth. "Look at you. So pretty and naughty on your knees."

She blinked slowly and gave him the lopsided smile.

"C'mere." Tell hauled her across his lap and kissed her, his tongue dueling with hers. "Mmm. The taste of my come on your tongue is a fuckin' turn-on."

"You do seem more relaxed."

"Thanks to you. You sucked all the tension and all the poison right outta me, baby."

Laughing, she swatted him.

Tell stretched out on the couch, bringing her on top of him. Running his fingers through her soft hair as her head rested on his chest. He was totally content. "What's on your agenda for this week?"

"Work. I've set up radio interviews for upcoming events. Getting competitors to agree to talk on live radio is a pain, so I've lined up a stock contractor and a committee member in case there's an issue." She sighed. "With just me here, I don't have backup for anything, from event staffing issues to breakdowns in communication with committee members."

"Any problems with the rodeo this weekend in Pine Haven?"

"No. But it's tiny and so last-minute they aren't expecting miracles on the PR front." Her face turned thoughtful as she buried her fingers in the dark hair on his chest.

"Something else on your mind, sweetness?"

"Nothing big. It's just weird. People I knew in passing, or who knew RJ, or my parents, or from school approached me at the community center."

"What did they want?"

"Seems once I volunteered for something, they assumed I'm interested in volunteering for other community projects. Before I knew what was happening, I agreed to help with a fundraiser for the chamber of commerce and help organize a workshop for the competitive cheer squad."

What had these people said to Georgia to garner her interest in community activities? It had to benefit the PR company in some way.

Not nice, Tell. Be happy she's not sitting at home.

"There's a meeting about the cheerleading workshop on Tuesday night."

Tell frowned. "Does that mean you're skipping out on meeting me at Ziggy's for dart league?"

"Shoot. I forgot. I can cancel—"

"Don't sweat it. We can meet up afterward."

"You sure?"

"Yep. As long as you're in volunteer mode, I could use some help with the rodeo club fundraiser week after next."

"Done. Anything else?"

"Yeah." He let the tips of his fingers follow the planes and angles of her face. "Bring that mouth over here. I need another taste."

She kissed him with such fire his cock hardened.

"Sweetness, you got way too many clothes on."

She raised a haughty eyebrow. "And whose fault is that?"

"Yours. Strip."

Chapter Twenty-Two

Georgia stood beneath the bank sign in Moorcroft, debating whether to cross the street to have lunch at the Mexican joint or head down the block to the greasy spoon, when the door to the bank opened and her father stepped into the sunshine.

She blinked at him for a second or two, wondering if her eyes were playing tricks on her.

He seemed equally stunned. Then he wrapped her in a bear hug. "Georgie! My goodness, girl, I was just thinking about you and here you are."

"Hey, Dad."

"Lookit you. No bigger than a minute. I forget what a shrimp you are," he teased. Then he added, "But damn, girl, you are a beauty. Lucky thing you got your mama's looks, huh?"

"And Mom says I got your temperament."

"Bet she didn't say you were lucky getting that trait. What're you doin' in Moorcroft?"

She held her breath, expecting he would demand to know why she hadn't called him to say she'd be in the area, but he just looked at her expectantly. Happily. "I made a few sales calls."

"Have you eaten?"

"No, but I have to get back—"

"You ain't even gonna let your old man buy you lunch?"

Hello guilt. "Sure. I'll let you buy... As long as it's Mexican."

He scowled. "That'll work."

Her father hadn't argued or insisted on eating at the restaurant of his choice? That was different.

Maybe he was different.

They walked together, her father making small talk about the weather and hinting about big news in his life.

After they were seated with menus, Georgia studied Robert Hotchkiss as he slipped on a pair of reading glasses.

It'd been two years since she'd seen him when he'd shown up in Dallas, out of the blue. He didn't look much different. Same pale brown eyes. Same shaggy gray hair. Same rotund carriage.

He glanced up with a small smile. "Whatcha havin'?"

"The beef enchilada platter. What about you?"

"Steak is probably the safest, although my doctor wants me to eat more green shit."

Georgia smiled. "Mom tried to get you to eat more green shit for years."

"She finally did develop my taste for all the different ways she could cook beets."

"My borscht never tastes as good as hers."

"Your mama's cookin' is just one of the many things I miss about her."

The waiter served their drinks—iced tea for her, a beer for her father—and took their order.

They snacked on chips and salsa. The restaurant had typical Mexican décor—piñatas hanging from the ceiling and gaudy sombreros on the brightly colored wall. Plastic cactuses scattered throughout. Mariachi music playing in the background. Strands of chili pepper lights draped from the ceiling.

"Speaking of your mother... I talked to her the other day."

"I heard."

His bushy eyebrows rose. "What'd she say about me?"

"Just that you called." She stirred a packet of sugar in her tea. "She's coming to visit." Why had she told him that?

"Is that right? She didn't mention it to me."

"I was surprised to hear that you call her regularly."

He honestly looked perplexed. "Why? Irina was my wife for twenty-five years."

"I figured after the ugliness of your divorce..."

"Look, Georgie, after RJ...everything got way out of hand. I never expected..." He sighed. "It's complicated and I never was good at uncomplicating things. But I'm awful good at makin' them worse."

Georgia bit her tongue. Changing the subject would be the safest way to finish this lunch. "What's this big news you mentioned earlier?"

"I'm gonna retire."

"Really? When?"

"Soon as the paperwork is sorted out. I sold the hog farm to a corporation outta eastern South Dakota. Shocked me how good of a deal they offered. And, well, I ain't getting any younger."

"You just turned sixty-eight, right?"

"Yep. That sounds old to a twenty-eight-year-old, huh?"

It did sound old. Her dad had been forty when she and RJ were born and her mother only twenty-two. During her childhood she hadn't noticed the eighteen-year age gap made a difference in her parent's relationship. But she wondered if that was why she'd never dated older men.

"I tried to call you on your birthday last month."

"I know." She aligned the bottom of the knife with the bottom of the spoon. "I don't celebrate or do anything anymore. It's just another day."

Her dad chuckled. "Your mom used to go all-out for your birthdays."

"The year we got the squirt guns was the best."

"Really? Didn't you break yours right away?"

"No. RJ busted his. He was so upset I gave him mine and we swore we'd never tell."

His eyebrows rose. "I never knew that."

"We were pretty good at covering for each other."

"And sticking up for each other. I remember the summer you two were seven. We'd just moved to the farm and I caught RJ climbing on the barn with a quilt that he intended to use for a parachute when he jumped off the roof. The kid like-ta give me heart failure. I paddled his ass good." He shook his head. "Then you marched up to me, bold as brass, and told me I'd better spank you too, since it was your quilt and you planned to jump off right after him."

Georgia smiled. "I don't know if you noticed I wore extra clothes as padding."

He laughed. "Nope. I didn't catch that."

"It was RJ's idea. He wished he'd thought of it."

"I imagine. You two were always thick as thieves."

That comment kicked her grief to the surface, not that she'd ever buried it deep. She scrambled to change the subject. "So retirement, huh? What will you do with yourself when you don't have to slop hogs?"

"Maybe I'll end up baby-sitting Deck and Tara-Lee's kid," he said with a laugh. "But since he's getting a cut of the profit, Deck will likely be takin'..." He glanced up sharply. "Sorry. I know Deck is a sore subject."

Do ya think?

"But now that the cat's out of the bag, I want to explain—"

Georgia held up her hand. "Don't go there. Please. We were having a nice lunch and I don't want my appetite spoiled."

"We do need to talk about this at some point, Georgie. It's been seven years."

The food arrived.

"So what's your main responsibility in this job?" he asked.

Grateful that he'd switched topics, she smiled. "I'm at the rodeo grounds to make sure our portion of the event is handled properly. Working with the committees beforehand. Selling ads. Lining up radio spots."

He sliced off a big chunk of meat. "What happens when the summer rodeo season ends?"

"I return to Dallas. But keep that to yourself. I don't want any of our contractors afraid I'll bail out early, since we're the new kid around town."

He grunted and steadily demolished his steak.

The conversation lagged, but not due to tension.

"Thanks for inviting me to lunch, Dad."

"You're welcome." He leaned back in the booth, folding his arms and setting them on his belly. "So am I gonna get to see you again before you take off?"

"I'll try. The road runs both ways. You could venture to Sundance."

"I'll keep that in mind."

Her father was looking at her in a way she'd never seen before—with regret. "What?"

"People change, Georgie. Holdin' a grudge ain't no way to go through life."

Was he talking about her forgiving Deck?

Maybe he's taking about you forgiving him.

She inhaled a slow breath. "I'm listening."

"Took me a while, but I'm finally starting to realize what anger cost me."

"Who were you angry at?"

"God. For takin' my boy away. I lost my faith."

Robert Hotchkiss had always been a man of faith, not merely paying lip service to being a Christian. He'd tried to lead his life according to God's rules and by example, expecting his family to follow suit. It hadn't been the easiest way to grow up, but she hadn't questioned it. Not until RJ had died. Although she'd veered away from the teachings of the church, she still didn't judge those people who abided by the tenets of their religions, just as long as they didn't try and push their beliefs on her.

So his response about losing his faith startled her—maybe that's why her father had become so unrecognizable in the wake of RJ's death. He'd had no one to turn to. So he'd turned on everyone.

"But the worst part?" he continued in a small voice. "Because of that anger, I also lost your mom. And you. I lost everything and everyone that mattered to me." He looked down. "It ain't right. And I don't know what I can do to make it right."

Neither do I.

"But I'm willing to do anything, Georgia."

What did it mean that he wanted to try and make amends?

Her phone buzzed, reminding her of her next appointment. She said, "Dad, I have to go."

"I understand. Thanks for makin' my day. I...hate that it's this way between us. I don't know you as an adult, Georgie. That makes me sadder than anything in the world," he said gruffly.

Completely at a loss, Georgia mumbled, "See you," and practically ran out of the restaurant.

Tell's week started out on a sour note and went downhill from there.

He hadn't seen Georgia at all on Monday and when he called her, she sounded preoccupied, although she swore she was just tired.

Tuesday night was a wash. She'd invited him to her place after his dart game ended, but the way she'd gone on about how much fun she'd had with the new people she'd met and the old friends she'd reconnected with had brought out a jealous streak and he'd just gone home. Alone.

Wednesday night was Georgia's girls' night with Stephanie. And Leah and Roxanne. And a bunch of other women. Evidently she'd had a great time, a fact he'd heard Thursday morning from Ned. And even Dalton.

Weren't you the one who encouraged her to cut loose? Have fun. Make friends. Get involved?

Yeah. Might make him paranoid, but now that Georgia had found a new crowd, maybe a cooler crowd, was she ditching him?

The niggling doubt was confirmed Thursday night when Tell tracked Georgia down at the Golden Boot—thirty minutes after they were supposed to meet for supper at Fields. He leaned against the wall and watched her as she chatted with the mayor, the superintendent of schools, the owner of the local real estate company, and the lawyer for a methane gas company.

All single men.

All gazing at Georgia with lust-filled eyes.

All dead men, as far as Tell was concerned.

But rather than storming over and hauling her ass out like he had before, he hung back. Just as he had in high school. Waiting for her to notice him.

You're still a wannabe, McKay. Nothing has changed.

Bullshit. But tuning out that voice of doubt and reminding himself to act like a mature adult in this relationship didn't spur his feet to move. He was stuck in hell, seeing Georgia laughing with these clowns, oblivious to the fact she'd missed their date.

Thirty minutes passed while he remained in the shadows, nursing a beer. Thirty long minutes in which he didn't cross Georgia's mind once because she'd made no effort to contact him.

Sobering and humbling.

He texted her.

I must've mixed up my nights. Thought we had a date at Fields. I'm tired and going home. Catch up with you later. T~

Maybe it was perverted, but he hung around to see her reaction.

Georgia fished out her cell from the pocket of her suit jacket and glanced at the screen. Guilt crossed her face and she swore. She immediately began punching buttons. Soon after his phone buzzed in his hand.

No, it was tonight. Sorry! I didn't mean to stand you up. I got sidetracked. Are you still waiting at Fields?

Tell waited a solid five minutes before he responded.

No worries. We'll go another night. Got a busy day tomorrow anyway. See you @ the Pine Haven Rodeo Saturday.

Georgia frowned and texted furiously, ignoring the men at the table.

I'm really sorry. Can I come out to your place and make you supper?

Probably made him a petty dick, but he just wanted to be mad at her.

No. I can't text and drive, so I gotta go. See you.

Tell finished his beer. Wondering if Georgia would stay at the bar and drink with these guys or if she'd head home.

But he didn't stick around to find out.

He dreamt of her that night. Dreamt of being back in high school. Dreamt of being invisible. Dreamt of gazing at her adoringly from the sidelines.

Georgia. Beautiful, perfect Georgia. His Georgia. Not the unattainable Georgia from the past.

He approached her in the lunchroom. But she wouldn't deign to look in his direction or even speak to him.

He pulled her hair and called her name in history class, but she wouldn't acknowledge him at all.

In the next dream frame, Georgia was surrounded by his cousins. Strong, strapping McKays. With those black Irish good looks. Rich men. Successful ranchers. Oozing confidence. Spreading charm.

When he wormed his way through the throng to get to her, he was roughly jerked back. Put in his place at the end of the line.

"She doesn't want you," Kade sneered.

"She never has, she never will," Colby hissed.

"She's too good for you," Colt added.

"You ain't man enough to handle her," Ben warned.

"She's using you, and you're a loser who lets her," Dalton said with derision.

His father appeared—all mean attitude and ugliness. "You're an embarrassment to the McKay name." Casper turned his back on Tell, shunning him.

Then, one by one, his McKay relatives started laughing at him. Pointing. Whispering. Making fun. Taunting him. He tried to run away but his feet were buried in the earth.

The real kick in the balls came when Georgia looked at him with pity and contempt. "You didn't really think *you* had a shot at me, did you?"

He woke up angry. Irrational anger from a stupid dream, but he hated there were some truths in his fears. That he'd never be good enough for her. In her eyes and everyone else's eyes. Truths that made him feel raw and helpless. Truths that made him a little desperate to dispel those fears by any means.

Chores kept him hopping all Friday morning. So when his caller ID said *Chase*, he almost didn't answer, but curiosity got the better of him. "Omigod! Is this really Chase McKay? World champion PBR bull rider? Callin' me? I'm so honored!"

"Yes, it is, and why don't you just go ahead and pucker up to kiss my famous butt for that smart-ass comment."

Tell laughed. "What's up, cuz?"

"I'll be in town for the Upton Rodeo tomorrow afternoon. Pressing the flesh, passing the word about safety helmets. I got to talkin' to Verna, the Upton Rodeo secretary, and she told me they're short a judge for tomorrow. I told her I'd call and see if you're interested in subbing."

Hell yes he was interested. Then it hit him. He couldn't. It was too bad Georgia had hired him to work the Pine Haven Rodeo tomorrow.

It's too bad Georgia has blown you off all fucking week.

Whoa. Seemed his subconscious was still bitter.

But the bottom line was the Upton Rodeo was a PRCA-sanctioned event. More money, more prestige than a dinky-ass nothing rodeo. Not to mention he'd get to share the spotlight with his celebrity cousin for an afternoon.

No one would fault him for taking this opportunity.

Well, Georgia might.

Well, she could just suck it up.

"Tell? You there?"

"Yep. Sorry. That sounds great."

"Awesome. I'm sure you know the drill by now. Lookin' forward to seein' you."

Georgia didn't check her phone Saturday morning until after she'd weeded her vegetable garden, showered and finished half a pot of coffee. She smiled, seeing a text from Tell at six a.m. She loved the pictures he'd text from his early morning ranch chores. Or just the sweet things he'd text because he'd been thinking about her. Those messages had been scarce the last three days. She'd just chalked it up to them both being busy. She scrolled through the text:

Sorry, but I have to back out of judging the Pine Haven Rodeo today. A family thing came up—don't worry it's not serious and I'll text you when I can. T~

What was she supposed to do now? Two judges were the minimum requirement. She tried eight numbers on the judges list and no one was available.

That's when she panicked.

Think, Georgia.

One solution occurred to her. She dismissed it. Several times. Until she just went ahead and made the call, pacing as the line kept ringing. Then a gruff voice said, "Hello?"

"Hey, Dad. How are you?"

"Georgie! I'm okay. I'm happy to hear from you. What's goin' on?"

"Is Deck around?"

Silence. Then, "Oh. You didn't call to talk to me?"

His hopeful tone had dimmed and she felt guilty. "I'm actually in a time crunch. I need to talk to Deck and I didn't have his number. It's strictly a business question."

"Georgia, dear, is there coffee left?" her mother trilled as she entered the kitchen.

"Your mother is in Sundance?" he asked.

"Yes. I told you she planned to visit. Now is Deck around or not?"

"Yeah. He's here. Hang on."

Muffled voices mixed with the sounds of hogs going hog wild in the background and then Deck came on the line. "Robert said you needed to talk to me?"

Cut right to the chase. Be professional. "Yes. I'm short a judge for the Pine Haven Rodeo today. Would you be willing to sub?"

"Who backed out?" A snicker. "It was McKay, wasn't it?"

Dammit, Tell, you owe me for this. "Yes. Look, the event is two-and-a-half hours, tops. It starts at one."

"What's in it for me?"

"Standard non-PRCA pay rate. There's food for contestants, judges and committee members. Plus, I could swing a companion ticket for Tara-Lee."

"When do I need to be there?"

"One."

A pause. "I suppose I could help you out. Just this one time."

She closed her eyes, glad he hadn't tacked on *since you're desperate and McKay left you in the lurch.* "Thank you, Deck. I really appreciate it. The paperwork will be in the secretary's office."

"I have done this before." The phone clunked. "Hang on, Robert wants to talk to you again."

"Will your mother be at this rodeo?" her father demanded.

Georgia held her hand over the phone and glanced at her mom, leaning against the doorjamb. "Are you coming with me today?"

"Better than sitting here doing nothing. Why?"

"Dad wants to know."

Irina Hotchkiss slowly sipped her coffee. "Is he going?"

For the love of God.

"I am *not* the go-between. You two are adults. Figure it out. But I'm leaving in half an hour." She handed her mother her cell phone and ran upstairs to finish getting ready.

When Georgia returned downstairs, her mother waited by the door. In a new outfit. A cleavage-baring outfit.

Do not ask why she's got the girls out in full display.

"Ready?" Georgia asked brightly.

"Yes. But I've decided to follow you in case I get bored and want to leave."

"Fine." Georgia handed her mother a spare house key and a complimentary ticket. "I'll be busy. Just text me and let me know what you're up to."

That way she wouldn't have to run interference between her parents *and* deal with her ex-husband.

As Tell slipped on the official black-and-white PRCA judge's vest, he heard Verna calling, "McKay?"

Both he and Chase said, "Yes?" then they laughed.

"I'm looking for judge McKay, not rider McKay," Verna said, handing Tell a clipboard. "We're just glad you're here and didn't have anything else goin' on today."

Nothing else going on. Right. Backing out on Georgia was a shitty thing to do, but he hadn't lied exactly. Being here *was* a family thing. This was the first time he'd be a judge when his world champion bull riding cousin, Chase McKay, took to the dirt.

Chase had agreed to ride as an expo at the last minute. The promotion company was all over the place, scrambling to make the most of the opportunity. Which made him wonder what Georgia was doing.

Cursing your name, most likely.

He signed off on the paperwork. "What now?"

"We hang tight. There are a couple camera crews setting up for interviews."

"Seriously?"

Chase shrugged. "Welcome to my life."

He snorted. "Yeah, it sucks to be you. Married to a gorgeous movie star, livin' the high life on a beach in California, and let's not forget that teeny tiny PBR World Champion belt buckle you're sporting."

A big grin split Chase's face. "It is good to be me." He ran his finger over the big buckle. "I still can't believe I won last year."

"You deserved it. You had a great season. Are your brothers and folks here today to cheer you on?"

"Actually, no. Mom and Dad are in Phoenix, staying with Sierra since Gavin has a week-long conference in Atlanta." He frowned. "That girl is givin' Gavin fits and he can't trust his ex with her anymore either. Ben and Ainsley are in Gillette for a wedding. And Quinn and Libby are in Spearfish today for Adam's T-ball game."

"How long are you stayin'?"

"Just tonight. I'm crashing at Ben's place."

"Ava's not with you?"

"I wish."

"How is she?"

Chase smirked. "Fuckin' spectacular. I'm the luckiest man in the world."

Tell punched him in the shoulder. "Lookit you, all in love and shit. Never thought I'd see you pussy-whipped."

"And now I wouldn't have it any other way." He crossed his arms over his chest. "Speakin' of pussy... I stopped into AJ's place early this mornin' for a massage. She mentioned you were makin' time with one Georgia Hotchkiss. Ain't she the smokin' hot cheerleader from your class? Her boyfriend was on the rodeo team?"

"Yeah. We're hanging out sometimes. No big deal." He gave Chase a cool stare. "How in the hell did that come up in conversation with AJ?"

"Evidently AJ is tryin' to marry you off."

"To Georgia? Jesus. It was just last week all them women were all gunning for her, afraid she'd break my poor little heart while she reached into their purses."

"That's changed. They're singing her praises now. AJ thought with me bein' the former bad boy McKay that you'd listen if I spewed hearts and flowers about how much happier my life is now that I've settled down." Chase shrugged. "All true. But I remember bein' pissed off when our cousins tried to tell me the same thing."

"The McKays are a meddling bunch," Tell grumbled.

"That ain't gonna change. So is she here?"

"Nah. She's working another rodeo event today."

"Chase?" A smartly dressed woman stepped into the tent. "You ready?"

"As I'll ever be." He clapped Tell on the back. "Come on, cuz, it's time for your close-up."

An hour later, Tell had no idea how Chase did this bullshit every day, cameras filming and photographers snapping shots and microphones shoved in his face, recording his every word like gospel. Tell resisted sneaking behind him and making bunny ears. That would just be immature. Funny as hell, but definitely juvenile.

Finally the PR woman ended the interviews.

They wandered behind the chutes and split up. Tell got his head in the game, and it was time to rodeo.

Every event went like clockwork. Chase was last to ride. His ride was an exposition, but that didn't mean it was a gimme. The bull they'd paired him with hadn't been ridden and was a beast at almost two thousand pounds.

The bull went vertical out of the chute.

Chase held on. He spurred, one with the animal through every twist, turn and jump. The crowd went nuts, aware they were witnessing a textbook, picture-perfect ride.

Tell scored the bull and the rider very high. Not because Chase was his cousin, but because the man was sheer poetry on the back of a bull.

Final score was ninety-three points.

After the buckles were awarded, Chase gave his spiel about helmet safety issues, and a good portion of the crowd stayed to listen.

Tell checked out with the rodeo secretary, waiting for Chase to finish yet another interview. And he wasn't the only one waiting. He casually checked out the women hanging on the corrals, anticipating Chase's appearance. As if Chase was gonna look twice at any of these bunnies when he had the stunning Ava Cooper in his bed every night.

"That was some ride," a busty blonde said.

Her redheaded friend nodded. Then she gave Tell a once-over. "Hey. You're one of the judges."

He smiled. "You caught me."

"You're really cute. God, I love them dimples." Her gaze dropped to the waistband of his jeans and seemed disappointed he wasn't wearing a buckle. "Didja used to compete in rodeo?"

"A few years back."

"Ooh. I can tell," the redhead cooed. She squeezed his biceps. "You've got the body for it."

The blonde, not to be outdone, thrust her tits in his face. "You're used to ranking bulls and riders. What would you rank me?"

He bit back the *damn close to desperate* comment that popped into his head. He let his gaze travel over her. "On a scale of one to ten? Pretty lady, you're a solid fifteen. And that's before I see how well you can ride."

She tittered.

Next thing Tell knew, he was surrounded by half-a-dozen women. All laughing at his jokes, pawing at him. Making sexual promises with their mouths and their eyes.

What about Georgia?

What about her? She's not here. And all these lovelies wanted to do was hang out with him.

Because they like you? Or because they're hoping Chase will show up?

And for the first time ever, Tell didn't dread that scenario. Wouldn't that be sweet? Seeing the surprised look on his famous cousin's face when he finally realized that Tell wasn't the scrawny runner-up in everything? That Tell had his own moves and his own group of hot chickies vying for a down and dirty piece of him?

Shallow, McKay, really fucking shallow.

"I'm thirsty," brunette number one complained.

"Me too," said the busty blonde.

"Ditto," said the redhead.

The expectant looks leveled his way prompted him to say, "I can't stand to see you beauties suffering from dehydration. How about if you all head on into Moorcroft and save us a table at Ziggy's? The first round is on me."

Chapter Twenty-Three

"Outstanding job, Georgia. We can't thank you enough for going above and beyond for our little rodeo."

Georgia beamed at Esther Theel, committee chair. "It truly was my pleasure. I hope the Pine Haven Rodeo continues for many years."

"You can bet we'll be moving it from this weekend next year, so we ain't competing with the Upton Rodeo." Esther gave her a shrewd look. "I should be glad that Barb Wyre PR isn't promoting that one. Or else you wouldn't have had time for us."

Today had been full of lucky breaks. Not only that Deck had agreed to sub at the last moment, and he hadn't been nasty, but due to her PR efforts the attendance at this rodeo exceeded initial expectations.

"As happy as I am with the gate, concession stand and beer garden receipts, I can't help but wonder if our take would've been higher if we'd hitched our wagon to a celebrity rider like Chase McKay."

"Why would you say that?"

"'Cause Chase was featured at the Upton Rodeo today."

Instead of blurting, "He was?" Georgia meticulously straightened a stack of papers and wondered why Tell hadn't mentioned it.

"All sorts of media coverage from what my spies tell me." Esther ran her hand through her short gray hair. "Especially after that ninety-three point ride. But I gotta say, it's a good thing the ride was for exhibition, because that score would definitely be called into question, bein's Chase McKay's cousin was a judge."

Georgia stilled.

Tell. You lying piece of shit. A family thing my ass.

The Upton Rodeo was a much bigger event and PRCA-sanctioned to boot. Had he really thought she wouldn't find out why he'd blown her off? Or didn't he care that his defection had left her scrambling to fill his judge spot at the last minute? Especially after she'd gone out of her way to find him more judging gigs?

Or maybe this is finally payback for all the times you left him high and dry.

The knowledge lodged in her belly like a boulder.

Esther said, "I wasn't gonna bring this up, but wasn't Tell McKay supposed to judge here today?"

Now she had to try and save face for both of them. "Yes. He'd gotten double-booked and…"

"Oh, I ain't surprised this dinky event wasn't his priority since his cousin is big-time. I was just curious."

"I understand Chase McKay is generous with his time and celebrity, especially with rodeos in his home state. You should look into booking him for next year before Upton gets ahold of him."

"Or maybe we should have you look into it, so we've got you locked in for PR for us," Esther said slyly.

Georgia forced a laugh and looped the messenger-bag strap over her shoulder. "Who knows where I'll be next year."

"If you are interested in having an early word with McKay, Ziggy's is the hangout spot for the rodeo crowd after a performance. I was thinking of heading over there myself."

No way. Georgia was not going to Ziggy's. Forcing a public confrontation with Tell wasn't smart, given that last time they'd had words he'd thrown her over his shoulder and carried her out of the bar.

So she'd head home, make plans with her mother and have a quiet evening. With lots of wine. With lots of whining.

The staunch self-warning did no good.

An hour later, Georgia found herself looking for parking in Ziggy's lot.

She paid the cover charge at the door. As she made her way through the crowd, she caught her first glimpse of a familiar face: her father's. That was weird. He'd never been the type to hang out in bars, even before RJ died. Georgia inched forward to see who shared his booth and her eyes bugged out.

What the hell? Her parents were having supper together?

She watched them for several more minutes. Although they were talking, neither looked happy about the conversation. Maybe it was better she wasn't there to mediate; heaven knew she hadn't done a great job in the past.

Still, the whole thing left her unsettled. Today's issues and events left her out of sorts and on edge.

Of course, that's when she heard his laugh. Deep, rich and strong.

Georgia turned toward the sound and saw Tell in a circular booth, surrounded by women. Laughing with them. Drinking with them. Charming them. Lapping up every bit of female attention.

A jealous rage rose in her. She wanted to punch him in his handsome face for his part in her tension-filled day.

But she had no idea how to handle this. Standing here, secretly shooting eye daggers at his female tablemates, was pointless. Should she storm up and introduce herself as Tell's...what? High school crush? Or go all hard-ass businesswoman and demand an explanation of why he'd blown off a professional engagement?

The longer she wallowed in indecision, the more she understood...she wouldn't do jack shit. That reaction sent her spiraling back in time. When Deck had done or said something wrong and she'd kept her mouth shut rather than confronting him.

When the single guys who'd been circling her started moving closer with that *hey baby come here often?* gleam in their eyes, Georgia decided to go. But in trying to avoid the sharks eyeing her like chum, she'd snagged Tell's attention.

Their eyes met. She expected him to look away quickly. Guiltily. But he kept focused on her. Part challenge, part some other fucked-up male pride thing that she didn't want to deal with.

Now she'd look even more pathetic if she fled.

Her fight or flight decision was postponed when a male voice said, "Georgia?"

Then she was face to face with Chase McKay. The man was built like a bulldozer. Eyes—the same mesmerizing blue as Tell's—stared back at her. His wide smile was pure McKay too. She blurted, "You remember me?"

"Of course." Chase didn't shake her hand; he hugged her. *Hugged* her. "You look fantastic."

"Ah. Thanks. So do you."

He grinned at her like he had a big secret. "My cousin is a dumb-ass. Bein' pigheaded is a rite of passage for us McKays, but this one is gonna be especially sweet to pay forward."

Confused, Georgia just blinked at him.

"We won't have much time, so we've gotta get maximum play outta this play." He stepped to the side so they were both within Tell's view. "I heard from Dalton that Tell got pissy when he thought you were hittin' up our relatives for sponsorship money? Can you imagine how much it'll eat at him, wondering if you're tryin' to sweet-talk me into makin' an appearance at a rodeo for your PR firm?"

"Why do you want Tell to think that?"

"Because he needs to wake the fuck up. And since what goes around comes around, I'm doin' him a favor. So, darlin', look like you're pouring on the charm."

Georgia slapped on a smile. "Even when I'm ticked off at him?"

"Because he's surrounded by them bunnies?" Chase scoffed. "He ain't hanging around them chicks to make you jealous. It's got something to do with me, which is all kinds of fucked up. Why are you so ticked off at him?"

"Because he left me holding the bag." She told him about Tell backing out of the Pine Haven Rodeo.

"To be honest, I'm shocked. Two years ago, Tell wouldn't let me compete in a PRCA event under another name. He's always doing the right thing."

"Not this time."

"Let's use it against him." Chase mimed signing a document on his hand. "Wanna play a game?"

"What game?"

"Make Tell's head explode." Chase's eyes twinkled. "Come on, it'll be fun. We'll just casually walk out the front door as if we're deep in conversation."

Georgia didn't know what purpose this would serve. This wasn't a sexual flirtation between her and Chase McKay. She'd followed his career and knew the bull rider was happily married.

They stopped in the middle of the parking lot.

"Won't be long now," Chase said.

"What am I supposed to say?"

"The bitchier you are, the more he'll try to get you alone to sweet-talk his way outta the doghouse. But stay firm, Georgia, because he's gotta learn how to do some serious groveling."

"I will never understand men."

Chase laughed. "Now that you've said that...I ain't feelin' manly. It's fuckin' bizarre that I just channeled exactly what my wife would say."

And as Chase had predicted, Tell barreled out, straight toward them. "Just what in the hell is goin' on?"

"I'm talking to Georgia."

"About what?"

"None of your damn business," Georgia snapped.

"The hell it's not. What does she want from you?"

Despite the fact Tell towered over Chase by at least six inches, Chase herded his cousin back. "Are you always so damn suspicious?"

"Of the two of you becoming buddy-buddy? Yes. You're a celebrity, Chase. She's in PR. Do the math."

"I did do the math and came up one judge short for the Pine Haven Rodeo today," Georgia said sweetly. "Ring any bells?"

Tell froze. He blushed. He opened his mouth but no sound came out.

Chase shook his head. "Not cool, cuz. You ain't the type to shirk your responsibilities."

"I'm a PRCA judge. I should've been on the roster for the Upton Rodeo in the first place. Besides, the Pine Haven Rodeo is small-time."

"Them cowgirls and cowboys who paid money to compete in it didn't think it was small-time," Chase said hotly. "Jesus. When did you get to be a rodeo snob, Tell?"

"Don't you talk to me about bein' a snob, Chase."

Chase focused on Georgia. "Who'd you get to fill in as a judge on such short notice?"

"Deck Veldekamp." She felt Tell's angry eyes trying to melt her face.

"So because Tell backed out, you—"

"Had to beg my ex-husband to help me? Yeah." She looked away. "Which was humiliating because Deck knew Tell was the one who cancelled on me at the last minute. Oh, and so did the rodeo committee secretary, so it was an all-around fabulous day."

Tell's learning to grovel curve was short because immediately he was in Georgia's space, forcing her to meet his hangdog gaze. "Shit, Georgia. I'm sorry. So sorry."

She stared at him coolly.

"I never thought... Goddammit. I'm such a fuckin' bastard for doin' that to you."

"I'd guess you're pretty fucked," Chase said cheerfully. "Lyin' to your woman for personal or business reasons is never a good idea. And from where I stood in the bar tonight, you looked awful close to cheatin' on her, too, with some of them horny toads known as bunnies."

"Not. Helping," Tell said through gritted teeth. "Why don't you get the hell out of here before I lose my sense of humor."

"Fine. I'll go. But remember, Georgia. I owe you a good PR turn. Just name it."

"While that's generous, Chase, it's not necessary."

"It is partially my fault Tell wasn't at the Pine Haven Rodeo. I asked Verna to bump one of the judges and requested Tell as a replacement. I had no idea he had other judging duties lined up for today."

Silence.

"Of course the only reason I got the gig was because of you."

Tell's embarrassment softened her temper. Why hadn't she considered it would still bother Tell to be in his cousin's shadow? That if he had the chance to step out of it and into the spotlight, he'd take it?

Georgia wanted to look at the gravel beneath her feet or the streetlight or the stars above—anything but the misery in Tell's eyes. But she forced herself to stay firm.

"So, cowboy, what do you want to apologize for first?"

Georgia was asking him. Like he had a clue. Wasn't like he could ask the self-centered teenage boy he'd reverted to for advice.

Man up. Think.

"Tell?"

He didn't reach for her, as much as he wanted to. "Can we go someplace where I can explain in private?"

Her eyes flashed a warning. "I don't want an explanation, I want an apology."

"I mean give you an apology. Even if it takes all night."

"If by *takes all night*, you're thinking that you and I will get naked and have wild sex—"

"It doesn't. I mean, yes, I wanna have wild sex with you all the fuckin' time." Shit. That hadn't come out right. Tell shoved his hands in his pockets and took a step back. "I swear. I just want to talk."

"We can't go to my house because my mom is staying with me."

Was that part of the reason she'd been so scarce this week? And why hadn't he known? *Because you got your feelings hurt and you've been sulking.* "How about my place?"

"Fine. I'll meet you there."

The short drive would give him time to figure out what the hell to say to her.

He opened the windows in his trailer to let in the cooler night air. He poured two glasses of tea, setting a sugar canister and a spoon beside hers. By the time he'd changed clothes, she was coming up the drive.

His heart beat as loudly as her knocks on the door.

"Hey. Come in."

She kicked off her shoes, making herself at home like she always did. After stirring three spoonfuls of sugar into her tea, she sat in the corner of the couch with her feet tucked under her.

Tell gulped half his tea, wishing it was whiskey, and perched on the coffee table across from her. "First off. I'm sorry for bailing on the Pine Haven Rodeo. It won't happen again."

"Because you're only scheduled for three more rodeos in conjunction with Barb Wyre PR?"

"No. Because it was a shitty thing to do. You deserve better after all you've done for me. I can't apologize enough, Georgia."

"Keep going."

"And if I'd known Chase was pullin' the strings in Upton, I definitely would've been in Pine Haven." He set her tea on the side table and took her hands in his. "I'm sorry you had to call Deck. Was he a prick to you?"

"Not bad, actually."

"Good." Tell rubbed her knuckles on his cheeks. "I missed you this week."

"Same here."

"Really? Didn't seem like it."

A tiny frown line appeared between her eyebrows. "Why would you say that?"

"I didn't see you Monday. You didn't come to Ziggy's Tuesday night."

"But I did ask you to come to my place."

"True. But you stood me up Thursday night."

"You know that wasn't intentional," she said softly.

"Do I? Because I went lookin' for you. And I saw you cozied up in a booth with the movers and shakers in Sundance. Every one of them slick dudes was flirting with you. Made me crazy. I knew if I stuck around, I'd end up in a bar fight with one of them, so I took off."

Her eyes cooled. "If you were there, then you know I wasn't flirting back."

"All my brain saw was those successful guys. And how freakin' beautiful you are. And then I wondered what the hell you're doin' with me. I figured you had the same thought and were finding new people to hang out with as a way of ending it with me." He had to look away. Christ, he'd already said too much.

Georgia's fingers were firm on his chin as she turned his face toward hers. "It was a business meeting over cocktails. Not my idea. And trust me, it wasn't fun. Even though I had to pretend it was."

"So if I would've interrupted your meeting to remind you of our dinner date?"

"I probably would've kissed you. Just like this." Her lips met his in a hard kiss. Then her grip on his chin tightened. "As long as we're on the subject, what was up with you and those rodeo groupies? Were you hanging out with them to make me jealous? As a payback for the jealousy you felt Thursday night?"

Feeling his cheeks heat, he jerked his chin out of her grasp. Then he pushed to his feet, grabbed his tea and retreated to the kitchen. Tempting to pour a slug of Irish in it.

"Tell?"

Her soft voice was directly behind him, but he didn't turn around.

"Talk to me. Please."

He hated to talk about this stuff. He hated acknowledging that he had personal insecurities, so why point them out to others? But for some reason, laying himself bare to Georgia wasn't as unnerving as shutting her out. She might not understand, but the fact she was here meant she cared on some level.

A fact Chase had shoved in his face. His cousin had been lying in wait for him by his pickup, grabbing another chance to chew his ass. Reminding him that one good woman was one in a million, but Tell didn't have to go through a million women to find her.

Sometimes Tell hated that fucking bastard.

Mostly because he knew Chase was right. Tell had found that one woman in Georgia. And he hadn't mustered the guts to let her know how he felt. But maybe showing her that he could talk about his feelings and shit would be the first step.

Tell inhaled a slow breath. "Do you have any idea what it's like to be so deep in someone's shadow you disappear? That's how it is with me when it comes to Chase. He's the star. Here, there and everywhere else. I'm not sayin' he doesn't deserve it. He's always had the talent, the women, the fame, the money, the charm, the good looks. I pale in comparison to him on every level.

"Chase let me tag along to rodeos when I was fifteen or sixteen. Didn't matter if it was because he felt sorry for me because of my family situation, or that I was nowhere near him as far as ridin' skills. I felt cool...until some asshole tossed off a stupid comment about I wouldn't be allowed to hang around with Chase if I wasn't his poor, wannabe, butt-ugly relative. I didn't have the life experience to let it roll off me, so it ate at me."

"I can imagine."

"It wasn't just my cousin's ridin' skills I envied. He always had all these women around him. So the night this older chick was all over me and I thought I was hot shit. I had the moves, right? Come to find out, she was one of Chase's castoff bunnies. She wanted to fuck a McKay, and since Chase was unavailable she made do with me. I never wanted to feel second-best again. But I have. So many times. So today I wanted him to see that I had my own posse. I wasn't that scrawny kid stuck with his seconds."

A gust of wind blew so hard it rattled the screen door.

"Has that been a big life goal of yours? To have your own pussy posse?" Georgia asked without sarcasm.

Tell spun around, ready to deny it, but something in her eyes curbed his intent to lie. "Not my only goal, but a pussy posse was definitely one of them."

"Did you reach it?"

"A long time ago."

"Thank God you crossed that one off your bucket list."

Thank God she wasn't pissed off and throwing things at him. "I'm sorry, Georgia. I was a fuckin' idiot today. Remember when you told me that selling advertising to my relatives had nothin' to do with me personally? This is sorta the same situation. Me flirting with those women had nothin' to do with you personally. And you hafta believe I didn't plan on takin' any of them women up on their offers."

"I believe you. I surprised myself by how much I wanted to challenge them all to a hair-pulling, eye-scratching cat fight."

Nice boost to his ego that she had been jealous. He rested his chin on top of her head. "So are we okay?"

"I guess. Once again we dropped the ball on that adult relationship thing."

"Yeah. Fightin' with you sucks. I hate it. I've never been in a relationship long enough *to* fight."

"Now I feel special."

You are special. So special it scares the crap outta me.

"But I'll point out the weeks we've had fights is when we haven't spent time together."

"A simple solution would be to spend all our free time together."

"Mmm."

"Georgia, darlin', will you stay with me tonight?"

She tipped her head back to look at him. "Yes, but no sex, remember?"

"Are you really gonna hold me to that?" Tell feathered his thumb over the pulse point in her neck. "I haven't touched you all week. It's makin' me crazy. I've been thinkin' about the wild, raunchy, kinky things I wanna do to you."

"Then another night will allow you to add to those fantasies, won't it?"

He groaned. "It might kill me."

Georgia laughed softly. "You'll survive. We'll find something else to keep us occupied."

"Like what?"

"You could teach me how to play poker." She held up her hand. "Not strip poker."

"Spoilsport."

"Or we could watch a movie. Heckle bad TV shows."

"Would that include makin' out on the couch and letting me at least cop a feel?" Tell waggled his eyebrows with such exaggeration she giggled.

"You're such a guy."

"And I can prove it. Three or four times at least." Then he blew in her ear and felt her shiver from head to toe. "Am I changing your mind, sweetness?"

She shook her head. "As much as I love slipping between the sheets with you, I just like being with you. You make me laugh. You're easy to talk to. And you don't treat me like a dumb cheerleader."

"Who the hell ever said that to you?"

"Lots of people. Not just kids at school. I heard someone say it was a good thing I was a pretty girl because I'd never get by on my brains." She smiled sadly. "One time Smitty made that kinda crack around RJ. My brother clocked Smitty so hard he broke Smitty's glasses. So you're not the only one with self-doubts, Tell. As much as I'd like to pretend I overcame it, some of those attitudes and comments have stuck with me."

"Why is it we have a better memory for the bad things that are said?"

She shrugged. "Maybe because it makes us appreciate it more when someone says something nice?"

He smooched her nose. "You're so smart."

The sweet-smelling scent of woman roused him.

Handy that she wasn't wearing panties.

Tell squinted at the clock. Four thirty. He had to start chores in another hour anyway, so he may as well use this time to his advantage.

Georgia slept on her side, curled into a ball.

He slipped his fingers beneath the hem of the T-shirt she'd borrowed, finding her warm, soft skin. When his hands began the thorough ascent of her spine, her back bowed and she made a humming sound. A sound which traveled straight to his dick.

"Georgia," he whispered, breathing in the heady scent of her hair.

"Mmm?"

"It's morning. Do you know what that means?"

"We went to bed too late?" she murmured sleepily.

"No." His mouth found the shell of her ear and he followed it with his tongue. "It means I can make love to you since night is over."

She half-rolled into him, tangling their legs and rubbing her smooth, muscular calf over his. "But I'm tired."

"I'll wake you up." He kissed the corners of her eyes. Her temples. The edges of her smile. "I want you like this. Warm and sweet and barely awake in my bed."

"M'kay." She rose up enough to ditch the shirt. "You always have such great ideas." Then she rolled onto her back, keeping her arms above her head and her eyes closed.

Tell nuzzled the outside curves of her tits, inhaling the fragrance of her skin first thing in the morning. The underswell tasted tangy—of her sweat and sleep. He sucked a tiny love bruise on the upper curve, then he focused his attention on her nipples. Sucking. Licking. Biting. Pinching. Pleasing himself with her body and turning her into a squirmy, sighing mass.

His fingers trailed over her slit, finding her core hot and wet. He swirled those digits into the sweet cream.

"Someone's awake now," he murmured and tapped her hip. "Turn over."

"Someone likes to take me from behind," she murmured back as she rolled onto her belly.

He made a place between her legs and hiked up her hips. His hands roamed over her arms, her strong back, her hips and her ass. Goddamn she had the finest ass. He scattered kisses down her torso. Tracking the line of her spine from her shoulders down, pressing openmouthed kisses in the dimples of her ass. He rubbed his morning whiskers on her cheeks, then traced the crack to her tailbone, loving the hitch in her breath when his tongue dipped down to circle her anus.

Then he caged her body beneath his and aligned his cock. His need to rut on her nearly overtook him as he slid home. But he paused just to breathe, just to absorb this perfect union of bodies as he made love to her. Savoring her every moan. Savoring every connection of his hard flesh into the softness of hers.

All at once he ramped up the tempo. Pounding into her. Going primal at the visual of his big, rough hands gripping her ass cheeks. His rigid cock disappearing into her wet and welcoming cunt.

Georgia pushed her hips back, taking every slamming thrust.

He could go for hours in the morning, so a quick rise to orgasm caught him off guard. He released a soft snarl as jets of hot come shot out of his dick. White spots, black dots all danced behind his eyelids, and he kept up the rapid rhythm until he felt dizzy and realized he'd been holding his breath.

That's when he also realized he hadn't worn a condom.

Falling onto his hands, he sucked in air and didn't bother to try and stay the trembling in his limbs. "Dammit, Georgia, I'm sorry. I forgot a condom."

"It's okay. I'm on the pill, so we're protected."

"Thank God."

He pushed back to his knees and gently rolled her over, knowing she hadn't come yet. Running his palms up the outside of her legs, he stopped to span the sexy curve of her hips. Then he moved his hands up her belly, molding her compact ribcage, squeezing those plump tits and cupping her slim shoulders. "So perfectly beautiful. Everywhere."

"I'm not dreaming?"

247

"No. But bein' able to touch you like this, anytime I want? Is a dream come true for me."

Georgia wreathed her arms around his neck. "Are you always such a sweet talker at the butt crack of dawn?"

"I could learn to be. If we did this every morning to start the day out right." He shoved his cock in deep on the first stroke.

"Yes." She arched. "I love that you're still hard. Even after you come."

"You do it to me. I can't get enough of you."

"Good. Because I'm so close. Don't slow down." She moaned when he angled his pelvis, brushing over her clit.

Tell buried his face in her throat. "It's there, baby. I can feel your pussy tightening around my cock." He panted as he rammed into her hard, bottoming out with each thrust. "Take it."

Georgia's body arched so much he could only see the tip of her chin as she unraveled. Her nails were digging into his ass so deeply he knew he'd bear gouges on his butt cheeks.

That's when he fused his mouth to hers and lost himself in the taste of her kiss. That's when Tell knew he'd do anything to keep her.

Chapter Twenty-Four

Hello, walk of shame.

With her mother in the house.

But worth it. *So* worth it.

Georgia tiptoed up the stairs, noticing the door to the guest bedroom was closed. She stripped and crawled between the sheets, drifting to sleep with a smile on her face.

She woke up three hours later and brewed a pot of coffee to chase away her lethargy. Tempting to laze in the sun like a contented cat today. But since she hadn't spent time with her mother yesterday, she wanted to do something fun today.

Fun. Tell McKay was definitely rubbing off on her.

As she crossed the foyer to get the newspaper, she heard a loud thump in the guest bedroom. She glanced at the clock. Strange that her early-bird mother wasn't up at nine o'clock. Maybe she was sick.

Georgia scaled the stairs, pausing outside the door. She heard more thumps. "Mom? Are you all right?" She opened the door and froze upon seeing her father's bare back and naked butt bouncing as he nailed her mother from behind.

"Omigod! What are you doing?" As if it wasn't obvious.

Her mother shrieked and her parents collapsed on the bed, her father valiantly yanking the covers over them.

That was the last thing Georgia had ever expected to see. Or wanted to see, quite frankly.

"Georgia, it's—"

"None of my business and I'm..." *Running like hell.* She slammed the door, racing downstairs and outside.

The sky was blue, the grass was green, the sun was yellow. Nope, she hadn't somehow wandered into another dimension.

Good. God. She'd walked in on her parents having sex. Her divorced parents. Robert and Irina Hotchkiss hated each other. Didn't they?

There'd be hell to pay if she lost her deposit because her amorous *parents*—for the love of God—had put dents in the Sheetrock from the headboard banging into the wall.

How long had this been going on? And what did it mean?

Georgia had no idea how long she sat curled up in the swing, random thoughts bouncing in her head. She jumped when the screen door creaked.

"Georgia?"

"There's coffee in the kitchen."

"Look, about what you—"

She held up her hand. "I don't ever wanna talk about it. Ever. Or think about it. Ever. I'm sorta hoping the sun will fry my retinas and burn out the images no child should ever see."

"You're being ridiculous," her mother chided. "It's not the first time your father and I have had sex since we divorced."

"Omigod, Mom. I don't need to know that!"

"What? That I still like sex? Or that I still like sex with Robert—"

"Stop talking! Stop talking right now." Georgia stuck her fingers in her ears and said, "La la la I can't hear you," just in case her mother kept blathering on.

There was some maturity.

That sent her mother stomping off, and she slammed the back door.

That wasn't exactly mature either.

She should've stayed with Tell until he finished chores. Then she wouldn't have known her parents were some sort of fuck buddies.

Fuck buddies.

Her parents.

She'd laugh if she didn't feel like crying, yelling and hiding—all at the same time.

"Are you done with your snit?" her mother asked with that imperious Russian inflection.

"Maybe."

Metal scraped across the cement and her mother parked herself in front of the swing so Georgia couldn't escape. "I'm sorry you walked in on us."

"Not as sorry as I am," she muttered.

"For heaven's sake, you're a little old to be traumatized by this! Especially since chances are high you and Tell McKay were doing the exact same thing last night."

Do not blush. "But you didn't have to see it, did you? And what am I supposed to think? Are you and Dad getting back together?"

Her mother looked shocked by the question.

Or was that guilt because she was just using her ex-husband for sex?

"The truth is I don't know what happens next. Robert and I...have issues. Too many, it seems. And then when I see him again, it's like those issues disappear."

Good Lord. Was she talking about...lust?

"That's why when I left him I had to move far away. Because when we're in those intimate moments, everything else fades into the background. Then reality sets in and I..."

"Do you still love him?"

Her mother's eyes met hers. "I never stopped loving him, *moyah doch.* I just couldn't live with him anymore."

Georgia felt the shock of that statement clear to the marrow of her bones. "I didn't know. Neither of you..."

"Things that happen privately between a husband and wife aren't meant to be shared. Especially not with children." She shoved a hand through her hair. "Robert and I were both so raw and angry after RJ died. He wanted a fresh start. I was too mired in grief to question him. When I woke up out of that fog, he and I immediately started playing the blame game."

"About RJ dying?"

"No, about you. I hadn't realized how much you'd pulled away from everyone. Robert blamed me for that. I blamed him for making us move to a hog farm."

"But I didn't pull away from anyone. I tried to be the glue that held everyone together. You and Dad. Me and Deck."

She shook her head. "You were a mess. Such a mess that you don't remember it. Sweetie, you're still a mess. You don't let anyone get close to you."

Her mouth opened to deny it but she honestly couldn't. So she deflected. "Are you saying the fact my husband was banging another girl is somehow...my fault?"

"Good God, no. We shoulder a lot of the blame in accepting Deck into our family. We thought he made you happy. And he wanted to marry you...you never said otherwise."

Her parents hadn't seen anything wrong with encouraging her to get married right out of high school. Early marriage was the norm for women in her family. Her mother had married at nineteen. Both her grandmothers had been married off by age seventeen. And she and Deck weren't the only couple from their class to exchange *I do*s the summer after graduation.

"I can't undo any of those past mistakes, Georgia."

That sense of surrealness washed over her again. They'd never talked about any of this.

"Then after RJ died, your father relied heavily on Deck because he couldn't count on me. Robert lost his faith and I'd always used his unwavering belief in God to bolster mine. Without his convictions...I had none. So we both lost our way. We're slowly but surely finding it again."

"Are you finding your way back to each other?"

She shrugged. "Perhaps. But regardless what happens, I believe it's time you mend fences with your father." She held up her hand. "And no, he didn't put me up to this."

"I don't know where to start."

"Ironically enough, neither does he." She frowned. "But he has mentioned making an effort, not that I know what that means."

"We had lunch together."

"That's it? Robert made it sound much more involved than that."

Georgia didn't need to point out her father's grandiose schemes to her mother. "Well, if I see Dad, I'll make the effort too. For as long as I'm in the area."

"Is it all right if I let him know that?"

"Sure." She stretched out on the porch swing. "So what do you wanna do today? It's not supposed to be too hot. We could hike the long trail around Devil's Tower. Or maybe head to Spearfish Canyon to see Roughlock Falls."

"Ah. Well. I promised Robert I'd help clean out the house. I left things there and he doesn't know what to do with them now that the place has been sold."

Her mom was ditching her? For her dad? Unbelievable.

"I hope you're not mad."

"No. That's fine. I tentatively had plans with Tell anyway."

"You haven't said too much about him." Her mother sipped her coffee. "Makes me think there's more to this thing with him."

"It doesn't matter because I'm not sticking around. I have a life in Dallas."

"Hmm."

She hated it when her mom said *hmm.* "What?"

"I don't think you're being honest with yourself. It feels to me like you came back to Sundance because you've got unfinished business here."

"My boss didn't give me a choice. I certainly wouldn't have chosen to return."

"But now that you've been here awhile, has that attitude changed?"

Yes. And I don't know what to do about it.

Her mother laughed. "You and RJ both had that look. When I see that stubborn tilt to your chin, I know the subject is closed." She stood. "I have to meet your father and I don't know how long this will take. So, umm...don't wait up."

Georgia waited a whole hour before she called Tell.

"Hey, sweetness, what's up?"

"You know how you're always surprising me with spur-of-the-moment fun? Today is your lucky day, cowboy, because I'm returning the favor."

"That right? And what fun stuff can I look forward to?"

"Me in a bikini. Wear your sexy board shorts and bring a towel."

When Tell didn't immediately respond, she worried she'd taken it for granted he'd have Sunday afternoon free. "Look. If you don't want to—"

"Don't get your panties in a twist. It's not that. I'm more surprised than anything." His voice dropped to a deep rasp. "And I'm feelin' a little cocky that you're takin' the lead. Admit it, hot lips, you like that I've helped you unleash your fun side."

She pressed her forehead against the closet door. "I appreciate it more than you can possibly know."

"How soon do I need to be ready?"

"Half an hour."

Tell's rough-tipped index finger trailed up the inside of her arm, sending ripples of gooseflesh from her wrist to her shoulder. "Come on. Please."

"No."

"But you're always up for trying something new."

Don't blush.

"Think about it. You're breathing hard. Sweating from the effort. And when you're in the moment, feeling weightless and boneless, you never want it to end."

Georgia gave him a droll stare. The man made everything sound like sex.

"I see them wheels churning, Georgia. You want to. You *know* you want to." He rubbed his mouth across her knuckles. "Please say yes."

"Explain something to me."

"Anything, baby."

"Why does a grown man have a gigantic trampoline?"

Tell shrugged. "I got it for Landon. He loves the damn thing."

"Sure. You got it for *Landon*. Like you got the zip line for *Landon.*"

When he offered that completely sheepish, totally charming grin, she melted. "Busted. I always wanted one when I was a kid and Dad never let us have one. So I'm makin' up for lost childhood opportunities."

"That's sad." She frowned. "What else did your father deny you?"

"Visits from Santa."

"No. Really?"

"Uh-huh. No Easter Bunny, Tooth Fairy or the Great Pumpkin either."

"Poor baby." Joking aside, it caused a dull ache to imagine a young Tell, missing out on some of the best aspects of being a kid. That sense of wonder. And the possibility that magic existed. Her parents had given her that.

"The weird thing? We had dirt bikes. Guess Pop didn't care if we broke a bone or cracked open our skulls bein' reckless boys, but stockings filled with candy and toys were dangerous." He smiled but it didn't quite reach his eyes.

"My dad was furious when I made the cheerleading squad. He said it was too dangerous being tossed up in the air. But he had no problem with RJ getting on the back of a bull or a buckin' horse."

"That sucks. But on the bright side for me, my dad was an equal opportunity hater. No one got special treatment—we all just got bad treatment."

As soon as Tell said that, she knew he regretted his honesty. He tried so damn hard to be the happy-go-lucky guy. If she kept thinking about the sweet little boy who'd never gotten a visit from Santa, she might start weeping. So she offered up her own recent parental issues.

"So in the rush to see your half-naked, totally-buff body glistening in the sun, I forgot to share what I saw this morning after I got home."

Tell kissed her fingertips. "If I didn't say it, I had an awesome time with you at the waterslide park. Damn near perfect day—you prancing around in a tiny bikini. Me getting to slather sunscreen all over this creamy skin." He grinned. "I still can't believe you went down the Turbo-Slam. Twice."

"I almost lost my bikini bottoms on that butt buster," she muttered. It had been a great afternoon. Tackling the various slides. Racing him to the bottom. Spinning down the white water "river" in inner tubes. Swimming with Tell was an experience in itself. His hot, wet, muscular body sliding against hers. Being weightless in his arms. Kissing him underwater.

"Earth to Georgia," he said silkily.

"Sorry. Just flashing back to some of today's high points." She smiled. "Anyway, I heard strange noises in the guest bedroom. When I went upstairs to check, I caught my mom and dad banging the holy hell out of each other."

"Are you kidding me?"

"Nope. I asked if they were getting back together and she couldn't answer. But she had no problem admitting she still loves my dad. And evidently she still loves having sex with him."

He rubbed soothing circles on the base of her thumb. "Are you freaked?"

"A little. She said some other things about the time after RJ died that caused me to wonder if I didn't see things clearly because I was in shock. Not Deck stuff, but family stuff."

"So you needed a dose of fun today."

She shook her head. "I needed a dose of you today."

"Anytime." Tell placed a gentle kiss on her lips. His eyes were all soft and she felt that melting sensation again.

"Do you ever wonder what it'd be like if your parents got back together?"

"Ain't happening. My folks hate each other. Even when things were shitty at home, they never said the kind of mean crap to each other that they let fly in public now. My mom went through a major transformation and she's happier, but she's also very self-involved. I understand why she's that way, since she did everything for everyone else for so many years and little for herself. But she's not the same person. Makes me sound like a bratty kid, but sometimes I miss the mom I used to have."

"I know what you mean." Georgia's mother had gone from a reserved Christian homemaker who deferred to her husband in all things to a Russian interpreter with the INS and a vocal supporter of MADD.

"I figured you of all people would." He tugged on the bikini string hanging around her neck. "Do you know how much I love bein' able to talk to you? About anything? You never tell me to grow up or chill out."

Georgia's stomach flipped at Tell's admission, and it scared her too because she was starting to rely on him. She'd sworn she would never be that type of woman again, even when her subconscious reminded her she'd never relied on Deck. It hadn't been love for either of them; it'd been a marriage based on convenience and family expectations. She steered the conversation back to where they'd started. "So do you think all our familial issues could've been avoided if we'd had a trampoline?"

"Possibly. After seein' your mom and dad doin' the nasty, there's all the more reason for you to go crazy and bounce that image right out of your head."

"How often do you jump on it?"

"All the damn time." He grinned. "Especially if I've had a shit day. Hard to be in a pissy mood after bouncing around in the air for a while. So whaddya say? Hop on up. Show me some of them cheerleading jumps."

"If I pull something, you'd better be willing to rub out any kinks."

Tell's blue eyes went from flirty to fiery. "Oh, darlin', I can get all the kinks worked outta you and then some."

Her heart rate spiked when he lifted her arm to his mouth and kissed the sensitive skin of her inner forearm. Tell kept his panty-melting gaze on hers as he licked the bend in her elbow. Just the tip of his tongue tracing the crease of her elbow like he was tasting her slit and Georgia felt the answering pull in her sex.

"I wanna see you."

See me what? Come unglued from you licking my damn elbow? Sure. I'm already there. "See me what?"

"Letting go." Tell angled forward, dragging his mouth down the side of her neck. "You taste good. Like sweat, sun, suntan oil and chlorine. And wait... Do I detect the taste of...*fear*?"

She shoved him. "Not funny. I'm not scared. I have been on a trampoline many times."

"Trust me. I know. But I ain't gonna believe you're not scared until you hop on up there and show me some hot moves, hot lips."

After expelling a heavy sigh, Georgia crawled onto the springy surface. The sides of the trampoline were enclosed with flexible posts and netting to keep bouncers from flying out.

Tell hung on the outside of the net, a silly grin on his handsome face.

Her heart skipped a beat. *Heading into dangerous territory, Georgia.* This was starting to feel like more than just a summer fling.

Wow. You're just figuring that out now?

The black material was taut and warm beneath her bare feet. She'd bounce a couple of times to get her bearings. Perform a few basic jumps and call it a day. But once she started jumping, she wanted to keep jumping. Seeing how much more air she could catch. Using each landing to propel her higher. Testing her limits.

She threw her arms up like she was diving into the sky. Then she threw her arms out into a T. She bounced and spun a circle in the air. She bounced and landed on her knees, quickly twisting her body before the next bounce so she landed cross-legged. Performing that move faster and faster so she looked like a Cossack.

Tell watched her, his fingers threaded through the mesh barrier.

As Georgia bounced and twirled, she felt light as a feather. Carefree. Happy. Especially when she looked at Tell, knowing if he hadn't pushed her, she'd still be sitting at the table, yammering on about family problems she had zero control over.

"Show me some cheerleader jumps."

"What kind?" she asked, breathing hard.

"My favorite was those splits in the air."

"Yeah? Like this?" Georgia bounced twice, extending her arms and her heels simultaneously.

Tell whooped. "Goddamn. That was perfect! Do it again."

Grinning, Georgia bounced harder and caught more air as she stretched herself out like a starfish.

With Tell egging her on, she performed a couple herkies, pikes, figure nines and back flips, ending with a backscratcher and a reverse twist.

Feeling lightheaded and giddy but amazingly juiced up, she slowed the bounces and crawled on her knees to where Tell stood. On impulse, she kissed him through the netting. The only places they touched were mouths and fingertips. Erotic and somehow intimate.

But he broke the kiss far too soon. He rested his forehead against hers. "Will you do something for me?"

"What?"

Then his fingers were on her chin, forcing her to look at him. "Take off your bikini."

"Right here? Why?"

"Because I have another fantasy involving you."

"Which is?"

"Very adolescent." There was his sheepish grin again. "But I've always been a simple guy."

"So tell me this simple adolescent fantasy."

"You. Jumping on a trampoline. Nekkid."

It took a beat for that to sink in. "Omigod. You cannot be serious."

His dimples winked when that bad-boy grin emerged. "I'm totally serious."

"But...why?"

"It's fuckin' sexy as hell. Seeing all those nekkid girl parts bouncing. Makes me crazy to think of seein' every bit of your sweet pink pussy when you do a split jump."

She was pretty sure her eyes bugged out of her head.

He laughed. "Shocked?"

"Yes. My God. How long have you been thinking about this?"

"For. Ever. Since the first time I saw you in that itty-bitty cheerleading skirt getting thrown in the air, givin' everyone in the stands a glimpse of your sweet little ass cheeks. I jacked off to that image more times than I can count." He actually growled. "So yeah, I've been dreamin' about this a long damn time."

"So you've been out here in the buff on your trampoline with your dangly male bits bouncing?"

"Hell no." He smirked. "I could hurt myself. Bruising my chest when my hard-on bounced against it."

She snickered. "Your *chest*? Cocky much?"

"Haven't heard you complaining much about me bein' cocky." Tell just grinned. "Look, Georgia, darlin', I wasn't gonna ask you."

"Why? Because you know it's a ridiculous request?"

"No. Because I knew you'd say no."

Her eyes narrowed on him. This was one sneaky-ass man.

"What?" he said with such an angelic expression she had to laugh.

"Oh, don't try and pull that innocent look, McKay."

"What?" he said again. "*You're* the one who said you're not very adventurous."

"I'm not."

"So? I've made my case and my point. You won't do it."

Do not fall for this. Do not.

She poked his chest. "You know what, cowboy? I'm about to get daring. Very daring. Like Criss Angel kind of daring."

"That right?"

"Yep." She shimmied her swimsuit bottoms off and threw them at him. "But...if you want me to strip the rest of the way, you've gotta do something for me."

"Name it."

Georgia cocked her head and focused on his crotch. "I wanna see you whacking off like you did *more times than you can count* when you were thinking about me bouncing on a trampoline."

Tell's cheeks turned pink. "Funny, Georgia."

"I'm not kidding. If you want me to jump nekkid, then you will be stroking yourself while you watch me."

Ten whole seconds passed until Tell yanked down his board shorts. "Take off the top."

She untied the swimsuit top, spun it around her finger and tossed it at him. The hook caught on the netting.

Tell wrapped his hand around his girth and started to stroke slowly.

She fell onto her back and bounced a couple times before spreading her legs as she moved her pelvis up, directly in line with Tell's eyes.

"Oh yeah. Sweet Georgia has left the building. Bring on Bad Georgia." He whistled a few bars from "The Strip" and she laughed.

Put on a good show. Make him drool. Make him shoot. Make him yours forever.

Tell's left hand was curled into the mesh; his right hand firmly jacked his cock. His eyes were that deep blue as he stared at her from beneath lowered lashes. His lips were parted, releasing broken breaths.

Rolling to her feet, Georgia began to jump. Her boobs jiggled and immediately her nipples hardened.

And his focus zoomed to her chest.

Imagine that.

After a few high jumps, she spun around. Letting him watch her ass shake.

He groaned behind her.

She performed a frog leap around the perimeter of the trampoline. Then she did a few twists and faced him again.

Bouncety-bouncety.

That hand started moving faster after her first straddle-split jump. She did jumping toe touches. Pikes. More straddle splits.

Her wiggle, jiggle, flounce and bounce routine really got to him because he let go of his dick and croaked, "Stop. Goddammit, stop, I can't take any more." Then both his hands were white-knuckling the netting.

When Georgia dropped to her knees to catch her breath, her body started to stiffen up in places. She'd be sore tomorrow. Really sore in more places than her little-used gymnastics muscles if she had her way.

She crawled across the trampoline, but Tell didn't open his eyes. But his gaze did snap to hers when she licked his fingers through the mesh. "So? Did this live up to your fantasy?"

He shook his head.

A tiny spark of fear began to burn.

Then his fingertip was tracing her lip. "This is a million times better."

His words stirred the bad girl into action. She sucked his thumb into her mouth, swirling her tongue around it. Moaning that she could taste his musky essence lingering there.

He groaned, "Fuck. Me."

The digit slid out with a wet pop. "Good plan." Georgia rolled herself up, letting her nipples poke through the mesh.

When Tell tried to capture one, she pulled back and laughed seductively. "You can have me any way you want me, McKay, but you've gotta catch me first."

Tell scrambled over the edge of the trampoline like a primate scaling a banana tree.

God he was amazing. All focused, aroused male.

He yanked his shirt over his head so they were both naked. Wild. Circling each other like wrestlers in the ring.

Then Tell said, "Fuck this," and launched himself at her, taking the brunt of their bounce on his back as he knocked her off her feet.

She shrieked and he spun her facedown, resting on his haunches as he hiked up her hips.

"I caught you." He slid her knees out, making a place for himself behind her. He spread her thighs and impaled her to the root on the first deep stroke. "And you're all mine now. Say it."

"I'm all yours." Georgia pushed back to meet his thrusts. Losing her balance when they bounced together, but it felt too good to stop. He'd find the rhythm; he always did.

He pulled out and she whimpered. He sat back, legs out in front of him, and brought her on top of his lap. "That ain't workin'. You drive."

She took his hard length in her hand, aligned it to her core and dropped her hips until he filled her completely.

Tell groaned against her chest, his mouth following the damp curve of her breast to her nipple.

Georgia threw her head back and dug her nails into his shoulders. Trying to find the right tempo of when to lift and lower. Every time she tried to bring that thickness in deeper, they'd bounce—not in a productive way, but in a way that sent them off-kilter. Tell tried to balance them by keeping his hands on the trampoline behind him, but between the suntan oil, the sweat and the bouncing, they slid sideways whenever she moved.

He winced and said, "Stop."

"What's wrong?"

"This is pinching my balls."

"Oh. Sorry." She carefully scrambled off him.

Tell reached between his thighs and readjusted himself.

She was sweaty, frustrated and she needed a goddamn orgasm. Now. Maybe they should just go in the house.

Georgia looked up to see Tell stalking her on all fours, planting random kisses on her quivering flesh as he positioned his body over hers.

The heat in his eyes made her mouth dry.

He scooped her up, clutching her butt cheeks in his hands and said, "Wrap your legs around my waist."

As soon as she did, he slid her onto his straining dick in one sure and sexy move.

Yes. She glanced down, his knees splayed wide, his flat belly rubbing against hers with every roll of his hips as his shaft disappeared inside her.

He murmured, "Goddamn you feel good on me."

She surrendered to the sensations of hot, sweaty, intense sex. Feeling those big hands of his squeezing her ass as he helped her ride his cock. Feeling his mouth attacking her throat as their slick bodies glided in opposition.

When their joined bodies bounced, it drove him deeper inside. Every. Time. And she cried out every time. Despite the heat of his body and the rays of sun beating down, her entire body was a mass of goose bumps.

So close. The tightening sensation started in her tailbone and radiated upward.

"You're there, baby. Take me with you."

And when Tell gently bit on her earlobe, she lost it.

The orgasm hit her with the force of a hurricane; no storm warning, it just swamped her. Wave after wave of pleasure crashed over her, making it hard to breathe, to think, to hold on as the power of it inundated her.

The roaring in her ears stopped. Her body quit vibrating from the last storm surge and she slumped against Tell. Sated. And sleepy. The climax flattened her completely.

Then Tell's hands were holding her face. His sweet, hot mouth was on hers, kissing her with that perfect mix of reverence and gratitude.

"Holy fuck," he whispered against her lips. "Did you get the name of the coal train that hit us?"

She snickered. "No, but at one point I'm pretty sure I heard circus music."

"Damn, woman. Once you started to come, you kept coming, and I was toast." He placed soft kisses on wherever his lips could land. "So fuckin' hot."

"I think you broke me. I'm pretty sure I have trampoline burns on my knees and elbows."

"At least you don't have them on your balls," he muttered.

Georgia thrust her hands into his hair, tilting his head back to gaze into his eyes. "Buck up, cowboy. The trampoline was your idea."

"You really think I'm gonna complain about a sex injury that I got after fucking on a trampoline?" He grinned and punctuated each word with a kiss. "Not. On. Your. Life. Baby."

"You're such a guy."

"And I just proved it." He swatted her ass. "Come on. Let's go in and get cleaned up."

Although the suntan oil and sweat was scrubbed clean from her body, Georgia wasn't anxious to leave the enclosed shower. Hot water, hot man, after hot sex—what more could she want?

"God. Your skin is amazing. I could spend all day just touchin' it. So soft. So perfect." Tell's finger followed the arch of her spine from the middle of her back, down the crack of her ass.

She didn't move.

Those hypnotic blue eyes never left hers. The shower pelted her shoulders, spraying fine water particles on his face. The misty droplets caught on the dark hair on his cheeks and on his long eyelashes. In that moment, with his intense gaze, he was the most breathtaking man she'd ever seen.

Oh, he was dangerous. She'd do anything he wanted, be anything he desired, if only he'd look at her like that forever.

But you're leaving, remember?

She didn't want to think about it now. Not when Tell was setting her blood on fire with the heat in his eyes and turning her world upside down with the addictive power of his touch.

His finger stopped on her anus. He insistently stroked the pucker. Pressing a little harder, inserting just a fingertip inside, continuing to gently swirl against the clenched muscle.

She couldn't look away even when her cheeks turned bright red. No man had ever breached that part of her.

"Ever been fucked here?"

"No."

Tell made a soft snarl. "This is mine. If you hadn't noticed, I ain't a patient man when it comes to what I want from you. And I want everything."

Georgia lost the ability to breathe.

"You will give it to me, won't you?"

She nodded.

"I want it now." He angled the shower spray so it hit the floor. Then he reached for a small tube, cracked it open and coated his fingers.

"You keep lube in your shower?"

"Yep. I like to jack off in here."

Her heart raced when he lowered his head.

He allowed two soft brushes of his lips over hers and whispered, "Relax." Then he plunged his tongue into her mouth as he slipped his finger into her ass.

That felt weird. Not bad, just not normal. She kissed him as that slippery digit moved in and out, her body tensed with anticipation and a little fear.

His mouth slid to her chin and he scattered kisses up the line of her jaw, dipping down to suck on the spot on her neck that made her crazy. Dizzy. Mad with want.

Those warm, full lips feathered across her ear. "Come like this. Touch your clit."

Reaching between her legs, she reveled in the eroticism of Tell's hand already there. She placed her hand on his, feeling him slide his finger deep into her anal passage.

"Fuckin' hot as hell, Georgia. Give me more."

She let her fingertip pass over the strip of skin separating the two openings. She wiggled her middle finger into her pussy, coating it with her juices and dragging her fingertip to the swollen flesh.

"When I fuck your ass this first time? I'm gonna take you from behind. That way I can pull your hair and bite the back of your neck because I know that drives you wild."

God, it turned her on when he whispered such raunchy things. Soft moans began to drift from her mouth as she fingered her clit and Tell worked another finger into her ass. Stretching her. Building another level of anticipation to the point she began to shake.

When she realized the head of his cock was rubbing on the inside of her arm, she moved her arm faster, increasing the friction for both of them.

Tell snared her mouth in a blistering kiss.

Georgia lost herself in this moment. Touching. Tasting. Absorbing the new sensation. Feeling hot, wet flesh sliding together. Hearing harsh breathing and the patter of water droplets against the glass shower door.

Her finger flicked her clit rapidly until the tingling energy gathered momentum at the base of her spine.

Tell ripped his mouth free and rasped, "Eyes on mine as you come."

That demand tipped her over the edge.

She moaned his name as the pulsations overtook everything. Her ass clenched around his finger. Her pussy spasmed and her clit pulsed. She gasped with each throb of pleasure, watching satisfaction flare in Tell's eyes.

Then his fingers were gone and he ground out, "Turn around."

Her heart still crashed against her chest as she braced herself.

He spread her ass cheeks and the thick cockhead slipped over her anus. Back and forth until she had the burning need for more contact.

"Tell."

"Relax and let me in, sweetness. It'll feel amazing. I promise."

She nodded. One, two, three prods. On the fourth stab, the tip breached that resistant ring.

"Breathe, baby. I'm gonna go slow." Then his mouth was skimming her shoulder as he eased in, inch by inch.

Her ass burned. But an odd sort of burning that wasn't painful, just constant.

"So tight. Goddamn. It's like having my dick in hot velvet. You okay?"

"Mmm."

"I'm gonna move now."

He withdrew, not fully, and pushed back in. Slowly. Carefully. Methodically.

Tell was the mindful lover, even when she felt his shaking and his need to unleash the power of his body on hers. The burning had faded and again, Georgia had that unnamed need for more.

"Tell?"

"Yes?"

"Fuck me. Like you want. Remember when you said you wouldn't have to worry about breaking me when you fuck me hard? Do it now."

A warning growl was all she got before his hand was fisted in her hair, pulling her head to the side so his mouth could latch onto her neck.

That's when he withdrew past the tight muscle and slammed back in.

Goose bumps erupted as he fucked her. Pausing at her sphincter, rimming it before pushing his thick shaft into her bowels. The bite of pain in her scalp matched the bite of pain in her ass and she liked it; she liked letting go.

His hips pistoned faster. Harder. Drilling into her anal passage with every deep plunge He released a hoarse shout and wet warmth bathed her swollen tissues. He pumped and pumped until he had nothing left. Until he was panting. Until he muttered nonsense into her hair. He cranked her head around and took her mouth in a brutal kiss. A kiss that was the perfect end to this dark pleasure.

His spent cock retreated and he turned the water spray on them, although it was nearly ice cold.

Georgia faced him, curling her hand around his nape, resting her damp forehead on his chest. Letting his body hold hers up because she felt as solid as a noodle.

Then those rough hands swept up her back, making her shiver anew.

"Had enough water games for today?"

"Uh-huh."

She didn't move much as Tell tended to her. Lifting her out of the shower. Toweling off every inch of her body. Spreading her out on his rumpled sheets.

He kissed her with pure sensuality. Soft, wet and slow. "Don't think for a second you're not adventurous. That you're anything less than fuckin' perfect."

And that's when she fell in love with him.

Chapter Twenty-Five

Georgia Hotchkiss was his girlfriend.

For real.

He grinned at himself in the mirror as he shaved, repeating the phrase out loud. "Georgia Hotchkiss is my girlfriend."

And if that didn't beat all.

They'd been damn near inseparable over the last three weeks. Georgia's job responsibilities had tapered off, leaving her with free time. Time she preferred to spend with him. If she stayed overnight, she'd get up at dawn to help him with chores. Then they'd have the rest of the day together.

She loved exploring the ranch on the back of his ATV. He'd always figured she was a girly girl, but she didn't mind getting dirty.

He'd taught her how to ride a dirt bike, but his heart had almost stopped when she'd wiped out and skidded across the ground. By the time Tell had removed her helmet and protective gear, she'd regained her breath. She batted at his hands when he insisted on checking for broken bones and bruises. The damn stubborn woman had climbed back on the bike, determined to make the tight corner. Which she did.

Georgia had been so pumped full of adrenaline, she'd fucked him like a wild cat on the hood of his truck. And that'd been a sight to behold—her beautiful skin glowing as the sun's last rays kissed her damp flesh. Her lips open as she cried out in passion. Her nails digging into his forearms as he made love to the woman who'd captured his interest like no other. A woman he'd started to need like a drug. She was a painkiller, a mood enhancer, an aphrodisiac all wrapped up in one tiny, potent package.

If Tell really thought about it, he might consider that feeling was love. But never having been in love before, he wasn't sure.

He scraped another layer of whiskers from his face. Georgia's skin was so delicate he had to shave twice a day or he'd leave beard burn on her skin. He flashed back to the day last week she'd forbidden him to shave because she wanted to see those marks on the inside of her thighs and her breasts.

She'd been awful damn squirmy at dart league that night. But knocking back shots with Roxanne and Leah dulled the discomfort, because he'd looked over to see her performing a herkie off the end of the bar.

Little Miss Georgia had gotten her butt paddled good for that one.

And she'd loved every minute of it.

Steam fogged up the bathroom mirror and he swiped it clean. Just thinking about her raised his temperature. Sex with Georgia? Beyond spectacular. More exciting, spontaneous, comforting, fun and hot than he'd ever dreamed it could be with one woman. But as much as he lived to get that sexy woman nekkid, the times they spent out of bed were beyond ordinary too. He'd never imagined she'd be so insightful. She didn't expect him to always slap on a happy face. If he had a shit day, he didn't have to hide it. But his shit days were few and far between recently. And he credited her for that.

She fit in with his friends. Being part of a couple bridged a gap he hadn't known existed. Almost like his buddies took him more seriously since he'd settled into a steady relationship. Which was ironic, since he found himself wanting to stay home with her more than going out on the town. Over the years he'd secretly sneered at his cousins and married buddies and their seemingly limited amount of free time. But now he understood why the guys wanted to stay home with their wives.

Even Brandt and Jessie encouraged Tell to bring Georgia over for supper. Her bout of shyness vanished when she held baby Tucker, and she and Jessie chatted like old friends. Tell was fascinated by how babies pulled women together. When he started to imagine a black-haired little boy with Georgia's pale-blue eyes and his smile, he figured Dalton would whap him in the head for thinking like a girl.

He turned the taps on and sluiced away the shaving cream. As he patted his face dry, he tried to remember how he'd agreed to help chaperone the dance put on by the Sundance High School Booster Club. Right. Georgia. After assisting him with rodeo club fundraisers and helping the cheerleaders, she'd had the great idea to bring together all the school clubs for one fun event. Everyone was excited and Georgia was creating positive buzz.

The only sour note was their parental situations. Georgia's mother had started pressuring her to work on rebuilding a relationship with her father. Tell couldn't fault Georgia for her trepidation. Only a person who'd suffered through family dramas understood that forgiveness wasn't automatically given. Sometimes it wasn't earned. And sometimes letting go was the best option. Not politically correct, but often necessary.

Not that Tell's situation with his father had changed much. Casper only called to rail on Tell about something. And he hadn't heard from his mother beyond a couple of short texts. She must not have needed a baby-sitter.

As far as Tell was concerned, out of sight, out of mind was the best way to deal with his folks. He couldn't change them or their behavior, so why even try now? He was beyond pretending it would make a difference. The only control he had in the situation was not letting his past ruin his future.

A future he hoped to have with Georgia.

After he'd tried her phone for the twentieth time and the call was immediately kicked over to voice mail for the twentieth time, he drove into town. His panic increased when he pulled up in front of her house and saw her car parked in the drive. What if she was sick? She didn't answer his knock.

Tempting to break in, but he found a space between the fence and a lilac bush that allowed him to enter the backyard. He hoped she'd just lost track of time and was sitting on the swing, enjoying the late afternoon sunshine on this mild summer day.

No sign of her.

Tell tried the handle on the back door and discovered it was unlocked. He stepped into the kitchen and called out, "Georgia?"

Silence.

The coffee pot was half full of cold coffee. One bowl, one spoon and one cup were in the sink. Just as he decided to check her bedroom upstairs, he noticed her cell phone on the table. Right next to a calendar.

He didn't pay much attention to dates, and most days he'd be hard-pressed to answer if someone asked him the actual date. He saw that she'd written in events for all the days of this month except for one. This day, the third of August, was devoid of any marks.

A punch of sadness hit him as well as guilt.

Now he had a pretty good idea where she was.

It was so like Georgia not to mention it. He hoped she wouldn't reject his comfort because he hadn't remembered what today was.

Although it wasn't far to the cemetery, Tell opted to drive. The gates were still open and he parked in the empty visitors' lot. Gravel crunched beneath his boots as he started on the first path.

This was one of the few places in Sundance where deciduous trees grew. Weeping willows, which were appropriate, he supposed. Soft breezes stirred the branches. Dappled sunlight threw shadows on the manicured grounds and across the headstones.

Tell avoided the cemetery as a general rule. The McKays had their own section in the far corner, in the oldest part, since his great-great-grandfather Jonas McKay had been one of the first settlers in Wyoming Territory. The odd thing was he'd only been in this cemetery twice. For his grandfather Jed McKay's burial and when they buried Luke. He remembered his surprise at seeing how few McKays were buried there, and feeling sadness at how much space was available for the existing McKays

He'd never understood why his mother came here bearing flowers and tears—because Luke wasn't here. Were visits solely a reminder of the finality of death? Or some weird prompt for survivors not to forget the loved one they'd lost?

Trying to keep his morbid thoughts at bay, he scanned the neatly ordered sections of grave markers, some elaborate, some simple, some so weathered by the harsh Wyoming elements the names and dates were no longer visible.

Then he saw her, five rows over, sitting cross-legged, her back to him. Her glorious black hair shone in the sunlight.

Part of him wanted to leave, to let her have the private moment, just relieved he knew where she was.

But a bigger part of him wanted her to realize he was there, ready to give her whatever she needed, whenever she needed it.

And that's when Tell knew that he was in love with her. Not the beautiful girl from his past he'd put on a pedestal. But the beautiful, complex woman she'd become, even when she swore she wasn't sure who that woman was. The woman he'd cherish every damn day of his life, if she let him.

Confessing his love while she wept at her brother's grave could possibly be the worst timing in the world.

He approached her cautiously.

Georgia glanced up when Tell's shadow fell across her. She wiped her tears and managed a wan smile. "I don't know why I'm surprised you found me."

Tell crouched down, within touching distance if she was so inclined to reach out for him. "As far as hiding places go, this is a pretty good one. Or a pretty bad one, depending."

"Bad, mostly. But no one looks at you funny if you're sitting alone crying." She sniffled. "Mostly they just leave you be."

"Do you want me to go?"

She shook her head.

He watched her, not shocked by her grief, but by the fact that she wasn't chasing him away. Maybe she did need him for more than sex and good times.

"I haven't been here since a year after his accident." Her fingers plucked pieces of grass, turning the blades into green confetti. "I don't know what I expected to be different. Maybe if I started talking to him, like in the movies, his ghost would appear. But to be honest, I'd probably wet my pants and run away screaming if that did happen."

He had no idea what to say to that, so he said nothing.

"I miss him."

"I know you do, baby."

Georgia ripped up more grass. Tears streamed down her cheeks. Her chin trembled.

He felt so damn helpless, even when he knew exactly what she was going through. He dealt with the anniversary of Luke's death differently, surrounding himself with people—strangers usually—so he had no choice but to slap on a happy face and not dwell on the loss.

Several long moments passed. Then she blindly reached out to him. "I..."

Tell stood and picked her up like she was a child, cradling her to his chest. "It's okay. I'm here."

She melted into him, with a whispered, "Thank you."

"You're breakin' my heart, sweetness. What can I do?"

"Take me home."

He headed back to his truck, wishing he could wrap her in cotton batting and keep her safe from all the hurt the world inflicted. He rubbed his lips over her crown, breathing in the scent of her, murmuring assurances he'd be there for her, no matter what.

She'd stopped crying, but she clung to him.

By the time he reached the parking lot, a prickly feeling caused the hair on the back of his neck stand up. He turned and saw an older man standing at the opposite end of the path.

A man he recognized as Georgia's father.

Tell started in that direction, but the man shook his head. Then he pointed to Georgia, indicating Tell should continue as he was, tending to the weeping woman in his arms. Tell nodded, but it made him uneasy, given the strained relationship Georgia had with her father.

"Where to?"

"Your place."

Such a surprise that she preferred his crappy trailer to her house in town. Wait. Did she consider his place...home?

She stayed in the middle of the bench seat, tucking herself against his side so no space remained between them. Tell idly played with her hair, letting music from the radio fill the silence on the drive to his house.

Once they were inside his trailer, he noticed her cradling her arm. "What's wrong?"

"I keep forgetting about my tattoo and then I rub against it."

He frowned. "When did you get a tat?"

"Before I went to the cemetery. It's a memorial tattoo India did for RJ. So I don't forget what he meant to me."

Oh. Sweetness. You are such a beautiful woman. Inside and out. "Does it hurt?"

"A little." She blew out a long breath. "Okay. It hurt a lot. I cried while she was doing it. I cried when she finished."

"Maybe the tears weren't only from the pain of the needle?" he murmured.

Her beautiful eyes were wet again. "No. How did you know?"

He just stared at her.

"I'm sorry. Thoughtless of me, isn't it? Sometimes I'm so...selfish in my grief I forget I'm not the only one in the world who's lost a brother."

"But you're the only one who's lost *your* brother," Tell said gently.

Georgia touched his face, her palms lightly resting on his jaw as her thumbs stroked his cheekbones and his temples. "You are a good man, Tell McKay. Everyone underestimates you, don't they? Believing you're just a laid-back, fun-loving guy out for a good time. You keep things light because you don't want people to realize the intensity of emotion inside you."

How in the hell had she seen that?

"Thank you for letting me see that part of you. Thank you for letting me have some of your strength."

"Anytime, sweetness. Anytime."

She looked down and tears dripped on her jeans. "I'm so tired."

"I know. C'mere." Tell hauled her onto his lap.

She wiggled until she found her spot and sighed.

He kissed her crown. "Rest. I've got ya."

They both dozed off.

Georgia shifted and something sticky rubbed on his arm.

He glanced down and saw blood. He kissed her forehead, wanting to wake her up gently. "Georgia? You're bleeding through the gauze."

"Guess that's my sign it's time to clean the skin and change the bandage." She sat up. "Are you squeamish?"

"No. Why? Do you need help?"

"Probably."

Tell followed her to the bathroom.

She ripped off the gauze and surgical tape. She wet a big cotton square with water and squirted on antibacterial soap, dabbing at the crusted blood. After rinsing with clean water, she patted the area dry "Wanna see it?"

"Hell yeah."

Georgia showed him the inside of her forearm. Black block initials RJ outside a red circle. But upon closer inspection, the circle appeared to be in 3D, like a woman's rounded belly, with the yin and yang symbols at the center.

"This is perfect. Did you design it?"

"Just the rough sketches. India did the real design work."

Tell stroked the crease of her elbow. "This wasn't a spur of the moment thing for you."

She shook her head. "That's how you end up with bad tattoos, with random, meaningless Chinese symbols, according to India. I scheduled an appointment for today several weeks ago. Right after I decided to make a permanent mark on my body to match the permanent mark I've had on my soul ever since RJ died."

Poor woman had such deep pockets of sadness inside her. "I could've gone with you."

"I know. And I appreciate the offer. But it was something I had to do on my own."

She smeared A&D on the surface and he covered it with gauze. He kissed each side of the tattoo. When he glanced up at her, tears pooled in her eyes again.

"Thank you. It feels better already."

Tell tucked a strand of hair behind her ear, then followed the line of her jaw to the other ear. "Let me love on you a little while, Georgia."

"Do I look like I need extra TLC today?"

Yes. "Maybe after seeing you like this...I'm the one who needs it."

Her sweet, lopsided smile nearly undid him. "Okay."

He kissed her softly. Slowly. Waiting for that moment when she swayed into him. When that happened, he lifted her in his arms and carried her to his bedroom. He kept his mouth on hers as he undressed her, his hands lovingly caressing every section of skin he exposed. "Lie back."

While she stretched out, he stripped and rolled on a condom.

He positioned himself above her, loving how her arms immediately circled his neck, pulling him closer. His cock needed no guidance; it connected with her opening and he eased inside on a slow, wet glide. Resting his forehead to hers, he stayed still, losing himself in this moment.

Then Georgia's hands were gripping his hair, pulling his head back to look into his eyes. "Hey. I'm okay."

I'm not. She had no idea how everything had changed for him today. Realizing he loved her and hoping a part of her was attuned enough to him to sense the change. He held her gaze as he started to move, her tight channel such a perfect fit.

She rolled her hips up to meet his easy thrusts, not in an attempt to get him to increase the pace, but showing him this wouldn't be him making love to her—but them making love together.

Even when her climax was within reach, she didn't lock her legs around his waist, grab his ass and grind into him. She just let him, let the connection of their bodies take her there.

Tell watched her beautiful face awash in pleasure. When he couldn't hold back another second, he threw his head back, feeling her mouth on his throat, sucking in time to the pulses shooting out of his cock.

It was glorious, this love thing.

His damn legs almost wouldn't hold him when he scooted off the bed to ditch the condom. He scrutinized himself in the mirror as he washed his face and hands. Wondering if being in love made him look different.

Nope. He looked the same, except for the huge fucking hickey Georgia had given him on the side of his neck. He'd never understood the appeal of those marks until now. For the next couple days, he'd remember the woman he loved had given it to him in a moment of passion.

Georgia was propped on the pillows, the sheet clutched to her chest when he returned. Some of the shadows were gone from her eyes, and she smiled at him. "Hey."

He pounced on her. "You." He pecked her lips. "Rocked." Another peck. "My." One last smooch. "World."

"And thank you for... Omigod, is that a...hickey?" Her cheeks turned the same color as the mark she'd left on his skin. "*I* did that?"

"Yep. And I'm pretty sure it's what made me come so hard."

She blushed deeper. This woman was such a contradiction, Bold one second, shy the next. He loved that about her.

You love everything about her, you fucking sap.

"So what else do you wanna do tonight? We could hang out in bed. Watch a movie. I've probably got frozen pizza. There's beer and soda in the fridge."

Georgia set her hands on his face again, touching him with such tenderness and gratitude. "Thank you, Tell. I don't care what we do as long as I do it with you."

If he didn't keep it light, he might fall at her feet and beg her to stay with him every night. "Now that there are no limits, I'm thinking about breaking out the cuffs."

Chapter Twenty-Six

Georgia watched from the medical tent as Tell chatted with a group of guys before the performance started.

The man was magnificent. Not just his physique. Not just his face. Not just his charm. Not just his ease with people that put them at ease. All those things by themselves were pretty impressive, but were powder-keg potent wrapped up in one hunky cowboy package.

This was the last event they'd work together before the Devil's Tower Rodeo next weekend. That would be a tense situation since Deck was also scheduled to judge.

Not that she'd told Tell about it.

Not only that, she hadn't let him know she'd be leaving in two weeks. Every time she thought about broaching the subject, fear would overtake her. Imagining the accusations and hurt in his eyes sent a shiver of dread zipping up her spine.

She had no choice but to go back to Dallas. Her position wasn't freelance; she couldn't do it from here. She doubted there were any jobs for her in her field in Sundance, Moorcroft or Hulett.

If you could find work here, would you stay?

In a heartbeat.

Georgia couldn't think along those lines. Barbara was pleased enough with her job performance that she'd scheduled a review for two weeks after her return to the office to discuss her promotion.

What would a promotion mean? More money? Couldn't be much; she was still a lower-tier employee, which was why Barbara's insistence that Georgia relocate to Wyoming for the summer had come as such a surprise. A couple coworkers had been jealous, even when they had families and couldn't take the job anyway. Maybe it stung a little that the people she'd considered her friends hadn't bothered to call her in the last eleven weeks.

But Roxanne and Leah called her. So did Stephanie. She'd had lunch with Chassie. Domini made time for her when she dropped in to Dewey's. India called to see how she'd fared after getting a tattoo. Even AJ called and nagged her to come in for a massage.

What a change from when she'd first arrived in town.

She no longer dreaded going to the grocery store, worrying who she'd run into, even after she'd run into Tara-Lee. She could talk to people about RJ without breaking down. She liked exploring her domestic side, cooking dinner for Tell and working in her tiny garden. She looked forward to hanging out with the friends who'd become more than just drinking buddies. She'd discovered that volunteering gave her a sense of purpose as well as satisfaction.

The sobering part was when she realized that she wouldn't have any of that when she returned to Dallas.

But mostly, she wouldn't have Tell.

So she would have him now. She'd take him as many times as she could get him, in as many ways as possible.

Georgia felt the other men's eyes on her as she approached Tell. "Gentlemen, can you excuse us? I need to talk to Mr. McKay."

"Lead the way, Miss Hotchkiss."

Their formal use of titles wasn't fooling anyone, not that they'd tried keeping their relationship under wraps.

Wanting privacy, Georgia wandered to the far side of the corral, away from contestants and other rodeo officials.

The scenery was spectacular. Breathing in a lungful of clean air, she knew she'd miss the scent of sage and how scorching hot days were tempered into cool mountain nights.

When she turned around from admiring the view, another amazing view greeted her.

Tell's back rested against a corner section of the metal corral. His head was cocked at a jaunty angle, shadowing his face beneath the brim of his hat. "Did you need something official, Miss Hotchkiss?"

She shook her head. "You still pissy with me?"

His blue eyes trapped hers. "Maybe."

She'd broken down the night before last, guilt-ridden by her inability to give him the truth on any level. His immediate need to comfort her had increased her feelings of guilt and she'd taken off without explanation. She'd called later and apologized, making up a story about work stress, but she sensed he hadn't believed her.

She sauntered forward, wearing a you-want-it-bad-boy smile on her lips. "Will you let me make it up to you?"

His big hands curled around her hips and he yanked her against his body. "What do you have in mind?"

Her lips met his in a slow slide. She wanted a gradual shift from sweet kisses to fiery. But as usual Tell wrested control. Kissing her passionately. Trying to push her to the point where her need for him overtook her common sense.

Not this time. In a moment of spontaneity, she decided to see just how far she could push him. Georgia broke the kiss with a murmured, "Bad boy, McKay."

He smiled against her cheek, but didn't apologize.

She shifted her stance. Her right hand trailed down his vest, stopping at his belt. A quick tug and the buckle was out of her way, allowing access to his button and zipper.

"While I appreciate your intent to make this right between us, we should hold off—"

"Oh, I don't intend to hold off. I intend to get you off. Right now."

"Georgia. We're in public. Anyone could wander back here and see what you're doin'."

"Then you'd better keep an eye out, hadn't you?" She lowered the zipper and slipped her hand between his boxers and his warm skin until she found her prize. Tell's cock wasn't completely hard—she'd soon fix that. "Besides, it looks like we're having a private, intense conversation. No one will bother us. Westerners are polite that way."

"What's gotten into you?"

"A sense of adventure. My own personal brand of fun."

He groaned. "I deserved that."

"And more." She loved how his shaft swelled in her hand and she kept squeezing until he was fully erect. Then she began to stroke. Not slow and easy. Quick and hard, exactly how he liked it. She let her lips whisper across his ear. "I wish my hand was slippery with lube."

"Sweet baby Jesus," he hissed.

"Maybe you should kiss my neck a little, so it looks like we're making up from a lover's spat."

"You are gonna pay for this bossiness," he murmured, nuzzling the side of her face.

"Will you force me to my knees? So you can feel this—" she jacked his shaft twice, "—gliding across my tongue as you fill my mouth with every inch?"

"You're yanking on the devil's tail here."

"Really? I thought I was yanking on something else." The tip of his cock leaked steadily and she moved her hand faster. She lost herself in the moment—she'd actually taken Tell by surprise.

"Goddamn that feels good."

"Don't throw your head back and look like you're about to come."

"Don't squeeze so hard unless you're tryin' to keep me from coming," he shot back.

"I want you to come. I want to feel those pulses that make you groan and your body shake."

"Won't be long. You rev me up in record time, hot lips."

The husky voice wound around her body like a velvet caress. "Give it to me, Tell."

He let his head fall forward. His grip on her hips increased but he didn't buck his hips into her hand. He was completely passive, letting her control his pleasure. Trusting her.

She increased her rhythm. As soon as she heard a catch in his breath, she smashed her mouth to his. Swallowing his groan of satisfaction. Kissing him crazily as he spilled warm and wet over her fingers.

The pulses in his shaft stopped and he released one last shudder. Several tender kisses later, Tell leaned back to gaze into her eyes. Everything she'd ever wanted was right there.

Her heart seized up. How could she ever leave him?

"Georgia, what's wrong?"

She carefully removed her hand. "Nothing. You'll have to deal with fastening your jeans. My hand is a little sticky."

His laughter morphed into a masculine growl when she brought her fingers to her mouth and sucked. One by one.

Then he kissed her. His way. With such sweet deliberation tears threatened, and when he finally released her mouth, she was shaking.

"I don't know what's put that sadness in your eyes, sweetness. But you can talk to me about anything."

Tell's tender loving care the day he'd tracked her down at the cemetery had rocked her to her very foundation. He hadn't offered platitudes or tried to cajole her out of a mood. He'd just seen to her, accepting her pockets of sadness, offering her his comfort until she took it.

Just say it, Georgia. Flat out. I love you, Tell McKay.

The announcer's booming voice came over the loudspeaker, shattering their moment.

And when she retreated, Tell let her.

The sun beat down. Dust clogged his nostrils. Last he'd heard, the temperature had hit the one hundred degree mark. Usually the dirt in the rodeo arena registered ten degrees hotter, so it was a damn oven. Everyone suffered when it was this hot. The animals, the competitors, the crowd. His shirt was soaked clear through. Even his jeans were moist from sweat streaming from every pore on his body in an attempt to cool off. He mopped his face with a towel every chance he got, but it didn't help much.

Tell's day had started out with a pissing contest with the stock contractor, because he'd disqualified one horse and two bulls due to heat exhaustion. The contractor demanded the second judge reassess the livestock, but Tell hadn't seen hide nor hair of the other judge yet.

He hadn't seen Georgia either. The last couple days had been pretty hectic, but he felt as if she was hiding something from him. Probably just paranoia on his part, given both their tendencies to avoid conflict. They were still taking baby steps with their relationship. But if he had his way, they'd take that giant leap and move in together.

He paced behind the chutes, anxious for things to get started. Then he saw Deck. Since the man was headed straight for him, Tell couldn't pretend he hadn't seen him.

You really going to run and hide from this pompous prick like you did in high school?

No. *Hell* no.

He stood his ground, arms folded on his chest. "Veldekamp."

"McKay."

"Surprised to see you back here behind the chutes at this rodeo."

"Why?"

Tell shrugged. "Thought it'd be a bad memory for you, considering how publicly you crashed and burned on your home turf that summer after graduation. Gotta be a kick in the balls that your rodeo career never reached the epic proportion you bragged it would."

"How'd you..." He muttered, "From Georgia."

"No. It was all around town. Funny, ain't it, how happy some folks are to see others fail?"

"I didn't fail, I got injured. Big difference."

"Whatever."

"At least I tried. Unlike some people, I don't got nothin' to prove. I was a state champion. You know what they say. Them that can, do; them that can't are bitter pricks about others' success."

Such bullshit. But it was hitting the mark.

"Besides, I'm not here as a spectator," Deck said. He looked at Tell's vest. Then in his eyes. His lips twisted in a parody of a smile. "Guess Georgia forgot to mention that I'm the second judge today."

Tell felt every muscle in his body seize up.

Was Deck fucking serious? He had to work with this asshole? Tell fumed silently, knowing Georgia had made herself scarce today because she hadn't wanted to give him the news.

What else was she hiding from him?

Doesn't matter. Suck it up and do your job.

At least Tell was the senior judge. He gave Deck a once-over. "You're late. Get your vest on, and then do a quick stock check. Report back here immediately."

"You're getting off on bossing me around, ain't ya?" Deck said.

He offered him a shit-eating grin. "Like you wouldn't fuckin' believe. And it's a damn cryin' shame they took away my bullwhip."

Tell focused on his job and making sure Deck did his part. It surprised him how close their scores were on the rough stock events. It didn't surprise him that neither of them could contain their mutual hostility when they had to confer.

After the bull riding ended, the prizes were awarded. The crowd was huge this year. How much of that was due to Georgia's PR efforts? He hung around watching the contestants and the stock contractor loading up. Probably half his family was in the stands, but he didn't want to deal with them or mingle with his friends. He wasn't the brooding type very often and he tended to lie low when that personality tic appeared. He didn't want to do much of anything except talk to Georgia and get to the bottom of why she was acting so distant.

He headed toward committee headquarters.

Deck waylaid him outside the loading chutes. "Where's Georgia?"

"What do you need from her?"

"Not your concern." Deck crossed his arms over his chest. "Make you feel like a big man? Getting named most changed at the reunion and acting all hot shit here at the rodeo?"

Tell didn't want to do this, but Deck had been pushing his buttons for years and he knew this was about to get ugly.

"I'd say you becoming a judge was all about reliving your glory days, but you never had any, did you? All the glory went to your cousin Chase."

"Does it make *you* feel like big man again, talkin' shit to me like you did a decade ago?" Tell leaned in. "Grow the fuck up, Deck. You're only embarrassing yourself."

Deck's mouth flattened. "No more than you are, trailing after Georgia like a lovesick pussy."

Feet scuffled in the dirt around them as people gave them a wide berth.

"What's going on here?"

Neither Tell nor Deck took his eyes off his opponent to acknowledge Georgia.

About damn time she showed up. When Tell saw her move into his line of vision, he said, "Georgia. Why don't you head on out to the rodeo grounds. This doesn't concern you."

"Or so McKay wants you to think. But it's always been about you," Deck said with a sneer.

Tell's head said *don't take the bait*, but his mouth had already engaged. "Is your dick attitude because I have her now?"

"*Do* you have her? For how long?"

Saying *forever* seemed cheesy, but he wanted Deck to know what'd grown between him and Georgia this summer was the real deal. So he said, "For keeps."

Deck broke eye contact and looked at Georgia. "He doesn't know, does he?"

"Hey, talk to me, asshole, not her. Know what?"

Deck released a sharp bark of laughter. "The joke is on you, McKay. Georgia is leaving at the end of the summer, as soon as rodeo season slows down. She never intended to stay in Wyoming permanently."

No. That couldn't be true. She wouldn't do that—flat-out lie to him. Tell spun around and faced her, his eyes searching hers as he bridged the short distance between them. So when Tell saw that look on Georgia's face he hadn't been able to place before, he finally recognized it: guilt. He wished the hot dirt would just swallow him up right now.

You've been played for the fool again. When will you ever learn?

Automatically he started backing up, away from her, tempted to turn tail and run.

But she kept up with him, step for step. "Wait."

"Why didn't you tell me?"

"I was scared to."

"But you could tell your ex-husband?"

"I didn't tell him. My dad must have. No one was supposed to know."

"Well, that makes it so much better." He lowered his voice so only she heard him. "Do you remember when you asked me if I was playin' a game? Is that what you've been doin' this whole time? Stringing me along so you could watch me unravel when you cut ties here for good?"

"No. God no."

"Do you feel anything for me, Georgia?"

"Yes."

He could work with that. "Then can you really turn your back on this? On us? Return to Dallas and pretend this never happened?"

Her gaze shifted to the side, to Deck, and she sighed. "I only came to Sundance because I didn't have a choice."

A swift kick in the balls couldn't have hurt worse.

If he stood there another second, he'd probably break down. Beg her not to go.

In front of Deck Veldekamp.

That would only be slightly less humiliating than the fact he'd fallen in love, for real, with a woman he still couldn't have. His heartbeat slowed, becoming a dull thud in his ears as he turned from her and started to walk away.

No surprise Deck wouldn't let it go.

"She's just like the song, ain't she?" Deck called out. "Georgie Porgie kissed the boys and made them cry. Wasn't there a line in there about bein' a coward and running away? That fits you, McKay, don't it?"

Against his better judgment, Tell wheeled back around. "You are a fucking moron. But if you really want me to beat your face in, keep it up. I've been waiting for this for years. We'll see if you're tough when your buddies aren't holding me down so you can beat on me."

"You ain't man enough to take it. Never have been. Never will be." Deck took a blatant step forward. "Are you?"

Deck didn't expect the first punch so fast. The second punch knocked him off-balance. The third punch sent him sprawling in the dirt.

Tell pounced on him, his fists connecting with flesh and bone. He let fly with years' worth of pent-up rage.

Deck didn't defend himself at all.

Unfortunately, Tell didn't get many licks in before he was rudely ripped away from pummeling Deck's face.

"What in the world is goin' on here?" the man demanded.

Tell fought the adrenaline rush and jerked out of the man's hold. All he cared about was Georgia. Who was crouched in the dirt next to Deck. Her hand on his arm. Her angry glare aimed right at him. At *him*. Not at Deck.

All the breath whooshed out of Tell's body, along with that tiniest bit of hope.

"What has gotten into you?" she hissed. "Why did you attack him?"

Just out of Georgia's line of sight, Deck's lips lifted into a greasy grin that showed blood on his teeth.

The fucker had won. Georgia had chosen Deck again.

Tell stepped back.

When Deck opened his big, fat mouth, Tell turned and walked away.

Georgia had an overpowering sense of loss as Tell disappeared into the crowd.

She shook her head to try and clear the confusion. She'd been right there and she had no idea what'd just happened. Tell and Deck had been arguing about some past slight and then they were on the ground, Tell throwing punches that Deck hadn't attempted to defend.

Something was wrong with that picture.

"You gonna go running after McKay now? Dry his tears? 'Cause guaranteed the loser is crying. He always does."

She looked at him "Why would he cry? You didn't even land a punch."

"Not this time." He wiped blood from his smirking mouth.

"What do you mean, *not this time*?"

"You think that's the first occasion me'n him have locked horns? Nope. But I always beat his ass down."

"Always? When was the last time?"

"End of senior year."

All the blood drained from her face. She remembered Tell had come to school a complete wreck. He'd claimed the damage was from getting thrown off a bucking horse. "Those bruises on his face were your doing? You went after him? Why?"

"Because he gave you a ride home and he knew better than to touch what didn't belong to him."

"You stranded me at school. He drove me home. That was it."

Deck shrugged. "Not according to him. He tracked me down, said you were miserable and cryin' because of me and that you deserved someone better, so I oughta leave you alone."

She backed away. "I had no idea."

"Of course you didn't. Even McKay ain't stupid enough to brag about getting the shit kicked outta him."

Georgia wasn't talking about the fight. She was shocked that Tell had stood up for her years ago. A girl he barely knew.

"Seeing that look on McKay's face when I told him you weren't sticking around? Priceless."

God. She felt sick to her stomach and as confused as ever. "Why do you hate him so much?"

"I don't hate him. I just like putting him in his place."

So it hadn't been about her. Just another example of Deck getting his kicks out of being a bully. And Deck knew she'd take the side of the guy on the receiving end of punches, not the side of the guy throwing them. She'd played into his hands perfectly.

"The committee can hold on to my check for another week or so, right?"

Georgia refocused on her asshole ex-husband. "I guess. Why?"

"Me'n Tara-Lee are movin' to New Mexico."

"What? When did this come about?"

"As soon as Robert gave me money from the sale of the hog farm."

"Is my dad going with you?"

Deck snorted. "No. Why would he?"

"Because he's been like a father to you."

"Whoa. Robert ain't my dad. And it's always been a little creepy how he acted like he was."

But only up to the point where it benefited Deck, when Robert forked over a pile of cash to a guy he'd considered his son. "After all my dad did for you? You're just gonna take the money and run?"

"I earned every penny of that money for the years I slaved at that hog farm," he retorted hotly. "Robert and I are friends, Georgia, but

285

mostly we're business partners. Now the business is sold, we're parting ways."

"Business partners?" she repeated. "You've always been much more than that." Hadn't they?

Deck shook his head. "I like Robert. He's a great guy. I know you need someone to blame for how things ended up with your father after RJ died, but your dad didn't choose me. Your mom left. You left in mind and spirit months before your body did. Robert didn't have anyone else *but* me. I never tried to take RJ's place, Georgia. I never tried to take yours, either. Robert's been a broken man for a long time. Maybe it's time you step up to the plate and help put him back together."

Deck's accusations settled in and he walked away for good.

Georgia had a weird punch of anxiety when she pulled up to the house she hadn't seen in years. The house she'd fled from and never looked back.

It's concrete and wood. Neither the structure nor the memories contained within have power over you.

As she started up the sidewalk, she caught movement out of the corner of her eye. She saw her father sitting on a pile of tires, staring at the house. Even from a hundred feet away, an aura of defeat surrounded him.

"Dad?"

He turned his head toward her as she erased the distance between them. "Georgie?"

Her retort, "Does anyone else call you Dad?" came out a little harsh.

"Nope."

"I saw Deck at the Devil's Tower Rodeo. I'm a little shocked he's just up and moving to New Mexico."

He grunted.

"Were you surprised he's leaving?"

"Nope. Deck's been restless and lookin' for an exit since he knocked up Tara-Lee. After nearly nine years, we were both ready to move on." He spit a stream of tobacco juice on the ground and squinted at her. "What brings you here?"

"I came to see if you're okay."

"I see you've still got that sweet streak you inherited from your mother." He sighed. "I'm not okay. Haven't been for quite a while. I'm tired. Some days it's just too much. And now... It ain't like I've got anywhere to go."

Georgia didn't know what to say. Her father was the most closemouthed person she'd ever met. So he must really be in distress if he was opening up to her.

"Things between you and Mom...?"

"Irina ain't invited me to live with her in Boulder if that's what you're asking. I'd go in a heartbeat if I thought there was a chance she'd take me back. But I'm sure you don't wanna hear about that." He squinted at her. "Today was the last rodeo for that PR company you work for?"

Who had he heard that from? She hadn't told him and it wasn't common knowledge. "Yes."

"So when are you going back to Dallas?"

The idea of getting in her car, leaving Tell and Wyoming, made her stomach hurt, her eyes burn and her heart heavy. Her life had changed these past months. Changed for the better. Although if she talked to Tell, she doubted he'd see any change in her at all, since she'd kept the truth from him again.

"Maybe the question oughta be *are* you going back to Dallas?"

"I don't know. My time here has turned out differently than I imagined."

"Has Tell McKay played a part in that?"

No reason to lie now. "A big part."

"He's a good man. I saw him...makin' sure you were okay on the anniversary of RJ's death."

She stared at him in shock. "Tell never said anything about you being at the cemetery."

"I wasn't there for you any more than you were there for me. It's a day I'd like to forget, but I can't seem to, no matter how hard I try." He pointed to her tattoo. "Your brother would like you done that in his memory."

Georgia saw his expectation—he wanted her to say something poignant, but the words wouldn't come.

"Look, I'm sure whatever you decide about stayin' here or returning to Dallas, Barbara will understand. She's a tough old broad, but she's able to look at things from different angles. It's why she's been so successful."

The hair on the back of Georgia's neck stood up. "Whoa. Are you telling me you know Barbara Wyrelinski?"

Her father nodded.

"How long have you known her?"

A pause. A heavy sigh. "Forty-some years. She's the sister of my army buddy who got killed in Vietnam. She sorta adopted me as her big brother. We both had interest in the western lifestyle and we stayed in touch."

"Why didn't I know that?"

"I've been around the world and I've got lots of friends you aren't aware of," he said tightly.

"I get that. But this is my boss we're talking about, Dad. In the four years I've worked for her, she never once mentioned knowing you. Why?"

"Because I wouldn't let her tell you."

Georgia frowned. She thought back to her conversations with Stephanie. About the odds of getting assigned a job in Sundance, Wyoming. So what were the odds that Barbara, a business owner from Dallas who just *happened* to be a friend of her father's, just *happened* to be one of the employer interviewers in Laramie, Wyoming, four years ago?

Astronomically slim.

Then she knew. Her father had set up the entire thing. He'd always run her life with a heavy hand and it seemed no matter how far away she moved, she'd never be out of his reach.

She stood and paced angrily, kicking up dust that reeked like pig manure. "I always believed I'd nailed that interview with Barbara on my own merits. But now I find out you..." Her entire body burned with humiliation.

"You did get hired on your own merits, Georgie. Yes, I asked Barbara to do the official interview at UW, but she does that all the time. And she wouldn't have hired you as a favor to me—she's too shrewd a businesswoman for that. Barbara liked what she saw in you—that's why she offered the job. And I've not meddled in your life since."

Her head spun. "Did Mom know about this?"

"No one but me'n Barbara knew."

"Didn't you think it was wrong if you had to keep it a secret? From everyone? Especially me?"

"What would you have done, Georgie, if I'd told you that I'd asked an old friend to interview you? You would've refused the meeting out of anger and resentment, just because that option came from me."

She opened her mouth. Closed it. That wasn't true. Was it?

"I'll agree some of your anger toward me is justified. But you are my *daughter*. I care what happens to you. As your father, you can't fault me for tryin' to help you secure a job so you could provide for yourself. I'll repeat, the only part I had in this process was getting you the first interview. The rest you did on your own. And you should be proud of that. God knows I am."

Georgia was too mad to acknowledge his pride in her. "And what part did you have in convincing Barbara to assign me to a job in Sundance?" she demanded.

He looked away.

"Not meddling in my life anymore? Bullshit."

"I know what it looks like. But Larry and Kim Pradst, who own L bar K, are friends of mine. They've stuck by me when no one else did. When they hit tough times because of Larry's cancer, I gave them Barbara's name for a possible buyout since rodeo promotion is part of her business. Barbara handled it from there, but the Pradsts knew you worked for her."

"How?" she demanded.

"Because I told 'em." His voice dropped. "They got a promise from Barbara that you'd take over their events in Wyoming, if only for this season."

Throughout her realizations and recriminations, one question kept repeating in her head: had her life ever been her own? Had she ever been allowed to make her own decisions?

Her father's gruff voice roused her. "Georgia Lou. Please. Stop cryin'. You're gonna make yourself sick."

She reached up to find her cheeks were wet. And although the sun beat down, she was cold. So cold. She shivered.

"I've gotta go. I've gotta..." What? Where did she go when her life was in shambles?

Then her dad did the strangest thing. He hauled her into his arms, hugged her tightly, patted her back awkwardly and released her abruptly. "I know you're upset. But that was the last thing hanging between us. Now that everything is out in the open, we can start fresh. I don't wanna lose you, now that there's a chance we can fix this."

Georgia nodded numbly, trying to ignore the pleading tone. The only thing she wanted to fix right now—was a drink.

Chapter Twenty-Seven

At the Golden Boot, Georgia poured her heart out to Stephanie.

Stephanie made sympathetic noises, patted her hand, handed her tissues, ordered her another drink. "G, you know I love you, right?"

"Yes. And can I just say the day we became college roommates was one of the luckiest days of my life?"

"Such a suck-up," Stephanie said dryly. "But that sweet sentiment doesn't mean I'll sugarcoat my observations."

"I know." Georgia wiped her eyes. "Which is why I had to tell someone who'd have an unbiased opinion."

Stephanie thoughtfully stirred her drink. "I'm usually the first to point out there's no wrong way to grieve, but the way your father handled RJ's death? Was the wrong way. Many families implode after that type of event. Yours is no exception. It's always seemed to you that your dad chose Deck over you. I can't speak to the logic of that, except to point out that if your father had kicked Deck to the curb, would you have pitched in and helped him with the hog farm?"

Georgia wrinkled her nose. "No."

"Your dad, who was grieving, threw himself into a new enterprise to take his mind off his loss and pain. He needed help, but he didn't get it from his wife or his daughter. Who was the one person that did support him?"

"Deck."

"Yes, Deck. His son-in-law, the man you married, the guy he considered part of his family. That's natural, Georgia. Maybe it wasn't natural for you to leave and Deck to stay, but that's how it played out. And wishing it was different won't change anything."

"Never crossed my mind to ask Deck to come with me, because it was him I wanted to get away from." She winced. "I wasn't exactly a good wife."

"You were too young to be saddled with the responsibility of marriage. Add in the other stuff... I'm surprised you lasted two years. You bailed only a few months after your mother. Didn't change the fact your dad still needed help. Deck stood by him. I highly doubt your father agreed with Deck's treatment of you."

Hadn't her father tried to explain, in his gruff way, that a woman leaving a man makes the man do stupid things? Strange to think her dad hadn't been talking about Deck and her. He'd meant that *he* hadn't been thinking straight when his wife had left him.

How could Stephanie be turning this issue on its head and making Georgia sympathetic toward her father?

Maybe you're finally growing up and putting those perceived slights in the proper context. Seeing it from your dad's point of view. Seeing that the tragedy of RJ's death made everyone act irrationally. Including you.

"His only option was to somehow make it up to you. When it came time for you to spread your wings, he wanted you to have a safe landing, so he brought in Barbara."

"But isn't that controlling and manipulative?" Georgia asked.

Stephanie sighed. "Only if he told you he'd brought Barbara in especially for you and expected you'd take the job offer no matter what it was, because refusing it would ruin their friendship, and he'd gone to all the trouble for you, so you'd better fall in line.

"But he didn't tell you he'd set it up, probably because you'd refuse a great opportunity on principle. Yes, you scored the interview because of him, but you scored the job on your own. And sweetie, you're really naïve if you think that type of nepotism doesn't happen all the time, in every corner of business."

"What about this summer rodeo gig? He basically set that up too."

Stephanie rolled her eyes. "Yes, you're having such a lousy time in Wyoming. Not stuck in a stuffy office. Reconnecting with old friends. Proving yourself in sales and event management. Having fun. Acting your age for a change." She leaned closer. "Need I point out that you've fallen in love with Tell McKay?"

"No. It's scary, these feeling I have for him. But whatever he might've felt for me? I destroyed by lying to him. I saw it on his face, Stephanie. Distrust, disbelief and disgust." Georgia briefly closed her eyes, trying to blink away that image. "Him washing his hands of me is probably for the best."

"The best for who? You're the happiest you've ever been—or you were up until today. You can just snap your fingers and forget all that, like it never was?"

Georgia shrank back in the booth. "God no."

"But you expect Tell can forget it? And he will?"

"That's not a fair comparison."

"It is fair, because it's true. Tell loves you. I could see it that night at the reunion regardless if he was ready to admit it yet. You're so worried about everyone making decisions for you that you don't realize by walking away you're doing the same thing to him."

That stunned her. "What am I supposed to do?"

"Take control of your life. Nothing is predestined, Georgia. People make major changes in their lives every day."

"But my job is in Dallas. My life is there."

Stephanie smacked her hand on the table. "Can you please admit that you only really started living your life when you returned to Wyoming?"

That stung, but didn't make it any less true. She'd been going through the motions in Dallas. Work. Sleep. Weekends that she largely spent by herself. Living in limbo. Waiting for...what?

A man like Tell to come into her life?

No. She didn't need a man to make her complete.

If that was true, why had she felt so hollow? So incomplete? Didn't she have what every college grad wanted—a job, a decent place to live and a little money in the bank?

Yes. Wasn't that enough?

No. It never had been. Just like being Deck's wife hadn't been enough.

Being with Tell gave her something she'd never had from any person or place or job—a feeling of home. An intimate bond that grew stronger every day. The kind of connection she had been too afraid to forge, fearful she'd lose it once she found it.

That's when Georgia knew she'd do whatever it took to keep the happiness she'd found here. Taking such a scary leap made her stomach roil, but if she didn't have faith in her ability to choose her own path, she still was letting everyone else pull the strings. And she was done with that. Starting now. At least if she fell flat on her face this time, she'd know exactly who tripped her up.

She glanced up and saw Stephanie grinning at her.

"I knew you'd make the right choice. I'm here for you, whatever you need. Now go get your man and start your happily ever after." Stephanie hugged her and left.

As Georgia headed toward the door, she caught a glimpse of a black-haired man on the outskirts of the dance floor. Her heart skipped a beat. Had Tell shown up looking for her after all?

But after watching the guy, she realized he was a McKay, just not her McKay.

It was Dalton. A drunk Dalton. He'd sway one way, catch himself, and snap his body straight. He was trying to pay attention to a slender brunette giving him the mother of all lectures.

He reached out to stroke the woman's hair and she dodged his hand. When that motion sent him falling forward, she grabbed the front of his shirt and jerked him upright.

That's when everything went to hell. Dalton trapped the brunette's face in his hands and kissed her. Not a gentle peck, but a tonsil-scratching kiss.

She broke his hold and pushed him. Dalton's arms flailed and he landed hard on his ass. She stepped over him before stomping away. A couple bar patrons helped Dalton to his feet, but he angrily waved them off and staggered down the hallway to the back door.

Concerned, Georgia followed him outside.

Dalton wasn't leaning against the building or lying in a heap on the ground. And in the state he was in, he couldn't have gotten far. She saw him standing beside a white pickup.

Surely he didn't intend to drive home?

Despite three-inch heels, she ran. He had the driver's-side door open by the time she reached him, but he'd dropped the keys on the ground.

She swooped down and plucked them up. "Looking for these?"

"Yeah. They musta fallen outta my hand." He swayed and kept one eye shut as he looked at her. "Georgia! Hey. It's the hot chick banging my brother, that lucky bastard."

"So nice of you to point it out," she retorted.

"You still got my keys?"

"Yep. But I'm keeping them because you are not driving."

"Fuck that. I'm fine ta drive."

"Bullshit."

He loomed over her. "Gimme my goddamn keys."

She lost her mind on him. She shoved him against the cab and stood on her toes to get in his face. "You don't get to do this. It would destroy your brothers if something happened to you. You're a fucking idiot to even think about getting behind the goddamn wheel when you're drunk." She stepped back, her breath coming in hot, angry bursts. One fist clenched around the keys, one fist ready to knock him the fuck out if he made a move for them.

"Shit." Dalton's belligerent stance vanished. He dropped his chin to his chest, probably to hide his embarrassment. "Sorry. I don't know what I was thinkin'. I'd never..."

"You're right *you'd never*. Get it through that thickheaded McKay skull of yours: you are *not* driving. I'll call Tell to come and get you."

Dalton's head snapped up. "No. Keep my family out of it. I don't want them to see me like this."

"What? Drunk?"

He shook his head. "Like a fuckin' chump."

Confused, Georgia stared at him. "Dalton. Honey. You're kind of a mess. Will you let me drive you home?"

"Really? You'd do that?"

"Of course."

"Because of Tell?"

"No. Because of RJ."

Another moment of silence passed between them, broken by the shouts of partyers exiting the bar.

He said, "Thanks. I'll take you up on that ride."

She eyed him. "I walked here from my place, so I don't have my car. You're a big guy and there's no way I can help you into the cab of this monster truck."

"S'okay. I can get in on my own." He hoisted himself up. Then he slid across the bench seat to the passenger side.

Georgia had driven her fair share of pickups, but this one was jacked up, tricked out, and she could barely reach the pedals. With her luck, Dalton would pass out before he told her where he lived. Driving aimlessly around rural Wyoming at eleven o'clock at night with a brokenhearted drunk wasn't her idea of fun.

So call Tell.

No. Dalton had asked her not to. Which left her with one choice.

She parked his rig at the curb in front of her house because she feared she'd take out the neighbor's bushes if she attempted to park in the driveway.

Dalton staggered out of his pickup and into her house on his own. She directed him to the living room couch.

He yanked off his boots out of habit and flopped on the sofa with a weary sigh. He draped his arm over his eyes. "I'm gonna be payin' for my damn pity party the rest of the night and most of tomorrow. Christ. My head is spinning like a fuckin' tornado."

"Do you want coffee?"

"Nah. Thanks. I'm just gonna sleep it off."

She brought him a pillow and a blanket. "The bathroom is down the hall, across from the kitchen."

"I ain't gonna puke, if that's what you're worried about. I can hold my liquor."

"Well, I'd prefer you didn't pee on my sofa either. So you know where the toilet is in case you need to use it."

He snorted. "You're funny. And sweet. Not at all what I thought you'd be."

Georgia perched on the edge of the coffee table. "I'm afraid to ask what Tell has told you about me."

"Nothin', really. That says a lot."

"Why?"

"If my brother ain't talkin' about you, it means there's something there to talk about."

That made no sense.

"You ain't playin' him, are you?" Dalton said softly. "He deserves better."

"Tell deserves the best because he's the best man I've ever known."

"Have you told him that?"

"Not yet. But I intend to."

Dalton groaned. "Good. But fuck. I'm really gonna be the last single McKay standing, ain't I?"

Yes, if Georgia had anything to say about it.

"Night, Dalton."

"Night, John-Boy."

She froze. "What did you say?"

"Nothin'. Drunk talk. Me'n Tell and Brandt and Luke always pretended it was stupid the way the Waltons said goodnight to everyone at the end of the show. But we really thought it was kinda cool 'cause we never did that in our family. So we started doin' it as a joke."

"You know what's weird? RJ and I did the same thing. 'Cept he always wanted to be John-Boy."

"So did Tell. Bastard made me be Mary Ellen."

Georgia laughed. "Night, Mary Ellen."

"You and Tell are two peas in a pod."

By the time she asked, "What do you mean?" she saw Dalton's breathing had slowed and he'd passed out.

Chapter Twenty-Eight

Sunday morning, Tell feigned sickness and skipped helping with chores.

He'd spent Saturday night after the rodeo dozing off between shitty reality shows on the Discovery Channel. Point for him that he hadn't drunk until he passed out. His mind had just shut down on its own and his body followed. He wondered if this was how his days and nights would be if Georgia was out of his life for good.

He couldn't live like this. He couldn't go back to the way he'd been. Well, he could, but his heart wouldn't be in it, not since Georgia took ownership of that motherfucker before she'd stomped the piss out of it.

This brokenhearted shit sucked.

Being without Georgia sucked.

The rest of the day and all of the night sucked too.

Monday morning, Tell and Dalton started and finished chores without talking, which wasn't unusual. Sometimes they'd go as long as a week without discussing anything besides ranch work. Working with the same people every day, and knowing that would continue for the rest of his life, made it easy to shove things aside, figuring they'd have lots of time to talk.

But that didn't hold true with Luke, did it?

"So you didn't get to help out with the bonfire yesterday," Dalton said.

Tell's gaze snapped to him. "What are you talkin' about?"

"Colt, Kane, Ben and Brandt torched the bunkhouse yesterday morning. "

That floored him. "What? When was that decided?"

Dalton shrugged. "Spur of the moment. Colt showed up to do his check of the place and found a dozen kids passed out in there. Was the same kids everyone's been seein'. Guess they got mouthy. Colby found trees they'd cut down and a fire pit out in the middle of the damn field.

Appears everyone's had enough. Kane and everyone else are kicking themselves because we shoulda listened to you sooner. They were gonna let you do the honors, but Brandt said you were sick and he'd take care of it."

"Huh. Well, I'm glad to hear they don't think I'm always jokin' around and they take my suggestions seriously sometimes."

"None of 'em think you're a clown. It was just an extreme solution to the problem. So points for you, bro, in the McKay hierarchy."

Tell rolled his eyes. "Were you there yesterday morning?"

"For a little while. Then I had something else goin' on."

The way Dalton fidgeted, Tell knew something was up. "Spill it, D."

"We got it."

"Got what?"

"That parcel of Charlene's land." Dalton reached into his back pocket and pulled out a slip of paper. "Got her notarized intent to sell. We didn't get it as cheap as I would've liked. Five hundred acres with highway access. Plus she's giving us the option of buying some of the corrals and equipment."

Tell just stared at his younger brother, a mix of pride and fear filling him. "But how?"

A sheepish grin stole over his face. "I've been takin' advantage of your workhorse ways as much Brandt has. But it's paid off for all of us. We'll own that land free and clear."

"Free and clear? Where'd you get the money?"

"From poker tournaments. When you stopped goin' with me, I upped my bets and stopped playin' it safe. In the last year and a half I...ah—" he laughed self-consciously, "—been flyin' to Vegas in addition to hitting all the big tournaments around here. And I've done well."

Tell frowned. "But you didn't take money out of our joint account."

"Yes I did. I took out half over a long weekend. Used it as seed money and doubled it in three days. So I returned the money and have been usin' the profit from that to gamble with." Dalton held up his hand. "No, I ain't addicted to gambling. It was a tool to get us what we needed. And a way to prove myself."

"Dalton. You've gotta know..." How did he say this without getting his brother's back up? "I never expected that from you."

"Which was why I needed to do it. Look, Brandt is the oldest, you're the smartest and I've always been the youngest. That's how everyone sees me." He kicked a clod of dirt. "I needed to prove to myself and to you guys that I could contribute something to the running of the ranch besides manual labor. Money is something we always need."

"Amen to that." Tell elbowed his brother. "Ya little lyin' sack of shit. How much money you got squirreled away?"

Dalton grinned. "Plenty. Even after buyin' the land. We'll bring Brandt in on the plans for the feedlot, but I think we'd better keep it from everyone else until it's a done deal."

"I hear ya. But I gotta ask if Rory Wetzler has anything to do with your reason to keep it on the down low?"

"Partially. I just don't want our cousins to get a jump on our new enterprise. But I did hear an interesting bit of gossip from Ben yesterday morning. I guess Rielle is scrambling to find another place to live because Gavin got sole custody of Sierra and he's movin' to Sundance. In the next couple weeks before school starts."

"Holy shit. Really? That's a shocker. It's gotta make Ben and Quinn happy though."

"We'll see. Gavin ain't exactly a McKay—in more ways than one. I guess Sierra has been runnin' with a bad crowd and Gavin has had it."

This was the opening Tell had been looking for. "Speaking of running with a bad crowd... I heard an interesting rumor about you awhile back."

Dalton looked him in the eye as he swigged from the water jug. "What did you hear?"

"You were havin' some sort of gang bang in a motel in Hulett, where you were the bang-ee. Rumor says you had thirteen women with you, and you fucked every single one while the other women watched."

He rolled his eyes. "Christ. No wonder the McKays have such a bad reputation for bein' man-whores with a taste for multiple partners. Not that them rumors weren't partially based on fact. But the facts get distorted. Big-time. Yes, I was with some women in a motel room. But it sure as fuck wasn't thirteen. It was only three."

"Only?" Tell repeated.

"This is gonna sound really weird, but two of the chicks were lesbians."

"And the third?"

"The woman I'd been seein'. Willa."

Tell frowned. "This is the first time you've mentioned her."

Dalton focused on digging a rock out of the dirt with the toe of his boot. "That's because I ain't exactly proud of her. I met her and her friends in a strip club. That right there shoulda been my tip-off they liked T and A a little too much. Willa had just gotten out of a relationship and was lookin' to have some fun. Right up my alley. She pitched this foursome idea to me. The horny bastard that I am, I agreed.

"It was fuckin' bizarre, bro. After I was with each one of them, then they were with each other. Doin' stuff I ain't ever seen even in porn. And then it was like I wasn't even in the room. Willa dumped me Saturday night. I shoulda let it go but I didn't. That's when she told me she was goin' back to her ex. Her ex-girlfriend."

"No," Tell breathed.

"Yep. Evidently I'm so fuckin' bad in bed that I can turn a woman back into bein' gay."

"Come on. You don't really believe that."

He kicked a clump of clover. "I don't know what to believe anymore. And as long as I'm confessing shit, you oughta know... I had a pretty good lyin' streak goin' there over the years about how many chicks I banged. Pretending to be a McKay stud who knew everything about sex backfired on me big-time. I ain't gonna go into details about what happened, 'cause it's the most embarrassing thing I've ever done and I have been forgiven by the person involved. In the meantime, I've been tryin' to get all the sexual experience I'd been pretending to have. Which is how I ended up doin' it with three lesbians. I should just stick to poker. I'm one helluva lot luckier in cards than I am in love."

Seeing his little brother so dejected and his face so red from embarrassment, Tell attempted to lighten the mood. "So Dalton and three lesbians walk into a strip club..."

Dalton said, "Fuck you," but he smiled. "That brings me to the next point. I was at the Golden Boot Saturday night. Georgia saw me make a drunken idiot of myself and she took my keys."

"You were gonna drive?"

"I guess. She took me to her place to sleep it off." Dalton looked him in the eye. "I take back the shitty things I said about her. She didn't have to help me; she coulda let me sleep it off in my truck. But takin' in a stupid cowboy like me showed her generous nature. That's not the type of thing a user does. She's sweet and fierce and smart and loyal. She is something special."

Don't I know it.

"You're a lucky guy, bro. She's perfect for you."

"Did she say anything about me?"

301

"Just that you're the greatest guy she's ever known. She seemed sorta sad. Did I miss something? Why weren't you guys together Saturday night after the rodeo?"

"No. We had a big blow-up when I found out she never intended to stay here permanently."

Dalton raised his eyebrows. "You're just gonna let her go?"

"It's not like I've got a choice."

"Bullshit. Don't be a dumb-ass, Tell. Convince her to stay. Wow her with some of that McKay mojo I'm lacking."

He snorted. "Right. Like that'll work."

"Then maybe you oughta tell her the truth."

"Which is?"

"Christ. You're really gonna make me say it? Tell her that you love her and can't live without her."

It couldn't be that simple. Could it?

It was worth a shot.

Tell grinned at his brother. "Thanks, bro. You know, you've got a romantic streak. There may be hope for you yet. Now if you'll excuse me, I'm goin' to get my woman."

Tell cleaned up and dressed in better clothing than he normally wore on a Monday afternoon. On the drive into town, he cautioned himself not to ask what the hell she'd been doing whoopin' it up in the bar after the shit that'd gone down between them at the rodeo Saturday afternoon. He composed snappy comebacks—a mix of charm, snark and wit. Then he practiced keeping his face a blank mask when he imagined her saying *it was a fling, I'm returning to Dallas and never coming back,* but he knew he'd never pull it off because he'd be crushed beyond repair if she left.

So what would he do to get her to stay?

What would it take for him to follow her?

He'd never considered that option. Could he seriously pull up stakes and leave his family and everything he'd ever known? Just to be with a woman?

Yes. If that woman was Georgia.

Whoa there. Before he started packing his shit and looking for cowhand jobs in Texas, he'd better find out if that was something Georgia wanted.

Tell fought a massive wave of anxiety as he knocked.

The door swung open and Georgia froze.

His heart began that slow, sad tumble to his feet until Georgia threw herself into his arms and squeezed him so tightly his heart stopped beating entirely. "Cowboy hottie, I am so happy to see you. If you wouldn't have come to me today, I was gonna drive out to your place."

"That right?"

"Yes." Georgia tugged him into the living room and shoved him on the couch. "I didn't call you because I had some important things to deal with first, not because I was waiting to hear from you first. We're beyond that behavior, aren't we?" She perched on the edge of the coffee table, facing him.

"I hope so. What's goin' on?"

"I know we need to talk about a lot of stuff. But before we get all this out in the open, I have to ask you one thing." Her eyes searched his. "Did you mean it when you told Deck that you wanted me for keeps?"

With all my heart. With everything I am. "Yep."

"You sure? This thing with us was supposed to be a fun diversion with some smokin' hot sex thrown in and it turned into so much more than that. I don't think either of us was prepared for how fast everything changed. Although it's pretty obvious it never was casual. It's always been something special between us. Something I've never felt."

Georgia was babbling? He put his hands on her cheeks. "Sweetness. Calm down. And if you're sayin' what I think you're sayin', well, I need to hear every word. Loud and clear."

She blurted out, "I love you."

There was that falling sensation again. "Run that by me one more time."

"I love you. I love you so much it scares me."

"Why does it scare you?"

"After RJ died, I closed myself off from all relationships. I couldn't lose anyone else I cared about if I didn't bother to care about anyone—a friend or a lover.

"I've needed to deal with this for a long time. It's not surprising it came full circle in Sundance. When I was forced to take this job, I swore I'd come back here, exorcise my demons and move on. Then I got involved with you. You changed everything. You challenged me. You accepted me. You freed me."

He had to breathe slowly, steadily, because the roaring in his ears threatened to drown out the sound of her words.

"I only just realized I'm tired of blaming everything that's wrong with my life on someone else. On my early, crappy marriage to Deck. On RJ dying. On my parents splitting up. On the way my dad grieved. On my job. Over the last day, it's become obvious I need to take responsibility for myself and my own happiness and live my life on my terms.

"The God's honest truth is you make me happy. Happier than I've ever been in my life. And isn't that feeling worth something when making a life-changing decision? Shouldn't that feeling of happiness determine *everything*? Yes. So I quit my job yesterday."

His voice was barely above a whisper when he asked, "Are you sure that's what you want?"

"Yes. So my decision to give up my life in Dallas to be with you here in Sundance is not politically correct. I'm supposed to believe I don't need a man to make me happy. But you know what? That's crap. That's me listening to other people's opinions instead of listening to my heart. My heart is telling me to stay here with you, Tell McKay. My heart loves you. I love you. I love everything about you.

"I can't imagine anything better than waking up with you every morning. I love how much you make me laugh. I love how you've taught me how to have fun. I love how you've shown me what a sense of community means. What friendships mean. I love how you understand family issues and don't believe everything has to have a quick fix. I hate that we've both dealt with sadness and loss, but I love I have you to talk to about it. You accept it all. Every part of me."

If Tell's mouth weren't so damn dry and his heart weren't beating a million miles an hour, he might have thought he was actually dreaming.

"I've had so many choices made for me throughout my life. This time I'm taking a stand and making my own choice. This time I'm choosing you."

As calm as he appeared on the outside, on the inside his inner teenage boy was yelling, *In your face, suckas, this girl is mine!*

She blushed and fiddled with the collar of his shirt. "So, ah, please don't tell me you were coming here to break up with me or something."

He laughed. He laughed until he cried. Or maybe he was crying because this woman had just made him the happiest man alive. He brought her close enough to stare into her eyes and feel her stuttered breath on his lips. "I'm not breaking up with you, but you should understand that I'm not good at this because I've never said it before."

"Tell, you don't have to—"

"Yes, I do. I love you, Georgia. I've come to some of those same realizations too. I wanna be with you so much that I was ready to move to Dallas if that's what it'd take for us to be together."

"You'd do that?"

"In a fuckin' heartbeat. I want a lifetime with you. Marriage, babies, havin' our family and friends over for dinner, goin' out on the town, planting a garden and sinking our roots in deep. I've seen my cousins so happy, and they've each built their own family. I've wanted that for myself, but I didn't think it was possible until you. You make me feel so much. Make me feel things I've never felt before. And yes, it's scary as hell for me too."

They stared at each other.

She grinned and said, "Wow. That's some grown-up stuff."

"Yeah. Mushy stuff too." He kissed her fingertips. "I love everything about you. I love that you get everything about me, and apparently you still love me anyway."

She laughed softly.

"You make me happy, Georgia. And I will spend the rest of my life makin' sure you don't regret choosing me."

"I already don't have any regrets." She kissed him with passion, heart and fire; he sucked it down like a narcotic. Drugged on the taste of her, the feel of her, this woman who loved him.

He broke the kiss to murmur, "And don't take this wrong, but you don't hafta get a job right away if you don't want to. I'll support you."

"See how sweet you are?" She nipped his chin. "Thank you. I appreciate it, but I've got a few offers."

"Already?"

"Leah and Roxanne have offered me a job at the beauty shop. Stephanie said she'd hire me to organize her filing system. Domini mentioned they're always shorthanded at Dewey's, so I could probably wait tables. At the fundraiser, the cheerleading coach said there was an assistant cheer coach's job for me at the school if I wanted it. And the Sundance Chamber of Commerce might be looking for a part-time PR person. So I've got options. The job doesn't matter as long as I get to come home to you every night."

"Well, now that you mention it, I was sorta kicking around the idea of takin' on a roommate."

"That right?"

"Uh-huh. But it's gotta be someone special. A woman who doesn't care that I'm gonna be a rancher the rest of my life. A woman who is okay with me judging the occasional rodeo. A woman who knows I can't cook. A woman who understands that once she moves in, she ain't ever movin' out. A woman who knows that I'll love her and cherish her and protect her every day of her life. That this is for keeps."

Georgia's eyes filled with tears. "I'm so ready to sign on the dotted line for that."

"And ain't it lucky I just happen to have a pen?"

She laughed. "God. I love you, Tell McKay. My very own cowboy hottie. I will take you up on your roommate offer, if it includes trampoline and zip-line privileges."

"Absolutely."

"I have to go to Dallas and load up my stuff and cancel the lease on my condo, but that should only take a couple of days."

"I'm goin' with you."

Her eyebrows rose. "Really?"

"I sure as hell ain't gonna let you drive across the damn country by yourself dragging a U-Haul. You'll need help loading your stuff. And I wanna see where you lived and worked because that's part of who you are."

"Who I *was*," she corrected. "You also want my colleagues and former boss to know exactly who I'm leaving Dallas for."

He grinned. "That too. You're mine now, hot lips, and I'm gonna take great pride in letting everyone know it. Especially letting you know it." He brushed his lips over hers softly. "Despite you actin' so tough, I suspect you'll shed a few tears, sayin' goodbye to that life, and you'll need me around for comic relief on the long drive back home."

"I need you for a lot more than comic relief."

"That's good to know. I love you. You're gonna get mighty sick of hearing me say that."

"Never."

"And I'm pretty sure I can find a whole bunch of fun things to do between here and Dallas. Amusement parks and the like."

"Oh hell no. You're never getting me on a roller coaster, McKay."

Tell just grinned and kissed her, knowing how sweet it would be when they teetered on the edge of the first drop, seeing the loops and turns ahead, and then experienced that sudden fall. She'd be screaming her head off, hanging on for dear life, but having the time of her life because she was with him.

About the Author

To learn more about Lorelei James, read her Author Notes on this and other titles, and see a McKay family tree, please visit www.loreleijames.com.

Send an email to lorelei@loreleijames.com or join her Yahoo! group to join in the fun with other readers as well as Lorelei:

http://groups.yahoo.com/group/LoreleiJamesGang

His rough touch makes her lose control...

Cowboy Casanova
© *2011 Lorelei James*
Rough Riders, Book 12

In Sundance, Wyoming, you can't throw a boot without hitting a McKay cowboy, so Ben McKay is used to fading into the background. Except on weekends, when he's Bennett, imposing Dom at The Rawhide Club, surrounded by a bevy of female subs eager for the attention of his long...whip.

As for the curvy brunette eying him from across the room? He'll eat his Stetson if she's the experienced Domme she claims to be. Bennett offers her a deal—he'll let her call the shots for one night. But the next night he gets to prove to her how freeing it'll be when he takes the reins.

Ainsley Hamilton is amazed by how well Bennett read her every secret yearning during that one explosive weekend—and she's stunned when they come face to face in their everyday lives as rancher and new bank president. Now Ben's urging her to explore her submissive side outside the club, and there's something in his commanding gaze that makes it too easy to let him take control—of her desires and her pleasure.

Can Ben help Ainsley overcome her fear that a relationship built on dark sexual appetites won't survive the light of day?

Warning: This book contains a lot of kinky sex. No, seriously, there's A LOT of kinky cowboy sex in this Rough Riders installment. You've been warned.

Available now in ebook and print from Samhain Publishing.

It's the perfect plan...until the ties that bind reach into their hearts.

Flanked
© 2012 Cat Johnson
Studs in Spurs, Book 5

Garret James doesn't need a woman tying him down. Not when the number of buckle bunny notches on his belt—and his position in the pro bull rider standings—are both on the rise. Just when he learns he's this close to blowing out his bad shoulder, Silver Jordan roars into his life, long, leather-clad legs straddling her Harley. Hell, he might not mind being tied to one woman, if that one woman was her. There's one problem—she's his friend's sister. But once their eyes lock, resistance is futile.

Then Silver offers him a smoking-hot deal. They both get the hottest sex of their lives and he gets access to her health insurance for his career-saving surgery—all wrapped up in a marriage of convenience.

For a while, dodging questions and hiding their arrangement is easy. But in private, they battle emotions between them they never expected to grow. After all, the marriage is only temporary...isn't it?

Warning: Contains body piercings guaranteed to make you squirm, a very intimately placed tattoo, one clandestine wedding and even more secretive sex.

Available now in ebook and print from Samhain Publishing.

SAMHAIN
PUBLISHING

www.samhainpublishing.com

Green for the planet.
Great for your wallet.

SAMHAIN
PUBLISHING

It's all about the story...

Romance

HORROR

Retro
ROMANCE

www.samhainpublishing.com

11/17 (9) 6/17

CPSIA information can be obtained at www.ICGtesting.com
Printed in the USA
LVOW12s2128231114

415250LV00001B/55/P

9 781619 211339